To Sheri —
Good luck!

Martin

BREAKING
POINT

VILLARD / NEW YORK

VILLARD / NEW YORK

BREAKING POINT

POINT

MARTINA NAVRATILOVA

AND LIZ NICKLES

Library of Congress Cataloging-in-Publication information is available.

ISBN: 0-679-43391-0

Printed in the United States of America on acid-free paper
24689753
First Edition
Book design by JoAnne Metsch

Here is to all the Sherlock wannabes and tennis-champion never-has-beens.
Keep trying and, most importantly—
have fun.

—MARTINA NAVRATILOVA

ACKNOWLEDGMENTS

The authors would like to thank all those who helped bring this book to life, especially Annik La-Farge, Craig Nelson, Joe Blades, Julian Bach, and Trish Lande. Special thanks also to Stephanie Tolleson, Andrea Jaeger, Craig Kardon, Kathleen Stroia, Rich Rose, Dr. Scott Powell, Dr. Irving Glick, and John Nelson.

BREAKING POINT

ONE

$\mathbf{I}$ am living the nightmare again, as I have so many times before. It is always as frightening as when the events actually happened, and never less disturbing, replaying endlessly like a video on a loop, all the details frozen in place. . . .

It is Paris, eight years ago. The day is unpredictably warm, as it is likely to be in May during the finals of the French Open. The wind is ruffling my hair. I look down at the skid marks and footprints, patterns in the red clay. My white shoes, their laces, and the crevices of my socks are smeared orangey-red, as if dusted with the dried blood of an alien. Beneath me, clay clots the herringbone pattern of my rubber soles, decreasing my traction.

I look up, squinting into the sun, past Perrier, Lacoste, and Peugeot signs, beyond the green and white awnings of the glassed-in press booth and the flags of many nations flying against the brilliant Kodachrome-blue sky. I hear the voice over the loudspeakers: *"Avantage, Mademoiselle Myles."* I think of the ball.

All around me are the sounds of a hundred thousand people

hoping I will fail. I am being vilified. Crucified. Fried. There are cries, cheers—an audible sigh of love for my opponent.

"Allez, Kel-lee!"

"Yay, Kell!"

"Kel-lee!"

The crowd takes up a rhythmic clap. Over the PA system comes a soothing, almost dreamy voice, reciting the score in French. The ball boys stand at attention on the sidelines in front of pots of red geraniums. Their arms are stick-straight in the air, balls in each hand at the ready, awaiting even the most microscopic signal from me or my opponent. The net judge leans low as he touches the net with one finger, like God anointing the angel in the fresco on the ceiling of the Sistine chapel.

Clay is a very honest surface. The great equalizer, they call it. Of all the surfaces in tennis, it brings out a player's best, worst, and most unexpected elements. Clay exposes the human emotional quotient. You can mask almost anything on any surface except clay, where spin can overcome power and strategy can eradicate technique. You have to think through each point, rather than rely on instinct and training. Clay's granular grit bites into the big serves and ground strokes that play so well on other surfaces. Clay slows things down, gives that extra split second to hit a passing shot.

It's an advantage that serves me well, and today I have exploited it. Still, I feel like a charlatan. I am not the better player, but I am the superior strategist. And tennis is often more mental than physical, especially at the championship level when both players have so many gifts.

I bounce the ball, and in the space of that moment I know I will win. Today we are like the poles of two magnets, the ball and I. We will find each other and connect, because today this match, this game, and this point—this championship point—are all mine. I'm in the best shape of my life, tapping into the wellspring of ungodly endurance that clay calls for. On grass, my opponent would certainly beat me. But on clay I have a chance.

I will bring her to the net, lure her so far inside the court that she can't run back to the baseline.

I scope out the woman across the net. Her face is calm, focused, smooth, devoid of emotion. Nothing will surface; it never does. Her makeup is perfect. She doesn't even seem to sweat.

Her white tennis dress has mint-green scrolled appliqués; her drop hoop earrings dance with every step. Around her wrist a dainty diamond bracelet glints in the sun. I wear plain white shorts, which I find most practical and comfortable, and a simple blue-and-white shirt. I look like a camp counselor.

I concentrate on the next shot. *Don't rely on your serve so much. Just get the first serve in play. Don't try serving hard until you have to. Hit the ball to her strength, open up her weaker side.* I reach up, toss, stretch, connect with the ball—and it begins again.

And then it is over, like a movie you understood so well until the last scene, when the plot suddenly becomes incomprehensible. There is the line judge in his dark suit, the disputed call, the derisive whistling from the crowd. And then there are the cheers.

"Kel-lee! Kel-lee! Kel-lee!"

And the entire Central Court at Roland Garros Stadium is on its feet, cheering wildly for the woman I, Jordan Myles, have just beaten in my first Grand Slam final. I have done the unthinkable—beaten Kelly Kendall, queen of the clay court, at her own game—and the crowd will not forgive me.

Kelly is smiling and waving graciously, accepting this tidal wave of adulation as her due. We meet at the net, and she pats me on the head. Perhaps she thinks I am a spaniel.

The trophy is presented, and I stand there holding it, an elaborately tooled, heavy-based urn engraved COUPE SUZANNE LENGLEN, named for the balletic French champion who never played this stadium, the cup for so long the undisputed possession of Kelly Kendall. Kelly holds the unbeaten record of five consecutive victories on Roland Garros clay. It's her surface, staked out, bought, and paid for by victory after victory. Today I have right-fully and proudly won this trophy, wrenched it forcibly from her grasp at the baseline. But it is Kelly for whom the crowd cheers, as I stand there, smiling to myself at my accomplishment, refus-ing to acknowledge the crowd's rejection. She is the winner, in spite of losing.

I hear individual voices in the crowd—"Kelly! You should have won!" *"Vive la Kendall!"*—and, when I step forward, a smattering of applause accompanied by a chorus of derisive whistling.

The lenses of the battery of courtside photographers swing past me toward Kelly. Will I be a fuzzy figure in the foreground when the pictures appear in the newspapers and sports maga-zines?

I am a professional; I try not to take it personally. This is my first Grand Slam championship but not my first win over Kelly, so I can't say I'm surprised. It is always this way. The crowd adopted her ten years ago, when she was a dimpled pink-cheeked sprite with a murderous two-handed backhand. No-body beats their Kelly and gets away with it.

I had hoped that this impossible victory over her, my first Grand Slam, would at least gain a toehold for me in the rarefied firmament inhabited by the stars. All the months of building up my endurance for clay with wind sprints and distance running, the endless hours of developing an offensive arsenal, practicing my topspin forehand, my slice backhand, and my drop shot, the mental rehearsing of every variation of strategy, have paid off. When I was little, I used to believe that the kid who tried hardest would get the most notice. And so I tried harder. Today, of all days, in the hot sunshine on the edge of the Bois de Boulogne, I willed myself to be a winner.

I turn away from the crowd, towel my face, zip up my warm-up jacket, and shoulder my tennis bag. Kelly and I walk off the court, escorted by security the few steps across the grounds, past the green-latticed souvenir and food stands toward the long tunnel that leads to the locker rooms. I cradle my trophy. She carries her smaller silver tray. At the entrance to the tunnel we are intercepted by Kevin Curry of the LaserGlass Company, accompanied by another barrage of photographers. A master of product placement, Curry is the guy who put the sunglasses on teen idol Sam Preston in the smash hit movie *Fish Crazy*. The entourage pauses briefly.

"Congratulations, Jordan—great game," Kevin comments absently as he walks straight past me and slips a pair of sunglasses on Kelly. Accompanying this gesture, I know, will be a monolithic endorsement check.

Kelly Kendall collects endorsements like some women collect charms for their bracelets. A tennis racket, a sportswear line, an athletic shoe, a vitamin, a hair color, a fragrance, a pain reliever, a car rental company—the list runs for pages. I, on the other hand, have had exactly one endorsement in my entire career: a sweatband company that went bankrupt.

The guards separate Kelly and me and, mistaking the target of the crush, hustle me down toward the long path into the tunnel. Looking back over my shoulder, I see the woman I have just defeated signing autographs as she is interviewed by CNN. I want to throw up, and, when I get to the locker room, I do.

This nightmare needs no dark shadows or B-movie monsters to jolt me out of a sound sleep. It is monstrous enough. Maybe the recollection is completely out of proportion to reality. Maybe that eight-year-old event wasn't as bad as I recall. But it doesn't matter. This is how I remember it. And whenever I am overworked, overtired, overstressed, or sometimes for no reason at all, it resurfaces: a picture-perfect playback of the day in my life when I realized that a win is not a win is not a win. Just as you never get over some losses, it's possible to win and never recover.

For a few years after my victory at Roland Garros, Kelly and I were positioned as head-to-head rivals. Actually, I never really approached her record, but nobody seemed to notice. Tournaments were promoted around the fact that we would be battling it out, women gladiators of the courts. Commentators compared and contrasted our playing styles and strategies. She was known for her steadiness, accuracy, and consistency; she just kept hitting from the baseline until she wore down her opponent. I was always characterized as the more physical. But I always felt I had a mental advantage that nobody picked up on. I could change strategies on a dime, which allowed me to win many matches that nobody quite understood. My tactics were so subtle that people—including my opponents—often didn't know what had caused a match to turn around in my favor. But I knew.

There were stories written about Kelly and me, enough to fill the five scrapbooks that my mother still has somewhere in the basement. My particular favorite was an article titled "Beauty and the Beast." Guess who was the beast. The serious reporters usually treated me fairly, but the trash press pegged me as Darth Vader. For instance, one time I had a bad shoulder. My arm hurt so much I couldn't even brush my teeth, and during my match that day I had to have the shoulder muscle injected with a painkiller. The next day, when I was scheduled to play Kelly in a final, I absolutely could not do it, so I dropped out of the tournament. Of course, this produced headlines claiming that Jordan Myles was afraid of losing to Kelly on clay so she defaulted. I became resigned that there are always certain elements of the press who will say whatever they want.

Off the court, Kelly and I were cordial if never close. Kelly Kendall would never allow herself the luxury of truly befriending a tennis competitor. There are some very real rivalries and feuds in tennis, but, ironically, the media people often miss them. You read about so-called friends who you know really hate each other's guts. Actually, most presumed feuds are just amplifications of a remark that might have been taken out of context—in the heat of an emotional moment, after a win or a loss.

When Kelly retired two years ago, the French Tennis Federation erected a statue to her on the Roland Garros grounds, right across from the life-sized bronze of Suzanne Lenglen. She is the only non-French player so honored. And my one win is suitably noted, etched on the trophy.

This morning, sometime in the purple Palm Springs predawn, the Roland Garros nightmare came back, so vivid that in my semiconsciousness the hair on the back of my head was wet and curly with sweat and the pillow was damp with tears.

When I was living with Gus, my ex-friend, mentor, lover, doctor, and boss, depending on when you asked me, he used to wake me gently, with soft nudges and caresses in places impossible to ignore. Then he'd hold me till I fell back asleep. But that was a while ago. Gus's name is still above mine on our business letterhead: Dr. Augustus Laidlaw, founder and one of my associates at the Desert Springs Sports Science Clinic, where our professional colleagues are the best doctors, sports scientists, therapists, trainers, and nutritionists in the business. But the relationship now is not one where I'll be calling him anytime soon to rush over in the middle of the night because I'm having a bad dream. In fact, he has another woman in his life, a local artist who is single-handedly trying to revive macramé. But that's another story.

I was leaving for Paris in the morning to revisit Roland Garros, but not as a player. My mind was saturated with memories. The phone rang, forcing me to open my eyes, and although the glowing numerals on my radio alarm clock said it was 4 A.M., I was glad. It was reassuring to pat my down coverlet and remind myself that I was in my own town house in Palm Springs, no longer playing professional tennis, so the call was probably some medical emergency. You buy into phone calls when you enter any medically related field. I'm a physical therapist, not a doctor, and I specialize in sports injuries and treatment, but there are occasional emergencies. When it comes to their bodies, professional athletes can border on the obsessive—understandably. Even a strained muscle will put a career at risk if it's not treated correctly, so these issues take on critical proportions.

I fell back onto the pillows, cleared my throat, and reached for the phone, instinctively hoping, as you always do when the phone rings in the middle of the night, that it wasn't a family disaster.

"Hello?" I groped the perimeter of the night table for my glass of water.

"Jordan," rasped a voice, "it's Woody Solister." He broke into a coughing fit.

"Mmm," I mumbled. Woody Solister. How many years had it been since I'd seen him? Yet even over the phone at this hour, his sandpapery voice and smoker's cough were unmistakable. He had won many Grand Slam titles in his time and had evolved into a fixture as a USTA coach, but it was common knowledge that at this point in his career he was just collecting checks and walking through the motions. I'd watched Hilton Head on TV, and when they cut to the players' box there he sat, reading a newspaper. It didn't matter. Woody made six figures plus just for being who he was.

"Now listen, kiddo." Woody called everybody kiddo, even if you were past eighty. "I'm coaching Dag now."

Dag. That would be Dagmar Olafsen. Her record ran through my head: good player, incredible serve, had a few career high spots, won the U.S. Open once a few years back, but never one of the greats.

"Mm-hm." I cleared my throat. "Woody, excuse me. It's four in the morning here, I'm leaving for France today, and isn't Dag kind of winding down her career?"

"Past tense. She *had* a bad shoulder injury, but we're getting that under control and she's got her old serve back. We're working on the rest. Here's the thing, Jordan: Dag needs some serious shoulder work. That damn rotator cuff. She tore it last year at the Lipton, had the microsurgery, and it all healed up nice as can be.

But then CiCi McBain—her last coach—didn't make her get the right therapy. Babied her, if you ask me. Now we're paying the price. She hasn't got her full range of motion back without pain. She needs you. Can you jump on board with us in Paris?"

"Well, Bill and I will be there for the clinic, Woody, but we've got a lot of commitments. I'm not sure I'll have much time."

"Do me a favor. Just talk to Dag. Watch some of her matches. You'll see for yourself. She can win. She can pull her ranking right back up there—higher, even. The girl has always had the talent. It's just that damned injury."

Even in my half-asleep state, I had to wonder why Woody was pushing so hard. He was not exactly the Sisyphus type, forced to roll huge boulders uphill. True, he had once been a Davis Cup captain, and he'd won a string of Grand Slams in his prime, but these days Woody was best known for his 7 A.M. Bible study meetings, usually attended by a small group of men players, held in hotel lobbies of the tour. I'd come across him many times on my way to breakfast, intently discussing some variation on how the Scriptures related to winning in tennis. This fervor was all the more notable for its stark contrast to Woody's marathon stints at bars and clubs. His enthusiasm for Dagmar's career resurgence was admirable but hardly typical. However, he was not insensitive to the lure of a substantial fee. And I had to admire Dag for not fading away, like some players, but giving her all at a time when others might coast.

"And you—well, frankly, Jordan, she insists on you. You know the game. You know the players. You've been there. She respects that. If she's going to win, she needs you."

I yawned. The middle of the night is never a good time to make any decision. "We'll talk. Gotta hang up now, Woody. I'm taking the company jet to New York, and then the Concorde to Paris. I'll be at the Méridien."

I sat up in bed, in the dark. I could make out the shapes of my soft-sided suitcase and garment bag, already packed. A.M.'s carrier was also set out. I always took Alice Marble, as my Jack

Russell terrier was officially called, in honor of my tennis hero, to France with me. Unlike England, they had no irksome pet quarantine. For the first time in my life, however, I was not taking a tennis racket to Paris.

Other people know Paris for the Eiffel Tower, the four-star food, the vintage wines, the couture fashions: the romantic city of the guidebooks. I have never seen this side of the town. For me, Paris was always clay, clay, and more clay—the culmination of the clay court circuit for women. Paris was the big event after Hilton Head. Paris meant endless hours of practice to develop the finesse and endurance it takes to serve and volley, to blast past the baseline in those relentless rallies.

To me, Paris meant staying in the player hotel—usually a large commercial place on the edge of town—shuttling back and forth to Roland Garros in the courtesy van, and hanging out between matches in the bowels of the player lounge, which, while well equipped, has the ambiance of a cement bunker. If you were a client of theirs—which I was—there was always a lovely meal available at one of the greenhouses owned by Global Sport, the world's biggest sports talent agency, but by the time I managed to get there they had usually stopped serving. Most often, I found myself tossing down a quick veggie meal hours later in an Indian restaurant.

As for diversions, there was always some sort of organized player entertainment. Stuffed into my journals are flyers and tournament reminders about a party at the Hard Rock Café, a tennis exhibition and concert at the Palais des Sports, a gymnastics exhibition at the Hermès Museum, the Kirov Ballet at the Théâtre des Champs-Élysées, a concert by Kiri Te Kanawa, even horseback riding at the Champ-de-Mars. And then there was the unofficial entertainment, like forays to the live sex shows near the Moulin Rouge that were particularly popular with some of the players. Although some of the competitors made a point of doing the town, I don't think I ever attended any of these events.

One year, however, a group of us who were out of the running took a consolation sightseeing cruise down the Seine. Another year I bought a bicycle and had a special pouch made for A.M. A Jack Russell terrier is not a large dog, which is fortunate, since I like to take A.M. wherever I go. That is, when she agrees to accompany me. A.M. has a mind of her own. I strapped her to my chest like a baby and biked wherever I could, to restaurants and parks. This was doubly rewarding because I was able to work off everything I ate just by biking around. I never did it again, because it seemed to rain every year.

That was about it. There was never time after the tournament to be a tourist, or even to rest. Win or lose, as soon as you put your racket down after the French, it was time to switch gears and start thinking about grass courts, specifically Wimbledon. So I was looking forward to finally seeing Paris as a civilian, shopping and spending free time exploring charming streets and discovering the Louvre.

Sleep at this point was impossible. I pulled myself out of bed to finish packing. A.M. slept on in oblivion, snoring doggie snores. Some people say dogs don't snore, but I've actually taped A.M. to prove otherwise. If she were a man, I'd kick her out of bed, but she's my baby, she's certainly outlasted the men in my life, so I let her get away with it. As many people have pointed out over the years, I have a soft spot for this dog. Yes, it's possible that she is spoiled, but she's my family, as I see it. Once, when she was sick in Rome, I dropped out of a tournament and hand-fed her chicken broth from an eyedropper, progressing as she got better to teaspoons of Gerber's junior beef. Our life together has been one big bonding experience.

I reached down and rubbed her ears, and she wagged her tail in her sleep. Her paws were scurrying in place. When this happens, I always think she's dreaming that she's loose in the woods, running free and chasing a squirrel. And I wish I were there with her.

· · ·

The Global Sport greenhouses are located directly across from Roland Garros, in a meticulously groomed public park that is usually the sun-dappled habitat of mothers pushing children in strollers, old men taking the sun, or young couples meandering along hand in hand. Just one cobblestoned street away, the cement complex that is the home of the French Tennis Federation is a blur of activity: milling crowds; elegant sponsor pavilions with gatekeepers in couture suits; dozens of food, refreshment, and souvenir booths; climbing ivy mingled with pink and red roses; white Peugeot vans discharging players in sweatshirts and warm-up jackets, equipment bags slung over their shoulders; police from the Service National in their short-sleeved blue shirts—all punctuated by the roars and screams of the crowd as a point is made, a match is won, or a star appears, or is created, on the clay courts.

The average fan would never guess that behind the high iron gates that border the complex is a parallel universe of stratospheric deal-making, celebrity shoulder-rubbing, and a commingling of the agents who control the sport, their clients who inhabit it, and the sponsors who pay for it.

The cocktail hour was almost over as I arrived, slightly jet-lagged, at a gate marked by a brass plaque: JARDINS ET SERRES D'AUTEUIL. OPEN EVERY DAY 10–18. 3 FRANCS. The garden was closed to the public for the duration of the Open. I showed my engraved invitation to the guard, and she nodded me through. I walked quickly along the gravel path, under the trees, and up the poppy-flanked walkway to the greenhouse complex. Birds chirped, and there was the peaceful sound of running water. This place was like another world, not even a part of Paris. Entering the park, you stepped into a different age, another dimension. I felt transported to an earlier time—when women in rustling skirts swept along these same paths under fine parasols, escorted by gentlemen in bowler hats. It was almost impossible to believe that the place that caused me so much anxiety was just across the street.

The three towering Victorian greenhouses, each as big as a small hotel, are elaborate constructions of intricate mosaics of glass laid into rococo oxidized-metal skeletons. They loomed against the sky, their panes reflecting the clouds and colors of the low-hanging sun. The main greenhouse, where Global Sport was holding its reception, had a mammoth domed central pavilion, giving it the shape of a keyhole. It was topped by a huge weather vane that seemed to slice into the air.

I was late. The reception had already started, and a scant handful of well-dressed men and women hurried ahead of me as I crunched along the gravel path. A man in a business suit with a black leather backpack rushed by, a motorcycle helmet tucked under his arm. Another man, in a red baseball cap and tinted glasses, seemed vaguely familiar, but he walked briskly past me toward the gate, away from the greenhouses. One or two couples sat sipping drinks on green-slatted garden benches. Music filtered out from the largest greenhouse, a jewel-box setting where Global Sport always holds its most elegant lunches and receptions. The smaller greenhouse, directly across the path, hosted the less formal Global Sport player reception area, reserved for G.S. player clients and their families and guests. Both are actually working greenhouses, with an impressive array of horticultural specimens cultivated for the park.

Other agents and sponsors have courtesy rooms within the Roland Garros complex in an exclusive area called Le Village, but Global Sport's greenhouses make all other accommodations at the French Open seem like low-rent motels across the street from the Taj Mahal.

Stepping into the main greenhouse, where a sign pointed me toward the reception in progress, I was instantly transported to the tropics. The air was humid and heavy, and there was a constant chatter of parakeets and exotic birds. Tiny nests lined the walls. The domed ceiling soared a hundred feet overhead, and huge palms draped sweeping fronds from majestic trunks. Gigantic goldfish with lacy tails swam lazily in a shallow flagstone pond. A sign in French noted that one hundred and twenty varieties of palms were cultivated here. Turning left, I went through tented canvas doors. The floor turned from stone to sisal carpet; the walls became a stage set of soft peach strung with climbing bougainvillaea. A thin haze of cigarette and cigar smoke wafted through the room as waiters in black jackets circulated through the elegant crowd.

The immediate entrance to the room was blocked by a four-deep clutch of Global Sport agents, surrounding tennis's newest and hottest sensations: the McAlisters. Identical twin brothers from southern Florida, they were good-looking, red-haired, freckled, not yet seventeen, not yet pro, and, most critically, not yet signed by an agency. *Sports Illustrated* had already run a feature on their sweep of the junior circuit, including their colorful penchant for wearing pit crew shirts on court. They and their parents were clearly being heavily courted by both Global Sport and its rival, World Cup.

I checked in at the registration desk with Marcie Greenwald, who was an assistant at Global Sport's headquarters in New York when I was a client.

"Jordan!" she exclaimed as we exchanged hugs across the desk. "The champion returns! Finally, we got you here!"

"You look great, Marce." She had lost that postgrad aura and was now polished and sophisticated in a sleek pantsuit and yellow silk blouse, an expensive-looking scarf casually tied across her shoulders.

"So do you," she said. "I like the super-short haircut."

"Hairdresser got carried away." I laughed, running my fingers through what was left of the black curls. In my never-ending quest to "do something," as my mother would say, about my hair, I'd had it snipped off to about an inch long all over my head, with long bangs left to brush my eyebrows. My muscular build made it hard to look like anything but a tomboy, but I admit to enjoying nice clothes and unusual jewelry. Tonight I was wearing rose quartz earrings that set off my dark eyes and complexion. "So what are you doing these days?" I asked.

"I live in Paris now," Marcie said.

"You work in the Paris office?"

"*Mais oui*. Publicity. Come by and visit." She motioned to a waiter carrying a tray of champagne glasses, plucked one for me, and silently directed him to an empty-handed client.

"So who's here?"

Marcie handed me her guest list. "The usual suspects. Alan, Ed, and Maurice—"

"The unholy trio." And three of the richest men in the world, the founders of Global Sport. They always kept a low profile and their names were hardly household words, but they had virtually invented the concept of the sports agent.

Starting thirty years ago with a few handshake deals with up-and-coming stars, they had built the business to include most of the major names in most of the major sports—with a special concentration in tennis. Alan had represented me when I was at the peak of my career, and to his credit he had remained loyal and supportive even after the mountain-climbing accident that ended any hope of my playing again. Ed was the financial wizard—I never did know much about that side of the business, nor did I know Ed particularly well, although I recognized his signature from my checks. Maurice was French and handled the European operations.

"We have a big Japanese contingent this year, sponsored by Equinox. That's their star player, Micki Takashimaya. She brought a gigantic entourage."

I noticed a hulking man shadowing Micki. "Her bodyguard?" I asked.

Marcie laughed. "No, her acupuncturist. And of course Kelly's here," Marcie said. "With a camera crew."

"Tell me where they're set up so I can go in the opposite direction."

Marcie laughed and pointed. "Over there with John McEnroe. She told me to tell her when you came in, but I see her producer has noticed you."

I could see Kelly in a pink suit, microphone in hand, conversing animatedly with Mac. I had to admit she looked better than ever. Her hair was a sleek short cut and nearly platinum blond. Her figure was still slim. I'd heard that she and her husband were trying, so far without success, to have a baby, but any strain certainly wasn't showing. Kelly looked radiant. I felt the familiar twinge of jealousy, even though I knew it was irrational.

As Kelly concentrated on her interview, a woman with a clipboard and headphones broke away from the camera crew and dove through the crowd in my direction.

"Jordan! Jordan!" She waved as if flagging down a passing car. "How about a two-shot, you and Kelly—the greatest rivals ever to set foot on French clay?"

I guess I'd had enough sound bites in my career in association with Kelly. I turned away and pretended to be engrossed in my conversation with Marcie.

A raucous laugh erupted from a group of men a few feet away. "Who's that bunch?" I asked.

"Don't you recognize him? Well, maybe if he turns this way a bit more. It's Woody Solister, with the people from Prime Rackets."

I stared. Woody was only in his mid-forties, but he seemed to have aged twenty years since I'd seen him last, which was not that long ago. His face was mahogany tan, weathered and liver-spotted, with a jaundiced undertone. His skin hung loosely over his skull like a bad slipcover. What was left of his hair had gone completely gray.

"He's on the last year of his Prime contract, and I hear they're not renewing," Marcie whispered. "Check out the snow job."

The snow job came easily to Woody. He knew every story in tennis and every story behind the story. The Prime people had reason to be enchanted by him, except I could see he had over-imbibed and was about to spoil his own illusion.

Marcie leaned close. "Did you hear? Woody's signed on to coach Dag Olafsen."

"He told me. I thought she was about to retire."

"She did well at Hilton Head. Maybe that encouraged her."

It wouldn't be the first time that Dagmar had managed to change the tide of her life. A Danish-American, she had moved to California from Denmark years ago in hopes that her consistency, 120-mile-an-hour serve, and staying power would make her a star. For a decade or so she was a top doubles player, so versatile the players used to joke that the best women's doubles team in the world was Dagmar Olafsen and anybody. She won many Grand Slam titles in doubles, but in singles she seesawed around the top twenty, never really making it to the top despite occasional stunning victories over players like Steffi Graf and Chris Evert.

Dagmar showed she had it in her to be a factor when she set herself to it. Then a shoulder injury dulled her searing serve, and her career sank into a decline. Her ranking slipped steadily, and for the past three years Dagmar had not been ranked in the top ten even in doubles. It seemed like her retirement was imminent.

Marcie shrugged. "Maybe Woody's teaching her to be a prima donna. She threw a tantrum on court during her doubles match. She made the ball girl cry—chewed her out because she said it was taking her too long to get the ball. The poor kid didn't speak English, but she got the drift, particularly after Dag threw her racket. The umpire gave her a warning for racket abuse."

"Good grief." Intimidating the ball kids was considered particularly ugly and oafish behavior.

"Then, in the press conference today after she lost, Dag claimed they had watered down the clay improperly, which caused her to slip on the lines." Marcie grimaced. "It made the press, of course. The tabloids are already smelling blood. Oh, well, I can't control every word out of the players' mouths."

"That surprises me, Marce. Dag used to be so quiet."

"*Used to be* is the operative terminology. Still, I can't say it's all bad. Everybody wants to see her play now, just to catch the fireworks—especially if she's up against Heather Knight. Then you can practically smell the smoke."

"Maybe it's part of psyching herself to be more aggressive. Sometimes that can carry over into your social behavior."

"Is that Jordan the therapist talking or Jordan the player?"

"Both, I guess."

"Jordan! There you are!" My partner Bill Stokes, co-founder with Gus of the Springs, was motioning across the crowd, his silver-gray hair in its usual velveteen crew cut, his clothes perfectly tailored. Bill could walk into a raging hurricane and emerge with knife pleats in his pants, unwrinkled.

I waved to Marcie and set off through the crowd, but Woody Solister grabbed my elbow.

"Kiddo! Just the person I was looking for," he rasped. His breath smelled boozy, and instinctively I backed away.

"Hi, Woody."

"Where's that pedigreed rat of yours?"

"Please, Woody. A.M. is a member of the family. She's back at the hotel, probably ordering up room service and costing me a fortune. This is not a way to get on my good side."

He grinned. "We need to talk business."

"What kind of business?"

"I'm coaching Dag now. Waiter, more champagne."

"I know. You called me, remember? But I'm happy to hear it, Woody. I wish Dagmar the best. Where is she?" I arched my eyebrows at Bill, hoping he would rescue me, although from the intensity of his conversation it seemed unlikely. Actually, I was stalling, hoping to avoid a commitment. Working with Woody Solister was not an appealing prospect.

He motioned with a morsel of puff pastry. "Over toward the back at a table with some prospective sponsors. Maybe you two can talk later."

"I'll think about it."

Suddenly there was an explosive crash and the splintering of glass. I ducked into a crouch in a reflex action, as the noise shuddered through the room.

Solister continued sipping his champagne, scanning the

crowd. Most of the others looked around curiously, tentatively frozen in place, the buzz of multilingual conversations snapped off in mid-sentence.

The shocked silence was broken by a scream, and as a group we all turned toward the front tented doorway where Marcie Greenwald stood, swaying in place as if the slightest movement of air would topple her, one hand clamped over her mouth.

I ran toward Marcie, still holding my champagne glass, the liquid sloshing over the side and splashing onto my feet. As I grasped her arm, I looked where she was staring and saw a scattering of broken glass on the ground and someone lying facedown in the goldfish pond: a young woman in a short black cocktail dress, her feet bare, her blond hair fanning out around her in the rippled water.

I looked up in the direction of the crash, dropped Marcie's arm, and ran to the edge of the pond. A gaping, jagged hole had been made in the greenhouse skylight, splintered glass etching a border around a patch of sky. The parakeets had escalated their chatter to hysteria level. A crowd of people pushed cautiously around the fishpond, edging me closer to the water. In the crush, I felt a cigarette burn my arm. There were muffled screams and gasps.

"Au secours!"

"Oh, my God!"

"Somebody call an ambulance!"

"Call Emergency Services!"

"A woman has collapsed!"

Looking over my shoulder, I saw a clearing in the crowd. Marcie lay motionless in the center, but someone was already kneeling over her. The crowd closed around her, separating us. I could only hope she had just fainted.

I charged into the water, going on autopilot. There was no telling the exact extent of her injuries, but I knew I had to get the blond woman face up, support her neck, and get her head out of the water. The pond was shallow, just knee-deep, and I crouched low to get leverage. Her arms were slippery, heavy and unbending, like algae-covered tree limbs, and she rolled onto her back with a small splash. I moved her as far as I dared, to a flat ledge at the edge of the pond, still in the water but level for her neck.

The woman appeared to be in her mid-twenties, slim and in good shape but not an athlete. Her eyes were open, the pupils fixed, as she stared straight at me, unseeing, water beading on her dark eyelashes. Her long hair clung in wet clumps to her forehead and across her face. At one side, a rhinestone-studded barrette shimmered incongruously, and somehow her lipstick was perfect—bright red and lined with a practiced touch. Her skin was still warm to the touch, and her face was flushed from the force of the impact.

I reached for a pulse in her neck; every second was precious. A large reddish bruise was imprinted on the skin of her throat. The pulse, if it existed, was so faint I couldn't feel it. Without extreme measures, this woman would be dead within minutes. Crouching on my knees on the stones and cement in the shallow water, I tilted her chin back, held her lower jaw open with one hand, and cleared her mouth and throat with the finger of the other. Then I bent my head low to her lips and began the rhythmic breathing and pushing of CPR. *Breathe. Breathe. Push. Push.* I counted it out, only dimly aware of the commotion in the room.

Others emerged around me, and someone tried to yank the woman out of the water by her feet, an action I knew could paralyze or even kill, if she wasn't already dead. The water was warm, her face was in the clear, and for now that would have to do. I turned my head between breaths to gasp, "Don't move her!" I couldn't help but notice Kelly and her camera crew, at the front of the crowd. The producer was gesturing wildly to keep rolling as the video operator knelt by the fishpond, his lens trained on my resuscitation effort. Kelly stood frozen in place, clutching her microphone, no words coming out of her open mouth.

In the distance, I could hear the *hee-haw* of French sirens. But now as I blew the breath of life into the woman's still lips, I knew it was hopeless. Her neck was oddly limp, probably broken.

The big goldfish circled us, lazily oblivious, their fins rippling like soft chiffon, as water seeped up the back of my black silk dress.

TWO

In front of the stairs to the Village enclosure, across from the crepe and strawberry stands of Le Buffet de Roland Garros and beneath Court Central, are the Infirmerie and the office of Roland Garros's Chief of Medical Service. There are actually infirmaries in each of the three stadium structures at Roland Garros, but this one is the domain of Dr. Jean Delaye, chief physician of the French Tennis Federation, who presides over this mini medical kingdom. The beds, neatly made up with crisply spotless white sheets, stood ready to receive patients. An EKG machine, plasma stands, stretchers, wheelchairs, a complete pharmacy, and the finest high-tech medical equipment on the tennis circuit waited at the ready. Ironically, the person who needed this help most was beyond it.

"What do we know about this young woman?" Dr. Delaye asked as he sat at his desk. He scrolled through his computer terminal, searching for data that would make sense of the blond girl's tragedy. Of course, she had not yet officially been declared dead, but there had been no heartbeat, pulse, or breath when she was rushed in an ambulance to the trauma center at the

Clinique de Choisy. You don't have to be a coroner to know death when you see it.

The greenhouse complex is not under the jurisdiction of the Roland Garros staff. Technically, the minute you move one inch outside the stadium gates, the City of Paris takes over, but Dr. Delaye had stepped in to assist. Unlike Grand Slam facilities in other countries, Roland Garros is the home of the national tennis federation of France, so it is in operation all year long and the medical staff is always in attendance at some level. The infirmary rooms are large, modern, and well equipped. Milling around outside the glass-walled office were Dr. Delaye's assistant; Bill Stokes; two or three young officials from the tournament, still in their red jackets; a clutch of police and blue-jacketed security guards; several tournament officials; and the head of tournament public relations.

Marcie Greenwald lay on one of the cots under a blanket, her feet elevated on pillows, being treated for shock—thank God it was only shock. I stood wrapped in another blanket, waiting for someone to bring me dry clothes.

The infirmary is well equipped for most of the injuries and illnesses that can happen at a major Grand Slam—anything from nausea to fevers, from sprains to heart attacks and strokes. Dr. Delaye and his staff oversee the three facilities located under Court 1, Court A, and Central Court. "Take a town of forty thousand people—even if it's a healthy town, anything can happen," Dr. Delaye was fond of saying. And he is prepared. Some stars, like Boris Becker, fly in their own doctors, but most players—and fans and media members—find the medical care at Roland Garros to be unusually competent.

I had always been impressed by the facilities here, and when I first went back to the tennis tour after my mountain climbing accident, as a physical therapist with the Women's Tennis Foundation, I had many long talks with Dr. Delaye about my career.

He himself led a multifaceted professional life, working with corporate sponsors and international scientific grants as well as on the sports scene. The precision of his organization's planning was as exacting as any surgeon's. For example, in case of a mass emergency, Roland Garros is divided into areas for carrying bodies or holding people in groups, and procedures are in place to deal with these kinds of situations. Roland Garros is really a city in miniature. It has its own restaurants and bars, its own post office, newsstand, magazine, and bank. The French tennis authorities thought they had considered every contingency, but they had certainly never imagined a woman falling through the greenhouse roof next door.

"You know, her neck might have been broken before the fall," I said, thinking aloud.

All eyes turned in my direction. Almost everyone here spoke English relatively well, and they all understood what I had said.

"Why is that, Jordan?" Dr. Delaye looked up from his terminal.

"She had red marks on her throat. I could see them as I gave her CPR. Sharp red marks. Not the kind you'd get in a fall."

"Well, the police will determine that," said Bill, a little too quickly. "We don't even know who she is yet."

"I think she's American," I said.

"How do you know?" asked Dr. Delaye.

"She was wearing a Donna Karan dress. The neck was ripped and I saw the label. It's not a designer most Frenchwomen—or anybody who was not an American—would usually wear. Unless, of course, she traveled a lot and picked it up on a trip."

"Well, nothing is certain at this point." Bill shot me one of his I-am-the-boss looks, which basically warned me to keep my mouth shut before I created an international incident. A former Olympic marathoner, he now sought funds and sponsors for the clinic.

Suddenly the glass door of the infirmary pushed open, and security guards escorted in a short man in a dark tailored suit and red baseball cap—the man I had seen leaving the greenhouse area as I arrived. Accompanying him was a man I knew very well, Dr. Richard Skenk.

"Just what we need," muttered Bill under his breath, but his face was nothing less than professional as he added, "Hello, Richard."

Dr. Skenk had been a tour fixture for as long as anybody could remember, and now, moving into his late seventies, he leaned heavily on his trademark cane. Dr. Skenk possessed a wardrobe of canes, which he used to assist his arthritic steps. He never missed a Grand Slam tournament on any continent, and he seemed to travel with a suitcase full of various braces which he applied to arms or legs in a kind of universal treatment. Currently, I had heard, he was utilizing the controversial procedure of prophylactic rehydration with an intravenous saline infusion. There were those who swore this treatment helps the body retain fluids and recover more quickly from a grueling match.

"Who's in charge here?" asked the man in the baseball cap. I knew his voice immediately.

Dr. Delaye nodded. "I am the chief physician," he said. "Hello, Richard." He and Dr. Skenk shook hands.

"Where have they taken Catherine? Nobody will tell me." The newcomer stood in the doorway, twisting the brim of his cap, as Dr. Skenk made himself at home behind a spare desk.

The entire room sprang to attention.

"Catherine?" Dr. Delaye stood up. "You know her, then?"

"Of course. She's my assistant. Actually, my former assistant. She quit a few days ago." He smiled thinly. "She met some guy. It was love. Paris, you know. Is she going to be okay?"

I looked at Dr. Delaye. Bill stared at me with a look that said *butt out.*

"They are doing everything they can for her," said Dr. Delaye quietly, a sensitive answer that revealed nothing. He walked over to the man's side. "If you would please help us? We need to know the young woman's full name, her nationality, whom we may contact. Any bit of information may help. Please, won't you sit down? May I ask your name?"

"Bennett. Jimmy Bennett." They shook hands.

Jimmy Bennett. How could I forget? There was a time when I had talked to Jimmy at least once a day, although I must admit we conversed more by phone than in person. He used to be my agent's assistant at Global Sport; he spent most of his time at the office while my agent was on the road with the players. Jimmy had been a hot young MBA who was willing to work his way up handling correspondence, running off copies, wrangling Fed-Exes, answering phones, doing whatever needed to be done. Once or twice, he'd even walked A.M. for me. About the time I left G.S., he'd been made an agent in his own right, but then I'd lost track of him.

I poked Bill. "Didn't Bennett just launch some new tournament?" Bill was always up on anything that involved sponsorship.

Bill nodded. "I heard he had formed his own agency and was promoting tournaments with private sponsors. He's got a big new one called the Crown Jewel."

I'd heard of the Crown Jewel. It was going to be played on all surfaces—hard, grass, and clay—in Las Vegas. That in itself was news, but this was also supposed to be the richest tournament in tennis history. I hadn't realized that Jimmy was involved. I stared at him, trying to remember what it was like to work with him. Of course, he didn't look the same: he'd put on some weight, his face had a meatier look, and his sandy hair was thinner and shorter. Then again, no doubt I had also changed. At any rate, he didn't seem to notice me, which was quite understandable under the circumstances.

"Jimmy?" He turned toward me. "It's Jordan. Jordan Myles."

His eyes widened behind the tinted lenses, but he didn't smile. "Oh, God, Jordan. This is just horrible. The poor girl. How bad is it?"

One thing I now remembered about Jimmy was that he liked to deal with facts. He'd never gone in for small talk or gossip.

"Bad," I said. He read my eyes; then he rubbed his hands down the sides of his face.

"Jesus, poor Cath."

"I'm sorry, Jimmy. There's nothing official yet, but you could go to the clinic."

"What do we know about this clinic? Is it a good one?"

I tried to reassure him. "I think they specialize in trauma."

"I want the best treatment for her," Jimmy snapped. "Anything. I'll cover the cost."

"But if you could just tell them who she is? Then maybe they could find out if there's anything in her medical history."

"Sorry. Sure." His lips were a tight white line. "Catherine Richie. Twenty-something. I was never sure; she only worked for me for about six months. Comes from Steamboat Springs, Colorado. Lives in LA now, in Santa Monica. Parents, younger brother. Not married. Career girl, a real go-getter. Very attractive. Nice person, too. I thought she had a future with my company, but she met some guy here in Paris. I never did know his name. She was a pretty private person. What can I tell you? She just up and quit."

"Any idea how she got to the top of the greenhouse?"

"I wasn't there. Maybe you don't know, but I've just formed my own management company, TalentMasters. We have a suite in the sponsors' village, and I was there with the Rolex guys. When we heard the sirens, I ran out to the road and saw them working on her. That's how I knew."

"We were hoping you'd have some information that would help us figure out what happened," I said. "She either fell or was pushed through the glass dome. For what occasion would you climb to the top of a greenhouse in the middle of the Bois in a cocktail dress?"

Jimmy shook his head. "This is just terrible," he said.

Bill stepped in. "The gendarmes are waiting out there and I'm sure they'd appreciate any information." It was clear Bill wanted us to have minimal involvement in a situation that was growing messy. He hated messes, and he always preferred a low profile.

"No need to become alarmed," said Dr. Skenk.

I looked at him. He seemed a sad figure, trying to insert himself into the situation. I imagined that when he left the infirmary, Dr. Skenk would tell all his friends and associates, not to mention his patients, how he had been at the hub of the investigation.

"I can't believe this happened to Catherine," said Jimmy sadly. "How am I going to get along without her?"

"Didn't you say she quit?" I asked.

"Well, technically, yes, but I thought she'd reconsider. I was prepared to offer her a substantial increase. And we were gearing up for the Crown Jewel, our big showcase tournament in Las Vegas. I don't know how I'll get through this without her. All the details are in her files."

Bill tapped me on the arm and we stepped aside. "They just got word from the clinic," he said quietly. "She's dead, and they've opened a murder investigation. They're notifying the U.S. consulate. After the autopsy, somebody has to claim the body and arrange for it to be shipped back to her next of kin. Do you think Jimmy should do it?"

I nodded silently. I was still digesting the idea of murder. That it had happened so near so many people seemed especially horrifying—all of us sipping champagne and eating hors d'oeuvres while over our heads this young woman fought for her life. I shuddered under the blanket, which could no longer warm me.

"The police will want to interview you too," said Bill.

"I know." I hadn't seen anything or anyone, however—just that jagged hole in the glass roof.

The authorities gathered around Jimmy, conferring quietly. Jimmy looked shaken to the core, his face drained of color. Dr. Skenk appeared at his side with a glass of water and some pills, which Jimmy downed in a gulp.

"It's going to be a long night," I said to Bill. "What about our investors and sponsors? Shouldn't you be meeting them for dinner?"

He brushed off the question. "They'll understand." He remained rooted beside me as a French police official approached us with a notebook and pen.

The policeman introduced himself as Inspector Lemire and asked to see our passports. He smiled in recognition from behind wire-rimmed glasses as he stared at my passport photo, an old one from when my hair was longer. "Mademoiselle Myles. Of course. I was in the audience when you won here at Roland Garros. A magnificent match."

"Thank you," I said. "I'm a physical therapist now." Then I described the condition of the body as I found it and my observation of the tears around the neck of the designer dress.

"And what did you see exactly?" the officer asked, focusing on the business at hand and writing intently. He spoke perfect English, with only a trace of a French accent.

"Well," I said, "I heard glass breaking, and I ran in that direction and saw a woman lying facedown in the fishpond. I turned her over and administered CPR. I really didn't see anything but broken glass."

"And before the incident, when you entered the greenhouse?"

"Well, I passed a few people, including Mr. Bennett over there—at least I think it was him—on his way out. I really only glanced at the roof. I didn't see anybody up there, although I wasn't looking for anyone or paying much attention. I do remember a kind of gingerbread weather vane."

"The grounds were sealed at the time of the reception, and only people with invitations, park employees, and private guards were permitted on the grounds. Security is very strong. We have been extremely cautious since the Monica Seles incident."

"Someone might have come in earlier and taken cover," I suggested. "There are a lot of nooks and crannies around the greenhouses, and a person could certainly hide among the plants and trees."

He nodded and scribbled in his notebook. I realized that he was being polite, and I immediately regretted my Nancy Drew comments. What professional police officer of any nationality would not consider the possibility of criminal perpetrators sneaking onto a crime scene?

After another half hour of basic questioning, during which I told the officer my observations about the woman's neck and my thought that it might have been broken before she fell, we were free to leave. I patted Marcie on the shoulder on my way out.

She reached up and grabbed my hand. "They're taking me to the hospital and keeping me overnight for observation," she said.

"It's okay," I reassured her. "That's normal in cases of shock. You'll be fine. What happens is all the blood goes from the periphery of your body to the center, so your brain had a shortage. But it's just temporary." I squeezed her hand.

Jimmy Bennett was in the middle of a call on his mobile phone. He motioned across the room that he would call me. The officer who had questioned Bill and me walked us to the door of the infirmary.

"Here is my card." He turned it over and wrote something. "My home number is on the back. Please call at any time if you think of something that might be important. And—can we expect you to make a comeback, Mademoiselle Myles?" he asked.

"No, I'm sorry to say," I said. "I'm permanently out of the game."

He pushed the door open and held it as Bill and I walked out. "Never say never, mademoiselle." He smiled. "In my business, you learn that."

I walked beside Bill toward the door to the players' entrance. All of a sudden it felt as though there were concrete in my shoes, and my head pounded. In the madness of the evening I'd forgotten to drink anything, a cardinal sin when trying to elude jet lag. We detoured into the catering stands and grabbed two large bottles of Evian, which we drank as we walked.

"It's hard to believe that the tournament will just continue, as if nothing happened," I said.

"Nothing did—at the tournament," said Bill. He tucked his water bottle under his arm and wiped some condensation from his glasses. "Officially the unfortunate incident occurred completely off the grounds."

"Think about it, Bill, it's a really sad story. This girl Catherine meets Mr. Wonderful in Paris, quits her job to be with him, and ends up like this. I wonder who he is and when he'll find out."

"He obviously wasn't at the reception," said Bill. He showed his pass and mine, which he had picked up for me, as we turned into the players' area. We had both sent passport-size photos ahead to be laminated.

"Probably not. But if she quit her job with Jimmy, what was *Catherine* doing there? In a cocktail dress? If she was just attending socially, wouldn't she have gone with her new boyfriend, especially if she had quit her job to be with him? Or maybe she just gave that as an excuse. Maybe she was going to work for somebody else, one of Jimmy's competitors."

"All questions which, fortunately, you and I do not have to answer." Bill yawned. "Are you starving, Jordan?"

"Let's see. It must be breakfast time back home."

"According to the French, we're right on schedule. They never eat till late."

"You go right ahead, Bill. I'm just too tired."

We circled through the building, winding up downstairs in the waiting room, where several players in warm-up clothes were ensconced in easy chairs watching the remaining matches in the fast-fading light on a bank of TV screens. A woman at the desk, obviously alerted that we were coming, waved us through. The official transport car area was located, for security's sake, at the end of a short tunnel that ran beneath the roadway in front of the building. The tunnel stairs exit virtually at the car doors. That way, star players can be taken out of the complex with minimal crowd exposure and risk.

By the time we'd ridden back through the Bois and I'd been dropped at my hotel, I was practically falling asleep in the car. As

I stumbled into the elevator, it occurred to me that A.M. needed her walk. I pushed my floor, and the doors started to slide shut.

Suddenly a gym bag swung into the path of the closing door, causing it to bump open again. A tall woman with a baseball cap pulled low over blond bangs stepped into the elevator.

"Jordan, I have been waiting for you in the lobby," Dagmar Olafsen said firmly, slightly reprovingly, as if I should have known. Her voice was husky, with a trace of a Scandinavian accent.

"Hello, Dag. Sorry. I was—unavoidably delayed. But I wasn't aware that we were meeting." I punched my floor again, and the elevator doors closed.

"We weren't," she said. "By the way, I heard what happened at the greenhouse tonight. Now I'm *convinced* you must be the one to help me." She stared at me from behind tinted aviator-style glasses. At almost six feet tall, she was very imposing.

"You know, Dagmar," I said, "you can always make an appointment. It's been a long day, and I really hate discussing these matters in an elevator car."

Her eyes were pleading. "You've got to work with me. I've been to ordinary therapists."

"I'm an ordinary therapist too." The elevator stopped and a Japanese couple got on. Dagmar moved closer and leaned over, since I'm four inches shorter than she is. I noticed that her hands were enormous.

"The physical therapy part, perhaps," she said. "The mental part, no. You are not, you never could be. You were a player. You were a great champion, greater than you ever gave yourself credit. And then you were finished—and you came back."

"Not to tennis," I reminded her.

She shrugged. "Maybe not, this is true. But to something more important, or perhaps in the end you care about it more. You made a great success in a difficult situation. This is motivation I admire. And what I need from you. And more."

"I'm getting off here." The elevator doors opened on twelve, and I got out my room key.

"What a coincidence. So am I." She strode down the hall, keeping pace.

"I need to walk my dog."

"Fine. We will walk together."

From the set of Dagmar's jaw, I could tell there was no dissuading her—and no sleep for me yet.

A half hour later, Dagmar, A.M., and I were all seated down the street at a sidewalk table in front of a little fish restaurant. The restaurant had massive copper pots hanging from a rack over the front door and a sumptuous display of fresh mussels, clams, oysters, and langoustines artfully arranged on a tray of crushed ice and seaweed. A perimeter of fat pink hydrangeas in waist-high window boxes cordoned off the tables from the busy street.

A.M. ignored the seafood extravaganza and sat at my feet, lapping up a tiny chopped steak prepared specially for her by the chef, who had stepped out of the kitchen to make a fuss over her. One thing I've always loved about France is the way they treat dogs like people. I ordered *pommes frites* and *haricots verts*. Dagmar ordered a glass of wine.

"I'm not playing tomorrow," she explained, pushing up her glasses until they held back her hair like a headband. She had a strong-boned face with high cheekbones and thick unplucked eyebrows.

"Okay, Dagmar," I said. "Why the full court press from Woody—and now you? All you had to do was call me at the clinic and come to Palm Springs for an evaluation. Why the panic?"

"Panic is an overstatement," she answered calmly, sipping her wine. Always the strategist, she was now trying to jockey for an advantage. "However, I am not happy with myself. For a long time I have not played to my potential, and that is what I wish to do now, this season. It may be my last. But if that is so, I don't want it to be because of my shoulder. And I know you can help me. *Will* you help me?"

"I don't know. It's not that I don't want to, but you're talking about an intensive program."

"That is right. I want you to join my team until I'm back on my feet."

"But, you see, I'm scheduled through summer."

"I will pay you double your usual fee, whatever that is," she stated flatly, setting her glass on the table.

"Money is not the issue."

"I will donate the fee to your charity of choice," she said.

"That's not the issue either. It's just that my time is already booked. The clinic handles my schedule. I just want you to understand."

Dagmar blinked hard, and I could see tears well up in her pale eyes. She turned her head away from me. "I know," she whispered. "I'm sorry. This was not very professional of me. But, you see, I'm not totally unrealistic. I know this is my last chance. When I left Denmark and my family and friends, it was hard for me, but I did it for a certain dream. And now, many years later, I still have the dream but I have not achieved it. I know I did well at doubles, but I want to feel I had a successful career at singles too. You understand?" She sighed. "All right, I may never achieve it. That I can accept. And no one realizes better than I do that it is a long climb up, especially once you have fallen down. But I will never accept not trying until there is nothing left to give." She lifted her chin and smiled ruefully.

I had to admire her. This was not Woody talking. No coach can instill that kind of determination, especially at the end of a career. And she was right. I knew how she felt.

"I am trying some new things," she said. "I'm with Jimmy now, as you know."

"I bet Alan, Ed, and Maurice were heartbroken to lose you."

"Maybe, but I wasn't sorry to lose them. They'd lost their faith in *me,* you see. I have to qualify for every tournament. Every time they looked at me, I saw myself through their eyes: a loser, a has-been. They didn't want to give me this one last chance." She swirled the wine in her glass so violently that it sloshed over the edge, soaking the tablecloth. "My God, Ed wanted to turn me out to pasture, have me make fitness videos. Fitness videos! Like Jane Fonda! Can you imagine? What a little shit!"

"What is your goal now?" I asked.

"Well, I am playing quite well on clay, and I can play better still. I want to get my singles ranking back into the top ten, of course. That would be respectable."

If not impossible. "I should say so. But the clay court season is over."

"The Grand Slams, yes. But there is a new series that includes clay—the Crown Jewel. It's going to get a lot of attention because it's one of the richest."

I was always a believer that there was life beyond the Grand Slams. Too much is probably made of them, in proportion to the many other events in tennis. But the Crown Jewel championships were new, unproven, and, as Dag pointed out, lucrative. The series had surfaced just this spring, highly publicized, backed by Japanese sponsorship, and promoted by Jimmy Bennett. But the tournament sites were in places that nobody wanted to play. It was hard to lure big names to Oklahoma, where I heard that Dagmar had won the first tournament in the Crown Jewel, although the event had flopped because no promotable stars had signed on. "Dag, correct me if I'm not up-to-date, but none of the big names are playing that series."

"Precisely. So I can win. I won in Oklahoma; I can do it in Las Vegas. The prize money is incredible. Somebody will show up just for that. At the last tournament, the winners from the clay court circuit will be showcased in a winner-take-all. There will be plenty of publicity."

A flurry of flashes flared, and I rubbed my eyes, startled, as a photographer backed off, waving apologies.

"The press are rediscovering me," Dagmar said wryly. "Suddenly, at thirty-four, I'm a story again. Stay out there long enough, just standing up, and you gain a few points, I guess." She ran her finger around the rim of her wineglass. Her nails were bitten, her fingers long.

"Well, you did attract a little attention here," I said. A.M. had finished her meat and I hauled her up into my lap.

"Oh, that. It was ridiculous. It seems like every time I play Heather, there's some incident. Now the media have picked it up. We're supposed to be feuding."

"Are you?"

She shrugged. "We're pretty evenly matched. That's all it is. The press turns any two women in competition into a catfight."

"Well, they need to print something, I guess."

"You should come back and play Kelly again. If you were back on the scene, they wouldn't pay attention to us. You two were the original rivals of all time."

"Just don't take it too seriously."

"Oh, but I do. I have to." She smiled, but the corners of her mouth were taut. This tension, and her turbulent behavior on court, led me to believe that Dagmar had indeed invested a great deal of herself in this rivalry. The press may have flogged the issue, but it was clear that she cared.

"So why do you think you're playing better in spite of your shoulder?"

She frowned. "Well, CiCi and I broke up. It was a very unsettling relationship, trying to keep both the personal and the professional. I think I am more focused now that Jimmy is my coach." She took a piece of bread and twisted it.

Dagmar had been one of the first women players to openly admit to being gay. She and her former coach CiCi McBain had been one of the steadier couples of either gender on the tour. CiCi had coached Dagmar since I was on the circuit, and they had lived quietly together on and off the road. Still, the outspoken frankness of this relationship had cost Dagmar virtually any chance at an endorsement contract. If my own commercial prospects had been weak, Dagmar's were nonexistent. Sponsors with multimillion dollar contracts never take even the slightest risk. They want sure things, like Kelly Kendall. As a result, Dag's income had been seriously affected. It was rumored that, for some of the leaner years, CiCi had worked for free. I had to wonder whether the breakup of this once-stable relationship had impacted Dagmar's game. You try to wipe personal problems out of your mind when you play, but it isn't always possible.

Dag leaned back in her chair, stretching her long legs. "Well, I won't pester you about it." Her posture seemed to sag slightly, her eyes dropped, and with them, it seemed, some measure of her hopes.

Hope is something you can never lose. After I had the accident, I awoke with my leg tacked together with a hundred and sixty stitches and staples, hitched to a perpetual motion machine that mocked me for my inability to move. There seemed no hope left in me. My knee was in shreds. Not only would I never play again, it would be impossible to live. And then I met Gus, who was able to pilot me through the crisis, who had given me the gift of rebuilding my dreams. How could I not give back now, to someone else?

I mentally sifted through my upcoming commitments: a corporate golf seminar, a speech, catching up on my paperwork, my ongoing clients at the clinic. There was a lot of business, but there was only one person whose hopes involved me in any way, and that person was sitting across the table.

"Hold up your right arm, straight over your head like the Statue of Liberty," I said.

She pointed upward.

"Now turn your hand backward." A slight wince crossed Dag's face. Woody was right. She didn't have her full range of motion, for some reason.

"How does it feel?"

"Tight."

"You feel a weakness in your serve?"

She nodded. "I need my serve back. I also get exhausted halfway through my matches. I'm in great condition, but I can't sustain my game."

Something was very wrong about this. Complete recovery from rotator cuff surgery should take maybe six months, absolute maximum. Recovery from microsurgery was five times faster than with traditional surgery. I couldn't tell what was wrong under the skin without a serious workup, but, under the circumstances, I marveled that she could play as well as she did. No wonder her disposition was shot. It takes guts to play at world class level when you're in serious pain, but this was not the first time I had seen it happen. Veronica Mills was once in such bad shape she should have defaulted at the singles finals of the U.S. Open, but she hung in somehow and managed to win.

"It's better now," said Dag, lowering her arm. She rubbed it gingerly. "At first I had to sleep sitting up in a chair."

"Okay, Dag," I found myself saying. At the same time, I knew Bill was going to wring my neck. He had the entire season planned. I was committed down to the second. My every moment was scheduled on the computer. I was going to have to work with Dagmar on my own time. It was going to be a long summer. "Why don't you come back to the Springs after the French is over? I'll call Tony and set it up. But I do have one condition, and it's a deal-breaker."

"Yes?"

"Come on your own. Forget the entourage." I suppose I meant Woody, but it would be undiplomatic to specify him by name. Still, whether an entourage numbered one or ten, it was rarely a productive addition. There was a limit to how much one's family, agent, racket stringer, masseur, hitting partner, spiritual adviser, bodyguard, refrigerator cop, et al., could add to a training situation. Invariably, there was an unwieldy difference of opinion, an attempt to manage by committee.

"Whatever you say, Jordan," Dagmar agreed. "This is going to be great."

"What do you want to do?"

"I want to win that last big tournament of the Crown Jewel. It's not a Grand Slam, but it's an all-surface event. I know that when I get on clay I can win it, if I'm in shape."

"Whoa, let's talk about this."

It is always difficult for professional athletes not to think in terms of the short run; everything is very immediate for them. I understood that mind-set all too well. But physical therapy can never be rushed successfully. There is no such thing as an accelerated program. I suspected Dag had already tried to take some shortcuts to speed her recovery, possibly even steroids, which would have contributed to her present problems.

"I understand what you're saying, of course, but I prefer to work one step at a time. We'll be looking at daily goals, not tour goals. Can you live with that?"

"I'm sure I can."

"Good. We'll start with a complete examination and a new MRI. First things first. You'll have to prepare for some frustration. There's no magic needle."

Dag was grinning broadly. I must say, it isn't often that you see a person so happy at the prospect of facing a hard uphill road.

When we were back in the hotel lobby, Dagmar stopped at the desk for messages and I tucked A.M. under my arm and headed for the elevators. Sleepily, I pressed the button for my floor. Two American writers from *Sports Story* magazine stood beside me, talking in low voices.

"I wonder if he did it," one said.

"They say he was having an affair with her," replied his friend.

"I thought she left him."

"Fit of jealousy?"

"I don't know. There are easier ways to have a fit of jealousy than push somebody through the roof."

"Where is he now?"

"Oh, he's out. The embassy got involved before the French police could touch him. You can't accuse Jimmy Bennett of not being connected."

"Well, they must have something on him, or they wouldn't have taken him in for questioning."

The elevator stopped, the doors opened, and I walked down the hall toward my room. When he had spoken to me, Jimmy had implied that Catherine was simply an employee. I wondered how much more there was to the story. Was he really implicated in the murder?

I didn't have to wonder very long, though, because A.M. started barking even before I got the room key out, and when I turned on the light Jimmy Bennett was sitting there, slumped in a chair. He looked dead.

THREE

Dead. What else would you think about a man you find sitting motionless on a chair in your room in the dark? Either that or you might assume he was waiting to ambush you. It was impossible to believe the worst about somebody I thought I knew, but the events of the day hardly led me to believe Jimmy had paid a social call.

I shuddered in spite of myself and backed up quickly, opening the door to the hall. But A.M., still riding in my arms, jumped to the floor, trotted over to Jimmy in the chair, lunged her fifteen-pound body at his ankle, and started chewing on it.

Jimmy sprang to life. "Hey! Cut that out! Those are silk socks from Sulka!"

"For God's sake, Jimmy, what are you doing here?" I yelled with some degree of bravado as I stepped into the room. If he wasn't dead or going to kill me, I wanted him out of my room so I could get some sleep.

"I wonder how you get dog saliva stains out of silk." Jimmy frowned, sidestepping A.M., who was now wagging her tail furiously.

"You have some questions to answer, or I call security."

He held up his hands, as if surrendering to Wyatt Earp. "Jordan, I apologize for catching you off guard like this. God, I'm a rude bastard! I know people are talking. So I made a little business arrangement with the concierge." He flopped back into the chair. "God! I've had a terrible day!"

"You? Poor you. What about Catherine? I'd say her day was worse."

He dropped his head into his hands. "A tragedy, just a tragedy. I don't mean to be insensitive." He looked up. Without the tinted glasses, I could see his eyes were bloodshot. "But you surely don't think I had anything to do with it?"

"Did I hear that the police wanted to talk to you? Maybe they know something I don't."

Jimmy leaped up again and in a step was at my side. "Now listen! How should I know how Catherine got up on the roof? I wasn't even *there,* for God's sake. I was trying to hook up with Dr. Skenk. He'll vouch for me. But of course you know that. You saw me leaving. Or so you told the police—Miss Eyewitness."

"Well, I did see you leaving. That's the truth. But if you were leaving, what's the problem?"

He rolled his eyes. "Inspector Clouseau thinks it's entirely possible that I didn't leave the grounds at all. After all, did you actually see me walk out of the gate?"

"No."

"I was afraid of that. And did you stand watching the gate to be sure I didn't cut back in?"

"No."

"I rest my case." Jimmy walked over to the minibar and yanked on the door. "This thing have a key?" He rattled the handle with no results.

"Gee, do I have amnesia? I don't recall offering you a drink. Or even inviting you over. But if you could get into my room, the minibar should be a piece of cake."

He paced frenetically around the small room. "Listen, Jordan, if we weren't old friends I wouldn't have presumed."

"Come off it, Jimmy, we haven't been in touch in ages. You didn't even recognize me. You had no right to grease your way in here. You scared me, and I resent it." I walked to the door and held it open. "This way out."

"Wait." He pushed the door closed and blocked it, his arm inches from my face.

What if this guy is capable of murder? I thought. Impossible to believe of someone you know, but there was always a chance. The police had detained him. I found myself scanning the room for weapons. The glass ashtray on the desk? The ice bucket? The phone?

"Here's the deal, Jordan," said Jimmy tensely. "The French police pulled me in after you left."

"Why? You said you hadn't seen Catherine. She was just an employee who resigned."

"Well, actually, there was slightly more to it than that."

"Oh, really?"

His arm fell limply to his side. "It doesn't matter. It's irrelevant. She's dead, but I didn't have anything to do with it. You know that and you can prove it."

"Me? I'm not involved in this!"

"Oh, you're involved, all right. You were there. You were the first person to reach Catherine. And my good friends at the police say you identified me leaving the greenhouse area at the beginning of the reception."

"That's true. I did."

Jimmy grabbed my shoulders. "So you see I wasn't even there when it happened, and you are the one person who can prove it."

I wrenched away. "Let go of me. I can't prove anything."

"You didn't see me go out the gate?"

"No."

"Think hard. You'll remember."

"I was facing in the opposite direction, Jimmy. We passed each other, and that was it."

He started to pace again. "These police here, they've been

insinuating that there was some sort of lover's quarrel. All right, we'd been . . . involved . . . but it was nothing serious. She broke it off. *She* quit, and that was the end of it. It was *her* decision! She was going back to the States."

"Then why was she dressed up to go to the party?"

"Who knows why women dress up and go to parties?" Jimmy said, exasperation in his voice. "Maybe she had a date."

"With whom?"

"I hadn't seen her for a week, maybe more. How would I know? Maybe with the janitor, maybe with the guy who killed her." His upper lip beaded with a fine, shiny sweat. "The point is, if you didn't see me leave the complex, somebody else must have. Think! Who else did you see on your way in?"

"Jimmy, I've been through all this with the police. I saw a guy in a suit and a motorcycle helmet and a couple of people I couldn't describe milling around."

He shook his head slowly. "You know, I didn't have anything to do with Catherine's death. But somehow this witch hunt is going to leak out and poison my event. Who's going to support a tournament when the promoter is under suspicion? Even if they can't prove a thing. I have to know who really did it. They have to nail the guy or I'm never off the hook."

"Did you and Catherine see each other for long?"

"Maybe two months; it was never serious. We both under-stood that. It was more a convenience thing. Working together, traveling together. You know, it happens."

That I did know. "But you broke up. . . ."

"We broke up over career conflicts. She didn't like working so hard. Or the travel. I don't have to tell you; you've been there. It got to be too much for her, the living out of a suitcase. She wanted to settle down, have a less demanding job. Spend more time at home, maybe have a family. I wasn't ready for that kind of relationship, not with anybody, not at this point of my life."

"But you said she fell in love with somebody else in Paris. Was he French?"

Jimmy bristled. "For all I know, he was a chimpanzee from the

Congo. Our relationship at this point was professional. We never discussed her love life. Like I told you, Catherine had resigned."

"Jimmy, relax. If you're innocent, you have nothing to worry about. You don't have to be so defensive."

"I'm not defensive. I simply have a lot at stake here," he snapped. "I've got players, sponsors. My business is on the line. I've got to deliver." He threw his head back. "Don't you under-stand?" he shouted. "I'm fucked! I'm totally fucked!"

"Maybe you should call Dr. Skenk. Maybe you need a pre-scription sedative. What's his number? You take a deep breath." I picked up the phone. I had to get this person out of my room, even if it meant calling security.

"Okay," said Jimmy, "I'm going. I apologize for the intrusion. But I'm asking you. See what else you can remember. It could mean something."

"I'll try. Maybe after I get some rest I'll think more clearly."

"Good night, Jordan." He picked up his briefcase, opened it, and handed me a large white envelope.

"What's this?"

"A press kit on TalentMasters." He took the envelope from me, pulled out a red folder, and handed it back. "All my numbers are in there. I'm on satellite beeper if you have any news."

"Believe me, you'll be the first to hear."

As I double-locked the door behind him, I prayed there would be no more surprises tonight. I was so tired, I felt numb.

I reached down, dragged off my shoes and socks, and started to pull my sweater over my head. It seemed like too much effort, so I left it on and scrabbled a little space under the bedspread. I aimed for it and flopped over, fully dressed. The bedside light seemed like a million miles away. I reached for it, but my hand stopped at the slick, shiny press kit. Lying on my stomach, I flipped open the cover and pulled a sheet of paper from the pocket. It was a press release, listing the background of the company—FOR IMMEDIATE RELEASE: JIMMY BENNETT'S TALENTMASTERS SCORES ROYAL FLUSH WITH THE CROWN JEWEL TENNIS TOURNAMENT.

Skimming the page, I saw it was a typical press piece hyping the event and announcing the details: the breakthrough news that it would be the first tournament to be played on all surfaces; information on the new stadium at the Las Vegas Grand Olympus Hotel, where the matches would be held; dates and times; which players made up the field; the sponsors and prize money. At the bottom of the page, one line caught my eye: *For further details, contact Catherine Richie,* followed by a phone number. How could I not pick up the phone and dial the number? It had a 310 area code in the United States—Los Angeles. A good friend of mine manages a restaurant there, so I recognized the exchange.

After three rings, the line picked up. "Hello," said a sweetly friendly but professional voice. The tone was unexceptional, but it upset me. "You have reached the offices of TalentMasters, and this is Catherine Richie. I'm not available right now, but if you'll leave your name and message, I'll get back to you as soon as possible. If you need to schedule a meeting or conference call, please dial extension four-five-zero."

I hung up, my hand unsteady. I could still hear that voice, the sweet voice that belonged to the staring eyes, the unresponsive lips, the dead girl I could not save.

The Global Sport town house is located on one of the streets that intersects with Place Victor Hugo. There is a sparkling fountain at one end of the block, and smart shops mingle with charming sidewalk cafés and umbrella tables. The stone buildings are alternately buff and white, filigreed with black wrought-iron grillwork.

Global Sport was my agency for five years before I retired from the tour, and although some of the people I worked with had moved on, there was still a relationship there, one we hoped would help bring us some corporate sponsors for the clinic. Bill had concocted the idea of forming a loose partnership with G.S., maybe giving them a favorable package of services in return for delivering sponsors who were working with their clients. The sponsors would gain the credibility of attaching the Desert Springs seal of approval, as it were, to their products, and could also hold training events for their own staff members, as well as their athletes under contract, at our facility. It seemed to be a beneficial relationship for everybody concerned, and Bill had set up a number of meetings while we were in Paris.

Unlike their ultra-high-tech American offices, the G.S. Paris space was like something out of an Edith Wharton novel grafted onto a twentieth-century business. The heavy iron-grated door swung open to a tomblike marble lobby, with an arched, elaborately molded plaster ceiling and a slightly frayed oriental rug. At one time, this must have been the ground floor of an elegant single-family home. Here, Global Sport spearheaded their European operations, which included six events a year in France, plus events in Switzerland, Monte Carlo, London, and Milan. Bill and I took the small spidery cage of an elevator up two floors to the office itself.

"You haven't said a word this morning, Jordan," Bill said, patting my shoulder, a patronizing gesture I particularly dislike. "Are you all right? Last night was pretty rough, I know." Bill is well-intentioned, but sometimes he has this annoying paterfamilias complex.

"I'm just taking in the sights and enjoying the fact that I'm not out there practicing."

"You're sure that's it? There's no story beneath the story?"

"Actually, there is one, but I'll save the details about Jimmy's surprise appearance in my bedroom for lunchtime—when we've built up more stamina."

"Jimmy's quite the hustler."

"He's going to hustle himself right into trouble. They're interrogating him for the murder."

Bill shook his head. "I'll stay out of your personal life, Jordan, but to get involved with Jimmy—"

"There's nothing personal." I cut him off. "Quite the opposite." The elevator was taking an inordinate amount of time to rise about fifty feet.

"Jimmy is not on the best of terms with Global Sport, as I understand it," said Bill.

"I haven't kept up with the politics."

"When he left to form his own shop, he raided the ranks."

"I didn't think he got any of the really big stars."

"Worse. He took a couple of people from finance and talent who knew where the bodies were buried."

"Bad analogy, Bill, under the circumstances."

"Well, there was talk, that's all I'm saying, and you should be aware of it."

The elevator creaked to a stop and we were greeted by Ellen, Alan's long-time assistant. "How are you, Jordan? We miss you," she said, with a quick hug. She was one of those ageless people, exactly the same as when I first met her years ago.

"I'm fine, Ellen. What do you know about Marcie?"

"She's okay. She wanted to come in today, but Alan told her to take a few days off. Apparently she wasn't doing so well last night. Horrible situation, just horrible."

Ellen led us to a large room with twenty-foot ceilings, as elaborate as the lobby. In a small arrangement of armchairs flanking the fireplace sat Alan Kauffman, a founding partner of the firm and my former agent, along with two men, one of whom was Kevin Curry, of sunglasses fame.

I shot a look at Bill. He hadn't told me that one of the prospective sponsors was LaserGlass. They were a force in the sponsorship community, to be sure, but I'd never really forgiven Curry for his behavior when I won at Roland Garros. Now that a few years had passed, I had elevated it to epic proportions, propelled by my recurrent nightmare. Then again, I'd never told Bill about the incident, so I couldn't really blame him for setting up this meeting.

"Jordan! Welcome home!" Alan greeted me with a bear hug, then brushed my cheeks with his handlebar mustache as he bestowed kisses on me. He was a big man with thinning red hair;

as usual, he wore a white suit and deck shoes with no socks. Alan was so rich, he was beyond fashion. He broke our embrace to greet Bill similarly. "Look at you two!" He beamed. "We're all so proud of the work you've done at Desert Springs. Such an accomplishment! A real credit to the industry!"

Bill, who in his time had received thousands of accolades from important people, including three U.S. presidents who were personal golfing partners, thanked him quietly. He was well aware of what he had achieved, and he had it in perspective. Nothing in sports can replace the adrenaline of the winning moment. The rest of an athlete's life is usually an addendum, but Bill had turned it into something truly worthwhile.

Kevin Curry walked toward me, extending his hand, and I shook it, although not with relish. "You know, Jordan, I was in the stands when you won here—I'll never forget that match point, one of the greatest." He flexed his hands and cracked his knuckles.

"I'll never forget it either, Kevin." I'm sure he missed my ironic delivery.

"This is Andy Fiero, our EVP marketing." He indicated his associate, a younger man who I assumed was the business voice of the organization, since Kevin's main strength had always been the schmooze. We shook hands. Andy wasn't tall, but he was slim and long-legged, giving an impression of height that was reinforced by a quiet, controlled presence.

We drifted to the big sandblasted glass table and took our seats around it, Alan at the head with Ellen beside him. I passed out copies of Bill's proposal.

"All of us at the Springs are very excited about a possible partnership," said Bill. "You know, when I won the Gold . . ."

He proceeded to integrate his epic Olympic story with the outline of the basics of our plan. This, I knew, was for the benefit of Curry and company. Alan already knew everything there was to know about both Bill and his proposal. He had already given it a green light, or we wouldn't be here.

"The thing is, Kevin," said Alan, as Bill wound up his pitch, "instead of dissipating your funds in little dibs and dabs, endorsements that are pretty much known only by insiders, LaserGlass would be making a substantial and high-visibility alliance."

I noticed Kevin stiffen. Basically, if they eliminated the insider sunglasses endorsements, they'd eliminate his job. I had a feeling Andy wouldn't object to that too heartily, but I decided to give Kevin a chance. Why, I don't know. "Or," I added, "think of it as *augmenting* your basic program. The two could work in concert, double the impact."

Andy nodded, Kevin relaxed a bit, and the meeting continued with everybody on board.

Alan handed out a flier with the agency's client list. "This is pretty current, and you're all familiar with it, except for one change. Heather Knight is no longer a client." He took out a pen and drew a line through her name. "El, let's get this reprinted."

She made a note on a small pad.

I was slightly surprised. Heather Knight's career had been launched by G.S., giving them a prominent place in the young phenom category. When she was only fifteen years old, Heather had flashed on the tennis scene like a meteor. She was the one they compared with Jennifer, the American girl who could play like Monica and hit the cover off the ball; when her game was on—which wasn't all the time—Heather, a true natural, beat players far more experienced and technically better.

On top of all this, Heather was that rare commodity, a born performer, quick with a quip or a pun and loved for it by the media, whom she showered with handouts of her favorite candies, Tootsie Roll Pops. From the beginning, Heather had given it her all, and for a while she was everybody's favorite moppet, smiling from magazine covers and ads, her parents trotting along agreeably in a happy daze.

But if her teens had been blazing, Heather's star began to dim as she moved toward her twenties. Suddenly, she wasn't so cute anymore. There were younger—and more promotable—players. The media moved on to other mascots, and other players edged her off center stage. I remembered watching Heather's frustration at last year's U.S. Open as she stormed off court, fuming over a loss to Millie Ashton, a much less talented player who simply outplayed her.

Heather fell into a cycle of losing. Her ranking was thirty-something; if she didn't make a move now, the downward spiral would continue. Changing agents in midseason is one way of grabbing for a life ring—although it's always the player herself who has to swim to shore.

Kevin, however, seemed puzzled. "Heather? Didn't you discover her at Jake's tennis camp when she was a kid?" His expression indicated that he thought she owed G.S. a little more loyalty.

"Well, she's grown up now," said Alan with a shrug. "It was her decision."

A young woman in black pants and a white T-shirt walked in with a silver tray of miniature French pastries and passed them.

"Where'd she go?" asked Kevin, popping a tiny cream puff into his mouth. He wore gold cuff links in the shape of tiny sunglasses.

"TalentMasters," said Andy, leaning back in his chair. "I got a fax about it last week." He smiled at me, and I thought I saw something in it that was more than business.

After the meeting, a G.S. car and driver took us all down to Roland Garros for the women's doubles quarterfinals, which were already under way. I ended up sitting next to Andy in the car. The Arc de Triomphe and the Eiffel Tower were part of the scenery, but Andy seemed to be watching me as Kevin launched into a story about his latest trip to the Caribbean.

"It's exciting to be going to this tournament with a former champion," Andy said, leaning over. His arm stretched across the back of the car seat, skimming my shoulders. I noticed his straight black hair and pale blue eyes. He had a sensual cupid's-bow upper lip. He was very attractive.

"It seems so surreal now," I said. "Like a movie I watched once."

"I'm sorry I never got to see you play."

"Just watch TV. They do slo-mo replay of the time I lost Wimbledon about once a year. Is this your first time at the French?"

"It is. I just joined LaserGlass last fall."

"Where'd you come from?"

"Quaker."

"Oil or oats?"

"Oats."

"And before that?"

"I was getting my MBA."

"How long ago was that?" God. I sounded like I was interrogating him. I couldn't even imagine why I was asking all these questions, except he seemed like a nice guy.

"Not that long ago."

"So tell me, how do you go from cereal to sunglasses?"

"I signed Michael Jordan for Gatorade."

That would do it.

We didn't talk for the rest of the ride, but just before we got out of the car he asked me to dinner.

"This is a business dinner, right?" I said. "Because I only have time for business on this trip."

"Definitely a business dinner," he said earnestly. He had a very earnest expression, the eyes of a man you can look at and imagine as a little boy. I liked that. "Definitely business," he repeated.

We both knew otherwise, and suddenly I was acutely aware of the fabric of his sleeve against the back of my neck.

Alan had seats in the G.S. box for Kevin and Andy, so Bill and I adjourned for lunch in the players' restaurant. Generally, you have to be a player or be with a player to have access to this area, but our passes—one of twenty-four different types issued for this tournament—permitted it. Once inside, however, the atmosphere was hardly exclusive. The entire players' area resembled the simple facilities you usually find at colleges and universities: natural wood-trimmed decor and earth-toned fabrics. At Central Court under Stand A were the accreditation desks, car and hotel services, flight reservation facilities, stringing and locker rooms, massage rooms, and the restaurant. Under Court A was a hairdresser, video games, locker rooms, and a nursery for players' children.

Beneath Central Court there was also, unfortunately, a total lack of windows or natural light. At the back of the restaurant were stairs to the players' lounge and dressing rooms. It wasn't glamorous, just one step above utilitarian, but I felt more comfortable here than I had in the elaborate greenhouse pavilion. How many hours had I spent playing cards or just sitting around in players' lounges all over the world? This was like coming home.

Bill and I pushed our trays through the cafeteria line and settled in at an empty table. The tournament was always less crowded as the weeks went on, filtering out all but the stars and the upsets. Most of the food was uninspired, but the French usually had pretty good cheeses and strawberries, so I concentrated on them. TV screens were mounted overhead, including one monitor that just listed the scores of the matches in progress on the various courts, so upcoming players could know when to get ready. Before the advent of the video monitor and the beeper, players were on their own. Nobody called them when it was time for a match, so they had to physically attend the games to stay abreast of the schedule. It was not uncommon for players to default simply because they didn't realize it was time for their match. Now, of course, there are TV screens with the games and the scores in the locker rooms so players can keep track of the action on all the courts.

"Speak of the devil," Bill said, motioning toward the TV with a baguette. Heather Knight was battling it out with Mila Karacek—holding on by her fingernails, it seemed to me. There was no sound on the monitors, but from the looks of it just changing agents wasn't going to save this girl's game. The tiny sprite of a few years ago was replaced by a blurry, slow-motion version of her former self. She didn't have the speed or the power anymore, and she seemed to sag between points. Her opponent, however, was faltering even worse—in fact, she appeared to be suddenly and dramatically falling apart, sweating profusely and moving as if she had lead soles on her shoes.

"I think we're going to have a deal," Bill said, ignoring the screen as he squeezed a lemon wedge onto his salad. Bill believes in the therapeutic powers of citrus and adds lemon to everything.

"Has Alan said something?"

"He doesn't have to. Did I overhear that you're having dinner with Andy tonight?"

"He mentioned it. Will you come too?"

"Oh, I wouldn't want to jinx the deal."

Suddenly there was a murmur in the lounge, the sounds of surprise in many languages. Within seconds, talking stopped as chairs scraped and people jumped to their feet, straining toward the TV sets. Mila was on the ground, and the match had been halted. A handful of security guards stepped out onto the court.

"God, what happened?" I wondered.

Bill shook his head, looking up. "Didn't see it," he said.

I saw the physical therapist, Alice Kellerman, dash onto the court, followed by a French medical team, and I shoved back my chair. After all the years I had spent after my accident in Alice's job, it was as if some unseen beeper had paged me. Almost instinctively, I found myself running through the doorway and up the stairs toward Central Court.

I got there just in time to see emergency services rush a stretcher onto the court and carry Mila off—toward the infirmary, I was sure. "What happened, Bunny?" I asked Peggy Braun, a doubles player who had lost in an earlier round. Everyone called her Bunny because of the way she hopped around the court.

She shrugged, never taking her eyes off the drama that was taking place on the court. "It looked like Mila got some kind of terrible cramp."

Cramps can be the scourge of many players. In fact, some players, Jimmy Connors for one, are notorious crampers. Dehydration is often the cause of these cramps, and to help ward them off, some players rely on intravenous fluids before their matches.

I spun around and ran the gauntlet back outside and around the stadium, elbowing my way as I flew through the crowd until, once again, I found myself back at the infirmary. This time, however, the guard refused to admit me. I stood there in frustration, shoved by reporters jostling for position, until one of the other WTF therapists arrived, breathless.

"She's with us," she barked at the guard as we flashed our laminated passes. And in we went.

The scene was a far cry from the previous night. There was no panic, but the atmosphere was taut as piano wire. The room was packed. One team was monitoring an IV of electrolytes and fluids under the supervision of a young Federation doctor, while a nurse barked orders in French. Mila was lying on a wheeled cot at the back of the room, her shirt cut open, and even as I approached I could see her abdominal muscles roll in involuntary spasms. Her coach stood beside the cot, screaming at everyone in German.

"Where's Dr. Delaye, Ali?" I asked Alice, who was the calmest person in the room. She and I had traveled together on the circuit for two years, often rooming together.

"Lunch break. Wouldn't you know? I expect he'll be here any second."

"What's her condition?"

"Extreme dehydration. She's erratic and disoriented—doesn't know where she is, temperature's elevated, blood pressure's crashed. Plus as you can see, she's in extreme spasm. They're giving her Valium in the IV just to get her to the hospital."

"It's not hot enough for heat stress," I commented. In fact, it was chilly; I was wearing a jacket. You usually only see cases of extreme dehydration in places like Australia, when it is routinely over a hundred degrees on court, or the U.S. Open, which can have a saunalike atmosphere in late August. "Are you sure that's what it is?"

"No, but it sure looks that way," said Alice.

"I think she's verging on comatose," I said. "They'd better get her to the hospital."

"She's having a seizure!" one of the nurses announced. Mila was shaking uncontrollably, her eyes rolled back in her head. The nurse moved quickly to put something in Mila's mouth to keep her from biting her tongue.

Exactly then, Jean Delaye swept into the room, taking command. He had such a reassuring and authoritative presence that the frantic atmosphere eased instantly. The German coach continued shouting and ranting into a telephone, but everyone ignored him as Mila was swiftly rolled out on her gurney, an impenetrable phalanx of medical and security personnel surrounding her in a race to the waiting ambulance.

FOUR

"It doesn't add up," I said to Andy over dinner at Chez Francis, a jewel-box bistro on Place l'Alma. From the window above our leather banquette, we could see the Eiffel Tower in the distance, illuminated like a postcard. On the polished bar were huge arrangements of lilies and gladiolas. Small brass lamps with pleated peach silk shades gave the room a romantic glow, but I reminded myself that this was a business dinner.

The waiter placed lentil and langoustine salads in front of us. I pushed mine aside and reiterated that I had ordered lentils only. The waiter gave me a strange look; I've never thought they understand vegetarianism or cholesterol in France, the birthplace of pressed duck and *beurre blanc*. "Mila was in great condition, according to the trainers, and it wasn't a hot day. Dehydration just doesn't make any sense."

"But that's the diagnosis, isn't it?" asked Andy. He helped himself to a roll.

"According to the reports from the hospital, this was such an extreme case of dehydration that the player almost died. In fact, she's still in bad shape. If she hadn't been in peak physical condition, she wouldn't have made it."

"Was she exceptionally thirsty before the match?"

"That's the problem with dehydration," I explained. "The other symptoms occur first; thirst doesn't usually occur until later. It's actually a poor indicator of the body's need for water."

"Sounds like a medical person talking," said Andy.

"Well, this is a basic, and it doesn't add up."

"A lot about this tournament doesn't add up," said Andy. "Do they know any more about the girl who fell through the greenhouse roof?"

"I guess they're investigating. Nobody seems to know what the motive could be."

He sipped his wine. "Tennis isn't the white-glove game it used to be, is it? You know, when the big buzz was heads swiveling politely back and forth watching the game. My God, nowadays there are assassination attempts, murders, you name it. And now tennis is a billion-dollar-a-year industry. Does it seem like a different world to you?"

"I used to like the idea of playing for the fun of it. But that's become a quaint nostalgic memory, like the horse and buggy."

"It's hard to believe you were a tennis champion. Your perspective is so different. But I did my homework. You won three Grand Slams: the U.S., the French, and the Australian Open. You had an incredible serve-and-volley game. . . ." He stopped. "Am I making you uncomfortable?"

I poked at the lentils on my plate. They were tiny, not the kind you see at home. "No, it's just I prefer to live in the present."

"Fair enough. Do you know Mila?"

"No. But she's a pretty good player, I know that. She'll be all right when she gets over this, but it's too bad she lost her shot at the Open."

"Heather Knight moves into the quarterfinals by default. She's scheduled to play Dagmar tomorrow."

"Fireworks guaranteed."

Andy removed a langoustine from its tiny red shell. "People are looking forward to it. Feuds like this put some personality back into the game."

"The wrong kind of personality, if you ask me," I said testily. "This is tennis, not pro wrestling."

"You're not eating," Andy observed.

"Well, two days of death and near-death have a way of suppressing the appetite. Even in France."

"Sorry. I didn't mean to be insensitive." Andy put down his wineglass and looked at me. His dark eyes invited me in. "I just want you to enjoy yourself."

I sighed. "I apologize. I guess I'm not very good company, even at a business dinner."

He reached out and touched my hand, very lightly, just across the top of the fingers. "You're wonderful company. The best."

His meaning was unmistakable. For so many years, I'd been wrapped up with Gus, and before that there was tennis—the two loves of my life. I wasn't accustomed to men approaching me, wasn't even sure I'd brushed Gus's cobwebs away to make room for it.

"I did a data dive on you," Andy said.

"Excuse me?" I moved my hand to dust away a crumb. I've never liked having my hands touched, an aversion acquired from hands that are rough, dry, and heavily calloused from a lifetime of holding a tennis racket.

He laughed. "I mean, I checked you out on the computer— fed in your name and read everything it printed out on you. There was a lot. A list of tennis championships so long I almost ran out of paper. Some amazing statistics. You're the only one who ever beat Kelly Kendall on clay in a Grand Slam. There was a *People* magazine piece on your marriage to the sportscaster, another one on your divorce. But that was a while back. There was all the coverage of your mountain-climbing accident, and then things trickled off for a few years until you surfaced as a physical therapist, with all the credits, as a partner when the Springs was founded three years ago."

"Well!" I said briskly. "Aren't you full of information. Advantage, Andy."

"Jordan, it's not personal. Believe me, I wasn't intending to pry into your life. It's just part of the information discovery process when we get into new business ventures. The fact that you are an extremely interesting and attractive person is purely coincidental. And fortunate."

"Hmm. Maybe I *will* have a touch more wine." I studied the label for a minute. "You know, Andy, in spite of all your data, you really don't know anything about . . . what we do." For the next hour, I gave him a detailed rundown of the Desert Springs Sports Science Clinic, from the fifteen tennis courts on all playing surfaces to our computerized nutritional profiling capability, and I must say he appeared to be interested.

"Of course Desert Springs is a serious facility with a wonderful and growing reputation," Andy finally said. "It sounds like a perfect tie-in for Laser products. We could create a Desert Springs sports line that would fit our mutual expansion plans perfectly. I'm thinking exercise equipment, workout wear, perhaps an athletic shoe."

"You're going way beyond sunglasses, then?"

"Oh, yes, that's why they brought me in—to expand the brand franchise. Confidentially, I can tell you that in the next twelve months, the LaserGlass name is going to become simply Laser, to allow us to affiliate with other areas more easily, establish other profit centers. A seasonal collection of new eyewear styles can only take you so far. We're moving beyond that, and an alliance with Desert Springs is a strong first step." He nodded confidently. "The financial analysts are going to love it."

"What's that mean?"

"Our stock will go up."

"And you'll be responsible?"

"It's a team effort."

I toyed with my wineglass as the waiter, in a long white apron, cleared our plates. "Does that conclude the business part of the dinner?" I asked.

"I hope so," Andy said optimistically.

"In that case, I'll tell you something else."

"I'd love to hear it."

I looked at him. "What you don't know about me wouldn't fit on any computer." I signaled the waiter. "Check, please." Andy reached for it, but I blocked his hand. "This is on the Springs." I placed my Visa card firmly on the table.

Things were very quiet in the taxi on the way back to my hotel. We were each careful not to cross over the other's invisible borders.

"I hope you didn't take anything the wrong way tonight, Jordan," he said finally.

I sighed. "I think I'm just tired."

When I got out of the taxi, we shook hands.

The next day I joined Bill, Kevin, and Andy, plus a man and a woman from the French Tennis Federation, in the Desert Springs box. The man was in public relations; the woman was a black sports psychologist who had contributed a chapter to Gus's last book. The stadium was packed for the women's singles quarterfinals, as Heather Knight faced Dagmar Olafsen.

The PR man turned to me. "I wish I could say this was like when you played Kelly—incredible interest in both players. But I suspect we owe this turnout to the unfortunate events of the past few days. There's a lot of voyeurs in this crowd." He fingered the laminated badge that hung from a card around his neck.

"That's morbid," I said.

"Well, it sells tickets," he said, his eyes surveying the stands.

Dagmar and Heather were hitting balls on the red clay, warming up. After a few volleys, Dagmar stopped abruptly and walked pointedly to the players' box, where she planted her feet and stood briefly, staring. The crowd rippled in response as people strained to figure out what was going on.

One look told me the whole story. Sitting in the box a few feet away from Woody Solister was CiCi McBain, Dagmar's former coach and lover. "It's CiCi," I said. "Did they get back together?"

"Quite the opposite, I'd say," the PR man replied with a wry smile. "Relationships are so complicated these days, it's hard to keep up. But Heather had a press conference this morning to make the announcement. CiCi is now officially *her* coach."

The match basically degenerated from there, with Dagmar complaining constantly about line calls and looking pointedly at CiCi. In the players' box, a parallel drama ensued, as Woody Solister and CiCi demonstrated their hostility toward each other with pointed body language. The crowd became a Greek chorus, booing and cheering accordingly. In this match, the theatrics clearly outranked the level of the tennis.

"Brilliant," said the PR man. "She's turned herself into a full-fledged bad girl."

"What do you mean?"

"A female John McEnroe."

"Except she doesn't have John's talent."

"Doesn't have to. Think Madonna—the voice is no match for Dame Kiri Te Kanawa. Talent is beside the point. Dagmar's now the girl they love to hate. But there's a sympathy vote, too. The insiders know about her injury, and now her former coach-slash-friend has defected to the hated opponent. Dag's a real underdog. There's an element out there who loves it."

"And Heather?"

"Oh, she's definitely taking the high road. The white hat. Poor, long-suffering, steady Heather. The crowd's behind her. Whatever happens, there are no losers on this court." He rubbed his hands together and leaned forward. "Well, let's enjoy it for what it is. Aside from Martina and Chris—and you and Kelly—the women haven't had a good rivalry out there."

He must have seen the expression on my face, because he quickly added, "Of course, that's not to say these girls are in the same league. Times are different now. The public has different expectations. There's a show business element, don't you think?"

"I think everybody out there still wants to win," I said, a touch of irritation in my voice. Watching this match, having the inevitable comparison between Kelly and me dredged up, was disturbing. Or maybe the events of the past few days had rubbed my emotions raw. Of course, I could well imagine what Dag must have felt when she saw CiCi sitting in the coach's seat rooting for her opponent. It was hard to see how she could hold her concentration together. I got up and left and, for the first time in all my French Opens, decided to spend the day at the Louvre.

Walking through the marble halls of one of the most amazing art museums in the world puts everything in perspective. As I studied the carved marble statues and stood before famous paintings I had only read about, I felt more distanced than ever from myself as the girl who had played her heart out at Roland Garros. I realized I had come to a new point in my life, where the mechanics of the game interested me less than the people and what was physically and emotionally going on inside them. I had a clinical distance now.

There was a long line to view the Mona Lisa, but I waited, thumbing through my guidebook. When I was at the top of the pro tour, lines had not existed for me; on the few occasions when I went to see a tourist attraction or show in a city where I was playing, I was always whisked through as a VIP. Well, those days were long gone. When I finally stood in front of the legendary painting, the timeless smile and the beauty of the brush strokes and the richness of the colors were still there, of course. But I was disconcerted to find that the painting was not simply hung on the wall, like most of those in the Louvre, but sequestered in a box of thick, tamper-proof, bulletproof Plexiglas, which became part of the artistic statement. An armed guard stood close by, reinforcing the militaristic impression. It seemed that in art, as well as sports, there can be no great achievements without a risk or a price.

I was heading for the museum café when my beeper went off. This was not unusual. With business in every time zone, we use international-capability beepers at the clinic. Sitting on a stone bench, I called Tony, my assistant, on my mobile phone. It had to be 6 A.M. in Palm Springs, but he picked up right away. I never needed to worry when I was traveling, because he always had the office under control.

"Tony, what's up?"

"There's an emergency message, Jordan. I think you'll want to call back, but I didn't want to give out your number without your approval."

"Who's the message from?"

"Noel Fisher."

The Fish, as I called him, was a private detective, a man of many contradictions, to whom I owed my life. We had worked together on an unofficial basis two years ago, when my client Audrey Armat, the teen phenom, had been murdered and Global Sport had hired him to investigate. A notably unstylish guy and former Green Beret who lived with his mother in Brooklyn and held patents on some amazingly high-tech inventions, the Fish was soft-spoken and unassuming. You would certainly walk past him without turning your head. But during the terrible period of that investigation, when my career and my life had been on the line, he had been there. I would call him back as soon as I left the museum.

"Is that it, Tony?"

"Everything else is under control. How's A.M.?"

"She's barking with a French accent."

"Okay, I'm going back to sleep now. Call if you need anything." Tony clicked off.

I flipped my phone closed and reached to tuck it back into my purse, but the space on the bench beside me where my purse had been was empty. Impossible. I looked on the floor, around the bench. No sign of it. An old lady in black who had not moved for the past twenty minutes sat on the other end of the bench, and an armed guard was only a few feet away. How could it have been stolen? I quickly assessed the damage. My credit cards were in there, and about a thousand dollars in francs, plus some traveler's checks I could always replace. My passport and my plane tickets were gone too.

"You missing a purse?" The voice was unmistakable, the look even more so: large-sized, open-necked sport shirt printed with corny parodies of Toulouse-Lautrec's Moulin Rouge posters; synthetic sport coat with a stain on it; baggy khakis; camera case; clip-on sunglasses; double chin; "whomper" hair—a scant handful from the left side whomped across the bald head to the right. Standing there, my missing bag dangling on the end of his arm, was none other than Noel Fisher. It shouldn't have surprised me. This was vintage Fish. He'd probably made his "emergency" call from the next room.

"Still the show-off, I see." I grabbed the purse. The Fish's idea of a joke tends to be esoteric; the time he ran my car off the road to get my attention came to mind. I sifted through my bag to see if he'd planted any electronic instruments, explosives, or miscellaneous subversive or tracking devices, but everything seemed in order. After a conversation with the Fish, one could usually benefit from a trip through a metal detector. "This is taking candy from a baby. Why don't you try for the Mona Lisa? The case is bulletproof, but that shouldn't stop you."

The Fish shrugged. "Nah. I appreciate art. That's why I'm here. Did you see that statue with the wings? I am truly in awe. Just think what these guys could have done if they'd had high-tech equipment."

"Call me crazy, but from your message I somehow thought you might be here to find me."

"Pure coincidence. But now that we've run into each other, how about a cup of coffee? I gotta sit down. I've been walking for miles, and this marble is murder on the feet."

We found a café across the street from the museum where, as usual, we ended up ordering the greasiest food on the menu.

The Fish requires a constant stream of nutrients, preferably in junk food form, to stay alive. He was a terrible dietary influence, especially to a reformed junk food addict. I found myself reaching for a handful of *frites*.

"You realize these are probably cooked in animal fat," I said, blotting the fries with my paper napkin.

"I should hope so," said the Fish, enthusiastically smothering his plate with salt and pepper. "That's what gives them flavor. Just ask Julia Child."

"You've asked her?" Frankly, it wouldn't have surprised me. The Fish had friends where you'd least expect it. In fact that was one his major contradictions. He seemed to be a loner, without friends or romances. The only person he talked about with any regularity was his mother. He appeared to go no place beyond Brooklyn. Yet the Fish always seemed to know somebody who had access to the information you needed, or to have been where you needed to go, or to be at your side before you knew you needed him.

Now he just laughed and washed down his fries with some red wine.

"Not to digress, Fish, how about letting me know why you're really here?" Of course, I had some suspicions.

He put down his fork. "Why beat around the bush with an old friend? I was hired by Mariane and Harlan Richie, parents of Ms. Catherine Richie."

"I had a feeling. What do you know?"

"Catherine was a good kid, at least her parents thought so. Very all-American. The Richies are hippie types, moved to Steamboat years ago to escape commercialism and raise their kids in a natural environment—that drill. Then, what happens but Steamboat gets commercial as all get out and Catherine can't get enough of the glitz. She moves to LA, where she can be even closer to the glamour. She gets hooked up with our friend Mr. Bennett. I believe you had the misfortune to meet her under negative circumstances."

"Worse than negative. I was the first one to reach her when she fell—or was pushed—through the glass ceiling."

The Fish nodded. Of course he knew. "Must have been rough," he said softly.

"She fell a hundred feet. Her neck was broken, I could see that right away, and she was still warm, but I didn't think it broke in the fall, because there were strange marks on it. The autopsy will show what that was all about, I imagine." Suddenly I lost my appetite. I pushed my plate away.

"Her trachea was crushed," said Fisher. "And not in the fall. What you saw on her neck was a handprint."

"So she was strangled. How did you find that out?"

"I met with Inspector Lemire. He has some information from the report. And he has a few questions about Mr. James Bennett."

"Well, Jimmy had a fling with Catherine, or at least so he now claims, after initially denying it. And she worked for him."

"In that order?"

"I don't know."

"I suspect it'll sort itself out."

"So how are you fixed for sightseeing?" I asked the Fish.

"Well, I was thinking about going to Notre Dame. I read the hunchback story on the plane."

"I had in mind something a little less touristy—say, the greenhouses out by Roland Garros. Tonight, at the time the murder happened, or at least when Catherine fell through the glass, we could walk through what I saw. Maybe I'll remember something."

"Why? You told the police everything, and you have work of your own with the clinic. You're not involved in this." The Fish made a great Devil's advocate. Besides, I could tell from his face that he sincerely disapproved. "Do yourself a favor, Jordan. Stick to your day job."

"Yes, I *am* involved." I found myself echoing Jimmy Bennett.

"Because a girl who is dead and can't speak for herself is asking me to help."

As a physical therapist, I knew that people's bodies often reveal things that they themselves would not. I could tell when an athlete was undertraining or overtraining, pushing too little or too far. I could sense drugs or steroids in the system before the blood test revealed it. I could read on a body when a sports career was over—betrayed by muscle, ligament, bone, or brain—in spite of the athlete's wishes or goals or a coach's or parent's demands. With my hands I could sense reticence, fear, joy, aggression, defeat, or incipient victory. I had lived through my own body; now I lived through others.

A dead body, however, reveals nothing to me. I am not a coroner or a forensic pathologist. For me, there is no challenge, mystery, or opportunity in inanimate tissue, slides, and sections or in bottled blood—only helplessness and failure. Feeling a young and vital person grow cold beneath my hands was not something I could rationalize or accept, no matter what the circumstances. Now that it had happened, I knew the Fish was absolutely right: I should keep a professional distance and try to view this tragedy not as a defeat but as fate, a sequence of events beyond my control.

But I also knew I couldn't do that.

FIVE

"So this is the same way you came in?"

The Fish and I were walking up the gravel path to the greenhouses, just as I had done two nights ago, when Catherine Richie died. It was the same time as when I had hurried in, late, to the Global Sport reception. The weather had not changed; it was still chilly and depressing, and the sky was steel gray as it edged toward dark.

"Same way exactly. Let's consider why she was here. Did the parents have any information about the new boyfriend or about her relationship with Jimmy Bennett?"

"None," said the Fish. He zipped up his windbreaker. The wind was picking up. "As far as they knew, Bennett was her boss, period. She never said anything about a boyfriend. But the police found her shoes and panty hose at the side of the greenhouse, as if she were planning some sort of sexual encounter."

I remembered she'd been barefoot when I found her.

"What makes them think it was sexual?"

"It's a theory, since there was no evidence of blood or semen, but the panty hose were bunched up and ripped, like she'd pulled them off in a hurry, in the heat of passion, assuming she was involved in some sort of rendezvous—which, of course, we can't."

We retraced my steps, and I racked my brain, but I remembered nothing more.

"This is where I saw Jimmy Bennett," I said. "But we passed each other and I didn't look back." I stopped and looked around. "He said he went on through the gate, but I suppose he could have stayed on the grounds."

"Maybe he met Catherine coming up the path," said the Fish. "She could have been behind you, and you wouldn't have noticed her."

"It's possible."

"Did you hear anyone talking?"

"No. There was music from the greenhouse, chamber music. And there was a harp."

On this twilight, the greenhouses were dark and silent. Global Sport had a reception and dinner planned at a four-star restaurant after the matches, and those who weren't at Roland Garros were probably in the city resting or getting ready. A lone uniformed gardener coiled a hose on the lawn. We walked to the rotunda of the largest greenhouse. The door was still open, and we went inside and looked up. The gaping hole in the ceiling remained unrepaired, but temporary screening had been placed over it to keep the birds inside. Fisher looked up, then down at the goldfish pond at our feet, which had been drained, probably to search for evidence and clear out the broken glass. I wondered where they'd put the goldfish. "God," he said. "This is no ordinary roof."

"If she hadn't been dead already, the fall would certainly have killed her," I agreed.

We circled the inside of the greenhouse, but nothing seemed unusual and no new details occurred to me.

"That's it," I said.

We went back outside. "What about these other greenhouses on the grounds?" asked the Fish.

"The one directly across from here is used for player receptions for G.S. clients. The other is part of the gardens—equipment, plants, that sort of thing."

The Fish nodded. "I'll just poke around."

"Fine. I'll sit on that bench over there and wait for you. Maybe I'll remember something new if I concentrate."

I headed up the path toward the bench, thinking about Catherine and imagining her walking on this same gravel, in her pretty dress, listening to the music filtering out from the reception. Perhaps I had just missed her as I arrived. Or maybe she was already on the roof, fighting for her life. Had she decided to come that night because she'd had a change of heart about her job or her relationship with Jimmy? Whom did she encounter on this path? Who led her away from the reception for which she had dressed with so much style and care?

As I tried to imagine myself in her place, I continued past the bench to where the path split, the other direction heading to the far side of the structure, which was bordered by a stone wall and a row of tall, leafy trees. There was some gardening equipment neatly stacked at the fork of the path. I followed the path to the other side of the greenhouse, where it became narrow and very dark. This was not a public area, and there was no provision for lighting or lingering. It was impossible, I decided, that Catherine could have gotten lost and wandered here. It was clearly off the beaten path.

Halfway down the length of the structure, a small metal staircase, like a fire escape, almost blended in with the metal framework of the windows as it led to the roof of the greenhouse and what appeared to be a narrow open-railinged catwalk. No doubt the investigators were aware of it and it was not new information, but this was the first and, as far as I could see, only way to the roof of the greenhouse. Catherine surely would have seen it. I wondered how and why she would have climbed it. A chill prickled through me. She had been running, I was sure, from someone.

The iron railing felt refrigerated as I climbed the fifty or so rungs to the roof. Once I reached the top, the larger dome loomed ahead of me, and I inched gingerly toward it, as Catherine must have done. The main dome was huge, and I wasn't dressed to climb it. Still, I felt compelled to try, if only to see how difficult it would have been for Catherine. I stepped onto the side railing and carefully edged my way along, several feet above treetop level, trying to imagine the terror of knowing your life depended on this. The wind picked up and my jacket whipped from side to side. Ahead of me, the railing intersected in a dead end with the long side of the rotunda dome.

I was calculating the best way to proceed when the heel of my shoe caught with a sharp tug. It felt as if I had wedged it in an iron window casing, and I shook my foot, dropping the shoe. I minced and sidestepped along the catwalk, peering ahead so I wouldn't trip, my steps uneven and hesitant, since I had one shoe on and the other foot bare except for my nylon stocking. The slippery stocking material was causing my foot to slide around alarmingly. *Of course.* That was why Catherine's shoes and panty hose were found wadded up on the ground beside the greenhouse, and it wasn't for any sexual encounter. I was about to do the same thing, for the same reason. Holding on with one hand, I leaned over, pulled off my other shoe and my knee-high stockings, and stuffed them into my pocket. My toes, though cold, now gripped the iron rungs.

It was growing darker by the second, and I began to wonder if I should get down while I could still see where I was going. Catherine must have been desperate to come up here in her cocktail dress. Surely the police had combed this very same footage, but I wondered if anyone had done it in the near-darkness, picking their way along barefoot in a flimsy dress. Catherine had to have been chased or had possibly followed someone up here. It would be almost impossible to drag an unconscious or resisting person along this walkway.

The catwalk dead-ended at the rotunda ceiling, so I climbed outside the railing and stood on the ledge that circled the rotunda, balancing against the glass panes with the flat palms of my hands as I tried to plot a path to the top. This was turning out to be much more difficult than I had expected, but I could see the huge weather vane looming overhead, and reaching it didn't seem like an impossibility.

Something cold and hard clamped around my left ankle, so unexpected that it took me an instant to realize it was a gloved human hand. I knew if I leaned over to look at the person attached to the hand, I would surely fall, so I grabbed the railing as hard as I could and tried to wrench myself free. I managed to kick my left leg loose, but that left me standing on one foot and, when the hand grabbed it and yanked me backward, I veered off balance, grabbed at the railing, reaching only air, and fell.

I saw nothing as I went down, as I had seen nothing when I fell off the mountain eight years ago. In vertical descent, there is no sense of real time. You might be going off a diving board or out of an airplane. The last time I had almost died, and I had faced my death squarely. Now the sensation was familiar, nothing to fear. Dying was not the issue. The only question that raced through my mind was which parts of my body were going to be smashed this time, and whether or not I could survive it. In the few seconds I had, I tried to control my fall. It was the only thing left to do.

I landed with such force that the wind was knocked out of me, but all I felt was the impact on my face. How long after that I lay there, either too stunned or too winded to move, or some combination of both, I do not know, but I was brought back to my senses by something wet and cold in my face. In the split second that my eyes remained closed, I felt no joy of survival. Instead, I tensed and struggled, waiting for the cold gloved hand to close around my mouth, tighten around my neck. Now I understood all too well the terror Catherine must have felt. I struggled over onto my back and saw two dark eyes peering into mine. A German shepherd loomed above me, its nose traveling wetly along my face. At the end of its leash was a guard, and kneeling next to him was the Fish.

"How'd you get over here?" he asked, his tone suggesting I

had gone for a walk around the block. "I had to call out the goddamned dogs to find you. One minute you're on a bench; the next you're jumping off a building. This is nuts. Women around here seem to be making a habit of this, and not too successfully. So cut it out."

I struggled to sit up. Amazingly, I didn't feel seriously hurt, but I was lying half submerged from the force of the fall in smelly, granular muck, clutching handfuls in each fist. Slowly, I forced my fingers open. Moist clumps of goo fell out onto my lap. The smell was repulsive.

"You were lucky," said the Fish. "You landed smack in the middle of a pile of shit."

I blinked. What was he talking about?

"Fertilizer. This is the main fertilizer dump for the park. You don't smell exactly like geraniums in springtime, but it cushioned the fall, probably saved you. And you should be happy. It's organic. You know, once when I was in the Green Berets, we jumped in a drill and this one guy's chute didn't deploy. The safety snagged, too. The amazing thing was, the guy lived, and that was because he landed in mud. Same principle. Of course, with him we were talking three thousand feet. How do you feel?" He extended a hand.

I pulled myself slowly to a sitting position. "Somebody grabbed my leg," I said. "I think he would have been happy to see me break my neck."

The Fish translated to the guard, who immediately relayed the information through his walkie-talkie.

"He's calling the police," the Fish explained. "Our buddy Inspector Lemire should be here in about ten minutes. You get a look at this person who grabbed you?"

"He was wearing gloves, and I didn't see him."

"He?"

"Actually, I don't know. But it was a large hand."

"You were stupid to go grandstanding up there."

"I was not grandstanding. I just wanted to see for myself what it was like."

"And I was even more stupid to think you'd stay where you said you'd be." The Fish turned and conferred briefly in French with the guard.

I rubbed my shoulder and stood up shakily, sinking knee-deep into the heap. "Well, I think I'm fine."

"I'll be the judge of that. *You* are going to take it easy. After we report this, we're going back to your hotel." The Fish took my arm and guided me down the fertilizer heap.

"I'll tell you this much," I said. "Catherine didn't go up on that rotunda for a walk through the garden. You have to be a mountain goat to get up there." I spit a mouthful of fertilizer into my hand, then rubbed my palm on my skirt. My nostrils were clogged with the stuff. I felt like vomiting. Suddenly I had a thought. "Where's that gardener? I saw a gardener on the grounds, in a uniform."

The Fish and the guard stopped and conferred.

"The guard says there's not supposed to be anybody on maintenance after five. Only security. How do you know it was a gardener?"

"He had on a uniform, a kind of jumpsuit, and he was doing things with some equipment, hoses. But I can't tell you that was the person who came after me."

The Fish nodded. "They'll check it out in the log book, see if anybody stayed late. But I doubt it."

"Maybe there's some crazy gardener or person impersonating a gardener who hangs around French greenhouses terrorizing women—like the Phantom of the Opera."

The Fish snorted. "Maybe there's somebody who doesn't like people snooping around crime scenes."

"You really can't maneuver up there with shoes on, especially sling-back, spike-heeled dress shoes, which Catherine had been wearing that night. I say she knew she was heading up the side of the greenhouse, at least once she got there."

"Because?"

"Well, either she was chased by someone or she followed someone up. I'm sure she got up there on her own steam, and then she was killed at the top. I could barely make it myself, and I used to climb mountains. It would be too hard to drag a dead or unconscious person up there." I tried in vain to brush off my clothes, smearing more ooze into the fabric.

The Fish reached into his pocket and handed me a towelette in a little package. "The guard did spot somebody moving around on the grounds, just after you fell. He was at the gate with the dog. I didn't actually call the guard, he came to investigate."

"Really?"

"And there was a large extension ladder on the ground, out of place. All the ladders had been put away for the night." He pulled a penlight from his pocket and shone it into my eyes.

"Are my pupils dilated?" I stared into the light, hoping I didn't have a concussion.

"Nope. You got nine lives. But from now on, you're out of this. I get paid to investigate. You get paid to do physical therapy." He opened his jacket, showing me his shoulder holster. "You are not prepared to deal with these incidents. So I'll make you a deal. You do your job and I'll do mine."

"At last count, I have seven point something lives left. What would this person be doing up on the roof?"

"Circumstances strongly suggest he was trying to get you down."

"But why?"

"Scare you . . . or kill you. Take your choice."

"Do I have to?" Halfheartedly, I looked around for my shoe. As my body heat warmed the fertilizer, the smell intensified. I was completely coated with slimy excrement. All I wanted was a double dose of extra-strength water, a shampoo, and a soak in a deep tub full of water as hot as I could stand it. I ached, but that was nothing compared to how I smelled.

The next morning I decided to celebrate the fact that I was still alive by having breakfast on the small outdoor deck of my hotel, where croissants, coffee, tea, and fruit were served along with newspapers from all the major cities. The foul weather had lifted, and there was a nice rooftop view, capped by the Eiffel Tower in the distance. A.M. and I commandeered a table, and I helped myself to a bowl of fresh fruit salad and a little cheese from the buffet. I ordered coffee from the waiter and settled in with the *Herald Tribune.* I checked my watch. It was nine o'clock and I was due to meet Bill, Andy, and Kevin in an hour. I wondered if I should tell Bill what had happened last night. I could anticipate his reaction. He would tell me to leave town immediately and go back to Palm Springs. Then he would call the French ambassador and file a complaint. Bill always believes in going straight to the top.

"Excuse me, are you Jordan Myles?"

I looked up to see a blond woman standing by my table, a carry-on wardrobe bag over her arm.

"Yes." I didn't put down my paper.

"I'm Mariane Richie. Catherine Richie was my daughter." On second look, the woman looked very much like Catherine, the same kind of casual, non-made-up good looks and sun-streaked blond hair, although the mother's had faded and was tinged with gray.

I put down the paper and stood up. "I'm so sorry, Mrs. Richie. I don't know what to say."

"I wanted to thank you myself. Noel Fisher told me what you tried to do for Catherine."

"Please sit down, Mrs. Richie."

She set down the wardrobe bag carefully, sank into the chair across from me, and folded her hands over her denim skirt. Her cuticles were bitten ragged, with small scabs edging each fingernail. Her shoulders were straight, but the effort to keep them that way was obvious. Deep lines were etched on each side of her mouth. "My husband just couldn't come," she said, so softly I had to strain to hear. "He told me not to come either, that there was nothing I could do. But I had to. I had to bring my baby home."

It was impossible to offer comfort, so I sat quietly.

"I just got in this morning. The hotel is holding my bag until my room is ready. I came out for a cup of coffee and recognized you. We used to talk about you, Catherine and I."

"You did?"

"About how you made a new life for yourself after tennis. When Catherine was in school, I used you as an example of a woman who really had her life together. I showed her that piece in *People* magazine." She smiled and, seeing the look that must have been on my face, reached across the table and touched my shoulder. "Oh, please don't take that the wrong way. Catherine always did exactly what she wanted without any advice from her parents. Like taking the job with TalentMasters. With all her technical training, we thought she could do better than an assistant's position, but she loved the idea of travel, of not being stuck behind a desk. And she was young, so we supposed it couldn't hurt." A vein in her neck throbbed.

I motioned to the waiter to move Mrs. Richie's coffee to my table. "Catherine had technical skills?"

"Always. As a child, she could solve the most complicated puzzles—you know, the really infuriating kind with two thousand pieces, almost the same shape and all the same color?" She smiled gently at the memory. "Cathy loved math, took advanced classes in high school. And she was a whiz at the computer. She interned for Apple during college, and then she had a wonderful job with KRW for two years. A very good-paying position."

"What did she do at KRW?" I don't know much about the corporate world, but I did know that KRW performed credit checks and had huge government contracts.

"She was—let me see." She opened her purse, took out her wallet, pulled out a small, somewhat frayed business card, and read some writing on the back. "She was an assistant systems engineer in encryptions in standards and data transmission. She handled continuous maintenance network databases and communications and worked on transmission protocols for wide-area networking."

I stared blankly, and Mrs. Richie looked equally blank. "Don't ask me what it means, but one night we were out to dinner with Catherine and some of her friends and co-workers at KRW, and her boss wrote this down for me on his card. Catherine told him to do it, because whenever anybody asked me what she did, I never knew what to tell them." She handed me the card. The printing on the front read: JASON CAMPBELL, SYSTEMS ENGINEER. There was a San Francisco branch office address.

"This Jason Campbell was her boss?" I returned the card to Mrs. Richie, and she carefully replaced it in her wallet.

"Yes. He thought she had a big future at KRW."

"It sounds incredible. She was obviously very intelligent." And a very long way from the world of tennis.

"Very. But the work was tedious, and she never got away from the CRT screen. She told me she felt she was missing out on something. Some weeks she never even saw the light of day. She was putting in twelve–fourteen hours at the computer. What kind of life is that for a young person? It was like living in a capsule, she said. She was just itching to get out into the world, to be with people, not machines. Her father and I could certainly understand that. It seemed as if she had the rest of her life to be responsible." The irony of this statement did not escape her. Mrs. Richie paused sadly, took a breath, and continued. "And then she met Jimmy Bennett and he offered her a job, and she thought it sounded so exciting. Traveling to Europe, meeting famous people—" She stopped abruptly and sagged in her chair.

"Where did she meet Jimmy?" I asked gently.

"In San Diego, at a systems seminar."

I wondered what Jimmy would be doing at a systems seminar. But then, as he was forming a new agency, he probably had need for new technical equipment and expertise. A systems seminar in San Diego would certainly be the place to find both.

"Do you know anything about her relationship with him?" I asked.

Mrs. Richie steadied herself with a sip of ice water. "Mr. Fisher asked me that question, and so did the French police. Apparently they had a romantic relationship, but I can't believe Catherine would have endangered her job by getting involved with her boss." She shook her head. "It wasn't like her. Catherine knew better. She was too smart. For the daughter of two parents who disdained the corporate world, Catherine knew an awful lot about office politics. More than she ever let on. She'd tell us about it."

"What would she tell you?"

"Well, I remember she called home last month and said she was sure that TalentMasters was going to be one of the biggest agencies, because some very major backers were putting money into it."

"Did she mention who those backers were?"

"No. It wouldn't have meant anything to us anyway. But she sent us a check toward her brother's college fund. She said she'd gotten a bonus because they'd gotten this new tournament launched and she was partly responsible." She sighed. "Her dad refused to cash it, but that was typical of Catherine. At any rate, we don't know what to think. It doesn't matter anymore, does it? Since the accident—"

"Mrs. Richie, I don't want to upset you," I said, keeping my voice low, "but your daughter died under very unusual circumstances. It was not an accident, and it was not her fault."

Her voice caught. "I know. We intend to find out what happened. That's why we hired Mr. Fisher. A friend of my husband's in Washington recommended him."

"He's very good," I reassured her. "If there are answers, he'll find them." I handed her my card. "Please let me know if I can help in any way. I'll do whatever I can."

"I know you will. Thank you again for everything." She blotted her lips with her napkin and smoothed her skirt, as though she were a guest at a tea. "And now, if you'll excuse me, I have to spend some time with my daughter." She picked up the wardrobe bag gently. "These are the clothes I chose for her to be buried in." With great dignity and obvious pain, Mrs. Richie stood up and walked away.

Perhaps because I was depressed after seeing Mrs. Richie, my meeting with Bill got off on the wrong foot and I decided not to tell him about the events of the previous night. It would have almost certainly provoked an argument, and almost everyone who knows him avoids getting into arguments with Bill because he always manages to win. The man has a near-photographic sports memory which he uses like a data bank to back up his point of view with a statistic or an example.

You could never present an emotional case to Bill; he always had the statistics to prove you were, if not already wrong, doomed. If there was any doubt, Bill would throw in a conversation-stopper like, "Do you know that the chances of catching a foul ball in the stands are one in a thousand, but the chances of being hit in the head by a foul ball are one in two hundred?" This is one of the secrets to his success in the business community. Bill may lack a Harvard MBA, but he always manages to make precisely the right analogy—or at least to say something nobody can challenge without an encyclopedia.

Bill and I sat in the red and black fifties-style lobby of *Le Sport*, a glossy new sports lifestyle magazine that was planning to run a profile on Desert Springs. The reporter was running a few minutes late, so I asked Bill if he'd learned anything more about Catherine.

"No, I haven't, just what I read in the papers. And I'd advise you not to get involved." He unfurled his newspaper and riveted his attention on it.

"I met her mother this morning at the hotel," I said, carefully not mentioning my plunge off the greenhouse roof. I wasn't in the mood to listen to him tell me that this was not in my job description. "It's so sad."

"Tragic," he agreed, without looking up. "But you did what you could. Now it's time to get on with our work. For instance, I've got a surprise for you. CiCi McBain called late yesterday and asked if you would work with Heather, and I agreed. I thought you'd find it interesting."

I jolted upright in my seat. "What? But I just told Dagmar I'd work with *her*! She's coming to Palm Springs as soon as the French is over."

Bill crumpled up the paper. "How could you agree to that before we talked?" he said. "This is unacceptable."

"Bill, what exactly is the problem here?" I asked. "Helping someone train, taking on new clients, is hardly a crime. *You* never asked me about Heather."

"The problem is bigger that your personal commitments, Jordan, because LaserGlass has signed an endorsement deal with Heather."

"I had no idea. Since when?"

"Yesterday. And since LaserGlass is now one of our sponsor associates, it makes perfect sense to take Heather."

"Can't somebody else work with her?"

"Who? They asked specifically for you. You *are* our tennis specialist, after all."

I shook my head. Bill completely missed the subtleties here. Nothing prohibits a physical therapist, or even a coach, from working with two players simultaneously. The better coaches, trainers, and therapists often work with multiple clients. Off the court, the fierce rivalries hyped by the media usually don't exist, and players who battle each other at the baseline and the net like gladiators often leave the stadium to share a dinner or even a vacation. But CiCi McBain would not work that way. Her style was to instill a cutthroat vendetta instinct in her players so they would take the game, and their rivals, personally. At one point, when I was on the tour, I was frequently up against one of CiCi's players. The girl had been a friend of mine, but CiCi kept her away from me and refused to allow us to socialize. Surely, no one could be more personal for CiCi than her former client and lover Dagmar Olafsen.

"Well," said Bill, "we'll just have to work it out. It could be this rivalry angle is going to be just what women's tennis needs to pull some fans. You ought to be an expert on that. And we're going to want to cooperate with LaserGlass. It's to our mutual benefit. We certainly can't afford not to do everything we can to help their player."

"What about Dagmar? Can't we help her get a sponsorship? She's actually the better player."

Bill was silent. We both knew that was a rhetorical question.

"Well, you should have asked me," I repeated.

Bill tapped the red leather couch nervously, drumming his fingers. "I am in charge of this clinic, Jordan, and, believe it or not, there are times when I see the big picture and you do not."

"All I know is that Dag came to me and asked for help. I think I can help her, and that's all I need to know."

We sat there in silence until the desk phone buzzed and the receptionist lifted her head. "You can go in now," she said.

Bill adjusted his tie as he stood up. "You know, there have been some great comeback stories in tennis. There was a young French girl, Simone Mathieu, who lost in the finals at Roland Garros five times before she finally won in 1938 and '39."

This was Bill's subtle way of telling me that I would be working with both players at the Springs.

"Another thing you will find interesting," he said casually. "Kelly Kendall is going to be coaching Heather, along with CiCi."

"Kelly? Since when is she coaching?"

"Since now."

If Kelly was part of the package, I could understand why LaserGlass was so anxious to sign Heather. After her marriage Kelly had stayed on the sidelines—content, she said, with her husband and their horse-breeding ranch in Wyoming. Recently, however, she was emerging onto the sports scene as a commentator. Getting involved with the game again as a coach would make fabulous PR.

I was sure Kevin had had something to do with this. He had always been completely taken with Kelly. Or it might have even been Andy's idea, to make Heather's comeback more newsworthy and justify LaserGlass's investment. However it happened, LaserGlass must have assembled a significant package. Kelly always said she hated to leave her family and could make six figures a day just by showing up to shoot a commercial for a product endorsement, so a longer-term commitment must have been extremely attractive to lure her.

"How does Heather have the money to pay Kelly to coach, especially on top of CiCi's salary?" I wondered aloud.

"I'm sure LaserGlass is involved."

That was an understatement. As in any professional sport, there were many incestuous sponsorship marriages.

"I thought you'd enjoy working with Kelly," Bill continued. "You two used to be quite the hot ticket."

Of course, he was right. You can't deny that, beyond appreciation for the players' mastery of the sport, the public wants the personalities, the drama, the soap operas. The fans don't just go to watch a good match; they go to see Steffi win, or to be there when Pete beats Andre. Or vice versa. Bill was smiling to himself as we got up to meet the reporter for the interview, and I was sure he was imagining Desert Springs at the center of what were shaping up to be the most talked-about comebacks in tennis.

SIX

By eleven o'clock, a weather front had moved in and horizontal sheets of rain drenched the city of Paris. At Roland Garros, they did what they always do on a rain day—roll the green tarp over the clay and wait for it to end. Now that I wasn't playing tennis, I actually enjoyed the rain. Gray skies and water-slicked streets suit the city somehow, so much so that, according to my guidebook, the stones of the Sacre-Coeur in Montmartre supposedly ooze a milky substance when it rains. I enjoyed looking at the architecture from the taxi window as I inched along the Champs-Élysées in lunchtime traffic toward Le Drugstore, where I was meeting the Fish for lunch. He had chosen the place because he felt comfortable with it; it was about as American as you could get in Paris, right down to the name.

With the Arc de Triomphe looming at the top of the avenue, I'd always thought the Champs-Élysées would be the epitome of French culture, the elegant place described in Proust. Instead, the street was clotted with airline offices, lingerie emporiums, movie theaters, car showrooms, and fast food places. Le Drugstore was at the center of all this activity.

In its own way, Le Drugstore was a very funky place. It was a conglomeration of tiny boutiques with overpriced merchandise—books, watches, perfumes, bath and beauty supplies—arranged like a wheel around a restaurant in the hub. Luckily, I got a table right away. I ordered an Evian and settled in to dry off and wait for the Fish. I wanted him to know the company Catherine had worked for and the name of her former boss, in case he could shed some light on her death.

After thirty minutes of watching girls at the makeup counter try on eyeshadow, I ordered a salad. The rain hadn't let up and traffic was terrible; it was possible the Fish was running late. After an hour, I paid the check and left. It was impossible to second-guess the Fish, but the problem usually involved shaking him off, as opposed to his not showing up. I called my hotel and his, but there were no messages. Also, I knew he had my beeper number. I was concerned enough to decide to swing by his hotel on the way to mine.

After about twenty minutes of standing on the curb and getting soaked, I managed to grab the cab of an elderly couple who were arriving at Le Drugstore. The Fish's hotel, the Rodin, was only a few minutes away.

I swept, dripping, through the glass doors and went straight across the modern lobby to the house phones. The line was busy. I couldn't believe the Fish would have left me sitting in the restaurant while he was on the phone, but then again, if he was following up a lead or a source, anything was possible. I hung up, approached a studious-looking desk clerk, and asked him for the room number.

"We don't give out room numbers, madame," he said, not looking up.

"I'm his wife. He's expecting me, but he is on the phone."

"Oh, excuse me, madame." He finally made eye contact. "In that case—" He tapped the name Fisher into his computer. "Yes, here it is. Room 751. This is one of our concierge floors. We have a lounge with complimentary coffee, tea, soft drinks, a continental breakfast, and a gym. No one can get onto that floor without a seventh-floor room key." He handed me a key, which was more accurately a piece of plastic with a magnetic strip, like a credit card.

Purposefully, I made my way across the lobby, my umbrella still drizzling across the carpet. My plan was to knock on the Fish's door and give him a piece of my mind, but once I was there, banging on the door raised no response. I didn't want to intrude, but then again I was tired of waiting around.

As I stood there, debating what to do next, I smelled something burning. I inserted the plastic card, a green light clicked on, and I opened the door. Instantly, I was accosted by an acrid cloud of smoke so thick I coughed and choked, my eyes tearing as I peered into the room. I saw no flames, but, on the floor beside the bed, a pair of feet protruded. I dropped my purse on the carpet, clamped my hand over my mouth and nose, and dashed inside. There, under a bedspread, lay the Fish. His face was badly gashed and dark. Partly clotted blood oozed from his nose and puddled down his cheek. His lips and eyes were swollen, red and raw. Every drawer in the room was pulled onto the floor, his suitcases were open and overturned, and clothes and papers were strewn everywhere. The bedside table had fallen over, and the phone receiver, smeared with blood, lay near the Fish's head. Frantically, I looked around to see where the smoke was coming from, and it was then I saw that the bedspread was smoldering.

I yanked the blanket off the bed and threw it over the bed-spread, then beat on the smoldering fabric with a pillow. It was impossible to tell whether the Fish was dead or alive, but I didn't want to touch the telephone, so I ran out into the hall to a fire exit, where I found an alarm box and extinguisher. I grabbed the extinguisher off the wall and threw the alarm lever in one move, raced back to the Fish's room, and sprayed the entire blanket with flame-retardant foam. As soon as it seemed the fire was out, I heaved the extinguisher onto the bed and dropped down beside the Fish. I grabbed his arm, now wet with blood and foam, and felt for a pulse. Thank God there was one.

As the fire alarm rang, a couple with two young children stood in the doorway, transfixed. "Get help!" I screamed. I had no idea whether or not they spoke English, but my frantic voice and the scene in front of them communicated the message. The couple bolted down the hall, dragging the wide-eyed children behind them.

I told myself to remain calm. If I was going to help the Fish, I needed my composure. He seemed to be breathing, but shallowly. I tilted his chin up and checked his airway, my fingers catching on broken teeth. Luckily, the throat was clear. Then I lifted an eyelid. The pupils didn't react, a very bad sign. Suddenly, Catherine Richie's face, with the fixed pupils, floated in front of me, and I saw it transposed onto Noel Fisher's body, as if in a waking nightmare.

"Come on, Fish," I urged the inert form on the floor. "Hang in there! Please, please, be okay." I was pleading with an unconscious man, but I couldn't let him slip away. Last year, he had saved my life from a crazed fan on a vendetta through sheer ingenuity and persistence; what if I was unable to do the same? I braced myself, but I refused to accept it. There was no way he was going to stop me from saving him. I felt his pulse again, but this time it barely registered. With that kind of a drop-off, he had to be bleeding internally, God knew where. Praying, I grabbed for the phone—even if I was contaminating a piece of evidence.

Just as I screamed for the operator, a crowd seemed to fill the room, everyone shouting at once in French. Someone pried me away from Fisher's side as the paramedics dove in. Within minutes they had the bedspread off and the trauma routine under way: his shirt cut open to the waist, a tube in his trachea, a needle in his arm.

"What's his blood pressure?" I demanded. But the paramedics either ignored me or couldn't understand what I was saying.

The nervous manager from the front desk grabbed me by the

elbow and tried to escort me out of the room. "Please, Madame Fisher," he whispered. "The men need room to work."

The paramedics had the Fish on a stretcher now and were rolling him out into the hall. I broke free from the manager, grabbed my purse, and followed—down the service elevator, through the lobby to the waiting ambulance—and climbed inside. "How is he?" I asked, feeling frantic and helpless.

The only answer I received was a grim headshake.

The doors slammed and we lurched away from the curb, and only then, as I wiped my friend's blood from my hands onto my sweater, did I stop to wonder who did this to Noel Fisher—and why.

"**B**roken jaw, concussion, two broken ribs—the punctured left lung has collapsed, so he has only half his respiratory capacity, and we've inserted a chest tube, as you can see—broken wrist. He has regained consciousness, but of course he's in shock." The doctor at the American Hospital in Neuilly ran down a litany of injuries that were horrendous, especially since they had been purposefully inflicted in a beating by another human being. "He will recover. Your husband is a tough man, Mrs. Fisher. He put up one hell of a fight." He was American, like many of the doctors here, and he had a New York accent. The Fish would feel right at home.

"I'm not Mrs. Fisher. The hotel just thought I was."

"Of course." The emergency room doctor had no doubt seen his share of unusual relationships. That was the least of his concerns. "We are performing the MRI and more of the necessary tests tonight. We do not know yet whether Mr. Fisher will require surgery, but he will remain in the hospital for quite a while. According to the initial CAT scan, the concussion is very serious."

"What about the police?"

"They are in the waiting room."

"I don't think he should be alone. Someone tried to kill Mr. Fisher. They could try again." Or, I thought, they could try again to kill me.

"I will tell the officer in charge to come to the room immediately."

"When can I see Mr. Fisher?"

"Now, if you wish, very briefly. We've just moved him into his room. You understand, he's heavily medicated."

Hospitals all over the world are the same—the medicinal scents, the hushed atmosphere, the footsteps in the hall, the lack of perception of time, except as tracked by doctors' rounds and meals on trays. I had clocked so many hours in hospitals as a patient, any of these sensory cues could reawaken the experience, and I knew how it felt to be lying there, immobile, wondering if you would ever live a normal life again. Of course, there were worse alternatives, and one was to be dead. I was grateful the Fish had survived. And grateful, now that I realized what we were dealing with, that I had escaped.

I walked quietly into the room, which was small but private. The Fish lay in a bed with the side rails raised, although there was virtually no chance of his going anywhere. He was a mound of white: sheets, nightshirt, bandages. His face was almost covered in gauze. One blood-red eye squinted at me, open barely a slit.

"Hi, I'm here," I said. I wanted to pat his arm or hand, but there was a tube, needle, splint, or bandage everywhere I looked.

He mumbled something, but since his jaw was wired shut and his lips stitched and swollen, I could barely hear his voice.

I leaned over the bed. "It's okay," I said.

His hand moved weakly, motioning me closer. "Shit!"

I have never been so relieved to hear anyone swear. "Who did this?" I asked. "Can you say?"

But the eye had closed and the Fish was asleep.

Back in the hall, I encountered Inspector Lemire, out of uniform. "We have to stop meeting like this," I said, immediately regretting it. Where the hell did I think I was, a cocktail party?

"We will not be able to speak to him tonight, according to the doctor," the inspector said.

"Please assign someone to watch him. Whoever did this could try again."

"And probably will, Mademoiselle Myles," he added. "And it is not safe for you either. You should leave the country immediately. We will escort you to your hotel and then to the airport. We will get you diplomatic travel priority."

"But why would somebody be trying to kill either of us? The Fish didn't know anything. He'd just gotten to Paris. And I probably know less than he does."

"There you are wrong," said Lemire. "You clearly know far too much. The question is, about what?"

I went to get a cup of coffee and then to the bathroom. As I turned on the water, I noticed my hands were caked with dried blood. I put them under the faucet and watched as the pink-tinged water swirled down the drain.

When I got back to the Fish's room, a police officer had arrived and was standing outside the door with Inspector Lemire, who nodded me inside. Pulling the shade up a few inches, I noticed it was dark outside. A quick look at my watch showed it was 10 P.M. Suddenly I remembered I was supposed to have met Bill and the LaserGlass group four hours ago, to go to Roland Garros for the women's semis. It seemed totally unimportant. I sat down in the single chair in the Fish's room, took off my shoes, and settled in as comfortably as possible for the night—or as long as it took.

The police outside, though comforting, were not entirely reassuring. If someone wanted to kill me, he could easily succeed. I had none of the Fish's tricks of the trade: the sophisticated electronics and tracking devices, the network of contacts. But I was stubborn and had incredible persistence. I would find out who did this to him before they got to either of us again. Of course,

I had no idea how I would do this, but there I applied the Scarlett O'Hara Theory of Problem Management: I would think about it tomorrow.

I made one quick but critical call to my hotel, to make sure the concierge took A.M. for a walk and gave her food and water. Then I called Bill, who was in his room.

"Jordan, for God's sake, I had to cover for you today. Andy was asking for you. You missed seeing our client lose at the semis. Where were you?" he said, his voice irritated.

"Actually, I've been with a sick friend. I'll try to be there tomorrow."

"That won't matter. You're leaving tomorrow. Since Heather lost today, Kelly wants to start her training program right away. Tony's booked your flight."

"I can't leave tomorrow. I told you, I have a sick friend."

"Who and how sick is this friend?"

"Noel Fisher. He's in the hospital."

"The detective?"

"Yes. He was over here investigating Catherine Richie's death. Her parents hired him. And somebody tried to kill him. He's a mess."

"On second thought, Jordan, you are leaving tonight." Bill knew me too well. "Either that, or you're fired."

"You can't fire a partner. It's in the corporate charter. And I think it's my decision when I leave. Or don't. It certainly isn't up to Kelly Kendall; I don't work for her. If you're telling me I do, I quit."

"You can't quit," countered Bill. "It's in the corporate charter." This was technically true. You had to sell your interest.

The Fish stirred in his sleep, but even his worst nightmare couldn't have been worse than his day today. I reached over and adjusted his covers.

"Give me a week at least, Bill."

"Jordan, I'm sympathetic. This is terrible. But doesn't he have anybody else to sit by his bedside?"

"There's just his mother, and she's in Brooklyn."

The line was silent for a moment. "Give me her name," Bill said. "I'll have Tony send her a first-class round-trip ticket. The Springs will pick it up. I'm sure he'd much rather be with his mother. They sound very close."

Until I mentioned her, Bill had never even heard of this woman.

"What's her name?" he asked.

"Mrs. Fisher. In Brooklyn. That's all I know. He never told me her first name."

"No problem. She'll be on the next plane to Paris—and you'll be on the first plane out tomorrow."

"A week," I bargained.

Bill sighed. "Three days and that's it."

"Fine. Three days it is." It didn't matter what I said. I wasn't going to leave before Noel Fisher was out of danger and I could talk to him. And I figured if he was still in precarious shape or if his mother didn't come, I could always stay longer.

"What about Dagmar?" I asked.

"We've worked it out. She arrives in Palm Springs in three weeks, when Heather leaves. You've got your work cut out for you, Jordan."

Bill, I thought, if you only knew.

The first thing I did when I finally got back to the hotel at six the next morning was to check out. I asked a security guard to accompany me to my room, shoved my things into my suitcases, collected A.M., settled up at the desk, and left, making sure I told the clerk that I was going to Orly.

Instead, I went straight back to the hospital, where Inspector Lemire had pulled strings to get me a room adjoining the Fish's. While it wasn't the Ritz, it was safe, with a twenty-four-hour police officer stationed in the hall next door, and there was a private bath and room service. The French love dogs, but I suspected they drew the line at hospitals. Still, if no one questioned what—or who—was at the bottom of my gym bag, I wasn't going to volunteer any information. I stowed my suitcase in the closet and A.M. under the bed. Hospital closets are not very large, but neither was my luggage.

I stopped next door to check on the Fish. Mercifully, he was sleeping soundly. His chart was hanging on the back of the door, so I took a quick look. Luckily, it was written in English: *no change*. Before I left the room, I swiped a clean bedpan and a small stainless steel dish for A.M.'s food and water. When I travel, I always pack her special veterinary brand food and a can opener, so we were set for a week. I pulled out one of the cans and opened it, poured some water from the bathroom faucets into the bedpan, and arranged a small doggie buffet on a towel under the bed. On the floor beside it, I scrunched up a second towel for A.M.'s bed. She pawed at it a few times to get the nap just right and made herself at home. Since she's been traveling her entire life, A.M. could make herself at home on anything from a velvet pillow to a bed of nails. By the time I changed into a pair of sweat pants and a T-shirt and threw myself onto the bed for a little rest, I was so tired I slept for ten hours.

When I finally woke up, I made a quick run outside with A.M. hidden again in my bag. She had a little walk just outside the door and we returned immediately to the room. I felt bad about this—A.M. loves her exercise—but it was no time for either of us to wander around. To make up for this, I played a quick round of catch with A.M., using a wooden tongue depressor. After a few throws, she disappeared under the bed with it.

I showed my ID to the police officer on the new shift and peeked into the Fish's room. A nurse was changing some dressings, and his eyes were still closed.

"Will he wake up soon?" I whispered, already knowing what the answer would be.

"I don't think so," said the nurse. "We've just given him morphine in the IV." She was French, with short dark shaggy hair, and looked like she'd just gotten out of nursing school. I suddenly hoped the police were monitoring whoever came into this room. Slipping something fatal into the IV line or administering an overdose would be so easy if you were in uniform and looked the part.

As I sat there watching the Fish sleep, I tried again to piece together whatever it was I had forgotten that was the reason we were here in the first place. In my mind, I walked up that greenhouse path sixty or seventy more times, each time examining my mental sketch of the people I had seen. With the exception of Jimmy Bennett, they were all anonymous faces. Was one of these strangers Catherine's killer?

The difference between the Fish and me was that he could look at a normal-seeming person and see a cold-blooded killer. As a professional detective and former Green Beret, he had seen, worked with, or identified many such people. We had once had an argument about where to draw the line about killing another human being. The Fish threw out his personal statistic that 75 percent of adults in America are capable of violent crime or murder. I claimed he had an occupational bias. We never resolved the discussion. But what this meant to me, sitting there anticipating each shallow rise and fall of his chest, was that the Fish must have spotted a particular murderous underbelly in someone he could identify or threaten—and they knew it and reacted accordingly. In that case, I wondered how long it would take before they got me too.

The Fish, while appearing purposefully obtuse, is one of the smartest people I have ever met or worked with, and he was trained in surveillance and protection. If someone could succeed in getting him, they could certainly make short work of me. Inspector Lemire—and Bill too—had suggested that I leave France. As I thought about it, I doubted that departure would end the threat I now sensed so strongly. If I knew something, they would find me, because information in the wrong hands can be equally dangerous anywhere.

After an hour of sitting by the Fish's bed, I went back to my room, had some cold soup from my meal tray, fed A.M. some slivers of cold ham, and pulled out the WTF staff phone listing for the tournament. Before each event, a list like this is drawn up and faxed to all relevant parties. I still received a copy, basically as a courtesy, because the WTF physical therapists and I often collaborated on player therapies. Reading down the page, I saw that Alice Kellerman was staying at the Hotel Bristol. I picked up the phone and dialed. I didn't expect to find Ali in her room, but she answered.

"Jordan! Where'd you disappear to?" Her voice was low with fatigue.

"Just visiting a sick friend. Now, Ali, fill me in. How's Mila Karacek doing?"

"Much better. It was definitely severe dehydration—one of the worst cases I've ever seen. But she's responded to treatment, and she's out of the hospital and going home tomorrow."

I honed in on my hunch. "That's good news. Now, this is a weird question, Ali, but what happened to her bottle—the one she was drinking from on court before she collapsed? Did it get thrown out?" I prayed it hadn't.

"Actually, it's in her locker. She has a special squeeze bottle that she refills each time she goes on court. After she got taken off, we put everything in her gym bag. I was going to pick it up tonight and leave it at her hotel."

"Would you do me a favor?"

"Sure, Jordan. What?"

"Leave the bottle in the bag at the desk with Inspector Lemire's name on it—he's from the French police. And don't touch it."

"If you want. Is it evidence for something? Are there finger-prints on it?"

"I don't think so." Actually, I wasn't at all sure about this, which was the point of my call. "But would you leave it for him, please?"

"Will do."

My next call was to Inspector Lemire. His wife answered on the third ring, and when I asked for him she banged the phone onto a tabletop without responding. I could hear children in the background, and the sound of a television. The woman was probably sick of people calling her husband at home for police issues. I didn't blame her, and I hoped I hadn't disturbed their family time over something that was all in my head.

"Hello, Inspector?" I said when he finally came to the phone.

"Yes."

"This is Jordan Myles."

"Are you all right, Mademoiselle Myles?"

"Yes, I am. But I think you should check the contents of Mila Karacek's sport drink—the one she used just before she collapsed on court. The bottle is still in her gym bag, in a locker, and I've asked someone to save it for you at the hotel desk."

"But Mila Karacek is not a criminal investigation. That was dehydration," said the Inspector.

"It doesn't make sense. We have a very motivated person out there who is trying to kill Noel Fisher, and also me. I think the drink should be tested."

"For what? Poison, you mean?"

"Not poison. You wouldn't need it, actually. I had in mind some chemical form of salt, something to hasten dehydration."

"You believe this?" Lemire asked cautiously.

I was, in fact, certain of it. A player's on-court drink is like a custom-made outfit, tailored specifically to the player's needs. Usually, these drinks consist of glucose polymers with fat or protein that are formulated to get into the system and metabolize slowly. They seemed to come and go in fads and have had many formulations. One of the popular ones involved mixing two scoops of electrolyte powder with Evian; another was designed to keep you from feeling hungry. There always seemed to be a drink-of-the-month that was hot on the circuit, although some players kept their formulas secret and guarded them vigilantly— another toehold on the competitive edge. If a specific ingredient balance were somehow distorted, it would be easy to send a player into serious and very fast dehydration.

"Even salt and sugar can be lethal in the right circumstances and quantities," I explained to Lemire. "For any aerobic activity that lasts over ninety minutes—like tennis, basketball, or running—you have to make sure your fluid intake keeps the right balance."

"And what would that be?" he asked.

"Well, more than six or seven percent glucose in your drink, and you'd be better off having plain water. You'll get a sugar spike, or—"

"This is very technical. Someone knew exactly what to do, then?"

"I'd guess. The good news is that the doctors treated her very quickly and she responded, so if it turns out the drink *was* tampered with, there probably won't be any permanent physical damage."

"I will have it checked immediately," Lemire said quickly. I imagined he would place a call the instant he hung up the phone. "This is very helpful information."

"It could be nothing," I said.

"Possibly."

There was certainly a chance that I was overreacting. At the time Mila collapsed on court, it seemed to be a random episode. Now I was suspicious of everything. You had to be, in a world where lunatics surface from the crowd to knife athletes in the back while they are playing a game, stalk them, and are hired to kill or maim them. Professional tennis players seem to attract more than their share of crazies. Tennis is a game in which the crowd focuses on particular individuals and personalities, not teams, and this personal familiarity seems to engender both extremes of obsession: loyal adoration and phenomenal hostility.

When Kelly had been playing, she had inspired strong feelings, a love affair by the fans that had never been equaled. And I'd certainly experienced the backlash of being her opponent. I had to wonder if this sense of emotional excess had been the precursor of the madness that had turned tennis from a gentleman's game to a blood sport.

"The therapist will be picking up the bag and dropping it off later tonight at the desk at Mila's hotel," I said. "She'll be at the player hotel, the Méridien. Mila gets out of the hospital tomorrow, and then she's flying home."

"I'll get it checked," said Lemire. "However, she should not touch the bag at all. Please give me her name and number and we will secure the bag."

I gave him the information and hung up, knowing exactly what they would find and wishing I didn't.

The next morning, I was awakened by a loud Brooklyn accent that barreled through the door of my room. "Now listen here," a woman was insisting. "If you don't let me in that room I will call the police."

Pause.

"I don't care if you *are* the police!"

I threw on a pair of jeans, ran my fingers through my hair, and opened the door. There in the hall, berating the on-duty officer who was guarding the Fish's room, stood a tiny woman with one of the biggest voices I've ever heard. She was seventy-something and barely five feet, including her spike heels—with gray hair covered by a sprightly hat trimmed with pink flowers; however, her attitude was anything but demure. She looked like the kind of woman who could make mincemeat out of even a customs officer. The poor man on duty didn't stand a chance. She had him cowering.

"Madame," he stuttered. "The bag . . . in the bag."

"It's a cheesecake, not that it's any of your business—a cheesecake for my son. Now, let me in that room or there will be repercussions."

"Excuse me," I interrupted. "Mrs. Fisher?"

She whirled around, spinning on a spike heel. "Yes?" She lifted her chin a fraction higher. "And you are . . . ?"

"Jordan Myles." I extended my hand, but she flew past it, straight into my arms.

"Jordan Myles! Well, why didn't anybody tell me!" She plunked down her purse and a large shopping bag, reached up, grabbed my shoulders, and held me out at arm's length, as if she were surveying a dress to try on for size. "Of course I know you, my dear. Noel has shown me so many pictures, I can't tell you. All that time you spent with him in England, on that terrible case last year." Her flashing eyes teared up and she rummaged in a pocket for a tissue. "Isn't this awful. But we must be brave." Suddenly, her body sagged and she seemed like the old lady she was. "What are we going to do?" she whispered, blowing her nose on a lace hankie.

"Don't be alarmed, Mrs. Fisher. He's getting stronger every day." I signaled to the police officer, and he stepped away from the door. Mrs. Fisher and I went inside together.

To my amazement, the Fish was sitting up in bed. "How's a guy supposed to get any sleep around here?" he mumbled through his wired jaw.

His mother clacked across the floor to his side. Pursing her lips carefully to conceal any visible reaction to her son's condition, she sat down firmly in the bedside chair and patted his arm, then leaned over to kiss the patient's bandaged face. I knew that the Fish, who was divorced and whose daughter had died, lived with his mother and talked about her endlessly. There was no denying their closeness. Bill had been right. I was no longer needed. I decided to tiptoe out of the room.

"Where are you going?" Mrs. Fisher's voice intercepted me at the door.

"I'll be next door, packing. I'm leaving for the States—now that he's doing better." I gestured toward the Fish, grinning. "I can see you're in good hands, buddy."

"What, no cheesecake?" Mrs. Fisher demanded.

The Fish was smiling too, as best as he could with his broken face. "Nice hat, Mom," he mumbled.

"Thank you, dear. I trimmed it myself."

"Cheesecake? Well, one piece. A small one," I said.

"A sliver," said Mrs. Fisher, rummaging in her shopping bag. "I don't want to waste it, and I can see right off that cheesecake is not on his diet."

"Your mother is not to be messed with," I said to the Fish as his mother set up the cheesecake on his rollaway bed table with the dignity of a woman about to host the most elegant of tea parties. She adjusted her hat.

"Do you like it, dear?" she asked me.

"It's lovely," I said.

"I designed it myself," she said with satisfaction.

The cheesecake was definitely homemade. It had the traditional graham cracker crust. Still, the sight of it, not to mention his mother, caused the Fish to roll his eyes happily. They were still horribly bloodshot but at last alert.

I leaned over the bed. "Who did this to you?" I whispered. "Do you remember anything?"

He shook his head, barely moving it from side to side, never taking his eyes off the cheesecake. In that moment, I knew he would be fine—eventually.

The recovery had begun. It would be long and painful, but it would happen. And as it evolved, perhaps he would remember how this had occurred—and why.

I was zipping up my suitcase in the next room when Inspector Lemire called.

"We have the lab report back. I thought you might like to know," he said.

"And?"

"You were right, Mademoiselle Myles. The drink had been tampered with."

"How?"

"There was an extremely concentrated diuretic present."

I nodded silently. But which of these terrible incidents were related? Was there some master plan, which the Fish and I had interrupted, or were these random acts? Had we become the targets? One thing I knew for sure was that Catherine Richie had not climbed onto the roof of that greenhouse on a whim.

"I'm leaving now for the airport," I said. "I'm sure you'll keep Mr. Fisher under very close guard—and his mother."

"Of course."

"He may have a very lengthy recovery. The cast will be on six to eight weeks, I'd say. Also, they may have to operate on his wrist. Then there's the therapy. This is assuming there are no complications with the lung or the concussion."

"We understand the gravity of the case. We have spoken at length with the doctors. The French government is very anxious for this unfortunate situation to resolve itself peacefully. So far, it appears that there is no pattern to these incidents, but patterns can take their time emerging. We do not intend to take unnecessary risks. The Roland Garros tournament is a very important occasion in France. We need to keep it completely safe for our foreign guests."

That was true. Incidents like the Seles stabbing and the violence at past Olympics seriously jeopardize the commercial opportunities of sports events, and France had a major investment, both financially and psychologically, in this tournament and its stadium. The cement was barely dry on Court A, their latest addition to the complex. I could take some slim comfort from the fact that, as far as the government was concerned, a successful attempt on my life would be worse than a human tragedy; it would be the worst kind of public relations to have a headline declare: FORMER FRENCH OPEN CHAMPION MURDERED AT ROLAND GARROS.

"One of our men will escort you through customs and onto the airplane," Lemire said. "And Madame Fisher will move into your room now that you are leaving. Bon voyage, Mademoiselle Myles. Your friend will be safe in our hands."

"I'm sure he will."

"Please be cautious yourself. We wouldn't want anything to happen to one of our champions. After all, winning at Roland Garros makes you just a little bit French."

"So it does, Inspector," I had to agree. "So it does."

SEVEN

I love almost everything about working and being a partner at the Desert Springs Sports Science Clinic. When I was playing I always dreamed of having a place like this to go to work on my game or rehab an injury, a place that combined world-class tennis and sports facilities with an equivalent caliber of trainers, therapists, sports psychologists, nutritionists, herbalists, and medical doctors. Our premises are physically beautiful, with clean-lined white stucco buildings surrounded by lush green vegetation that emerges from the desert like a palm-studded oasis.

However, one of the least pleasant aspects of my job is paperwork. When I was playing, paperwork was kept at a civil distance, the domain of agents, managers, and lawyers. Now it's all mine to handle. Accordingly, when I walked into my office at the clinic on the morning after my return from France, my worktable was covered with a blizzard of papers stacked in piles so high that they almost hid my collection of framed pictures of A.M. with various celebrities—everyone from Bob Hope to the vice president of the United States to Billie Jean King.

"I tried to keep things organized," said my assistant, Tony, peering at the desk through his John Lennon wire rims. Tony specialized in organization. He was like a human computer combined with a neatness fanatic—in other words, the perfect assistant. With Tony, nothing slipped through the cracks, whether it was juggling fifteen or twenty meetings a week or setting up A.M.'s appointment to get her teeth cleaned.

I met Tony years ago, when he was a ball boy at the U.S. Open. He volunteered to run some errands for me, and right then he began to make himself indispensable. Over the years, we kept in touch and I followed his schooling and helped counsel him from time to time. Tony had a love of sports but absolutely no talent or desire to do anything but remain on the periphery. His main talent was his computer skills, which were formidable. After graduation from high school, he worked a few years in computer programming. When he read about my accident, he wrote me and we struck up a correspondence that eventually turned into this job. We'd been together ever since.

"This pile is your bills," Tony said as he walked me through the paper maze. "The ones on top are past due. You better get to them first thing. The pile to the left is updates on client files, just FYIs. Interoffice memos are in the pile over there. And this bunch, in the red folders, these are urgent. Letters that need a response are in the yellow folder. Form letters that just need your signature are in the plain manila folders. And this blue folder right in front is the data search you asked for on Dagmar and Heather. The pink folder on top is Heather's clinic file. You might want to look at that before you see her."

I stared at the stacks of papers and folders. Tony had done his usual perfectionist's job of sorting them. At the top of each stack, he had placed a neatly polished rock of an interesting shape as a paperweight.

"Let's face it, Tony," I said. "This is just rearranging the deck chairs on the *Titanic*. I'm never going to get through all this."

"Oh, you'll do it," Tony said reassuringly. "It may take months, years even, but you'll do it. I'll help."

"How can you help?"

"I can take out the trash."

"Right, that's helpful. There's bound to be plenty of trash."

"I can forge your signature pretty well by now."

"True."

"I can get you some mint tea. Get your juices running."

"That *would* be helpful."

"Here's your agenda for today." Tony handed me a neatly typed index card. "Your first appointment is in an hour. Heather is checking in." Tony disappeared in search of the tea, and I eased myself into the chair that was pulled up to the table I used for a desk.

The view from my office was always beautiful, even on the rare occasions when it was raining. The mountains usually had a calming effect. But today, looking out, I wondered if someone was there watching me through the glass, if someone had followed me from France or sent someone to harm me. I'm not paranoid, but just as insurance I have a personal alarm that emits a silent signal to our private security service on a cord around my neck, under my sweater.

That was one advantage about living in Palm Springs. It is a small city, but the large number of resident celebrities has caused some first-rate security companies to locate here. I was grateful for that now, because once somebody's tried to kill you, it's not easy to relax. In fact, I was feeling nervous for no reason, just thinking about it. For the first time since I'd had this office, I got up and yanked the blinds shut.

Back at my table, I braced myself and flipped through the pile of bills. The water bill was way past due, and my mortgage payment was coming up. Going through my expenses at this point would only slow the process to a halt. I made a mental note to have Tony install one of those automatic check-paying programs on my laptop for my personal bills.

Forging on to the next pile, I glanced at the correspondence that had come in while I was out of town. There were some notes from clients, an invitation to speak at a college commencement, a batch of invitations to various sports events and banquets. I turned to the data searches on Dagmar and Heather, then tucked this file into my knapsack for reading at home tonight, then opened Heather's clinic file, which included a complete medical and training history, including her current diet regimen. Scrutinizing her medical records, I couldn't find anything physically amiss. But peak performance is a complex issue, and I knew we'd have to examine every aspect of her physical and psychological state.

"Here we go," said Tony, placing the paper cup of tea in front of me.

I blew on the tea to cool it and dipped the bag in and out of the hot water. "Tony, what do you know about KRW?"

"In a word, big. They handle government contracts."

"If someone were an assistant systems engineer there, they'd be highly knowledgeable about computers?"

"Incredibly, I'd say. KRW deals with confidential stuff. Databases that make NASA look simpleminded. Even trainees at a place like that are usually the cream of the crop."

"Hm. Why do you suppose a sports agency would recruit a systems engineer from KRW?"

Tony leaned in the doorframe, rocking on the heels of his Nikes. "Maybe they were installing a data bank, like the Women's Tennis Foundation did a couple of years ago. Maybe they wanted to make up individualized programs for each of their clients, with cross-referencing capabilities. Or a billing and accounting system."

"Wouldn't they want a person with more than just technical expertise?"

"Possibly they had that capability on staff already. Or they didn't want to pay for the experience, so they went for the cheaper person. Or maybe they just didn't want a hotshot. Some of these technical people are in their own world. They can only talk to each other, and they tend to be very set in their ways. Maybe the agents wanted somebody they could mold to do

things a particular way, somebody without preconceived no-
tions."

"Somebody they could control?"

"They could try for it. But it's hard for somebody who isn't into
technical stuff to push around somebody who is. Most people
don't even know what happens on the computer, beyond the
basics of, say, turning it on. A good technical person can get in
there and somebody without the knowledge will have no way of
knowing what the hell they're doing, no matter what it is they tell
them to do."

I thought about Jimmy Bennett. He was the type to delegate,
and it seemed highly improbable that he had much technical
expertise in computers. He may have lured Catherine Richie to
his new company with some sort of siren song about celebrity
clients, glamorous travel, and growth opportunities, but he had
recruited her at a systems seminar. It was clear to me that he had
hired her for her technical capabilities. Of course, a start-up
company would require a lot of new systems designs and instal-
lations, but no matter how bright she might have been, it seemed
to me that Catherine would not have had the specialized background to handle this kind of thing. Besides, she'd been hired as
Jimmy's assistant, not as a systems engineer or supervisor. And
why would Jimmy specifically recruit an assistant with a systems
background? Wouldn't someone who'd worked at another
sports agency, or at least a talent or management agency, have
been more appropriate for the position? It struck me as a strange
match. I decided to call Catherine's former boss at KRW when I
had a little more time. Right now, it was time to meet Heather in
Bill's office.

I checked my watch. It was ten till the hour. "Do you think
Heather's there yet?" I asked Tony.

He raised his eyebrows. "Oh, yes. They've been setting up for
a while now."

"They?"

The eyebrows remained raised. "Well, it's going to be a media kind of day. Bill's in the meeting of course, and Jillian from PR, you, Heather, Kelly Kendall. And also Jimmy Bennett."

"Oh, no. Media?"

"Oh, yes. Let's just say I hope you brought your makeup person."

I sighed and propelled myself toward the door. Bill had never mentioned the media. I wondered what he had in mind—possibly a press conference or interview. Jimmy Bennett's presence seemed superfluous, but it was not unheard of for agents to accompany their clients.

"So what do you think of Heather?" Tony asked as we walked down the hall, past the glass-enclosed atrium with its desert planting. Some of the cacti were in bloom now, sprouting bright red and orange blossoms. A quick collage flashed through my mind: a tiny five-foot-two fireball of a teenager bouncing and blazing across Centre Court at Wimbledon, a blistering serve, a barrage of headlines and magazine covers. "At one point she had the best serve on the women's tour," I said. "And I think she was only fifteen."

"Do you know her very well?"

"Believe it or not, I played her when she was thirteen, but only once. She beat me."

"What happened? Why is she here?"

"She wants it back." We all do, in a way. The difference with Heather was that she was still fairly young. She had seemed overweight and sluggish in France, but the root of her problems might be more psychological than physical. Perhaps she was burned out, disillusioned. If she wanted it back badly enough, maybe we could help her make the adjustments she needed.

The entrance to the double doors of Bill's office was clogged by dozens of thick black cables that ran out the door and down the hall, fastened to the floor at intervals by thick swabs of silver electrician's tape. In the doorway stood aluminum light stands and reflectors, manned by technicians in blue jeans and supervised by a young man in a sport coat and tie.

"Excuse me," I muttered, picking my way through the cable jungle. "I need to get by."

Bill was sitting at his desk, frowning intently at a page of notes, as a woman in a khaki jumpsuit leaned over Heather Knight, patting on pancake makeup with a fat puff.

Unlike the rest of the people in the room, Heather seemed relaxed, but then she was used to being the center of attention, to charming the world by being herself. As a teen phenom, she'd grown up playing to the camera. Perhaps because she'd been born with so much athletic ability, she'd been able to get by with less personal application than many of the rest of us. She was a natural, a kid with a built-in arsenal of touch shots and a serve that belied her tiny size.

Across the room, CiCi McBain licked her lips nervously. Her eyebrows were thick and unplucked, shading piercing-blue eyes of obvious intelligence. Both women were dressed in the Springs' logo sweat suits.

I nodded to them, walked straight to Bill, and leaned close to his ear. "I thought we were going to evaluate Heather this morning and get going on her program."

"We are," he said. "And the crew of *Sports Final* is here to film it."

"This is a circus," I said through gritted teeth. "Can't we get rid of these people?"

"I don't think so," said Bill. "LaserGlass's PR people set it up. It's good publicity for the clinic. And it was part of the package."

"*Whose* package?"

I didn't have to wonder for long.

"Hi, people." In walked Kelly Kendall, her smile as brilliant as her makeup. She was escorted by Jillian Edwards, our corporate public relations director, and both were flanked by Jimmy Bennett, who was looking especially pleased, a crescent-shaped smile planted on his thin lips as if stamped there by a cookie press.

"Sit here, to camera left, Kelly," said the young man in the sport coat. "And you, young lady"—he indicated me—"sit right here, on the other side of Heather."

"Jordan, it's great to see you," said Kelly, waving across the room as she clipped on a lavaliere microphone.

"Hi, Jordan." Jimmy beamed.

"Isn't it something to be working together again?" Kelly enthused.

"Yes, it's great, except I guess I don't totally understand exactly what we're working *on* at the moment," I said.

"This is just a little color piece," said Jillian.

"A day-in-the-life kind of thing," said Jimmy. "It's going to be a lot of fun. And we've been promised a slot on *Up Close and Personal* this weekend. That's network prime time."

"I think I'm not prepared for this," I said. The makeup, the cameras, the director—they were all making me nervous.

"We will be very reality-based, so just act naturally," elaborated the director. "Eduardo, get a meter reading on her face. And make sure to frame the shot so we get that mountain view." He came to rest in front of me and smiled. "Hi. I'm Steve."

"Right, Steve," I said. "How about telling me what I'm supposed to do. I think I forgot to read the script."

"Oh, that's very funny. Actually, there is no script. Just do what you'd normally do. You've been on camera before, I understand."

"Once or twice." Probably when you were in diapers, I thought.

"The main thing is to keep it real. This is going to be a mini-doc."

"Mini-what?" I asked.

"A mini-documentary. Kelly Kendall returns to tennis, and how does she do it?"

"How?"

"By teaming up with her former rival—that's you—to coach a great player back to victory. We're going to follow the entire process for our viewers."

I wanted to say that Heather had never been a great player, but I couldn't. I wanted to say that Kelly Kendall's so-called return to tennis was not the point here, but I didn't. Certainly everyone else in the room knew that, but nobody corrected Steve.

"Can you see the Desert Springs logos on the sweatshirts through the camera?" asked Jillian.

"We can. Not to worry," Steve reassured her. "Now everybody quiet, please, let's get some sound levels."

Everyone had to go around the room and say a little something or count to ten. Things went on like this for about another half hour, and then the film crew told us we could begin our meeting.

"Try to forget about the camera," Steve reminded us. He was beginning to irritate me. "And—action!"

"Action!" repeated the assistant.

"Usually we begin our process by explaining that what we do here is help an athlete realize her individual goals," Bill began. "Let's talk about what you really want out of this, Heather. What are your needs here?"

Heather nodded intently. It looked like she had a double chin. Too many lollipops, Heather, I said to myself. In fact, she didn't look good at all. Even the heavy camera makeup couldn't hide the fact that her skin was broken out and blotchy. Her legs seemed a bit thick. There was nothing dramatically bad, but definite room for improvement. Considering the shape she appeared to be in, it was amazing that she'd done as well as she had recently.

"I think it's obvious that I peaked very early," Heather said. "I want to play like I used to. I want to figure out how I can improve on the game as I play it today, make corrections where I can. I know I'm not a teenager anymore, but I've still got my serve when I'm on. I don't know, maybe I overtrained, listened to my parents too much, or my former coach."

CiCi nodded silently. Her dark hair was pulled back into a

single braid, and her angular cheekbones gave her an exotic look.

"I was always trying to please somebody else, to break some record. Now I'm just trying to please myself."

"And how did you feel at the French? What was your state of mind?" Bill asked.

"I was nervous. It was a weird tournament for everybody, I know, but I got upset when I shouldn't have. I feel like I lost control."

"We need to target the emotions and abilities that will allow you to win, regardless of how you feel," Bill said. "And we're here to help you do that. We're going to give you the necessary weapons: confidence, positive energy, fight, spirit, and determination. Don't you think that's achievable, Kelly?"

Kelly nodded intently. "That's right, Bill. I'm sure we can. Believe me, I know how easy it is to get blocked on court, to let yourself get distracted. You have to look deep inside yourself for the answers. We'll help Heather isolate these factors and define them to improve her game."

The interview went on like this for about forty-five minutes, accomplishing nothing constructive as far as I was concerned. Bill pitched questions to Kelly, and Kelly answered them, and the camera recorded it all, making her seem like an expert. She'd been coaching—co-coaching—for approximately thirty minutes and suddenly she was an authority. There was no denying that Kelly was a great tennis player. But she had yet to prove herself as a coach. I suppose I was being petty and defensive, but the whole thing bothered me. This videotaped charade was a waste of time. I wondered if I was destined to be haunted by Kelly Kendall for the rest of my life.

Finally, it was over. I ripped off my microphone, which I'd never had a chance to use, and left the room. All the old feelings of resentment toward Kelly rushed to the surface. Now she was invading my home turf, dogging me into this phase of my career.

I wanted her to go away, back to the ranch, to center court somewhere, to the broadcast booth, anywhere but here.

To my surprise, Kelly was right behind me.

"I hope I didn't offend you," she said, catching up as I headed back to my office. "I didn't mean to come on like the Normandy invasion." Looking at her face, I could read nothing—as usual. It was impossible to tell whether she was sincere or just placating me.

"No. It just isn't the way we usually operate," I said.

"Well, as I was talking, I realized I was monopolizing the conversation. But Bill kept asking me questions." She rolled her eyes, as if to indicate that the situation was out of her control, and smiled the smile that could melt an iceberg.

She was so charming, I had to forgive her. Vintage Kelly.

"Come on in my office," I said. We ducked through the doorway. "Sorry it's such a mess. I haven't gotten through my mail."

I quickly pushed aside some of the papers on the table. A few things dropped over the edge and onto the floor, completing the picture of disorganization.

"So what made you decide to coach?" I asked. "I thought you wanted to stay on the ranch, do a little commentary from time to time."

She smoothed her hair. It seemed to have gotten several shades lighter since France. "Well, I thought I should give something back to the sport, you know? You should understand. You're certainly doing that in a much bigger way than I am."

"Of course," I said. It sounded good, but I knew Kelly. She was not the give-back type. Kelly Kendall never gave an inch, a point, or a pointer. There was another agenda, but I'd have to figure it out for myself.

"I think Heather has real potential to make a big comeback at Wimbledon," she said. "She may not win, but I think she'll do well, and that's the important thing."

"Is that Heather's goal? Wimbledon?"

"That's *our* goal. And the Crown Jewel series—mainly for the visibility. There's going to be satellite coverage of the final at Las Vegas. Heather needs to work with your team here to get back on track: get on a nutritional program, drop that weight, get remotivated. But she can do it. Her game's slow now, but it's definitely still there."

"What about CiCi?"

"Well, we're team-coaching. I'm basically handling the technical game, and she's working on the mental part. She really is excellent at psyching out the other players."

"Why did CiCi decide to work with Heather in particular? Was it a career decision or a personal one?"

"I don't know. We never talked about it," said Kelly.

Kelly leaned toward me. "Listen, I hear you had some trouble at the French. God, it sounded awful."

"It was—a girl was killed. And a friend of mine was badly hurt."

"Horrible, just horrible. You have to wonder, When will it stop, where will they draw the line? This is a crazy world. Listen, it's getting really depraved out there. Remember that guy who stalked me in Rome?"

"The one who was arrested after he lived in your closet for a week?"

She nodded. "He killed himself and sent me a video of it."

"Good God!"

"He set up a video camera on a stand, turned it on, and just kept it running while he blew his brains out. Then his best friend sent me the video—and a letter blaming me, of course. Apparently he thought I'd been ignoring him. The fact was, I'd never even met him. Apparently, he arranged the whole incident just to torture me." Her green eyes glittered with horror. "I have full-time personal security now. I have to. Jeff really doesn't know how to cope with this. It's so unfair to him. All he wants to do is raise horses."

"Then why are you getting back into tennis? You could just stay at the ranch with Jeff, out of the public eye."

"I could. And you had your chance too. You of all people should understand. I guess I'm just not ready to leave tennis completely. It's been my whole life for too long. I tried, but—well, it's a choice. And frankly I don't think either of us is the type to let some crazy person out there dictate our lives. I refuse to give in to it. And it looks like you do too."

"That's true, but it's terrible for anybody to live like this," I said.

"Well, you don't have to be a victim. Look at this." Kelly reached into her purse, pulled out a small handgun, and put it on the table.

I shuddered involuntarily. I'd always despised guns. Guns and reptiles. "My God. Is that thing loaded?"

"Don't worry, the safety's on—see?" She pointed to a little lever on the left side of the gun. "This is a twenty-five-caliber Beretta semiautomatic. Don't panic. You can't fire unless you flick the safety off." She demonstrated the mechanism. "It's perfectly safe if you use it properly. You should get one too. Face it, Jordan, somebody tried to kill you. Or did I misunderstand?"

"No, that was about what happened." I was irritated to have Kelly point it out. She had always made a point of bringing the obvious to my attention: defects in my serve, the fact that none of the major players showed up the year I won the Australian Open, now this.

"You should carry a gun for protection. Of course, mine is licensed. And I'm an excellent shot, by the way."

"I bet you are. You could always hit the line dead on." The image of wholesome Kelly Kendall packing heat was almost unimaginable. I stared at the gun. "It's a very small gun," I said, for lack of any other comment.

"It shoots a big enough hole on the target range," Kelly said briskly. She picked up the gun carefully, put it back in her purse, and daintily crossed her legs.

"Would you mind not bringing it around?" I asked. "Guns make me very nervous. And how did you get it in here? We have a security system."

"Really? I didn't come in through the gate. I took a helicopter from the airport. They usually don't check me anyhow. Besides, it's licensed."

I could certainly imagine a starstruck guard waving America's Sweetheart straight on through. Who on earth would consider Kelly Kendall a security risk?

"Well." Kelly collected her purse and stood up. "Time to get back to work. All those years ago on the circuit, who'd have predicted we'd be here together today?"

"Not even the psychics, Kel." I wondered if I resented her because she was intruding on my new life here, or because she had intruded on my life in the past, or because she'd done everything so perfectly it was impossible not to resent her. The fact that she'd managed not only one of the most brilliant careers in tennis, but also a life with a husband, was reason enough. I tried to avoid thinking about husbands—and children. As I approached thirty, that was the most painful area of all.

"Kelly, there you are." Jillian jogged into the doorway of my office, out of breath and looking slightly frantic. "We have a photo session set up for you in five minutes."

They breezed out together. Seconds later, Tony stuck his head in.

"The PR Princess," he said. "I saw them in the hall."

"Don't joke about Kelly," I said. "She's armed and—I don't have to assume—I *know* she's dangerous."

"Well," Tony said, "in case you haven't checked your schedule, your real work starts with Heather's evaluation in an hour, after she's seen Dr. Wexler. She's with him now for her baseline workup."

"Thanks, Tony. Would you mind holding my calls and closing the door on your way out?"

I put Kelly Kendall out of my mind and spent the next thirty minutes combing through Heather's case file. Other than the weight gain, her medical records and the notes from the WTF physical therapists didn't indicate anything unusual. Many phenoms, however, suffer from cases of early brilliance and subsequent burnout. The unique aspect of Heather's case was the sudden resurgence of motivation relatively late in her career. The phone buzzed and I picked it up, slightly irritated that Tony would interrupt me.

"Yes, Tony."

"Jordan, you have a call."

"I thought I wasn't taking calls."

"This one says it's urgent. His name is Jason Campbell. Do you know him?"

I was on the verge of hanging up when I remembered who Jason Campbell was: Catherine Richie's boss at KRW. Of course I took the call.

"Do you know who I am?" said a young, earnest voice.

"Yes, I do. Catherine Richie's mother told me about you."

"Yes, and she also told me about *you*. I had to come here to speak with you as soon as I knew you were in town."

"You couldn't call?"

"I owe this to Catherine. I blame myself for what happened to her."

"I can meet you here, in my office."

He paused. "No, I'd rather not, if you don't mind."

"Why not?"

"Well, actually, I'm not sure it's safe. I'm not sure it's *not* safe," he added quickly, "but just in case."

"There's a little coffee shop called Sandy's just across the highway before you come to the Springs," I said. I was already on my feet, pulling the keys to my motorcycle out of my bag. "I'll be there in less than five minutes." My motorcycle was parked in the lot. If I hurried, I could make it to meet Jason and be back in time for the meeting with Heather.

Actually, I knew I'd be late, but I didn't care.

EIGHT

I never go to the little white stucco restaurant across the highway from the clinic, and neither does anybody else that I know. Gus actually ate a hamburger there once and lived to tell about it, so I suppose it can't be that terrible. Still, the smell of rancid grease did permeate the place as I came in, looking for Jason Campbell.

It was too late for breakfast and not early enough for lunch. Jason was at a small booth by the window; I could tell because he was the only person in the place.

"You're Jason?" I asked, sliding into the booth.

He half stood and reached across to shake my hand. He was nice looking, not too tall, with dark hair and pale skin.

"So why isn't it safe in my office?" I asked.

"I wouldn't feel comfortable there," he said. "I don't trust anybody from that world after what happened to Catherine."

"Then why did you come to see me?"

"Her mother said you tried to help her."

"Yes, I did."

He nodded slowly, as if I were absolved. "You were the last

one with her, the one who found her. I owe it to Cath to talk to you in person."

"I understand Catherine worked for you," I said, as gently as possible. It was an unnecessary remark, but I had to start somewhere. The waitress approached with a pot of coffee, and I waved her away. Framed black-and-white photos of stars of this vintage were stacked on the walls as well. I wondered if James Dean had ever actually ordered chili here, or if Marilyn Monroe had lingered in one of these booths over a club sandwich. Somehow I doubted it.

"Yes," said Jason, "it was her first job out of school. She was a great girl. Did you know Catherine?"

"No, I didn't."

"She was brilliant. Just goddamned brilliant." He twisted his paper napkin. The corners of his eyes crinkled in a reflex reaction to the pain of remembering.

"What a waste," he said bitterly. He picked up his glass of water and drained it in a gulp. The paper napkin was balled into a damp pulp.

"Her mother said she did well at KRW," I said.

"She did better than well. If she hadn't left, she'd have had a real future there. And she would have been alive."

"Don't blame the fact that she left. That's not why she died."

"Do you know why it happened?" Jason asked bluntly, looking straight at me.

"No. Not really."

"Well, I'll tell you one thing. She was scared out of her mind." He rummaged through the backpack that was beside him on the seat and pulled out a small tape recorder. "This was the last message she left me." He pushed the play button.

Jase, it's me. Catherine's voice. The same voice I had heard on her message at work, but this time tight and clipped in tone. *I'm in Paris. I need your help with something. I'm trying to fax into a security program. I'll modem you the information and could you fax my program from your end. Please, don't let me down. Have to run. I'll call you tomorrow.*

Jason turned off the tape. "What this means is that Catherine was involved in some kind of systems activity, and she wanted to camouflage that she was the one who was doing it."

"That's not what she said."

"Please. Catherine could do anything on the computer. She modemed me the program. It was simple, a no-brainer. So why involve me? She didn't want it traced to her, that's all I can imagine. And I also think she was in a hurry to get out of there and come back."

"What was on the list?"

"That's the weird thing. It was nothing. Just a directory—a list of names, agency clients and prospective clients, something like that. It didn't make sense for me to get into it."

"Do you still have the list?"

"Yes, on my hard drive and on a disc."

"Could I please see a copy?"

"Sure, I'll fax it to you from the office. But it's nothing."

"Do you know why anyone would want to kill Catherine?"

"No. But I know she was scared or else very unhappy."

"How did you know?"

"Because she was coming home. She wasn't a quitter, believe me. I don't know, maybe she got bored with that stupid job. That's possible. Setting up meetings and events in tennis? You didn't need her brains for that."

"So why do you suppose she took the job?"

"Two reasons that she told me. One, she wanted to travel; two, they paid her a fortune. She still had a big college loan to pay off, and she was ambitious. She said she couldn't say no."

"How much did they pay her?"

"I'm not sure. But I tried to top it, and she said to forget it, it wouldn't be possible. It had to be six figures, at least."

"Six figures to be an assistant and set up meetings?"

"Well, they really wanted her. I don't know the pay scale in sports, but I know there's big money involved."

"It still seems very high. Can I tell you something? Tennis *coaches* maybe make six figures, if they're good. Something isn't right about this. Tell me, Jason. Other than that last message, did you ever hear from Catherine after she left?"

"Once, right before she died. She called and missed me, so she left a message. She asked for her old job back. That's how I know she wanted to quit and come home."

"I see. Did she ever mention Jimmy Bennett?"

"Yeah, she worked for him."

"Did she ever mention any love interests?"

"No, never."

"Jimmy Bennett said Catherine quit his company to be with some new guy she met in France."

Jason dropped his head into his hands. "It's news to me. And if that was the case, why would she want her old job back? It doesn't make sense."

I had to agree. It also didn't make sense that Jason had taken the trouble to track me down and come here. "Jason," I said, "why are you here? Please tell me the truth."

"I loved Catherine," he said. The statement in no way surprised me. He had been—and remained—too involved with her for anything else to be the case. "And she loved me too," he continued. "There's no way she would have been going off with some mystery guy in France. It's absurd. It never would have happened. Bennett's covering up something. He's a lowlife. If I ever meet him, I'll kill him."

"Do you think Bennett killed Catherine?"

"It almost doesn't matter. He's responsible, that's the point. He put her in that scumbag world of his."

"Hiring someone is not a crime, Jason. She didn't have to take the job."

"There was the money. And—well, we'd broken up. We'd worked together for three years when she left. I guess it got a little close. But we always kept in touch, and we were getting back together. . . ." He trailed off. There was no need now to elaborate on their plans for the future, on his heartbreak and regret.

"You say you don't trust anybody. Do you think Catherine was frightened?"

"Her? No, not at all, nothing scared her. She thought tennis was a game and a business, period. Everything was one big adventure, and that was how she liked it. She liked to take things on, grab them by the horns and shake them."

"What do you think she had by the horns this time?"

He shook his head slowly. "I don't now. I just don't know."

I had to get back to the clinic. "Listen, Jason, here's my home number." I scribbled it on a napkin and pushed it across the table. "Call me any time. Where are you staying? Maybe we can talk after I finish work."

"I'm going straight to the airport. There's no need for me to stick around here."

I left the waitress a five-dollar tip, since we hadn't ordered anything. Jason walked ahead of me to the door, his shoulders slumped. "It all seems so senseless," he said.

So far I had to agree.

"So," he said, attempting to change the subject, "are you working with any big stars now?"

"I've got Heather Knight as a client. She's here this week. Remember her? She was a big star a few years ago, as a kid."

Jason stopped suddenly. "Heather Knight? Her name was on Catherine's list."

"Well, she's a client of Jimmy Bennett's, so that's not surprising."

Jason frowned. He had pushed the door to the diner halfway open and he stood still, poised at the edge of a thought. "Catherine talked about her, I think. Yeah, she did. I don't really know the names of these tennis people, I don't follow the game, but I remember she said that this Heather was making a comeback and she was going to owe it all to Catherine."

"She said that?"

"I remember because she sounded so—bitter—about it. Like she really didn't like her and was doing her a big favor."

"What was the favor?"

"She didn't say."

"Maybe she helped recruit Heather as a client, so she could get a fresh start with Jimmy. Could that be it?"

"I don't know. We didn't dwell on it. She knew I don't care about these stars with their colossal egos."

"But how could Heather possibly owe her comeback to Catherine?"

"I have no idea," said Jason. "Why don't you ask her?"

I caught up with Heather in the office, as they were printing out her schedule on the computer. For the next ten days, this was to be her bible. Our goal was to tear down her game and give birth to a new one, a painful process, as change always is. The Desert Springs system was to dissect every aspect of a player's physical and mental situation, as well as her game. For the body and mind to connect, all aspects have to be in harmony. Otherwise, your body won't do what you ask of it.

As a physical therapist, my primary role involves treatment of injuries, but there's also the issue of making sure a player remains in a safe zone medically. In a case like Heather's, the added pressure and stress of attempting a full-force comeback, the effort of trying to recapture a level of play from her teenage years, could cause stress that in turn might tighten her muscles, a condition that could lead to injuries. I also tried to be sure there were no emotional issues that were having a physical effect. This is routine. You can't cut off a player's head; if she has problems, they can, and usually do, show up on her body and in her game.

Of course, I'm not a psychiatrist, and I usually wait for the player to say something to me, rather than vice versa. But today, when I went through my routine session with Heather, she volunteered nothing. She did, however, want to increase her power and her speed, so I gave her a series of exercises to build up her legs and her serving shoulder and arm, and exercises that supported her nondominant arm as well. Other than that, there wasn't much to do. It seemed to me that the issues with Heather, other than her age, were mainly mind-set and conditioning.

I opened my notebook and handed Heather a routine attitude assessment test that we administer to every client who enters our program. There were about five hundred multiple-choice questions and a page of open-ends. Once a player completes the form, we feed the multiple-choice results into the computer and print out a charted motivational profile that we can compare with those of the most successful high-level performances, which we also have charted and kept on file. The open-ended questions are for added dimension.

"What's this?" Heather frowned. "It looks like homework. I didn't even do homework when I was in school."

"It's very simple," I explained.

"But it's so *long*."

True. The assessment test was purposefully long, so a player couldn't scam the test and have it come out the way he or she wanted.

"Just relax and be open and honest," I explained. "Answer in the here-and-now context. There are no right or wrong answers."

The test took about an hour and a half, and I left Heather alone while she completed it. After the allotted time, I collected the test for Tony to run through the computer. Then we'd fax the results to Gus at his seminar for analysis. Gus actually preferred to receive the results on an anonymous basis, so he wouldn't be biased in his assessment in any way.

"Well, that was exciting," said Heather, her tone implying the opposite.

"Let's take a walk," I said, wrapping up our session. I didn't know Heather that well, but once you were outside, it always seemed easier to talk, and I was counting on this to get a real dialogue going. "So what do you think of the Springs so far?" I asked.

"It's a very nice place and an interesting approach, but to be honest I have faith in myself, in my own talent. It's always pulled me through. I just need motivation, that's all. After all these years, it's not easy to always be *on*." She sighed. Her face looked set, determined.

"Fine," I said. "I understand that. But we're going to try to get you back to your peak performance state more consistently. That's the goal, isn't it?"

"Right." She squinted into the sun, tied a bandanna around her hair, and picked up the pace.

We passed the white stucco bungalows where the clients stayed. "You know, Heather," I said. "You have absolutely incredible natural athletic gifts."

She made a face. "And here I am, after all these years, in a training camp and being compared in the press to the likes of Dagmar Olafsen. Please!" She stretched the last word into two syllables.

"Mental toughness is not something we're born with," I said. "You have to develop and nurture it. You've been lucky your entire career. You got by on your talent. Now it's not enough."

"That's what CiCi has been telling me."

"What's that?"

"That I can't be comfortable at the baseline anymore. I have to attack, be more aggressive, take my points."

"And you?"

"I understand, but I also know my own game."

"Why did you change coaches? Why CiCi?"

"It was time for a change. Jimmy helped me see that what I was doing wasn't working, and he suggested CiCi. I didn't think she'd be available—she was so tied in with Dagmar—but it turned out she wasn't feeling good about working with Dagmar after their breakup. I think she was bored, to tell you the truth. Anyhow, it seemed to be a good fit."

"You also joined Jimmy's new agency, right?"

"It's the smartest thing I've done. Jimmy believes in me," she said emphatically. "He has vision. To Jimmy, I'm not at the end of my career. He sees this year as a beginning for me, a new phase. His people are young and aggressive, real go-getters. I like that."

"Like Catherine Richie?"

"Catherine Richie?"

"His assistant—the young woman who was killed during the French. You must have known her."

"Sure. We talked on the phone, and I saw her at matches. She arranged the details for some interviews I did. And once, when I went to LA, she picked me up at the airport."

"That's it?"

"Uh-huh."

"You never spent any time with her other than that?" I kept thinking about Jason's comment that Catherine had told him Heather would owe her career to her.

"No. Why would I? She was just a secretary. Too bad about what happened to her, of course."

"She never did any special favors for you?"

"Once she got me some tickets to a rock concert. No big deal. I think it was actually Jimmy who got them. She just mailed them."

"Do you have any idea why anybody would want to kill her?"

"I can't imagine. Maybe there were drugs involved."

"You think Catherine was involved in drugs?"

"Anything's possible these days."

"True, a lot of weird things have been going on around tennis lately," I said. "Have you had any problems?"

"No, none at all."

"Except for what happened to Mila. You were there. Did you realize that somebody spiked Mila's drink? That's why she fell apart. It almost killed her."

Heather stopped and turned toward me, really attentive for the first time. "That's horrible. My God, I hadn't heard that."

"They're keeping it quiet. There's an investigation. Any thoughts on why this happened?"

"What are you, Nancy Drew?"

"I'm not blaming you, Heather. But it came close to you. You should think about that."

She shrugged. "I'm not going to live in a state of fear," she said, "but I've made what I think is a smart decision. I'm not going to play the Grand Slams anymore after Wimbledon. It's too dangerous. Security is a complete joke. Besides, Jimmy thinks I can make more money and increase my marquee value by playing exhibitions."

There was a kernel of truth in that. If you couldn't win on the Grand Slam circuit, you could be more valuable elsewhere. Second-tier or waning players had been known to opt for cutting down their public exposure at the Grand Slams and making guarantees of $100,000 or more per day in markets like Hong Kong, Korea, Singapore, Japan, and South America. The Japanese, in particular, were willing to pay big money.

"Are you referring to the Crown Jewel?" I asked.

"Yes, as a matter of fact."

"It's a rich event."

"The richest. A million dollars."

"I hadn't realized there was quite that much money involved. How do you think Jimmy pulled together that kind of funding?" It seemed a great leap from the Jimmy of a year ago, scrounging and begging to recruit players to the outskirts of Omaha.

"Investors. Jimmy has a commercial approach. He's not stuck in tradition. He's making his own rules, breaking new ground. I like that. Tennis is a snob sport. That's one of its problems. It's a sport for an inner circle—players as well as fans. Jimmy is expanding the circle."

"Well, I think it's a wonderful effort, and if he handles it right it will be good for the game," I said. "Tennis could use some broadening; I don't think anybody would dispute that. There's always room for growth and innovation. Do you realize that the Crown Jewel is an all-surface tournament? It's the first time ever where all the surfaces will be in play. When was the last time we saw that kind of creativity in this sport—or any sport?"

"That's right." Heather nodded emphatically. "And people are starting to see the light about Jimmy. Did you know that Celine Gilbert is signing with Jimmy?"

"Really?" Celine Gilbert was currently the number-three player, a real catch for a new agency.

"And Harriet Craig is going to play at the Crown Jewel."

Craig was the top-seeded player in women's tennis, sure to attract fans to any event.

"So you see why I'm working with Jimmy. It turned out to be a good decision, I think."

I strongly suspected that Jimmy had also slashed his commission to entice Heather into his fold—a strategy not unheard of among maverick agents trying to lure players away from the bigger and more established agencies.

"And there's another thing," Heather said.

"What's that?"

"I mean to put myself back where I belong. When I leave here, CiCi and I are going to practice on grass until Wimbledon. Now, what's next for me here?"

I ran through the system for her. "There will be a psychological profile on how you handle stress, your need fulfillment, your competitive skills. We'll be looking at the whole picture of your game—before, during, and between points—how you manage your changeovers, your preparation for tournaments, every area that can positively impact the performance outcome."

I watched Heather closely as we talked. There was something bothering me. Her motivation seemed ironclad, yet I'd seen her game in France and it didn't fit. For a player as motivated as she claimed to be, she was sloppy and undertrained. Still, the fact that she was here showed a strong level of commitment. Maybe her approach was uneven, or perhaps she'd simply realized that she couldn't lean on her natural talent anymore, she had to get to work. I had to give her the benefit of the doubt.

"We'd better get to the tennis court," I said. "You're set for a videotaping session in ten minutes."

. . .

The outdoor practice courts, as usual, were humming with activity when we got there. A junior group was just finishing up on most of the nine outdoor courts. The kids were cleared off as Heather approached, and I noticed that one of the courts had been covered. Obviously, Heather didn't want anybody observing her practice sessions.

While Tanner Axel, our top training pro, was working with Heather, I decided it'd be a good opportunity to talk to CiCi. She'd been a fixture on the tour for years, but I'd never gotten to know her. She tended to keep to herself, and her entire existence seemed to be wrapped up in her player. She and Dagmar had been a personal and professional couple for at least five years, so this experience was new for her in more ways than one.

CiCi had a weathered face the color of tarnished pennies, the result of years of being in courtside sun. A fine web of wrinkles lined her forehead, and she wore no makeup. At least a dozen turquoise and silver Indian bracelets were stacked from each wrist to forearm, and they jangled when she spoke and gestured. Her fingers were similarly adorned with heavy silver rings.

"This is a big change for you, isn't it?" I asked rhetorically.

"Yes," she said curtly. Subject closed.

We stood quietly for a minute before I spoke again. "CiCi, I was just wondering, did you know Catherine Richie?"

"Jimmy's assistant. Yeah, I talked to her sometimes, but I didn't know her personally. Terrible about her."

"Yes, it certainly is."

"You were there, right?"

"Yes. It was a real tragedy. So you don't think she had much to do with Heather?"

"Nothing except some administrative details, as far as I know. Why?"

"I had heard that Catherine was doing something or other for Heather."

"Maybe she made a plane reservation," said CiCi irritably. "Or fixed coffee for a meeting."

"Supposedly she left Jimmy before she was killed. Do you have any idea why?"

"Why does anybody leave anybody? You get sick of them, you want something different, you get a better offer. It was probably something like that. But who knows? I wasn't there." Her voice was getting increasingly irritable.

"Is that why you left Dagmar?"

She paused. "It was time. I needed a challenge."

"But what a coincidence. Dagmar's trying to make a big comeback too. The situations are similar."

"No, they're not. Trying to make a comeback and actually making a comeback are not the same. I know Dagmar. In the end, she'll peter out, lose her wind. That injury—well, I pushed her and pushed her, we worked on it, but she can't seem to recover completely, and she doesn't want to listen. Everything has to be her way. When that happens to a player her age, or any age actually, well—I think it's over for her."

"But not for you, now that you're with Heather."

She lifted her eyebrows. "I should hope not. Heather doesn't let her emotions get in the way. She plays by instinct, uses her natural talent. And we can get her back in shape. It shouldn't take much."

Cici's equation was simplistically optimistic, and I had to believe she knew it. But if Heather won, CiCi won. That much was clear without discussion. A coach's reputation is tied to his or her player. Regardless of their personal relationship, CiCi could have felt Dagmar's ship was sinking. There was a lot at stake, and a dollar value attached. The coach of a star player in the media spotlight can make five hundred dollars just by agreeing to wear a particular sponsor's patch during a tournament. And that's just the beginning. CiCi's motives for dropping Dagmar could have been emotional or purely monetary. Either was perfectly understandable, as was any combination. But the fact that she'd allied herself with her former girlfriend's arch rival did show tinges of spite.

"How do you think Dag feels about the fact that you're working with Heather?"

"I haven't asked her, but frankly it's not an issue." CiCi dusted off the question and did not meet my eyes. In fact, her glance had been evasive all along. "It's my career," she said. "This is my particular opportunity. She has her own career to think about. I tried to help her while I could. She wouldn't listen. She had to have everything her way. Well, now she can. I'm out of it." She swung around and faced me. "What business is it of yours?"

"CiCi, you have to understand that I'm not a competitor on the circuit anymore. I'm working with your player. If I'm going to do my best to help her, I need to understand the situation as well as I can. Let's face it, nothing that's going on right now is status quo. There's been a murder, there's been foul play involving a match that Heather was playing, you used to be very close to Dagmar, who is now Heather's rival—"

"That's the media," snapped CiCi.

"Well, I don't have to tell you that these things have an impact on her game."

"She's never played better in years. Just look at her."

That much was true. Heather's form was superb, but then it always had been. She was textbook excellence, but I knew it wasn't enough; she couldn't win in the Grand Slams. She was merely going through the moves. There was no passion for the game. And something else disturbed me most of all: Heather didn't have the kind of attitude it takes to win. She hadn't seemed vitally interested in what I was telling her or the various aspects of her training that we discussed. Taking the attitude test had been a boring chore, for instance, as opposed to the interesting exploration it should have been. I wondered again what Catherine, a virtual outsider in the world of tennis, had planned to do for Heather to clinch her comeback—and, whatever it was, if that could have cost her her life.

NINE

"I've got the results of Heather's test," said Tony, waving a fax in my direction. "Gus was taking a break from the seminar today. He got right on it and modemed back his report like this!" Tony snapped his fingers as he handed me the pages.

"Did you tell him whose test it was?"

"Of course not!" Tony looked wounded that I'd even ask.

I closed the door and settled in at my table to read.

> This player's motivation is problematical. There seems to be only a superficial interest in the actual game of tennis, while interest in pleasing others is disproportionately high. Motivation to capitalize on opportunities in the game is weak. This player seems to concentrate too much on the past, as opposed to the present. Although confidence is high, emotion is flat.

Gus's report went on to say that although the player professed interest and dedication in the open-ended questions, what she said and what she revealed about herself in the test did not mesh.

As soon as I read this report, I returned to the practice court. Heather's group was waiting to replay her practice tape, so I called Tanner Axel aside. "How was practice?" I asked.

"Disturbing, Jordan, to be honest." He mopped his brow with his trademark red bandanna. "She only works when people are watching and she thinks she has to make an impression. At least that's my take on it."

"What about the closed practice?"

"Fewer people to watch."

"Thanks, Tan." What he said was consistent with Gus's analysis and specific enough that I felt it should be brought up.

Kelly appeared, this time unaccompanied by cameras. She was now wearing navy blue slacks and a white silk T-shirt. A heavy gold watch circled with diamonds ringed her wrist. She conferred briefly with CiCi and then came over to me.

"I'm glad you're here, Kelly, because I'd like to discuss something with you and see how you want to handle it."

"What's that?"

"Frankly, Heather's motivation assessment is worrisome."

"I understand you found no physical problems with Heather, right?"

"She looks pretty good, I'd say, physically."

"That's fine." Kelly nodded. "Why don't you take a break?"

"What do you mean?"

Kelly's eyes were unreadable behind her reflective sunglasses. "We think it would be better if you didn't get involved with Heather's game," she said, smiling sweetly.

"Kelly, I work with all our clients here at the Springs. This motivation issue was brought up by Gus. As you know, he's our head sports psychologist, and his reputation is world class. I only administered the test; the results were submitted anonymously and then analyzed and interpreted by him. However, according to our pro, Heather's actions seem to bear out the conclusions. We need to discuss this if you want the best treatment for your client. You're going to need a month to rebuild her game, and Wimbledon is three weeks away."

Kelly blinked impassively. The ice princess was back. "Actually, Jordan, there's no real reason for you to be involved beyond this point. We've decided to keep Heather's coaching team very small."

"I'm not a coach."

"True, but you are going to be working with Dagmar, and there's no reason to take any risks just now."

"Working with me is not a risk, Kelly!" I was furious. Kelly was trying to ignore my expertise and edge me out on my own turf.

She sighed and brushed back a strand of golden hair. "Well, that's the way Heather wants it. And I'd have to say I agree. Of course it's irrational, but your presence could be a distraction. We can't have that. And this motivation thing. That's ridiculous."

"*We* can't have that, Kelly, or *you* can't have that? Who is the competitive one here, you or your player?"

"Don't overreact, Jordan," she said. "If I were you, I wouldn't take it personally."

I could see Heather and CiCi ignoring the monitor and watching me. There was no way I was going to show a reaction and give them that satisfaction.

"Whatever, Kelly," I said. "You're the coach."

She nodded curtly, as if I were a reporter who'd asked one too many questions after a press conference. I had to admit that if any other coach had asked me to absent myself from a coaching situation, I would have complied without emotion. Coaches and their players have been known to do strange things to keep their game secret and give it that added edge. Some players routinely request arenas to open for 6 A.M. practice times during big matches, just so they won't be seen. Others refuse to practice with other players on the tour, or insist that their hitting partners sign confidentiality agreements. Still, being asked to step back by Kelly Kendall was hard to swallow. It seemed incredible that, at this point in my life, at a facility where I was a partner, she could impinge on my career. Being caught in Kelly's backwash seemed to be my fate in life, and if there hadn't been bigger issues on my mind, I might have let this incident blow out of proportion. I decided to let it go.

I ducked out and headed back to the office to call Paris. I had barely sat down when Tony came in, waving an envelope.

"Oops, I think I'm in trouble," he said. "I forgot to give you this, and Jimmy came by to collect it."

"What is it?"

Tony played innocent, but I knew he knew what was inside, and I knew he had not forgotten to give it to me. Tony never forgot. If something curious came through the office, he had ways of figuring it out—even, I suspected, going so far as to steam open a sealed envelope or eavesdrop on an appropriate conversation.

"Hey, come on, Tony. Don't make me read it. What is it?"

"Oh, all right, beat me and flog me. It's a confidentiality agreement."

"A *what?*"

"Confidentiality agreement. Mr. Bennett asked that you sign it."

I ripped open the envelope and quickly scanned the two pages inside. Then I laughed, wadded up the document, and threw it out. As a physical therapist, all the work I do with my clients is automatically confidential, at least in my opinion. It was the same thing as medical privilege. I wasn't about to be force-fed some document that served Jimmy's promotional purposes.

"He made everybody sign these," said Tony. "Even the kitchen. Maybe Mr. Bennett thought one of the dishwashers was going to call the tabloids with Heather's celebrity diet tips or something."

"Well, covered courts are one thing, private practices another, but this is way over the top," I said. "Where is Jimmy? I'll tell him myself."

"Gone. He was out of here the minute they had his close-up in the can. I think I heard him say he was heading back to his LA office."

"Fine. Good riddance."

"And you got a message." He handed me a piece of paper with a phone number.

"This is an international area code—it's the hospital in Paris." I reached for the phone. "Who made the call, Tony?"

"I don't actually know. It was on your voice mail. Somebody left it last night, and I just picked it up."

"Is the message still on there?"

Tony looked alarmed. "No, I erased it after I copied it down. But it was a man."

"American?"

"Yes, I think so. I didn't recognize it."

I dialed Noel Fisher's line, and his mother answered. "Hello, dear," she said.

"How's your patient?" I asked.

"He's starting to complain, which means he's getting back to normal." She chuckled. "Why, just last night the nurse—" There was a loud *clunk!* and the phone went dead.

Sometimes connections to Europe are terrible. I redialed the number. Busy. I tried again. Busy. I put the phone on automatic redial, and the phone was continuously busy. I decided to hang up and try again in fifteen minutes. Meanwhile, I reviewed some files from upcoming clients. I got caught up in the reading, and then there were rush orders for supplies to approve, and one thing led to another until I realized with a start that almost an hour had passed. When I called Paris this time, the phone rang and a strange voice answered, a voice that spoke only French. Fortunately, Tony speaks fluent French, so I put him on the line.

"Ask him to put Noel Fisher on," I said.

After a few moments of conversation, Tony put the phone on hold. "He's not there," he said.

"What do you mean, he's not there? I just talked to his mother. Check the number." My stomach suddenly clenched.

"You dialed the right room. This guy's an orderly. He's cleaning the room or something. It's empty. He hasn't heard of Noel Fisher."

"Of course not. Nobody there has. They had him in the hospital under an assumed name for security purposes. But where is the man who was in the room?"

Tony got back on the phone. I had to admire his way with languages, a facility that came in handy in all our international dealings. After a few more minutes of conversation, he hung up.

"Why'd you do that?" I yelled.

"Relax. You're stressed out. Well, Mercury's in retrograde. What can you expect? The guy I was talking to knew nothing, or at least claimed he knew nothing, and there's no way I could strap him to a chair and beat a confession out of him from across the ocean, okay? Your friend Fisher, or whoever was in that room, is just gone—moved or checked out. Maybe you'd better call somebody a little higher up the food chain."

I opened my purse, yanked out Inspector Lemire's card, and placed a call to him, willing him to be there. He answered on the third ring.

"Noel Fisher is not dead, as far as we know, but he is gone, it's true," admitted the Inspector. "My man at the hospital has just called me, in fact. Unfortunately, we have no idea where or how."

"How could this happen? He was under twenty-four-hour police guard! I was talking to his mother less than two hours ago, and the phone went dead."

"At this time, I must admit, no one knows, Mademoiselle Myles. The guard did not see anyone come or go. I will inform you as soon as we have more information."

"And what about his mother?"

"She is also gone. The guard opened the door to each room, and both of them were gone."

"Oh, my God." My conscience whipped at me. If I had stayed, this would never have happened.

"We are classifying this as a kidnapping," said Inspector Lemire.

"How do you kidnap a man flat on his back in a hospital bed?" I said, through gritted teeth. "And his mother?"

"This is what we are now trying to find out," said Lemire, his voice flat with fatigue and frustration. "I will keep you informed. But I must ask you one thing, mademoiselle, if you wish to help."

"Anything, of course."

"Please stay out of the investigation. This is a police matter and very serious. Any interference, no matter how well-meaning, could jeopardize the entire matter. And it would not do at all to have a third person, one of our Roland Garros champions, missing—or worse."

"Just tell me this, Inspector. Do you know for a fact that the Fishers are not dead?"

"No," he said quietly. "We do not know that for a fact. And Mademoiselle Myles—"

"Yes, Inspector?"

"Of course you are now on American soil, but I think it would not hurt for you to be extremely cautious."

"Thank you for your concern, Inspector. I'll consider your suggestions."

Tony, sensing my mood, made himself invisible and crept out of the room as I ended the conversation. After I hung up, all I could do was sit there in a stupor. From across the ocean, it all felt insurmountable. Inspector Lemire would do what he could, but so far his efforts had failed completely. If I didn't help, who would care enough to think of Noel Fisher as anything but a statistic? The only other person I knew whose concern might exceed mine, let alone match it, was in her seventies and missing also. Still, I knew Lemire was being sensible, an approach that was rarely my strength. I couldn't ignore the facts that I didn't speak French, didn't know Paris, and would no doubt be in his way. I had to admit that to go to France and risk bungling the investigation would be neither helpful nor constructive. And it could do more harm than good.

But there was one place I *could* go.

I picked up my backpack and headed for the door.

"Tony," I called over my shoulder, "would you mind looking up the address of TalentMasters and leaving it on my voice mail? And please tell Bill that I suddenly feel very sick. I must be coming down with something." I faked a hacking cough. "I don't want to expose anybody to this, so I may not be back till it clears up."

Tony, who knew I was never sick, didn't buy it—and didn't even look up from the drawer of files he was rearranging. "Take two aspirin, drink a glass of juice, and I'll be over to walk and feed A.M."

I went home, changed into jeans and boots, threw a few clothes into my backpack, grabbed my helmet, and climbed on my motorcycle. Riding my bike through the starkness of the desert always makes me feel energized. And now, by heading straight for LA I was taking some sort of action, not just absorbing Kelly's shots and waiting for the phone to ring. I swore two things to myself as I edged past the speed limit: First, I would never again play second fiddle to Kelly Kendall; second, I would find out what linked Noel Fisher to Catherine Richie. Because I was convinced there was a link. And when I found it, I would find the Fish. . . .

Within three hours I pulled up in front of the black glass building on Maple Drive where Jimmy Bennett's TalentMasters Agency was located. The company did not occupy the entire building, but they had their own receptionist in the lobby.

"Do you have an appointment with Mr. Bennett?" she asked politely.

"Well, actually, no, but I believe he's expecting me," I said. A total lie, of course.

Within minutes, a young woman materialized and introduced herself as Jimmy's assistant. "I checked his calendar, and I'm so sorry, but there must be some confusion," she said, biting her lip. She seemed nervous about making a mistake, which meant that she was probably a very new hire. "He's completely booked. In fact he's leaving shortly for an appointment."

"Oh, I'm sorry," I said. "It must be my mistake." I smiled understandingly at the woman and went immediately to the garage. Nobody ever takes cabs or walks in LA. I figured Jimmy would surface on the way to his car.

As if on cue, ten minutes later the elevator doors slid open and he stepped out, wearing his usual baseball cap. "Jordan. I didn't expect to see you here," he said with a startled little laugh. "We've got to stop meeting like this." He clicked a set of keys, and a black Viper responded with a piping squeak.

"Well, I had to talk to you in person. I mean, knowing how busy you are, I might not have gotten through on the phone."

"What can I do to help you out, now that you're here?" He glanced pointedly at his watch, which in the style of many agents was a relatively modest timepiece. It was bad form to have a nicer watch than your client. "In brief, if you don't mind. I'm due at an appointment in fifteen minutes." He opened the trunk of the Viper and tossed his briefcase inside.

"Jimmy, I need to know what really happened to Catherine. Somebody's life may be at stake."

"Whose life?"

"A friend's."

"What really happened? You were there, if you'll recall."

"She didn't quit because she fell in love with a Frenchman."

"Really? Well, maybe she just said that to paper over my ego." He laughed. "She wouldn't be the first secretary in history to quit because I am a total shithead of a boss."

"Don't insult my intelligence, Jimmy. I'm getting some strange signals about Catherine."

"Sour grapes and idle gossip don't mix too well, especially in this business. There were some hostile people when I started TalentMasters. They're still out there, waiting to get me. Of course, I understand completely. I did what they wanted to do and didn't—or couldn't. I ignore them and so should you."

"What did Catherine have to do with Heather?"

"She was my assistant. She did the same kinds of things your assistant, what's-his-name, does for you, I'm sure. Now, if you'll excuse me, I'm late." He brandished his keys.

I stepped into his path. "No. I will not excuse you. How you got out of France I'll never know. However, I need some details, details you don't seem to care to share with anybody. Things are just a little too vague around here, including the whereabouts of two people I care about. So I'll just have to become an unbearable nuisance until you decide to tell me the facts." I grabbed the car keys out of his pasty hand. "Now, where shall we have our cozy little discussion?"

"Give me those keys, you bitch!" He lunged at me and clamped down on my arm, but not before I had dropped the keys down the front of my blouse.

"Fine. Take them. And be prepared for a charge of sexual harrassment. Attempted anything. You name it, I swear I'll do it. And he'll be my witness." I gestured toward an elderly gentleman who was getting off the elevator and stepped back as if I were intimidated by Jimmy, which I wasn't in the slightest.

"Is everything all right over there, miss?" the man asked.

I looked at Jimmy. "Is it?"

He was sweating. He gave me a vicious stare, glanced back at the man in front of the elevators, then turned on his heel and stalked out of the garage stairwell.

"Nice chatting with you," I called out.

The minute the elderly gentleman had pulled out of the garage in his Mercedes, I opened the Viper's trunk and took Jimmy's briefcase. It fit nicely in my saddlebag as I rode up Sunset Strip. Of course, I realized I was taking a risk. If Jimmy were really an innocent party, he would probably waste no time in charging me with stealing the briefcase, if for no other reason than it was an extremely expensive model made out of the skin of an endangered reptile. However, there wasn't much chance of that, in my opinion. Jimmy knew something, and he wasn't going to volunteer it. Somebody was going to have to force it out of him, and it might as well be me.

I checked into the Impressionist, a funky modern hotel sandwiched between the leather dress shops and comedy clubs on Sunset. The place was a rock 'n' roll haven that bordered on tastelessness, but it was my favorite hotel in LA.

The first thing I did, as usual, was call Tony and tell him where I was. I could count on him to keep this information confidential from everybody except really important people, like Inspector Lemire or the vet.

"So how did Bill react when you told him I was going to be out for a few days?"

"Relieved, actually, was my take," Tony said. "I think Kelly and company had gotten to him. I don't think she likes competition."

"Tell me about it. How's A.M.?"

"Mad that you didn't take her with you. She tore up a pillow in your living room. I got out the Dustbuster and cleaned it up."

"Was it the one with the needlepoint happy face?"

"I'm afraid so."

"At least A.M. has good judgment."

"Listen, Jordan, no word from France, but you got a fax from somebody named Jason Campbell. Do you want me to send it to your hotel?"

"That I want to see right away."

"Got it. Hang up, and it'll be waiting for you at the desk. But will you please take your laptop next time? I hate sending things to hotel desks. Anybody could read them."

"Does this look like something somebody'd want to read?"

"No, it's just a list of players. There's really no rush sending it."

I sighed. I should have known better than to hope this list would turn out to be anything.

"But you never know," Tony continued, segueing into his lecture mode. "Next time could be different. Besides, if you had your laptop, our modems could talk to each other."

"True, but I like talking to you in person. Your modem wouldn't be nearly as much fun. Now, do me a favor and take

A.M. on an extra-long walk, okay? She deserves a reward for taking out that pillow."

I hung up and opened Jimmy's briefcase. This required the assistance of a pair of cuticle scissors, twisted into the lock at exactly the right angle to spring the clasp. Because I had to use a tool, I did feel a little bit like a thief, but then again, a business card with Jimmy's home address was inside, and I resolved immediately to return the case as soon as I checked it out.

Inside I found a mobile phone, a folded-up miniature blow dryer, a sports magazine, and a number of folders. The first one I opened contained a paper-clipped sheaf of papers that turned out to be the confidentiality agreements from the Springs—excluding mine, of course. There were two other folders, and also a large address and appointment book. The folders were marked ITINERARY and SPONSORS. I flipped through each one.

The itinerary folder seemed routine, with dates and locations of most of the major tournaments, plus Jimmy's Crown Jewel series. I also noticed a section of the itinerary from the previous year. There were numerous trips planned to Atlanta and Miami, as well as to Europe. Typical agent fare.

The other folder included a four-page letter to each sponsor, awaiting Jimmy's signature, detailing the public relations program for the Crown Jewel, along with elaborate four-color brochures that made the tournament seem grander even than Wimbledon. A championship trophy, shaped like a crown and featuring the appropriate gemstones, was prominently pictured in the photo spread. The headline, in elegant type, proclaimed this THE WORLD'S RICHEST TENNIS MATCH. The details were fascinating. A matched pair of competitors, chosen by their standing in the tournament's exclusive ranking system, would play head-to-head at the glittering Las Vegas Olympus Hotel in a series of three matches on all surfaces: hard courts, grass, and clay. The winner would be proclaimed World All-Court Champion and given a one-million-dollar prize on top of the two-hundred-thousand-dollar guarantee.

The letter referred to four sponsors: Equinox, Fresh Horizons Yogurt, Calibre Automotive Company, and Pentacle Electronics. These sponsors were obviously coughing up big bucks to fund this event. A detailed program for the Las Vegas event was outlined. I only skimmed it, but the artist's rendering of the planned competitors' entrance parade stopped me: there were swags and flags, and the finalists were pictured entering the courts riding jeweled elephants, escorted by shapely actresses and muscled actors costumed as Greek gods. Fireworks exploded festively above the arena. There was certainly nothing subtle about the event.

There was also a copy of a deal memo to the Sports Network and one to Vernex Communications, cementing an international pay-per-view TV deal. In another folder was a fashion magazine layout of Heather modeling sportswear, awaiting Jimmy's approval.

The address and datebook proved interesting. Flipping through the time period around the French Open, I saw several mentions of Catherine Richie's name in the daily entries. Apparently, Jimmy had met with her frequently. On the day of her death, the notation read: *C—reception*. My hands froze, and my grip on the datebook turned leaden. Of course, this proved nothing, but did it mean that Jimmy planned to meet Catherine at the greenhouse reception? Or some other reception? Or did Jimmy plan to meet some other person whose name started with the letter *C* at the reception? It had to mean something. In any event, I certainly sensed that Jimmy had been lying about breaking off contact with her.

I dialed Jason Campbell and left a message on his machine. "Jason, I have Jimmy's datebook. He had a meeting scheduled with 'C'—I think that's Catherine—on the night she died, at the reception. What do you think? You can't reach me for a while—I have to return the datebook to Jimmy's house."

I pulled a light nylon jacket out of my backpack. It was getting late, and the warm air would be cooling down rapidly. Then I grabbed my helmet and left the room. Down at the front desk, the clerks were checking several people in and out, so I had to wait a few minutes before I was at the head of the line. I used the time to study Jimmy's datebook. There was an entire section of business cards in compartmentalized plastic sleeve pages at the end. "I'm in room 625, and I believe I have a fax," I said to a clerk. "Meanwhile, do you have a copy machine I can use, please?"

"Can I copy something for you?" he asked.

"I need to do this myself," I explained. He ushered me into the manager's office, and I spent the next twenty minutes copying the contents of Jimmy's datebook, including the business cards, front and back, and the letters. Then I collected the fax, which I looked at briefly. As Tony had said, it was just a list of players' names.

"Do you have an envelope?" I asked the desk clerk.

He handed me a large white one with the hotel logo embossed on the corner. I tucked the copies inside, sealed the envelope, and handed it to the clerk. "Can you please hold this in your safe for me?" I asked.

He gave me a slip to sign, and that was taken care of. I tucked the datebook and folders back into the briefcase, snapped the locks shut, and walked to the front of the hotel. After retrieving my motorcycle from the parking attendant, I headed down Sunset to Laurel Canyon and up into the Hollywood Hills—to Jimmy's home.

There's nothing better than zigzagging in the Hollywood Hills on a soft evening, when the air is fruity with the scent of night-blooming jasmine. You have to concentrate hard on the road at night, and even professional navigators can get lost in the curves, bends, and hairpin turns. Jimmy's address was almost at the top of the mountain, near Mulholland, and as I rode I almost forgot that I was a thief, participating in my own crime.

I remembered quickly enough when I found Jimmy's house. It was a hulking, white-cement, fortress-style structure, its face to the street a nearly solid wall, with only a few slitty windows high up and rounded turretlike structures bordering the tile roof to reinforce the fortress feeling. An electronic gate sealed off the driveway. Inside I could see three cars: a red fifties Corvette convertible, in mint condition from what I could tell; an Infiniti; and a Jag. Quite a nice collection, except they filled the driveway and the garage, so Jimmy's Viper was parked, slightly askew, outside the gate. There was no sign of activity in the house, although the structure was such that a full-scale war could have been going on inside and no one on the street would ever guess.

I rode a bit down the block from the house and then walked back with the briefcase. Reaching down beneath my T-shirt, I fished the keys to the Viper out from inside my bra, where they had been since my confrontation with Jimmy. The car unlocked itself when I pushed the button on the key, and I opened the briefcase, dropped the keys inside, then slipped it back inside the trunk and closed it quietly. Within seconds, I was on my way back down the mountainside.

I was only a few minutes into the ride when a bright light flicked onto me from behind, one of those high-intensity beams that police use on the side of their cars to spotlight criminals. For a second, I thought it was the police, about to arrest me for briefcase theft, and I slowed down. Then I saw and heard the car behind accelerate forward until it was right on my tail. This stretch of road is particularly treacherous in the best of circumstances, the dips and bends in the road forming a series of blind turns and continuous S-curves. A light rain had begun, and the pavement was slick. I pulled to the side of the road. So did the car. Since I could see in my mirror that this was no law enforcement vehicle, I came to the instant conclusion that stopping would probably be hazardous to my health.

Instead, I gunned the bike to get away from him. Los Angeles drivers are notoriously quirky. It was possible that this was one of them, or even a tourist with a map, searching the hills for movie-star homes. Although it was unmanicured, this was a very rich section of town, because the backs of the houses, invisible from the street, all faced a magnificent view of the city below, stretching all the way to the ocean. But the car leaped forward as well, again closing on my tail. The bright light in my mirrors nearly blinded me when I looked in them, and I could see very little behind me. I couldn't even tell what kind or color of car it was, and the driver was left to my imagination. It did not take much imagination, however, to wonder if Jimmy could be at the wheel. Ahead, the road reflected my own lights back at me as the rain glazed the blacktop. My bike skidded around a curve, and I realized that this car was actually trying to run me off the road—if not kill me outright.

A contest between a motorcycle and a car is really no contest. This driver could run me down any time he pleased. He was simply playing cat and mouse. I struggled to control the bike as I tried to decide what to do. The car edged closer, overlapping the bike until its front bumper was inches from my leg. A cross street was approaching, and I took a chance—possibly my last and only chance—and yanked the bike into a turn. The wheels skidded and I almost went down but somehow managed to recover my balance. All my years of physical conditioning and precise sensory response seemed to come to a head now, and just to keep my sanity, I imagined myself in a race. I shot up the street, another winding road heading who knew where, with houses set far back behind tangled branches and brush. Now I was heading back uphill.

The laser light reappeared behind me. No, this was no movie-star gawker. The car was hunting me down, and I was un-protected prey. I had the distinct feeling that while our previous tête-à-tête was a game, this encounter would be deadly serious. Sweat trickled down my back and matted my hair to my head beneath my helmet as I searched frantically for some way out.

The car came closer.

I knew I had only seconds to do something. Just ahead and across the road, I spotted a large house perched on the edge of a rare spacious lot, with a number of cars parked in front, obviously a party in progress. One of the cars was pulling out of the lineup and would soon be blocking my escape. I could hear the car behind me speed up, feel the flash of light intensify. Beyond the house was more road, winding into darkness and brush. In that kind of garbled darkness, any kind of accident can happen to a careless biker who loses control. No one would question such an accident. I had to take a chance, and take it now.

Clenching my teeth, I turned the handlebars and flew off the road, aiming for the just-vacated space between the line of parked cars. The bike tore through the opening, up and over an embankment, clearing a small hill in a leap and then, in an instant, flying through a border of waist-high thorny bushes. Leaning close to the bike, I tried to slow down, but it had a momentum all its own as it continued the race forward along the side of the house, a long, muddy downhill slide. The bike was now out of control. The wheels had no grip. At the bottom of the sloping yard, everything went into slow motion as the bike tipped over on the edge of its wheels, skidding. In my struggle to regain control and wrench this piece of heavy metal upright, it was now impossible to stop. I looked up just in time to see an iridescent patch of blue, the underwater lights of a swimming pool, as the bike skidded sideways over the edge of the patio. A patch of lawn furniture—umbrella, tables, chairs, and loungers—loomed ahead like a wall. I encountered them with a metallic crash, hooking the umbrella on the rear bumper and dragging it along in my wake. My eyes were wide open and unblinking behind my visor as the bike lurched a final time and surged into the pale, glowing water with a hiss like an angry snake, engine churning and sputtering, wheels spinning. Dazed, I pushed myself off as it sank to the bottom of the pool.

Struggling to stay afloat, I swam to the edge, gasping, and shoved up my blurred visor, half expecting to see my pursuer, probably now on foot and holding a gun trained on my skull. Instead, there were twenty people holding drinks and hors d'oeuvres balanced on cocktail napkins, staring in astonishment, as music blared from inside the house to the patio. Their expressions ranged from hand-on-mouth horror to blank disbelief.

As I hung on the tiled edge of the pool and pulled off my water-logged helmet, I noticed my hands. They were scratched and bloody, as if I'd been clawed by a giant cat in a terrible fight. The bushes I'd ridden through must have been filled with thorns.

"Are you all right?" someone asked.

"I think so," I said, coughing.

"Well, that's one way to crash a party," said the backlit shadow of a man. "If I'd known you wanted to come that badly, I would have sent you an invitation." He leaned down, pulled hard, and lifted me up and onto the side of the pool.

"I'm sorry," I managed to say, regaining my breath. "I was run off the road."

"Real far off the road, I'd say," the man said. "Are you drunk?"

Someone materialized with a towel and wrapped it around me.

A woman stepped forward. "You'd better come inside," she said.

"Should we call the police?" whispered a voice, as the group began to unfreeze and stir.

"I'm Jordan Myles. I was just up the hill, visiting someone, and—well, the bike . . ." I honestly didn't know what to say.

The lady of the house, a striking black woman wearing tights and a long cashmere sweater, introduced herself as Carla Ferrie. She put her arm around me and led me into a cedar-beamed living room. It was a unique combination of elaborate oriental rugs, cushy velvet sofas, and ottomans in jewel tones, tufted and fringed. A row of bronze, chrome, and Plexiglas awards lined the fireplace mantel. As I was dripping wet, we didn't dwell on the decor, and Carla gently guided me directly into the master bedroom, which featured a wall of beautifully lit, vintage black-and-white photographs of Hollywood stars: Greta Garbo, Marilyn Monroe, James Dean, Clark Gable, Bette Davis. Her husband was a record-company executive, she explained, and they lived here with their three kids.

"I think this will fit." Carla ducked into the dressing room and reappeared with a velour warm-up outfit.

"I feel terrible," I said to her as I towel-dried my hair. "Of course, I'll pay for the damage. And, if you don't mind, I'd like to arrange a towing service to come in tomorrow and get my bike out of your pool."

Carla handed me a tube of antibiotic ointment and a box of Band-Aids. "Well, it was a boring party until you dropped in." She sat on the edge of the beautiful bed, with its silky duvet and piles of pillows in varying shapes. I was careful not to let my hands bleed onto the linens. "Is there anyone you'd like us to notify? I'm not so sure you don't need to be checked out by a doctor." Her eyes focused dubiously on my bleeding hands.

"I'm fine," I assured her. "I'm in a medically related profession myself. But maybe I could borrow your phone to call a cab."

"That's certainly no problem." She handed me the bedside cordless phone. "And take off those wet things. I'll lend you something to wear." She opened a drawer. "What happened? Do you think there was a drunk driver, somebody weaving all over the road? Was that it?"

Terrible as that was, in my case it would have been preferable to the truth. This poor woman had been disturbed enough tonight, I decided. Why make it worse? "I'm not sure," I said.

There was a knock on the door. "Everything okay in there?"

"Yes, Al, it's fine. She's finishing up." Carla turned to me. "Are you in trouble, honey?"

"Actually," I said, "you guys saved me in more ways than you'll ever know. But I'm not in that kind of trouble. I just want to get your place back to normal right away."

"I wonder what our insurance will cover," she mused.

"Your pool is probably not insured for hit-and-run," I said. "Please send all the bills for the pool, the garden, and the patio furniture to me directly. I'll have your clothes cleaned and return them by FedEx. We'll exchange numbers, and my assistant will get in touch with you first thing tomorrow to make any arrangements." I fished my wet wallet out of my jacket pocket. Only the plastic credit cards were undamaged. "You've been very kind to help me like this. And I wrecked your party, too."

She laughed. "No, it's the opposite. People will be talking about this party for *years*. You're sure you won't spend the night in our guest room? You're welcome to." She wrapped my wet clothes up in a towel and rolled it to wring them out, then handed me a velour warm-up suit.

"Thank you, but I just want to get back to my hotel. I've had enough excitement, especially considering how bad it might have been." Actually, this was not something that I even cared to consider.

I came out of the bedroom to find a contingent from LAPD waiting. Our discussion didn't get too far.

"Who ran you off the road?"

"I don't know."

"Why did they run you off the road?"

"I don't know."

"What kind of car was it?"

"I don't know."

The accident report was duly filed for insurance purposes, but since there was no one to charge there would be no charges.

I went back to the Impressionist in a cab, an uneventful fifteen-minute ride down the mountainside which only hours before had been a death trap.

TEN

Back at the hotel, the first thing I did was book another room, which I had no intention of ever using. It was in my best interests, however, that anyone monitoring my activities at the hotel believe that I was still there. By now it was late, almost ten o'clock, and I realized I was hungry. I had a fruit plate sent up, and I sat with my Xerox copy of Jimmy's datebook as I took a deep breath and tried to make sense of what had almost happened.

Who could have known I would be on that hillside? Only someone who had followed me or was watching me—possibly from inside the house.

And why would they try to kill me? I couldn't answer that question any better now than I could in France—except to say that it was probably for the same reason. And why they tried to kill Noel Fisher, the same reason he was missing now.

This much was increasingly clear: If I didn't figure out *why* all this was happening, the people who were behind it were eventually going to succeed in their mission. Obviously, the normal channels of law and authority were not going to get to the bottom of this in time, if ever. I would have to save myself.

Was it possible the key was on my lap? I spent the next two hours poring through the photocopied datebook, but the only new information I unearthed were the names of Jimmy's facialist, acupuncturist, and personal trainer.

I went back to the fax Tony had sent. It was what it was, a list of player's names. Another dead end. At midnight I went to sleep, but I was restless all night, listening for the slightest sound. At six o'clock, I left a detailed voice-mail message asking Tony to please work out the salvage of my motorcycle and any damage payment or insurance papers. Then I called Jason Campbell at home and asked if he could possibly give me a lunchtime tour of Catherine's former office.

I had a cup of herbal tea and some melon, asked the hotel concierge to dry-clean and return Carla's warm-up suit, then left for LAX to catch a commuter flight to San Francisco. Soon I was in a cab heading over the Bay Bridge toward downtown San Francisco.

In my jeans and T-shirt, I was hardly dressed for the corporate world, but then again, I wasn't trying to impress anybody at KRW—I just wanted to learn more about Catherine, and it seemed to me that if Jimmy wasn't going to cooperate, this was a good place to start. The taxi took me along the Embarcadero and turned left near the Golden Gate ferry building. The KRW building was about two blocks off the Embarcadero, at the corner of Spear and Mission streets. It was a sweeping structure that was smoothly distinctive in the skyline, combining pink granite and dark reflective glass in a rounded tower. Jason's group was on the fourteenth floor, and they had their own receptionist. The corporate color seemed to be orange—the carpeting and walls were all the same shade of pumpkin, and the receptionist even wore a pumpkin-colored jacket.

Jason came out and shook my hand. "I'm so glad you came," he said. "I can't stop thinking about this." He pushed a laminated ID card into a slot in the door. A green light came on and the door slid open. We walked through a maze of hallways in which every office looked alike, with a glass partition, a desk, and a computer station—allowing the eye to sweep right through the building to the windows, with their partial view of the Bay Bridge. Finally we reached a characterless small office bearing Jason's nameplate. He closed the door as we walked inside.

"Nobody will bother us here. It's not a very social place. Nobody talks to anybody except on E-mail."

"So what happens in your department?" I asked.

"Not much that you can see," he said. "We do research on future needs and protocols and ways of transmitting and integrating databases. We try to find new ways to compress and send image data and to protect wide-area transmissions."

"I think I need a translation."

"It's sort of like being the computer cops. KRW has a satellite, and of course we're on the Internet, and we need to protect those databases. So we figure out how to do that. It's sort of like being in computer security. Would you like some coffee?"

"Never touch it."

"I can order in sandwiches." He stretched in his chinos.

"Great."

Over my avocado and sprout on seven-grain bread, we spoke about Catherine. Jason's face softened as he reminisced.

"She was just one of the all-time great people," he said. "Smart, nice, and pretty. For someone so intelligent, she wasn't stiff at all. She knew how to have fun—that's what I really liked about her. I could tell right away."

"How?"

He took a bite of a very unappetizing-looking hot dog. "Well, for instance, we played a game called NORAD."

"NORAD?"

He laughed. "Yeah, the point of it was, which one of us could break into the NORAD defense grid first."

"What? You were actually trying to break into the national defense system?"

"That's illegal, something a hacker would try to do, a very

sophisticated hacker. But it can be done. No, this was just a game, something we played with our E-mail. One of us would leave the other the most complex codes, and the other person would try to break them. Catherine could always figure out anything I gave her. She was better at it than I was. Our job here basically involved figuring out ways to keep people *out* of the system, not accessing systems."

"I still haven't figured out Windows," I admitted.

"That's okay," said Jason. "I haven't figured out how to serve."

"You don't play tennis?"

"I'm not very athletic. Well, I take that back. I swim. But I'm not a sports buff. Catherine wasn't either. I don't think she knew thing one about tennis. Maybe she'd heard of Chris Evert, or Navratilova, or Billie Jean King. But that was it, period." He sighed and crumpled up the wrapper from his hot dog. "So why did she go work for those guys?"

"Well, they were setting up a new business with a lot of systems," I said. "They needed a very skilled person. At least that's one way of looking at it." Even as I said this, it bothered me. Never in any of our conversations had Jimmy mentioned Catherine's computer skills. He always talked about her as a lowly assistant, somebody to make a plane reservation or take a message. If he'd been paying her a big salary, she would have had to do more than sharpen his pencils to earn it.

"Are you positive about the salary?" I asked Jason.

He looked disgusted. "That I'll never forget. She was so excited about being paid so much."

"Did she ever mention setting up systems for them?"

"She set up some. Kept client lists, databases—that kind of thing. To be honest, I think it was the glitz that attracted her." He gestured with his arms. "As you can see, it's not very glamorous here. Paris, it's not. Just a minute."

He opened his desk drawer, took out a framed picture, and handed it to me. It was a color photograph of Jason and Catherine together, laughing happily on the beach. Catherine held a shaggy puppy in her arms.

"That's Shippy. I adopted her—afterward."

I stared at the picture. Although Catherine's death had changed my life, I'd never seen her alive. She was vibrant and lovely against the blue summer sky, her hair blowing in the wind. A moment in time, light-years away from the still woman in the black cocktail dress, now gone. I handed back the picture.

"I used to keep it on my desk," Jason said. "But I got too upset every time I looked at it." He stood up abruptly. "Excuse me a minute," he said. "Use my phone if you need to make any calls."

I had to swallow hard before I picked up the phone and called Tony at the Springs.

"Thank God you called!" His voice was at urgency level 8.8. I had learned to gauge these matters. "You disappeared off the face of the earth again. I got your voice mail, but the hotel didn't have you listed."

"I'm still out of town," I said. "Can't say where. How's Heather?"

"I told her you were sick. She wanted to send flowers."

"That was sweet."

"Don't jump to conclusions. She didn't say what kind of flowers. You also got a postcard."

"Do we need to talk about it now?"

"Maybe. It was from Noel Fisher."

My chest tightened. "What? When?"

"Well, I take it back. The *signature* says *Noel Fisher.*"

"And the rest of the card?"

"It's just one line: *Not to worry.*"

"That's it? Where's it postmarked?"

"Monte Carlo. Maybe he's recovering there."

"Do we have his signature anywhere in the files?"

"Not that I'm aware of."

"Does it mention his mother?"

"I told you: *Not to worry.* That's it. Look, maybe it's real."

"I don't believe it. Why would he disappear, then send a stupid postcard? Fax it to Inspector Lemire. His number in Paris is on a card in my desk drawer. Maybe he can do something with it. Add a note that says exactly when we got it."

"Will do."

"And please tell Bill my fever is spiking or I'd be in."

"I'll tell him."

Jason was coming back into the room. "Later, Tony," I said, and hung up.

"Oh," said Jason, settling back into his chair, "I should have told you. You were recorded. Everybody is, for security reasons. I hope you don't mind."

"Was your last conversation with Catherine recorded?"

"No. She called me at home."

"Well, Jason, thanks so much. I won't keep you. I want to turn around and get back to LA before the rush hour. But I have some notes in Jimmy's datebook here, and I'd like you to make another copy and read through them, in case anything strikes you. Would you mind?"

"Mind? It would be very important to me."

We walked to the Xerox room together.

"That was her office," he said, as we passed one of the small cubicles on an interior wall. Inside, a young red-haired woman was working, fingers flying over the keyboard of her computer. There was a small plant on the edge of her desk, the only corporate concession to nature I had seen in the office. I wondered if it was Catherine's plant. I imagined all the times he must have stopped by for meetings, coffee, the casual conversation that ignites real relationships.

We stood there while a monolithic copy machine fed the pages through. Then Jason walked me back to the lobby door.

"I know this is hard," he said, "but without your help I'd just give up. Nobody else is doing one goddamned thing. It's like Catherine just vanished. Except she didn't—she was murdered in front of about three hundred and fifty people. Somebody is getting away with this, and it makes me sick."

"We'll do what we can," I said softly.

This time, we hugged. "Don't give up," I whispered. "Somebody's got to know something. We just have to figure it out."

I didn't tell Jason what had happened to me in Paris and in LA. He was too upset already, and what good would it do? The best thing he could do now was read Jimmy Bennett's datebook and see if he could unearth any information.

I flew back to LAX and checked into the Shutters on the Beach, a small hotel but one of the few right on the water in Santa Monica. There was a gorgeous view: a beach, an ocean, and lots of sky.

Across town, on Sunset, my room in the Impressionist was empty, which was just as I intended it. For the Shutters, I chose the name Nancy Saunders. As Nancy, I had a great time doing things I wouldn't normally have time to do—take a nap, walk at sunset on the beach, eat a three-course dinner on the terrace. After dinner, I put my call in to Tony.

"So where are you this time?" he asked, yawning.

"A beauty spa."

"Tough work, but somebody's got to do it."

"Did Lemire answer the fax?"

"Yeah, he did." Tony hesitated.

"So what did he say?"

"He faxed back. Said he'd been taken off the case."

"What? Why, did he say?"

"No. Maybe it was because of the postcard. If Fisher sent it, he's still alive, right?"

"Theoretically," I said dryly.

"Well, one piece of good news."

"Hit me with it."

"Your bike got hauled out of the pool, and insurance will cover it. I had them take it to a repair shop."

"Do they think they can fix it?"

"Not sure yet."

The next morning, I woke up blinking at the ocean and the brilliant sand of Santa Monica beach.

It was a perfect day for a walk on the beach, so I strolled out onto the Strand and headed toward the Santa Monica Pier. Close to the pier, a crew was shooting locations for an episode of a TV show. Crew members kept the area clear, but a crowd of curious bystanders had gathered, many hoping to get in the background of the shot.

The background of the shot.

I stood perfectly still. Why hadn't I thought of that before? There was a video record of the greenhouse reception in Paris, and Kelly Kendall, or at least her crew, possessed it. Analyzing the video, not of the crime but of the reception beforehand, might give a better clue as to who was—and wasn't—there. I pulled my mobile phone from my backpack.

"Tony?"

"Hi, Jordan."

"Do you have any idea where Kelly is now? I've got to reach her."

"Actually, I do. She left to do color commentary at an exhibition in Manhattan Beach."

"The Manhattan Beach Country Club, where they play the Slims?"

"That's the place. She'll be taking a chopper back here in the morning. Maybe you could hitch a ride."

"Coming back to work with Heather?"

"Wrapping it up is more like it. Heather's leaving."

"After less than a week?"

"Apparently she has some previous commitments in Japan.

"Aka, a big-money exhibition."

"You got it."

"How's A.M.?"

"She misses you. She tried to rip the leg off your couch."

"Tony . . ."

"I said she tried. I didn't say she did it. But who's to say she won't next time? I think she needs her mom."

"She's just sensitive, that's all. Don't heap a guilt trip on me. I spend quality time with that dog, and you know it."

"Fine. Have a latchkey dog. It's your choice."

" 'Bye, Tony." I was already on my way back to the hotel to get a taxi to Manhattan Beach.

Soon I was heading down the 405, past the airport, past El Segundo, to the Rosecrans cutoff. I knew the way well; I'd played many tournaments at this club. This was fortunate, since I had no pass to get behind the scenes.

"Jordan! How wonderful to see you!" Eddie Rice, a longtime photographer for *Sports Scene* magazine, spotted me at the front door of the clubhouse. He shouldered a huge camera bag with the longest lens known to man strapped on in a separate case.

"Hi, Eddie. I'm looking for Kelly."

"I saw her doing an interview on the balcony. It might still be going on."

"Great, thanks."

"Say, Jordan, you don't mind if I tag along here for a second. Maybe get a couple of shots of you and Kelly together?"

"I'm not here to talk tennis, Eddie." I moved swiftly down the stairs and ran head-on into a man so large, he seemed to take up the entire staircase. I tried to dodge past, but his oversized blue sport coat was an immovable object. Eventually, he tilted slightly sideways, and I slipped by, trailed by Eddie.

"That was Micki Takashimaya's acupuncturist. I swear the guy was a sumo wrestler," said Eddie, shaking his head as the huge man disappeared up the stairs.

The back of the clubhouse opened onto the courts, where a match was in progress. The dining room faced a covered porch that had a bird's-eye view of the courts. Kelly, in a tailored peach silk pantsuit, was doing an on-camera one-on-one with Billie Jean King.

I recognized the cameraman from Paris. He was thin, red-haired, and young, wearing a baseball cap—the same guy who was running the camera that night at the greenhouse, and obviously part of Kelly's permanent crew. As he was packing up his equipment, I approached him.

"I remember you from Paris, right?" I asked.

He looked up. "Right. Bob Riordan. You're Jordan. I saw you try to save that poor girl. You were great."

"Thanks. I remember you kept the camera rolling, even though Kelly couldn't talk."

He shrugged. "We couldn't use it. The family wouldn't give permission. Not that I blame them."

"I almost had an exclusive on that one, you know. She called me."

"Who?"

"The girl who died—Catherine. I had a message from her at the trailer at Roland Garros. She left her business card, in fact. She wanted to talk to me at the reception, said she'd see me there. Of course, she knew I'd be there, covering Kelly, as usual. I looked for her there, but . . . well."

"Why do you think she wanted to talk to you, Bob?"

He shrugged. "She was a PR person. They always have something to say to the press, don't they? I wasn't too excited at the time. I figured it was some promotional pitch. I mean, she left her phone number and all. . . ."

"When did she leave the card?"

"That day, the day she died."

The day she died, Catherine no longer worked for Jimmy.

"I was shocked when I found out it was her," Bob continued. "I barely knew her, just from seeing her around at press conferences. They were hyping the Crown Jewel pretty heavily."

"Is there any other reason she might have called you?"

"Not that I know of. Like I said, I barely knew her. Poor kid."

"What about the phone number? Did you call it?"

Bob shook his head. "I figured if she wanted to find me, she would."

"Do you remember what the phone number was? Where she was staying?"

"No. Like I said, I never called it. But if you really want to know, I think I kept the card. I stuck it in this big envelope I have back at the office in New York, where I put all the cards that people give me. You never know, in this business."

"If you find it, would you please let me know what it was?"

"Sure. But I'll call it myself first. You've got me curious."

"What happened to the rest of the footage?" I asked.

"What rest?"

"The stuff you shot at the reception, before the . . . incident."

"Well, this murder overshadowed it. That was a fluff piece. After the murder, it seemed frivolous and insensitive. We didn't use it for the show."

"Where's the tape now? Who's seen it?"

"Jimmy Bennett has it." His eyes drifted toward the court and the Rolex scoreboard.

"How do you know?"

"He asked for it that night. I handed it to him."

"So he has the tape now?" Bennett would never admit such a tape existed.

"Well, one of them."

"How many are there?"

"Two. We gave Jimmy a dub. The original's back at the studio. They may have another dub here."

"Why would that be?"

"It's a freak show. A novelty. Sometimes people keep stuff like that around. Besides, we keep a complete file of Kelly's interviews whenever she does a tournament. She had the exclusive on that one. It was her biggest so far, and we can't even get it on the air."

"Can I get another dub?"

"Sure. No big deal. I'll send you one."

"Actually, I was thinking, I'd come with you now to the trailer and we could just knock off a down-and-dirty copy. I need to check something."

The press trailer was at the edge of the parking lot. We stepped over a forest of heavy black electrician's cords and climbed up the stairs, where a man sat drinking a paper cup of coffee. Inside it was freezing cold, the air-conditioning turned up full blast. An attractive young receptionist sat at a computer at an ugly wood-grained Formica desk. She reached continuously for the jangling phone. A TV screen was positioned above her head, monitoring the action on the courts.

"Any messages, Steph?" Riordan asked.

She handed him a fistful of pink slips, which he stuffed into his pocket.

Beyond a small partition was a room with long tables for computers, a phone at each of about twenty stations. On the facing wall was a long foldout table with stacks of press kits in neat folders, photocopied press releases, and player stats.

Past that area, behind a glass door, was the editing bay. Six small screens analyzed every inch of footage, as a team of video and audio technicians spliced together a piece for their show.

"Hey, guys, do we have that stuff from the French on file?" Riordan asked. "Is there a monitor and a playback unit around?"

Standing off in a corner, I stared at the screen as Eddie slid the cassette into the slot and that terrible day at the greenhouse was replayed. The camera swung through the crowd, stopping only to scan the room and trail Kelly from interview to interview. The faces behind Kelly and her interview subject were mostly out of focus. With this equipment, it was tough to distinguish identities. At the Springs, we had cutting-edge video technology. I'd be able to slow images down, blow them up, play with them. For now, I was unable to do anything but stand and watch as the camera veered frantically through the crowd and came to rest on a woman in the water, trying to breathe life into someone else. I barely recognized myself as the woman, head bent down, looking up occasionally to yell past the camera.

Fifteen minutes later, my dub in hand, I caught up with Kelly. As usual, she was surrounded by a flock of reporters, tournament officials, and fans. A little girl stood shyly on the edge of the crowd, clutching her doll and staring up in awe, completing the celebrity tableau. A teenage girl handed Kelly a white visor, and Kelly signed the brim.

"Look over there," I heard someone in the crowd whisper. "Didn't that used to be Jordan Myles? The one Kelly used to play a few years back?"

I had heard this before, the Litany of the Used to Be's. Used to be a player. Used to be a champion. Used to play Wimbledon. Used to be good. Used to be somebody. And I usually felt like answering, "That's right, I used to be her. And who did *you* used to be?" For a long time, the Used to Be's upset me more than I liked to admit. When I first left tennis after my accident, I often asked myself the same questions, and I can't count the hours I spent wondering if I'd ever have another identity—or if Used to Be was all I'd ever be. Sometimes it still hurt to hear it. But today it didn't bother me. Today I knew who I was. Maybe it was the recent close calls, the chances once again to outwit the fates. I knew I was here, now. I was alive. The rest was gravy.

Kelly stepped through the crowd toward the door and the people parted respectfully, leaving her a clear path. I sprinted to catch up.

"Hi, Kel, I think I'm going your way," I said. "Mind if I hitch a ride back to the Springs?"

She finally realized I was there. "Oh, hi, Jordan." She leaned over to give me an air kiss. A few cameras flashed, recording the anything-but-historic greeting of the ex-rivals. "We're leaving any minute. The helicopter is already here. Are you ready?" She checked her watch.

"Sure am," I said. "Everything's in my backpack." I figured I could arrange to have my bike shipped back to me when it was repaired.

"We'll be leaving from the roof of the hotel next door. Let's go." She lifted her head, gave the fans a dazzling grin, and a hulking man with a walkie-talkie and a wary expression materialized at her side.

"We're leaving, Si," she said.

"Fine, Miss Kendall." He cupped his hand around the walkie-talkie and passed this news on to someone on the other end as he walked ahead of Kelly, cutting a wedge through the crowd.

"Si's great," she said, over her shoulder. "He even cooks, in a pinch." For Kelly, who was not the least bit domestic, this would be a definite plus.

Flanked by security, tournament officials, press agents, photographers, the generally curious, and a few people who were obviously angry that this entourage was blocking their path, we made our way out of the building. I found this excursion interesting. When you are on the circuit, security is erratic. At major tournaments, a phalanx of security often forms an ironclad grid around a player and literally washes her on and off the court in a human wave; however, when it comes time to leave the grounds, the same player is often left to her own devices, with minimal or nonexistent security. By arriving with her own personal guard, Kelly had spotlighted the issue, and this tournament was not taking any chances with their household name.

Although we were going only a few feet away to the hotel where the players were staying, a tournament car was waiting at the curb. Kelly, Si, and I got in and were whisked immediately to the hotel's entrance. Another crowd quickly gathered, and hotel security appeared to escort us to the service elevator, which had rooftop access. There a white Bell Jet Ranger helicopter sat silently, like a metallic gull poised for flight. In half an hour, we would be in Palm Springs. I had to admit it was exciting to be in the helicopter. I was looking forward to watching the pilot work at the controls. Then again, helicopters are known for being dangerous. I was torn between being apprehensive and wishing I could fly the helicopter myself.

Kelly, Si, and I were strapped in our seats, awaiting takeoff, I assumed, when Kelly suddenly swiveled in her seat and announced, "Okay, here he comes. We can leave now."

The helicopter door slid open, and in climbed Jimmy Bennett. He was carrying his briefcase. Had he ever noticed that it was missing? It was impossible to read his expression. He looked through rather than at me as he strapped himself into the empty seat beside me. Then he pulled out a Walkman, snapped on the headphones, leaned back, and closed his eyes. The engine hummed and the huge blades overhead began to turn. Apparently Jimmy and I were about to get to know each other much, much better.

ELEVEN

$\mathbf{I}$ wasn't sure whether being home was good or not. On one hand, if someone was trying to kill me, they no doubt had my home pinpointed on a map with a big red X. On the plus side, however, a lot of elderly VIPs live in Sandstone Canyon Villas—a handful of big-name entertainers, a former president of the United States, and some diplomats—so we have exemplary private security. The community is gated, and guards patrol on foot and on motor scooters. Because I live alone and travel so much, that was a persuasive reason to buy there. For an extra fee, you can also request stepped-up surveillance of your house or town house, and I signed on for that service immediately.

As a final safety precaution, I contemplated inviting Tony to move in with me for a short while. This was not as drastic as it sounds. Tony, who lived in a small studio apartment, considered house-guesting or house-sitting at my place to be almost a vacation, because then he had use of the membership-only pool, health club, and golf course. It's a very expensive membership, even for residents, but I moved in soon after they opened the community, and, since I was somewhat of a name in tennis, they offered it to me on a complimentary basis. Athletes didn't impress him, but Tony loved the idea of playing golf on the tee behind an ex-president. Beyond that, Tony and I were family. In my business, where you travel most of the time and have little time to yourself, the people you work with become your surrogate relatives. Tony was like my brother. He knew my weaknesses—better than anybody—but he unfailingly defended me and looked after me, as I did for him.

After I retrieved my voice mail, I intended to present my suggestion to Tony. His desk was in a small reception area just outside my office, and A.M. instantly wriggled out from beneath it and leaped into my arms, forgiving me instantly for not bringing her along.

We were enjoying our reunion when a curly-haired girl in her late teens appeared in the doorway. She had pale skin splashed with freckles, thick unplucked eyebrows, and large gray eyes that seemed to take in everything at a glance. She was wearing a white polo shirt and khakis, the uniform of our college interns, and she peered tentatively into the room.

"Meg, you haven't met Jordan yet," said Tony, ushering her inside the office. "Jordan, this is Meg Zaresky. She's our new intern, from Colorado Springs. She started while you were away."

"Hi, and welcome," I said as we shook hands.

"My mom used to play with you," she said.

"Who's your mom?"

"Janie Pierce. I knew you when I was little."

"Janie? Good grief, how can you be Meggie?" I remembered Janie quite well from my early days on the tour. She had been a terrific doubles player and had stayed on as an official for a few years after she retired from play. I remembered her great sense of humor. Since I'd only met her husband a few times, he was hazier in my memory, but I clearly remembered her little girl—now this young woman—running around chasing balls.

"Well, tell your mother to give me a call, Meg," I said. "I hope you're enjoying it here."

"I love it," she said. "It doesn't even seem like work."

Tony handed her a stack of folders. "Here, take these to the microfilm room," he said. "That should help it feel like work."

Meg dutifully scooped up the folders and disappeared down the hall.

"I wonder why Janie didn't tell me Meg was coming?" I said.

"I don't think they're very close," said Tony. "There was a divorce."

"What a shame," I said. "I should call Janie. Would you see if Meg has her number?"

"You got this fax." Tony handed me a sheet of paper.

It was from Bill Riordan—a copy of Catherine's business card, front and back. On the back was a handwritten series of numbers. Bill had added a note that there was no such number. "Check out this number in Paris." I told Tony. "Meg left it the day she died."

He nodded. "Before you do anything, you have to see this." Tony handed me the *Los Angeles Times,* folded back to a full-page ad on the second page of the sports section. The headline, in huge type, read THE PEOPLE'S CHOICE: YOUR VOTE COUNTS! "Jimmy Bennett took it out to hype the Crown Jewel."

I skimmed the ad. It listed the current top players in tennis, including Heather, and invited readers to call in their vote for the fan's favorite players via a 900 number. Of course, with a 900 number, in addition to collecting votes and publicizing his tournament, Jimmy would make money from every call. It was a brilliant public relations maneuver.

"He's running fifteen-second TV commercials too," said Tony. "And get this: the tabloid shows are going to run interviews with Jimmy—a first-in-sports kind of thing. The guy really is a maestro of the media. He's turning the Crown Jewel into a national issue."

"He knows how to manipulate, period," I said, tossing the paper into the wastebasket. "Now, Tony, I wonder if you would do me a favor?"

"If it involves animals, the answer is no." Tony folded his

hands on the desktop in front of him, the picture of immobility. "Uncle Tony needs some time off."

"Actually, I was wondering if you could move into the guest room for a while."

"You mean your office that has a couch in it?"

"Well, yes. But it's important." I hesitated. I certainly didn't want to involve Tony in anything that might harm him, but I also didn't think it was fair not to warn him. "Tony, you can feel free to refuse. Being around me may not be very healthy right now. It's a selfish request. Somebody may be trying to kill me."

"Like the inconsiderate person who ran you into the swimming pool?"

"Possibly."

"And you want them to kill me instead?"

"I know how they operate. They won't try anything if anybody else is around. They're just after me."

"If they're killers, Jordan, it goes with the territory that they are neither trustworthy nor predictable. Now, refresh my memory. Did you mention exactly how they have tried to kill you so far?"

"They tried to pull me off a greenhouse roof in Paris."

"Did they chase you up there?"

"No. I went up to check out how Catherine died."

"I see. And they ran you off the road. Anything else?"

"I think they also tried to kill Noel Fisher."

"I thought you said they were only after you."

"Well, other than Fisher."

"Isn't his mother missing too?"

It was difficult trying to explain something I didn't understand myself. "You're right, Tony," I admitted. "Forget it. It was a crazy idea. I have no business dragging you into this."

"That's the first sensible thing you've said so far in this conversation. But forget it. I'm there. I just wanted to reacquaint you with reality." He grinned. "And here I thought you were going to ask me to do something tough, like type a memo or take the dog to the groomer."

"Well, you could call Noel Fisher's office, and also his mother's home in Brooklyn. See if either of them has surfaced yet."

"By the way, Bill is looking for you."

"I figured. I have to run to the video studio. Then I'll catch up with him."

"You gonna tell him about this latest development?"

"I think I have to, at this point." I pulled the videotape from my backpack, hung the pack on a hook of the bentwood hat rack on my office door, and set off for the video studio, which was across the complex.

The studio was always dark and cool, even on the hottest desert days. As usual, Stan, our Director of Video Facilities, was extremely busy. He was sitting in front of a large monitor, comparing multiple images on the screen—all shots of Heather making a similar serve—in an effort to map a pattern. This was one of the most revealing things we could show a player. The images were all superimposed, one upon another, and coordinates were visually mapped, each successive image shown with a different color. Then, in an exercise that was almost like connect-the-dots, the various points of the serve or stroke were given a graphic pattern that could be compared or contrasted with other patterns to show strengths, weaknesses, or evolution.

Stan's fingers were flying across the control board, ferociously clacking the keys. He didn't even look up when I came in.

"Hey, Stan, what's up?"

"Heather's leaving any minute, and I gotta have this for CiCi."

"Stan, I can see how you're in the middle of this, but I wondered if there was any way I could just pop in this video and blow up a background."

"Sure there's a way. It's easy. But can it wait?"

"I'm sorry. I need to see it right away."

"Joey!" he yelled, without looking up. His young assistant materialized. The Springs often hired college students as summer interns, and Joey was one of them. He was about twenty years old, with a glasses and a blond ponytail.

Without looking, Stan reached out, I handed him my tape, and he handed it to Joey, who seated himself beside Stan at the control console. Seconds later, the image of Kelly Kendall at the greenhouse cocktail party came up on a screen to the left of the one Stan was working on.

"How many fields you want to go up, Jordan?" Joey asked.

"Enough to see the background more clearly."

Kelly's face blew up and blurred, and we spent twenty minutes scanning the tape at various points. Every time I saw any flicker of red, I asked Joey to stop the tape.

"What do you think that red spot is?" I stared at the images moving slowly across the screen.

"Flowers," he said.

"How can you tell?"

"You look at enough of this stuff, you can sort of tell. You want to be sure, I can send it out for digitized computer enhancement. We don't have that kind of equipment here, but they do in LA."

Another flash of red moved into frame. "Can you pause there?" I asked, leaning closer, scrutinizing the screen. "What's that? More flowers?"

"Judging from the positioning, I'd say maybe a head—or a hat."

"Freeze it there, Joey." I leaned in closer and squinted. Yes, it was a hat. A baseball cap? Possibly. But the image was too blurry to see for sure or to identify who was wearing the hat. "Can you make this bigger? Blow it up even more so I can see it better?"

"Well, what you're asking for is a contrast in terms, Jordan," said Joey. "If I blow this up any more, it's just going to get fuzzier and less clear."

"So what's the alternative?"

"We can get it enhanced, but I can't do it here."

"Can you get this part enhanced for me, please?"

"Sure, Jordan. When do you want it?"

"As soon as possible. It's a rush job. And can I get a printout of the frame, so I have a hard copy?"

"No problem. I'll call you when it comes in. It shouldn't be long. We have something new—maybe you don't know."

"I admit, high tech is not my specialty."

"We've just gone on-line with a couple of the facilities in LA, to cut down on all the messengering back and forth. You know how we used to have to ship our tapes there and wait for them to ship the results back? Well, we can do it all direct now, over the computer. It's an instant transfer. I could have this by the end of the day, depending on how booked they are."

My next stop was Bill's office. His secretary, Rowanda, informed me that he was in a meeting, but I decided to wait. Bill spent half his life in meetings, and entrapment was usually the best way to catch him. After about fifteen minutes, a young boy and a woman in her forties, obviously a junior player and his mother, emerged, and I stuck my head in the office door.

"Jordan," Bill said, smiling. "Good to see you back. Sorry you were under the weather, but you're getting back at the right time. Heather is leaving today."

"How can she have gotten any results in such a short time?" I said, trying to mask my disbelief.

"She's got to go to Japan to play a grass court event," said Bill. That explained it. Exhibitions in the Orient tend to pay huge money. "Woody Solister was on the phone this morning," Bill continued. "He's chomping at the bit to get Dagmar in here to work with you. I told him they could come any time."

"Thanks for your concern, Bill, but there's something we need to discuss. In fact, I wasn't really sick."

I proceded to tell him the whole story, winding up with, "So I think somebody wants me dead. Or at least very scared."

Bill shook his head slowly, and I noticed a muscle twitch in his jaw. "Are the police involved?" he asked.

"I have no proof of anything. It's just how it appears. Of course I reported the motorcycle accident, and in France I notified police too, but there's nothing concrete."

"Then how can you be certain? These are very serious allegations."

"I can't. But I'm telling you that I strongly suspect Jimmy Bennett is hiding something involving Catherine Richie's death."

"Good lord! Jimmy Bennett?"

"I'm not saying he's directly involved, just that I think he knows something. And I think certain players may somehow be involved too, but I don't know how. And there are people who do not want me to figure out what this is all about."

Bill stared at me intently. "Those people may be right, Jordan. It's none of your business. Why get involved?"

"Noel Fisher is involved as an investigator, and he disappeared."

"Fisher?"

"Yes, he's the man who worked on the Audrey Armat case."

"Audrey died."

"Yes. But he saved my life."

Bill reached for the phone. "I'm going to call the authorities."

"Don't, Bill. There's nothing they can do."

Bill's hand remained on the phone. "I'm not going to stand by and see people disappearing, you threatened, and this clinic involved in any way."

"Bill, the French police are involved. And believe me, if I can get any facts, I will be the first to call in the American authorities. I think I may have something for them to go on any minute. Until then, there's not much anybody can do."

"I hope Bennett's not involved in some sort of scandal," said Bill with a frown. "He's always been a loose cannon. Our relationship with Heather would certainly be compromised."

"I hope he's not involved too, Bill," I said. "But that's why I'm telling you. I know that this Heather–Kelly association has high visibility, and the Springs is a part of it."

"One shred of bad press and clients are going to bolt." It was a mantra Bill reiterated when even a whiff of scandal threatened. "Not to mention our investors." He shifted a fist-sized paperweight a quarter of an inch on the desktop.

Bill tends to be pessimistic this way. He's very attuned to

public relations, both negative and positive, and any hint of the former appalls him.

I promised to keep Bill posted and headed back to my office to tackle some paperwork. Until I heard from Joey, it was all I could do. I was shuffling through some parent reports from a junior client's files when I heard a commotion outside the door, which ended with muffled thumpings on the door itself.

The door banged open, and in strode Jimmy Bennett, his face flushed. "Jordan, if you're going to accuse me of something, do it to my face," he demanded.

Tony was on his heels, still attempting to head him off. "I'm calling security," he announced.

"It's all right, Tony, I said, holding up my hand. "But hold my calls—unless it's Joey from AV."

Bennett stood his ground, glaring at me. "Tell me what you said to Bill—only this time say it to my face," he said.

I groaned inwardly. Bill, in a nervous panic, must have demanded an explanation from Jimmy. It had not been smart of me to tell him my suspicions. "Sit down, Jimmy," I said.

"The hell I will."

"Fine. Have it your way. I will be brief. But don't tell me you didn't have something to do with the fact that I was almost run off the road in LA after I saw you in the garage."

"I don't know what you're talking about," he growled. "You've been on some kind of a goddamned jag against me and I'm sick of it. Now I suppose you're upset because Heather had you pulled off her case. Well, to my mind you're as unstable and irresponsible as all get-out, and that was a necessary and responsible move. I'll tell you what this is all about. It doesn't take a psychiatrist; I'll save you the money for therapy. You've always resented Kelly Kendall, and now that she's working with my client you can't handle it. You are completely unprofessional, but I never thought you'd stoop to lies. Bill should have you taken off the staff here. In fact, I'll make that a recommendation." He checked the buffing on his nails.

Tony buzzed my intercom, and I picked up the phone.

"Joey says come on over, he's got your stuff, and there's an identifiable image," he said.

"Did he say who?"

"He didn't know the person."

"Great. Thanks, Tony." I hung up and faced Jimmy. "You know, Jimmy, you're right. Call me crazy, but I do tend to get carried away, particularly when there are lives at stake—say, Catherine Richie's and especially my own." I put my hands on my hips. "But I know you like Las Vegas. You must be the betting sort. So I'll make you a bet right now. This minute. If you win, I back off. You'll never hear a peep out of me again. I'll sign papers, if you want. If I win, you still get off easy. You have to tell two people everything you know about Catherine Richie—the truth, not that charade you concocted. The two people are me and Inspector Lemire in Paris."

"You're out of control, but then I knew that in LA." Jimmy laughed. "What's this stupid bet?"

"It's about movies," I said. "We're going to look at a movie together. Follow me." We walked in silence across the compound to the studio, but with every step Jimmy was bristling with indignation.

In the dim light of the video studio, Jimmy and I stood together behind Joey's chair.

"I've got it cued up," said Joey, looking back over his shoulder. His glance bounced to Jimmy, then turned into a stare. Quickly, he turned back to the controls and I heard the clatter of the keyboard. The original blurred image came on the screen. Joey tapped his keyboard again, and a box appeared around the red hat. "Here's what we sent our technical friends in LA," he said.

"What's this?" Jimmy demanded.

"A souvenir from Paris," I said.

"Here's what they sent back," said Joey. He tapped some more keys, and the frozen image of a red baseball cap materialized. Beneath it was Jimmy Bennett's face.

"Well, what do you know," I said. "If it isn't . . . let me see,

Joey. Would you mind turning around and taking a look at this gentleman here?"

Joey gave a quick look, confirming what he'd seen when we walked into the room. "It's him," he said. "At least your friend here looks a lot like the guy on the tape."

"Thanks, Joey." I patted him on the shoulder.

"What's this all about?" Jimmy said tautly.

"Please print that frame out for me, if you would, Joey. And one for the files. Well, Jimmy, it goes like this. You *were* in the greenhouse the night Catherine was killed—and you were there just before she died. You left—I saw you leave—but obviously you came back. That's what the tape shows."

Jimmy's face stared back at us from the screen, the truth impossible to deny.

"Of course, the fact that you were there doesn't mean that much. It does show that you probably weren't with Catherine when she was killed. The question is, why would you go to so much trouble to say something different?"

Jimmy looked noncommittally at the screen. "This is what the hoo-ha is all about? Well, big deal. In all the confusion, it's hard to remember exactly when I came and went."

"We'll see if the French police think this is a big deal or not. Let's see. How do you spell e-x-t-r-a-d-i-t-i-o-n? In French."

Bennett turned on his heel and stormed out. I was right behind him. "Gonna keep running from this, Jimmy?" I called out, catching up. "That's constructive."

He stopped, and his shoulders sagged. Suddenly, his rubbery face looked worn, his eyes red-rimmed. "I don't think you're clear on a few things," he said softly. "I have no continuity in my life. How can I keep anything straight? I travel over two hundred days a year. Good lord, Jordan, I remember when you lived like that. I had to see to it that all your bills were paid, that the right dog food showed up wherever you were, that your passport got renewed—you needed a babysitter! But everybody understood, because tennis was your job, and that was your life. My job is my life. I live it. I'm always on call, always part of my clients' lives. And they're not just clients. I go through what they do, feel what they do. It's not a job I take home, this job *is* my home. It's where I live. I can't even sleep." His eyes were puppylike, large, brown, and pleading. "If something breaks about one of my clients, or my tournaments, in another time zone, and it's the middle of the night, who's the first one they call? But I don't mind. Do you understand what I'm saying?"

"Yes, Jimmy, I do. But what's your point?"

"So I'm guilty, I admit it," he said, shoving his left hand into his jacket pocket. He pulled out a Zippo lighter and flipped it open and shut, open and shut. "Guilty of getting overly involved in my clients' lives—and also at times my employees'. After all, we're like a family. Catherine was like family. After she quit, it broke my heart. I missed her like a daughter. And I was worried. After all, I was the one who had taken her to Europe. I felt responsible."

I waited.

"I was supposed to meet her at the reception," Jimmy said finally. "When she didn't show up, I went looking for her. That's when you saw me leaving the greenhouse area. I still couldn't find her, so I ducked back in, just to be sure we hadn't crossed paths. That was it." Jimmy lit a cigarette, held it, but didn't smoke it. Instead, he used it as a pointer, aiming it at me to punctuate his words, as if he were the lecturer savant and I the very ignorant pupil. "Tell that to anybody who wants to hear. It's the facts."

"So why did you say that something different happened?"

"To be honest, I don't know. It was such an emotional moment. There didn't seem to be any point to dwelling on it." A rim of white ash formed at the end of the cigarette.

No point—especially since I had the tape that proved he had been lying.

"And I don't suppose you had anything to do with the guy who almost killed me by running me off the road?"

Jimmy looked at me evenly. "Someone ran you off the road, Jordan? That's terrible. I wish I could help you, but I have no idea what you're talking about."

"And I suppose you have no idea where Noel Fisher is right now?"

"Why would I? I didn't even know the guy."

Jimmy tossed his unsmoked cigarette onto the ground and smashed it into the gravel under his shoe. I could see him looking at me, calculating how far his story had sunk in, like an actor gauging his audience, deciding whether or not to escalate his performance. Then he yawned.

"You know, I think I'm getting tired. Tired of your constant innuendo, Jordan—especially coming from someone I thought was a friend. Unless you have something concrete in the way of accusations, please do us both a favor and go bandage somebody's knee or something. Because the next person to answer your questions about me will be my attorneys. Can you spell l-i-b-e-l?"

I wondered how far I could push him. Sometimes, under pressure, people will blurt things out. This was strategy I'd used well in my competition days: Aggravate your opponents, peck at them, make them impatient, and they will often slip and make a mistake, or at least the surface will crack. "All I know is there are a lot of strange things related to Catherine's death, and they all come back to you somehow, Jimmy," I said.

Tiny pellets of moisture were beading above his lip. He nodded slowly, his eyes narrowed, and a sliver of a smile formed at the corners of his mouth. "You know, I think I get it. CiCi had you pegged. You can't stand it, can you? You can't stand not being the center of attention."

"This is not about me."

"I beg to differ. This is totally about Kelly Kendall working with Heather and me. We have a dream team here, and you're not on it. And you have never gotten over the fact that Kelly spent about five years basically wiping up the courts with you."

"Jimmy, I have news for you. Winning isn't what this is about, and neither is Kelly Kendall." These were words I never imagined I'd hear myself speak. For so many years, Kelly had virtually defined my life: me versus Kelly, that had been all that counted. Even when she had arrived at the Springs to coach Heather, I felt twinges of the old rivalry. But now they were gone. I couldn't define myself in relation to anybody else anymore—not Kelly, my rival; not Noel Fisher, my teacher; not Gus, my mentor. I was truly on my own.

"Take my advice, Jordan. This kind of behavior is destructive. Let it go. Get therapy if you need it. I'll even pay for it. This kind of bitterness can destroy you."

Meg pulled up beside us in a golf cart. "Mr. Bennett, the *New York Times* is ready to start their phone interview. And Ms. Kendall is waiting."

Jimmy kept talking—or, more accurately, lecturing. "I'm telling you this as a friend, Jordan. You are obviously distraught. You're not yourself." I wondered why he wasn't hurrying off to the interview. Surely the *Times* was more important. "Frankly, I'm concerned about you. You'll do yourself serious damage, and you could cost your organization a lot of business while you're at it. It's pathetic to have to say this to someone I have known so long, but frankly I think you've lost your sense of perspective. You forget you're not on the tennis court anymore. Wake up, Jordan, it's not a game." Shaking his head mournfully, Jimmy pulled the brim of his hat lower, climbed into the golf cart, and sped off.

I knew that in a few hours Jimmy would be gone, lifting off in the chopper with Heather, Kelly, and the entourage, and I would have no further proof of my suspicions. What's more, if you accepted things at surface value—and right now, that was the only way anyone could accept them—he was right: The videotape proved nothing, and I was jeopardizing my credibility, not to mention my safety, by continuing to press the issue.

There was, of course, the distinct possibility that Jimmy was guilty of nothing more than employing Catherine Richie and taking her to France on business. At this point, there seemed to be many possibilities and few courses of action. All I could do was send the printout of Jimmy at the greenhouse to Inspector Lemire, so he could forward it on to the person in charge of the case. Then I could comb through Jimmy's datebook again and search for something I might have overlooked. And I could wait.

Waiting was the one thing I learned to do well when I was in the hospital, flat on my back, recovering from my accident. For an A-type personality, which I am, waiting is akin to purgatory. But as part of my healing, I was forced to learn the power of patience. I found out that you cannot force events as if they were tulips in a hothouse. You have to ambush fate by waiting for it on a limb, alert to the slightest motion so that when it passes by beneath you, you are in a position to pounce. Sometimes, it is best to wait for your opponents to come to you. And if you do, they almost always will.

TWELVE

"**H**alfway through a match!" Woody Solister stormed, as Dagmar Olafsen, the object of his indignation, sat slumped in a chair in the examining room. "She poops out halfway through a match. It's always the same. Starts out strong, then *boom!* She crashes. All I'm asking is to get the back half up to speed with the front half. She has great stamina, so that's not it. It's the shoulder."

Woody chewed a wad of gum furiously, as if he could chomp the problem into oblivion. He must have had an entire pack, maybe two, wadded into his mouth; his cheek bulged, and I could smell the peppermint scent from several feet away. On his forehead was a fat gauze bandage, held in place by strips of flesh-colored tape, the result of a recent basal skin cancer excision. He spoke at a rapid-fire pace, on the theory that it forced those around him to listen. His client sat quietly in a chair beside him. Meg Zaresky came in with a tray of fresh-squeezed juices and passed them around. Woody took a carrot-and-apple combo and downed it in one gulp.

Ever since they had arrived—less than an hour after Jimmy,

Heather, Kelly, and their entourage had lifted off from the Springs helipad—Woody had been pushing for an instant answer, the magic formula that would solve all Dagmar's problems.

"You know what Dagmar said?" he said, leaning close and chewing ferociously. "She said we're gonna skip Wimbledon. That's right. Skip it. She wants to concentrate on this rehab. I can buy into that. I don't want her overexposed before she's ready. If people can see her at every tournament and she's not winning, what's going to happen to her marquee value?"

By this time, our clinic physician had already examined Dagmar and given me a complete report. As I had suspected, it was her rotator cuff. Biodex testing, which measures how quickly each rotator cuff fatigues, had indicated that the affected side was only two thirds as strong as the right. It was a common injury for athletes who use extensive overhead motion—those who play tennis, volleyball, and baseball. However, she should have recovered completely by this time.

"I don't understand." Dagmar sighed. "If the rotator cuff muscle is so bad, how is it I can still play?"

"The other muscles compensate," I explained. "They perform the function of the rotator cuff, which tricks you into thinking you're better, but actually this only makes the rotator cuff weaker. You need exercises that are specific to the rotator. The good news is you should see results within a few weeks. If you're conscientious, by the time of the Crown Jewel in August, unless there's a complication, you should be completely recovered."

"I've had so much therapy." Dagmar looked down at her hands, which were huge, with bulging veins. "You can't even imagine what CiCi put me through. She made me take the most horrible-tasting herbs. And I had these rubber bands for resistance exercises—"

"Yes, I know. My guess is that the rotator cuff muscles weren't isolated. CiCi is a coach, not a physical therapist. It may have appeared that the exercises were working, but in fact, you were continuing a substitution pattern."

"That would explain it, at least," huffed Woody. "McBain pushed Dagmar, if you ask me. She forced her to go too fast too quickly, and she isolated her from professionals who could have helped her. Woody Solister is not going to make that same mistake." Woody frequently refers to himself in the third person, a trait he shares with the Queen of England.

I showed Dagmar how to do the exercises correctly, and she winced.

"It hurts, so people avoid the pain. That's human nature, and that's what leads to the problems." I said. "But here's what we'll do now. To get started, I'm going to see if one of our therapists can give Dag a homeopathic massage with arnica, which will help alleviate swelling, and I'll give her some arnica tablets, and travmeel, which is a homeopathic anti-inflammatant, to help out."

"I'll try anything," said Dag. "Let's get going."

For the next two weeks, things were almost normal. Dag's therapy progressed according to plan, and she worked very hard, almost fiercely. I had to remind her not to overdo, not to push so hard. When she wasn't working on her physical therapy, Dagmar spent time in the gym or in the training field with Woody, building up her overall strength. There were sessions with the nutritionist, and Dagmar followed her diet rigidly. Although Gus wasn't at the clinic, his assistant worked with Dag on mental toughness training. She learned how to sharpen her focus; how to gain consistency by viewing each point as the most important of the year; how to sharpen her visual, auditory, and kinesthetic recall, replaying in her mind all the physical sensations she experienced when in her top winning form. She did all this with a thoroughness, professionalism, and dedication that won my respect.

To my surprise, Woody more than rose to the occasion. Because on summer days temperatures can boil up and over 110 degrees, a lot of our outdoor work is scheduled to bracket the heat, in the very early or twilight hours. Early hours were best for Woody too. He usually didn't start drinking until afternoon. Woody didn't try to hide his affinity for alcohol; he just worked around it. One morning he sat with me on the grass as we watched Dagmar running wind sprints with the Springs speed coach.

"It's always that drive to get back to something you were before," he said. "To play like you did at the French last year, or the Open three years ago."

"I know. But she has to look at each thing as a separate event."

"It's a process," said Woody, plucking a weed and chewing on it in lieu of a cigarette. "I told Dag, Stay focused on the process; that's all you can do. The rest will take care of itself."

"Easier said than done, especially if you've ever been number one or way up there. There are so many other factors involved."

Woody's eyes narrowed. "Being the best is the person who looks like the best. Dag has a chance. Look what Connors did. Sometimes being the best when you're young is a death knell. Look at Borg. Maybe she can't win the French Open today, but, hell, she can win the Crown Jewel. She's a born clay-courter; the girl grew up on clay in Holland and Sweden. All we have to do is get that shoulder back."

"And what about you, Woody? What made you want to do this?" It was common knowledge that Woody hurtled from one endorsement to another and rarely ventured into the fray anymore.

He never took his eyes off Dagmar. "The truth? It's been a long time since anybody asked me. Dagmar asked."

Tony moved into my guest room and at night, after work, we cooked pasta dinners and ran videotapes of old movies. I talked to Jason a couple of times, but he had no insight from Jimmy's datebook. I heard nothing from France. It was as if a black hole had opened up and swallowed up the Fishers. My calls to Inspector Lemire revealed that he was on an extended holiday. I contacted the American embassy and was told by an attaché that they were aware of the situation and were working with the French police; someone would get back to me. In England, in the small town about a half hour from London called Wimbledon, the All England Lawn Tennis Championships were under way.

I was home, lying on the couch around ten o'clock on Saturday night, reading a science fiction book—the story of how a deadly virus infested all the planet's oceans and polluted the global water supply—and waiting for Tony to return. He'd been putting in a lot of overtime lately, spending innumerable hours glued to the computer. I knew he was tracking down something important, but when I asked him about it he only shrugged. That much was typical Tony. One of the reasons he was so professional was his mania for detail. He liked to have all his i's dotted and t's crossed. I had just brought A.M. back from a walk around the yard when the phone rang. It was the front gate guard, announcing that I had a visitor, a Ms. Zaresky.

Meg came into my house white-faced and in tears.

"Meg! What's the matter?" When I reached out for her, I could feel her trembling.

"I don't know how to tell it or who to tell," she whispered. "So I came to you."

"Tell me *what*?"

Shakily, Meg lowered herself into a chair. "Something *terrible* happened."

"Tell me about it," I said. Meg was a quiet girl. She must be very upset to make so dramatic a declaration.

Meg burst into tears. I patted her gently until she calmed down. Then I sat her on the couch and made her a cup of chamomile tea with lemon. Meg took the cup and cradled it to her chest as if it were a soothing hot-water bottle. When she finally began to speak, she looked at the carpet, the furniture, the ceiling—anywhere but at me.

"I was in the locker room. Almost everybody had left, and I was changing to take a run before I went home." She looked at me briefly, then dropped her eyes. Her voice became almost robotic. "Dagmar came in and we started to talk and she was so nice, you know? She asked me where I went to school and everything. What I wanted to do. How I liked it at the Springs. She asked me if I might want to visit her sometime. Maybe we could hang out together. I—I thought she was just being friendly, so I said sure, that sounded like fun. We sat there awhile and she told me about her injury and how bad it made her feel, how much time she'd lost. And I told her about my parents' divorce. It was cool. I had somebody to really talk to me. She put her arm around me and we talked some more, and then she— she started kissing me." Meg took a sharp little breath. Her eyes riveted to the floor.

"Then what happened?"

"I tried to push away, but she's really strong. I had to really shove her. She—she got upset. She said she thought we were friends, but now she'd see to it that I lost my job." Meg looked up. "Can she do that?"

"This is very serious, Meg. Are you sure that's how it happened?"

"Yes. And that's what I told Bill. Just what I told you."

"You've already talked to Bill?"

She sniffed and nodded. "I thought I should see him right away, to be sure I don't get fired and lose my internship."

Bill would be forced to take action, I knew. "I'm really sorry this happened," I said, "but are you absolutely sure you didn't— misinterpret something? I know Dagmar is gay, but I've never heard of anything like this happening with her." I didn't know what to say. I didn't want to belittle or diminish or even distrust what Meg was saying, but I knew I had to be extremely careful. "What can I do to help?"

"Don't make me talk to Dagmar," Meg said, blinking like a little girl.

"Would you like to stay here tonight? So you won't be alone?" With Tony in the guest room, I could give Meg my own bed and sleep on the couch downstairs.

"Thank you."

I showed her to my bedroom and gave her a travel kit, one of several I always keep packed in plastic bags in case of sudden trips. I lent Meg an oversized T-shirt to sleep in. Then I took an extra duvet and pillow from the linen closet and set myself up on the couch.

Even before Tony came back, Meg was asleep, but I remained awake on the couch, bundled up under my duvet, flipping pages of my book but not really reading. I had left Tony a note, roughing out the evening's events. It was impossible to sleep, wondering what Bill would do about this, what position we would officially take. Most important, I hadn't talked to Dagmar; she might have a totally different version of what had happened. I called her bungalow, but there was no answer. I tried Woody. No answer there, either. I called Bill's house. His answering service picked up, and I left a message that Meg was with me. Then I checked on Meg. She was sound asleep, curled up around a pillow and looking like innocence personified. Then I padded back downstairs and let A.M. out for her last walk of the day. And finally I reclaimed my couch and fell asleep even before the eleven o'clock news.

I awakened to the sounds of eggs cracking and juice squeezing. Tony had decided to go all out and make his famous cornmeal pancakes with blueberry compote.

"Before Meg comes downstairs, you have to give me the details," Tony said, beating the eggs with a wire whisk he had brought along from his own kitchen. My culinary supplies are admittedly sparse.

"As far as I know, there are no details," I said. "It was very straightforward."

"What about Dagmar? What's her version?"

"So far nothing. I can't reach her."

"Is she still here?"

"As far as I know."

"Maybe she doesn't know about this yet."

"It's possible."

"You know, Dagmar spent all those years with CiCi."

"But she doesn't seem capable of something like this."

"You never know." Tony rinsed the blueberries in a colander and shook them into a saucepan.

Meg came downstairs, and we had a silent breakfast. The pancakes were delicious, but, aside from Tony, nobody had much of an appetite. The main beneficiary was A.M., who scored some juicy leftovers in her dog dish.

As Tony and Meg cleared the plates, I went upstairs to the study, closed the door, and called Woody's room again. This time, he answered, his voice soggy with sleep. "What!"

"Woody, it's Jordan. I'll get right to the point. Are you aware that one of our female interns is accusing Dagmar of sexually harassing her?"

"Tell me this is a nightmare." He coughed into the phone, clearing his throat. "Hold on. My throat. I gotta get some water." The phone clunked down, and I heard him moving around. In a few seconds, he returned. "Now what is this? Are you serious?"

"Meg Zaresky, a nineteen-year-old intern, says Dagmar tried to come on to her in the locker room."

"Oh, God."

"Dagmar had better be prepared to tell her side of the story, because Meg has already talked to Bill and there are going to be repercussions."

"Let me talk to her and get back to you," said Woody tersely. He hung up, and the phone rang. It was Bill.

"Jordan?" His voice sounded anxious. "What's the Zaresky girl told you?"

"She says Dagmar came on to her. She's considering filing a lawsuit. But we don't know Dagmar's side of it yet."

"We're going to go over everything in a meeting in half an hour. Meet me in my office, and bring Meg Zaresky."

. . .

"**Y**ou've been so nice," whispered Meg as we walked into Bill's office. "I'm sorry about this."

"We just want to get everything straight," I said.

"My dad is coming to get me later today," she said. "I guess I'm leaving. He's called some lawyers."

"Don't think about that, Meg. You just worry about you. The rest will take care of itself."

Bill was waiting in his office. With him was a lawyer I had never met before, a woman in her late twenties, wearing jeans and a crisp white cotton shirt. "This is Lisa Lenders," Bill said, introducing her.

Lisa was good, I had to admit. She chatted gently with Meg, acting more like a friend than a lawyer. Her questions were nonthreatening but to the point. Still, Meg's story remained unchanged. Dagmar had come on to her. She had resisted.

Finally, Meg said, "You know, my dad's on his way. I think I should pack." After she left the room, Bill, Lisa, and I reconvened.

"I think we can handle this situation," said Lisa. "There was no real incident. Dagmar didn't actually touch Meg. There are no physical damages."

"What about psychological?" Bill asked.

"Very difficult to prove, but it could surface later," said Lisa. "Time would have to pass before she could make any kind of claim successfully. And I doubt the parents would drag Meg through all that just to prove psychological damage. Besides, that's more of a long-term thing. True, she's shaken, but she's obviously functional. I think we just have to wait and see what the parents do."

"Dagmar denies everything," said Bill. "I talked to her before I came over here. She claims it never happened. Did you ever see any evidence of this kind of behavior, Jordan? Meg was working in your office."

"No, I didn't. Dagmar seemed completely focused on her therapy."

"Well, it's one person's word against another. These cases are almost impossible to prove, either way," said Lisa. "I think we have to wait and see what happens."

The meeting adjourned on an unsettling, unresolved note.

As I walked to the Jeep I was borrowing from the Springs, I realized I wasn't ready to leave this incident alone. I decided to swing by Meg's room and talk to her for a few more minutes.

As I pulled up in front of the low white stucco building, one of a handful that housed the clinic guests, I saw Meg outside, talking to two men I didn't recognize. I pulled over, wondering if one was her father. If they were having an emotional reunion, I didn't want to intrude, so I turned off the engine and watched for a minute, deciding what to do.

My eyesight is still as sharp as when I was on the circuit. As I came closer, I noticed that one of the men had a camera and the other a tape recorder. The man with the camera was taking pictures of Meg, motioning to her, positioning her so the Springs buildings were in the background. I'd seen enough of these types to know immediately what they were: the press. Probably the tabloid press—since the legitimate press usually goes through channels rather than garbage cans. My only questions were: How in the hell did they get onto the premises, and what was Meg doing talking to them?

I got out of the car, determined to keep the encounter lowkey. Reporters inevitably pick up the scent of discord or panic. "What's up, Meg?" I asked, as casually as possible.

She turned, startled. "Oh! Jordan. These are two—uh, friends of my dad's. They're here to help me pick up my stuff."

One of the men carried a huge professional camera bag. The other, I noticed, had pocketed his tape recorder.

"How do you do," I said. "Are you interested in the clinic?"

The men did not introduce themselves. I held my ground and the situation became uncomfortable—everybody standing fixed to the spot, nobody speaking.

Finally, the men backed down. "Okay, Meg, thanks," said the man with the camera bag. "We'll be in touch." With that, they scrambled away, got into a sedan with rental plates, and drove off.

"What was that all about?" I asked.

Meg's face reddened, and she ran her hands through her hair. "Well, like I said, they're friends of my dad's." She looked at her watch. "Gotta go." With that, she turned and hurried into the building.

I immediately went to see Dagmar, who was staying across the grounds. Her bungalow was curtained by a stucco wall, with tangled vines arched across the doorframe and windows, and set against the backdrop of a mountain view. The guesthouses on the clinic grounds were perfectly positioned, each designed for maximum peace and privacy.

Woody answered the door and led me to her. Dagmar sat on a stool in the small kitchen, her eyes bloodshot and swollen from crying. "It wasn't supposed to turn out like this!" she sobbed.

"Dagmar, tell me exactly what happened," I said.

"Nothing." She wiped her eyes and faced me in a fury. "I never even spoke to that girl. Nothing happened! She's a vicious little liar!"

"They can't prove a damned thing," said Woody, awkwardly patting her shoulder. "Mainly because there's nothing to prove. These young people today, they should read their Scripture!"

Dagmar looked up at me and laughed bitterly. An odd response, I thought, but understandable under the circumstances.

"We're talking about innuendo," said Woody angrily. "I admit, I'm over my head in all this legal mumbo-jumbo, but these days everybody's guilty until they're proven innocent. Isn't that the drill?"

Dagmar sat in stony silence, rubbing her shoulder mechanically.

Woody walked over and cupped her face between his hands, then put his eyes level with hers. "Now you listen to me. I've invested a lot of time and a lot of sweat in you, and you are not gonna let me down. Do you hear?"

She nodded glumly.

"Heather Knight is all over the press." Woody reached over, picked up a copy of *USA Today* from the countertop, and waved it at me. "Look at this! Heather Knight is quoted as saying that Dagmar is a bad example for American youth. Listen to this headline: 'Olafsen Poor Role Model, Knight Knocks.' And that's the high point." He tossed the paper into Dagmar's lap. "We have our work cut out for us. The question is, can you handle it? It's going to be a war."

Dagmar stared back at Woody. "She's a bitch," she whispered. "And CiCi, of all people!" Her eyes clouded with tears. "Don't let them do this to me, Jordan. They're trying to destroy me."

"I'll take that as an affirmative," Woody interrupted. "Fine, then we understand each other." He straightened up and turned back to me. "We *all* understand each other. We will see you Monday, eight A.M., as usual."

The old ramrod still had spine, I had to admit. I suspected that, all problems aside, he relished nothing more than a good gloves-off fight. As he saw me out, I paused in the entryway.

"What's your take on this, Woody?" I asked.

"I think it's a setup."

"But why?"

"Because that's the kind of cheap shot Bennett takes." Woody took a pack of cigarettes out of his shirt pocket, shook one out, and twirled it in his fingers. "Trying to quit." He stuck the unlit cigarette into his mouth, where it dangled from his lower lip as if stuck on with invisible glue. "You know, this poor kid has worked her butt off. She's better. She can beat Heather. CiCi probably knows that. She's going for the psychological advantage." He tapped his forehead.

"What about Meg Zaresky?"

"On something or on the take. Could be either."

"She's just a kid. It's hard to believe. Are you sure it's not true?"

His eyes narrowed. "I've seen a lot of liars, and Dagmar isn't one of them. She's all heart. That's her problem."

There was nothing more to be done, so I went home for lunch. The day wasn't half over, and I was exhausted. I had just walked in when Tony handed the phone to me.

"Is this Jordan Myles?"

"Yes. Who's this?"

"Steven Sweet from the *Intelligencer*. We have information that one of your clients, Dagmar Olafsen, has been accused of sexually harassing a young woman who is a minor. Would you care to comment?"

"No comment!" I slammed down the phone. "That was a reporter from that slimy supermarket tabloid, the *Intelligencer*," I told Tony. "How'd they get this number? And there were a couple of reporters—I'd bet money they were from this same scumpond—slinking around, talking to Meg today and taking pictures. God knows what they're going to print." I immediately called the phone company and asked them to change my unlisted number.

Upstairs in my room, I ripped the sheets Meg had used off my bed, and stuffed them into the hamper. Then I remade the bed and climbed into it. A.M. jumped on my chest. So far, things were not going well at all. I stroked A.M.'s ears and found myself talking to her, as I often did when things were really bad.

"Catherine is dead. The Fish is still missing. His mother is still missing. Inspector Lemire is off the case, and nobody else seems to care. The daughter of one of my old friends has made a terrible accusation against one of my clients. Somebody tried to kill me. What are we going to do about all this, girl?"

A.M. rolled over so I could rub her belly. One of the things I like best about her is that she never argues with me and rarely talks back.

I strongly suspected that Jimmy Bennett had something to do with this mess. *Innuendo*. Jimmy had used that word, and so had

Woody. How difficult would it have been for Jimmy to manipulate Meg as he had Catherine?

I was in way over my head, but that was hard to admit, even
to a dog. Maybe the solution was to remove myself from the
scene before any more damage could be done, to myself or
anyone else. I'd often thought about going into private practice,
where I could be more in control of my own life. Maybe now
was the time to do it.

I picked up the remote and turned on CNN. It was something
I do out of habit when I don't want to feel alone. I liked the fact
that CNN was on twenty-four hours a day; it gave my life a
feeling of continuity. The credible, serious news was always
interesting to me—and a vigorous contrast to the exploitative-
ness of the tabloids.

CNN was doing a rundown on the day's results at Wimbledon.
A crawl listing the players' names and match results and the draw
for the next day was running down the screen. Behind the
names, there was a montage of scenes of Wimbledon—the lav-
ender and green signature colors, the spire of St. Mary's Church,
the spectators in their prints and pastels, the strawberries and
champagne, the roses, the impeccably manicured grass courts—
all of which I knew so well that when I closed my eyes the
images continued.

In a shoebox in my desk drawer was the ball from my first
Wimbledon match, marked with the date in felt-tipped pen. I'd
been so excited, I hadn't followed tradition and given the ball to
the ball kid. Instead, I'd walked off the court in a daze, the ball
tucked into my pocket. I hadn't realized I'd kept it until I got
back to the hotel and unpacked my bag. That ball became my
charm, my talisman, and for the rest of the time I was on the tour
I carried it everywhere. The year I made it to the semis, my
charm almost worked.

As I watched, I fell asleep, the TV droning on.

At three-thirty in the morning, I awoke with a start. I wasn't
having my usual Wimbledon nightmare, starring Kelly Kendall.

This time, the crawl of the players' match draw and results kept rolling through my mind, over and over again—except that in my dream the list of names became the list Catherine had faxed to Jason before she was killed. Sitting up in bed, I turned on the light.

The draw. That was it! The list Catherine faxed Jason wasn't a list of players and clients. It was the draw for the women's matches at the French Open. I was almost certain of it.

When I got back from Paris, I had tossed all my materials from the French Open into a folder and left it on my worktable, to be sorted out later. Of course, I had never gotten around to it, and the file remained untouched.

I threw on my sweatshirt and leggings, pinned up a Post-It to Tony, grabbed my purse, and slipped out of the house. It was still dark, that purple dark that comes before dawn, and the grass was dewy and wet as I jogged across the grass to the white Jeep.

I reached the Desert Springs main gate in less than ten minutes. Steve, the night guard, was on duty. Steve was an ex-army officer who had decided to get his college degree. During the day, he took classes or slept. Weekends and nights, he worked on our gate, spelled two nights a week by somebody else.

"Getting an early start, Jordan?"

"Trying to." I nodded. "What're you reading tonight?" Security was so unproblematical at the Springs that the gate guards often read books or magazines.

He held up a paperback copy of *War and Peace.* "Term paper."

Following the policy for any of us after hours, I went through the formality of showing my laminated ID card, then drove across the parking area to the portico in front of the main offices. The building was locked up for the night, so I had to swipe my ID through a security machine to open the front door.

At night, without the people and the activity I was used to, the place reminded me of a stage set, everything in its place and waiting for the action to begin. There were no light switches in the halls—no surprise, as I knew that the entire overhead lighting system in the office building was computerized to go off automatically at 10 P.M. and stay off until 5:30.

I had a pocket-sized flashlight attached to my key chain, and I turned it on to navigate through the halls. I let myself into my office, closed and locked the door behind me, and turned on the desk lamp on my table. A pile of papers—mail and magazines—had accumulated on top of the French Open folder. I transferred the pile to my lap and, for a few minutes, dug my way through to the bottom. Finally, I found what I was looking for: the photocopy of the first-round women's singles draw. I had picked up the sheet in Paris on my way past the hotel's Players' Service desk.

Next, I opened my purse and pulled out the list Jason had sent me and placed the two lists side by side. Jason's page matched the opening draw list. However, I still couldn't be sure what this meant. Had Catherine just been keeping a record of the tournament? But why would she fax that to Jason, who didn't even follow tennis? And why would she ask him to fax it to a European modem?

A tiny sound jolted me to attention. There was a noise at the door of Tony's office. I reached up and flicked off the desk light.

A flashlight suddenly panned through the frosted glass transom of the office door and across the wall, and I froze. The light would have been visible through the transom, if anyone were looking for me. My scalp tingled, and it flashed through my mind that I had been insane to venture into this empty office building in the pre-dawn darkness, alone.

The door handle slowly turned left, then right. As quietly as I could, I gathered up my papers and bent over on my hands and knees. The light beam flickered across the ceiling, and I crawled quickly around behind a large leather chair, flattening myself as close as possible to the frame, hardly daring to breathe as I heard the click of the lock opening and footsteps moving into the office.

The footsteps came slowly into the middle of the room, and the flashlight washed back and forth across the walls and ceiling. Then I heard the footsteps approach the table. There was the sound of papers being ruffled. Then it was quiet, and I remembered: I had left my purse sitting on top of the table. I heard a clatter as its contents were emptied onto the tabletop.

"Jordan Myles," said a man's voice slowly and, it seemed, with a certain satisfaction.

So I had been discovered. It was still not four in the morning— at least two hours before anyone on the staff would come into the building, at least three before Tony might notice my absence from the house.

Silently, I went over my options. The man was between me and the door. My back was literally to the wall. The building was deserted. There was a fire alarm in the hall. If I could reach it, I might have a chance. I peered around the back of the chair, but all I could see was a pair of dark trousers.

With that, I launched myself from behind the chair, aiming for his knees. My shoulders connected full force with the backs of a pair of legs, I grabbed his knees with locked arms, and the man toppled over, like a tree trunk that has been cut in half. His flashlight crashed to the floor and landed facing us, like a spotlight, illuminating the length of the man's fallen form.

I was on my knees, vaguely aware that I had torn the fabric of my leggings, but before I could spring away, or even get a better view of my attacker, a heavy hand smashed down on my mouth and an arm of iron clamped around my neck, nearly choking me. I felt myself being dragged and choked, bile rising from my empty stomach into my throat, and I forced my mouth open and bit down as hard as I could on the hand, tasting the saltiness of blood as my teeth sank into the flesh.

He jerked his hand upward to my scalp, grabbing my hair and wrenching my head to the side so hard my teeth chattered as he dragged me to my feet. I brought up my knee as hard as I could, connecting with his groin, and as he doubled up I broke away momentarily and caught a look at him. Gasping, I realized that he was wearing a uniform, the uniform of our security company. In his hand was a revolver. Either he misunderstood who I was—or he understood all too well.

"Stop!" I tried to explain. "I'm—" At that moment, I heard the unmistakable click of a gun being cocked. It was not a noise I had ever heard before, but I knew it instinctively. This was no time for discussion; I had to take the risk. Mustering all my strength, I stomped the gun out of his hand, but he grabbed my leg as I scrambled over him, pulling me down as I fought my way toward the door. My mouth bashed hard into the edge of a chair as I tumbled over, landing on my shoulder with a jolt.

The struggle was grim and silent as we twisted and rolled on the floor, both groping for the gun, which had landed some-where in the shadows. The man was much stronger than I, however, and would overpower me within seconds. I saw the glint of metal. He had found the gun.

Suddenly, the office door flew open. "For God's sake, what's going on?"

Looking up, I saw another security uniform: Steve, from the front gate. "Police!" I panted. I had no breath left.

"Hold on, that's Mike Stills. Mike, that's Jordan Myles you're wrestling with. She works here, for God's sake. What's going on?"

From the floor, faces two inches away, the face staring back at me was blank, bland, with no hint of the ferociousness of only minutes ago. You would have thought he had done nothing worse than accidentally walk into the ladies' room. I staggered to my feet and stood up.

"I am so sorry," said the man who had tried to choke the life out of me moments before. His voice was low-key and smooth as he smoothed his jacket, and so calm it seemed impossible that he had even been in the room just seconds earlier. His back was to Steve as he slipped the gun inside. "This is just terrible. I hope you're not hurt. I thought somebody had broken into your office,

Ms. Myles. You didn't identify yourself. You're on a special-alert watch, you know. I had to err on the side of caution. I hope you understand." He dusted himself off, smoothed his hair, and extended a hand to steady me.

I refused his hand. Instead, I wobbled to a chair and straightened my sweatshirt, which had ridden up over my midriff in the struggle.

My former attacker, who was not as tall as he had seemed in the dark but was powerfully built, rubbed his hand gingerly. "She bit me." He held up his palm and displayed a set of teeth marks that would have done my dentist proud.

"Well, thank God for that," I said. "You do your job very— aggressively."

"These things tend to happen at three A.M.," he said. I surveyed him closely. He didn't seem unduly concerned about the fact that a few minutes ago he had almost taken my head off.

"Steve, your friend here got a bit carried away. Correction—he went totally overboard. But"—I planted myself firmly and faced Mike Stills—"among other things, you were going through my purse. Why were you doing that?"

He picked up my pass from the floor and handed it to me. The laminate had cracked in the struggle. I would have to get a new one. "I just opened it to see who it belonged to. It was pretty obvious that somebody was in here, and when I checked with Steve on the radio he said you had come in through the gate. So when I found that pass, I read your name to see if it was you."

"I'm sure you're now very surprised to discover—what a shock—that it was my purse in my office." There wasn't much else to say, except that I didn't believe him. He'd known exactly who I was, and his use of force was anything but misappropriated.

"So, net net, everything's all right here?" asked Steve. "Nobody's hurt?" He glanced anxiously at my torn leggings. "Maybe you need a Band-Aid. Or first aid?"

"I need an explanation. I think this got way out of hand. Your buddy here overreacted." I said. "Maybe he needs to go back to Security Training One-oh-one. Rule number one: Don't kill the person you're supposed to protect."

"Are you saying you want to file a complaint?" asked Steve.

"No." I didn't want to complain. I wanted information.

"Mike?" asked Steve. "What do you have to say?"

"Well, that's the last time I open a woman's purse. I apologize for frightening you, Ms. Myles. I was just doing my job."

"I'll let them know in management, and there'll be a report. Jordan, I wish you'd let me run you to the emergency room for a check-over," said Steve. "You look pretty shook up."

"I'll be fine." I had seen quite enough of hospitals recently.

"At least I can get you home."

"I'm not going home. I came in to do some work, and I'm going to do it."

Steve shook his head. "This is going to look real interesting on the report," he said ominously. "Let's go, Mike. I don't feel good about leaving you here, Jordan. You should get that lip looked at. And I'm going to call Dr. Stokes. He should know about this." The two of them left, rather stiffly. Steve gave one last anxious look over his shoulder before closing the door behind them.

I collapsed onto the couch and dabbed my lip with the back of my sleeve. Blood. My neck was throbbing, my hair was all over the place, and both leggings were ripped. Beneath the torn fabric, my knees stung. Gingerly, I picked off the shredded material that covered my left kneecap. A four-inch-square patch of skin was rubbed completely raw, peeled back like the skin of an orange. Blood oozed and beaded slowly to the surface. Mike had really tried to hurt me; his actions had been quite purposeful. Running my tongue along the inside of my mouth, I felt a jagged edge. I probed with a fingertip. The point of one of my eye teeth was broken off. The missing piece had disappeared; I must have swallowed it.

I grabbed the phone and called the twenty-four-hour number of the main office of Palm-Tech, our security contractors. There was a sticker with the number on the side of the phone receiver, in case of emergencies.

"Palm-Tech," answered an operator.

"Operator, this is Jordan Myles from the Desert Springs Sports Science Clinic."

"Is this an emergency?"

"No, but I need to get some details about the background and employment history of one of your security guards."

"I'm sorry, miss, but I can't help you. It's against our policy to provide that information."

"There must be someone I can talk to."

"The administrative office doesn't open until nine A.M. You'll have to call back then."

"Isn't this a twenty-four-hour number?"

"Yes, but for emergency response, not employee records, miss."

"I see. Thank you."

Outside the window, dawn was inching across the desert, the purple of the sky paling to pink, the silhouettes of the mountains as sharp as if they had been cut from a gigantic roll of black construction paper with an X-Acto knife, then glued to the horizon. I sat alone in the empty office, staring at the two pieces of paper with the opening draw for the French Open women's singles, puzzling about the significance of two identical lists of names, and wondering if Mike the guard had been assigned to protect me—or kill me.

THIRTEEN

"**F**or God's sake, Jordan," Bill grumbled. For the first time since I had known him, he was wearing a rumpled shirt, probably thrown on at breakneck speed as he broke his own Olympic record hurtling from his bed to the clinic. "What are you trying to prove? When Palm-Tech called me at home to report this . . . misunderstanding, I was very concerned."

Even though it wasn't yet 7 A.M., my office was crowded. Bill sat across the table from me; on the couch was a bow-tied vice president from Palm-Tech; Tony had rushed over as soon as he'd read my note; and Steve, the after-hours gate guard, stood propped in the doorway, his posture showing the fact that he'd been up all night. The only person missing was Mike. I had already recounted my version of the story for the report and fended off Tony's efforts to send me over to the hospital for a check.

"Where is Mike, exactly?" I asked. "And what do you know about him?"

The vice president turned to Steve.

"He went home to shower and change," Steve explained.

"I think he should be here," said Bill. "I'd like to speak to him personally."

"Use my desk phone," I said. Tony handed me some ice in a plastic bag, which I applied to my lip.

"Call my office and have my secretary look up his number and patch you in on a three-way," said the vice president, whose name I still didn't know or care to know. I kept running my tongue over the rough edge of my broken tooth and wondering when I would be able to get to the dentist. Although my lip felt as if someone had inserted a golf ball under the skin, amazingly, the tooth itself didn't hurt, but I knew it would have to be bonded or capped.

Steve frowned into the phone receiver, then pushed the hold button and motioned the vice president over. The two conferred in whispers, and the vice president got on the phone and turned his back to us.

"So what do we know about this Mike person?" I asked.

The vice president hung up and assumed an official stance. "We'd like to discuss this whole incident in detail and get back to you with a response. A knee-jerk reaction won't do anybody any good. Again, I apologize, Ms. Myles, but fortunately nobody was seriously injured."

"Just a minute," I said. "Where is Mike now? Exactly."

"I agree. How do you expect to avoid this in the future if we can't speak to the man involved?" Bill interjected.

The vice president looked uncomfortable. "I'm sure we'll locate him momentarily. But I think my secretary gave me the wrong phone number. The number she gave me belonged to some little old lady."

Why did that not surprise me? I didn't think we'd ever see Mr. Mike again. "How long has Mike been an employee of Palm-Tech?"

"According to the records I have available, he was a new man—about one month."

"I see."

"We are very careful about our hiring policies: screening, references, even fingerprint searches."

"I see you checked out his phone number."

"It's possible he moved and our records don't reflect that yet. I'm sure his phone number checked out when he was hired. And I'm sure Mike will answer all your questions when we talk to him."

"*If* you talk to him."

"I have no reason to believe that won't happen," the security company's vice president said confidently. "No reason whatsoever."

I, of course, had every reason to believe that wouldn't happen.

"You don't suggest there was something . . . untoward . . . about our employee?" said the vice president. "Why, Mr. Stills has our total endorsement. I can see why you're upset, but it was certainly an honest mistake. Of course he will be reprimanded. He may need some training. Perhaps he was a little precipitous—"

"Perhaps you should tell him not to pull a gun on a client."

"Did you say *gun?*" The vice president stiffened. Even Steve suddenly jolted to attention.

"Yes, a revolver. About a foot from my face. Cocked and, I assume, loaded. And his reaction was unnecessarily violent—I mean, my tooth is seriously broken here. Granted, that's not life-threatening, but this guy could have killed me."

"Did you see a gun, Steve?" the vice president asked quickly.

"No, sir. I didn't see it."

"That's because he was facing me, not you, when he put it into his holster," I said.

"It was dark," said the vice president. "It's possible to mistake, say, a beeper or a mobile phone for—"

"A gun is a gun, and, believe me, you know a gun when it's pointed at you," I said, exasperated.

The vice president was silent for a minute. He opened a small leather-bound notebook, took out a thin gold pen, and made a brief notation. Steve watched him carefully, waiting for him to speak. Finally, he looked up, focusing on Bill. "Our men aren't armed," he said.

"What?" Bill said.

"Palm-Tech on-premises and grounds security for the Desert Springs Sports Science Clinic does not involve armed response. None of our guards carries a weapon." He spoke slowly and quietly, weighing the impact of what he said.

"In other words, this was not a Palm-Tech employee?" asked Bill, half rising from his chair.

The vice president fluttered his hand. "Oh, no, he was—is— an employee. I can assure you of that. But he was not supposed to carry a gun. Our policy is to alert the police, if the situation reaches that level. A suspect wouldn't make it to the highway before he or she would be arrested. Our people are professionals; they're trained to de-escalate a situation. To use brains, not bullets. Only thugs wave guns around, or actors playing guards in the movies."

"So, help me out here. Why was this man carrying a gun?" asked Bill, struggling to ignore the obvious.

In my mind, there was only one possible conclusion. Mike Stills had not come here to forge a career path in the security business. He was on the grounds of the Springs at this specific time for one specific purpose: He was after me.

They had made their move. Now it was my turn.

By ten o'clock, Tony and I were sitting in a booth at the diner.

"I have to tell you, Jordan," Tony said, leaning across the booth, "I think they were looking for my computer files. I've been nosing around, and you can leave electronic footprints. An expert could trace them."

"Really? Can they get at your files? Is there anything on them?"

"Well, I'm working with some numbers from Roland Garros, but there's nothing concrete yet. I think the number on the business card that Catherine left for Bob Riordan may correlate to Roland Garros. If something clicks, I'll let you know. It'll take some work. And of course, there's nothing on the hard drive. I keep everything on discs, which are"—he patted his pocket—"in here. At all times. I never leave anything in the office."

"It's more likely they were after me again," I said. "Fits the pattern."

I remembered the approaching waitress from my last time here, with Jason, and hoped she wouldn't recognize me. I picked up a newspaper from the seat of the booth and buried my face in the financial section.

"You!" said the waitress, pointing at me with the laminated menus. "The one who doesn't eat."

"Oh, I'll eat this time. I'll have a"—I winced—"a Liberace special."

"With or without the candelabra?" Tony said. "Just coffee." He nodded to the waitress. She walked toward the kitchen and he leaned over. "What in God's name is a Liberace special?"

"I don't know."

"But you ordered it."

"Everything here is named after old-time stars," I explained. "I figured it had to be something."

"Why bother ordering at all, or even coming here?"

"The list that Jason programmed in for Catherine was the same as the opening draw at the French."

"So what? It sounds like she was keeping track of the players. Lots of people do that."

"Not via transatlantic computer program."

"Reporters and wire service people do." Tony's eyes narrowed. I could tell he sniffed something.

"True. But she wasn't a reporter or a wire service person."

"Maybe she was helping one out for some reason," he said slowly.

"In any case, I don't want to use the office phones, or my home phone, or my car phone," I said. "And I don't want to get thrown out before I use their pay phone. Watch for my order."

At the phone booth I placed several calls to Jason, finally reaching him in his car. "I figured out what the list was that Catherine faxed you," I told him. "It was the player draw for the opening round of the women's singles at the French Open. Why would Catherine have sent you that? What did she ask you to do with it?"

"Program it in. That was all. For her records."

"Jase, you said your company keeps recordings of all phone numbers called for security purposes."

"Yeah. It does. It also records the calls and even the computer transactions. We're a bit like the IRS."

"I remember. Could you reconstruct the computer activity for that call, when you programmed in the players' names?"

"I think so."

"Great. But don't call me. You were right. It's not safe. I'll get back to you."

"I hope this leads to something. Frankly, Jordan, I think it was pretty harmless. I mean, keeping track of the players was her job."

"Her job, not your job. Why would she involve you? There had to be a reason."

"Well, maybe we're about to find out. By the way, that number on the business card that Catherine left with the cameraman?"

"Yeah."

"I recognized it. It was one of her phone numbers."

"Okay. I'll tell Tony. He was tracking it down."

"Well, why waste his time?"

"Be careful, Jason. A so-called security guard just made a rather impressive search of my office. Tony thinks he's after some discs."

"Did he get them?"

"No. Tony keeps them in his pocket." I hung up and went back for my Liberace special, which turned out to be a towering fruit salad topped with a scoop of orange sherbet and a maraschino cherry. It didn't matter. They could have served me nuclear waste; I had no appetite.

I noticed that the TV suspended over the counter showed highlights of a men's match at Wimbledon. Andre Agassi, sporting a new hair look, was serving. Agassi is one of the few men known to take advantage of the complimentary hair salon services that are available for players at Wimbledon.

"Now will you hire a bodyguard?" asked Tony. "What's it going to take?"

"My experience with security has not been encouraging," I said. "Oh, and the phone number—Jason recognized it. It's nothing."

Tony nodded.

"Except," I frowned, "didn't Riordan say he checked it, and there was no such number? Maybe it was a temporary number, just for the duration of the tournament."

"I'll keep checking."

The Wimbledon coverage cut to a commercial. "We'll be back with a preview of the ladies and a word with Heather Knight, who is speaking out for women's tennis," said the announcer. Tony and I sat transfixed through commercials for running shoes, dishwashing detergent, and two different cars. At last Heather appeared on the screen.

"Heather." The interviewer, a woman in a Wimbledon-green jacket, beamed. "You've had a great year, the comeback of the nineties, some might say."

"I'd rather say I never left." Heather smiled. "Yes, it has been quite a year."

"Once, you were the youngest top-ten player on the tour. Now you've not only grown up, you've emerged as one of the tour's spokespeople for issues."

"Yes. I believe that as athletes and role models for young people all over the world, we can't just stop at our sport. We have to deliver character as well as performance."

"Well said. Can you give us an example?"

I felt it coming as the camera moved in for a closeup of Heather.

"There are certain players who, in my opinion, should be banned from the tour for the way they conduct their personal lives."

"Nice shot," said Tony.

"I'd like to get specific for our viewers, if you don't mind, Heather. You were quoted as saying that Dagmar Olafsen is a poor role model. Would you care to elaborate?"

Heather shook her head slowly. "Samantha, this is a family broadcast, and I'm not one to throw stones. I'll take the high road on this. I'd rather beat Dagmar on court, which I will if and when she ever sets foot behind a net again."

"Dagmar is sitting out this year's Wimbledon. Do you know why?"

"I have no idea," said Heather. "But my guess would be she knew she couldn't win. And I think her attentions were else-where. Her mind hasn't been on the game. It's been on her personal life. You can't play your best when you're distracted like that." She turned to the camera with the ease of a practiced media performer, addressing her audience with great sincerity. "But I challenge Dagmar's choices, because there is no place for that kind of behavior in tennis. Or anywhere. Tennis is a great sport. Women's tennis has had some truly heroic women. There's no place for what we're seeing out there today. It just gives everybody a bad name. That's what I think."

"And do you think you can win here at Wimbledon, Heather? Kelly Kendall seems to think you can."

Heather smiled modestly. "Well, she's the expert. And my idol as well as my coach, I might add. I just want to play my best."

"Do you want to throw up?" Tony asked.

"Tony, wait!" As the program segued to the commercial break, the camera panned a section of the queue, where people lined up for hours, even days, to get into the grounds. I could hardly believe what I was looking at. "It's Mrs. Fisher!"

"Where?" Tony squinted at the screen.

"That older woman, right there, talking to the queue ladies, the one in the pink hat." The straw hat trimmed with a froth of pink carnations was unmistakable. Hadn't Mrs. Fisher said it was one of a kind?

"Yeah, I see her. Are you sure that's her?"

"Positive." The camera moved on, and I lost her. But I knew it was Noel Fisher's mother. I couldn't have been more positive if she was carrying a cheesecake. Talking to the queue ladies, who were professional waiters-in-line and perennial fixtures on the Wimbledon scene, would be perfectly in character. She probably had struck up a fast friendship with them by now.

"That's very rude of her. If she's out tea-and-crumpeting at Wimbledon, she's obviously not missing."

"Clearly."

"Well, she hasn't been home," Tony said. "I've been calling the neighbors once a week, just in case. No sign of either of the Fishers. Nobody thought anything of it because she left word that she was going to Europe to visit him and wasn't sure when she'd be back. One of the neighbors has been taking in her newspaper and mail. He's still taking it in. But if the Fish was in the shape you reported, I can't figure out how he could be walking around."

Of course. There had been a purposeful veil of confusion at work all along. The sudden disappearance of two people under police protection, with the police conveniently unavailable to discuss it and the American ambassador sidestepping the issue, had to be part of a bigger picture, and Jimmy Bennett's evasiveness was the least of it. But what would be such a big picture that even the embassy would be involved?

"Maybe he's dead," ventured Tony.

"I doubt it. That woman wouldn't be galavanting around Wimbledon in a flowered hat if her son were dead. He told me last year when we were there investigating Audrey Armat's disappearance that his mother had never been to Europe. She'd barely been out of Brooklyn. She only went this time because her son was in such bad shape and Bill sent her a ticket."

"Maybe it wasn't her, Jordan. There are a lot of old ladies in hats at these kinds of events."

"It was her, believe me. And if she's there, the Fish isn't far away."

"You're not going over there to find him?" Tony's glass stopped in midair.

I pushed away my Liberace special. The orange sherbet had melted into a puddle, oozing over the fruit like a neon flood. "No. The Fish has connections you can't believe, and not just high-level types: maids, security people, cooks, somebody's brother-in-law. If the Fish really doesn't want to be found, nobody in the world could find him. And when he does want to be found, we won't have to look."

"It's your call," said Tony. "But I hope you're not talking yourself into something. I'd have to say that could have been any little old lady from Leeds on TV, and the Fish could be—"

"I think when we figure out what was behind that computer program, the rest of this will be a lot more clear to everyone. Waitress. Check, please."

"Does Jason have any ideas?"

"Not yet. Maybe you could do a little snooping too, Tony. Let's see if there's anything we can find on Mr. Jimmy Bennett."

Tony hummed a quick medley of old Beach Boys tunes, and we went back to surf the Internet.

Tony's specialty was medical research, but he could pull up just about any piece of information I ever needed from any of the computer on-line services. This time turned out to be no exception.

"Found him," Tony said, just minutes after he'd input Jimmy's name. He pointed to the screen. "I did a key-word search, using his name. This is a list of all the articles in print that mention Jimmy." He scrolled the screen. "As you can see, there's a lot of ink on this guy. There's a batch from last year, when he formed

TalentMasters. A bunch of titles on the Crown Jewel. Stuff on him and Heather. Here's something interesting, a mention in the *Harbinger Report*. That's a financial newsletter. I'll bring it up."

Quickly, I skimmed the column. It was speculated that a Japanese conglomerate, Hiro International, was rumored to buy TalentMasters.

"Tony, have you heard of a Japanese company called Hiro International?"

"Vaguely. I think they're into cars and electronics."

"Hm. Sounds very familiar. Could they be the same companies that sponsor the Crown Jewel?"

"Let's take a look." Tony pulled up a file on Hiro and the names of their holdings. The Calibre Automotive Company, Equinox, and Pentacle Electronics were among the companies they owned.

"These guys are three of the sponsors of the Crown Jewel. Now let's look at the stock."

The keyboard clattered beneath Tony's fingers. "Let's see. TalentMasters is privately held. Hiro's stock is holding steady at fifty-three, fifty-four dollars per share. That won't tell us anything."

"It looks like Jimmy has some major investors."

"If he sells his company, he'll make a fortune, especially if he owns all the stock, which I can't tell here, but it's a likely bet."

"He has a lot at stake," I said. "No wonder he's so nervous. I think I'll nose around a little more, if you don't mind."

There was a short knock at the door. It opened a crack and Bill stuck his head in. "Jordan, what are you still doing here?" He frowned. "Tony?"

"Right," said Tony, turning off the computer with authority. "You are going to have your teeth examined. We can't have you going through life looking like White Fang. Bill's called his dentist, who will take you whenever you walk in. So let's get with the program. No discussion about this. We insist." He stood up, took me firmly by the elbow, and propelled me to the door. "I am going to drive you. Let's go."

Leaving the clinic compound, I noticed a mobile news van parked across the road, in the Heavenly Hash lot, but I didn't give it much thought—beyond the realization that they were finally getting a few customers.

Dentists' offices are notoriously similar. There is the receptionist with the clipboard and the computer; the patients sitting in silence in the waiting room, contemplating their imminent discomfort and wishing they were anywhere else; the months-old magazines and medical journals; and, usually, one dismembered but current newspaper, left by an earlier patient.

I checked in with the receptionist and settled down with an *American Gazette*. It was turned to page four, so I had to reassemble it. When I did, I saw the headline in a special banner at the top of the front page: DID SHE OR DIDN'T SHE? TENNIS WORLD IN UPROAR. There was a small inset picture of Dagmar. I didn't have to read the article to know what it said. And I realized that for this news to hit the front page of a national newspaper—and probably sports columns across the country—this quickly, someone had to work very fast. If you were the cynical type, you might almost think this entire incident and its follow-up had been planned and executed with the precision of the Normandy invasion, and that an entire press campaign was rehearsed and ready to release—before the alleged incident had even occurred.

The dentist spent around two hours probing inside my mouth. Between the cut on my lip, the bruises on my body, and the Novocaine to numb the grinding on my tooth, I wasn't in the mood for anything but sleeping.

Tony and I went back to my place, and he worked on his laptop while I took a nap. I woke up at four in the afternoon and decided to swing by the clinic bungalows to check on Dagmar. And, as long as I was in the vicinity, I wanted to slip briefly into the office to look up the numbers for Meg Zaresky's mother. I wasn't sure how I'd approach Janie. Whatever the truth was, as a mother she had to be beside herself about her daughter's situation.

Pulling up at the clinic gate, I saw about ten photographers and the mobile news crew camped out on the grass opposite the gatehouse. I rolled down the window and leaned toward the guard. "When did these guys get here?"

"They've been arriving all day," she said. "They keep asking me when Dagmar Olafsen is coming out."

"Are they trespassing or anything?" I asked hopefully.

"Not so far. That's a public easement they're on. We can't do anything about them."

With a rush, the reporters dashed up to my car, brandishing microphones and trailed by cameramen hoisting equipment. "Jordan Myles, would you care to comment on the fact that a Desert Springs client is alleged to have molested a Desert Springs intern?"

"No comment."

"Is Desert Springs hiding Dagmar Olafsen?"

"No, we're not. Beyond that, no comment." I rolled up my window and drove on, but one reporter ran after the car. Through the rearview mirror, I saw the cameraman racing to keep pace. He looked like he might keel over in the heat. When I looked ahead, a third person, a woman, was vaulting onto my hood, snapping shots through the windshield. I slammed on my brakes and yelled into the windshield, "Please get off my car! This is how people get run over."

"Would you care to comment on the First Lady's remarks?" The reporter with the microphone knocked on the window.

I put the window down again. "The First Lady?"

"The wife of the president of the United States. She's a tennis fan. She said at noon today, and I quote, 'This kind of contro-versy is a sad moment for every child who dreams of a sports career.'"

"I have nothing to say." I jabbed the gas and sped into the parking lot.

I had made it as far as the lobby when I saw Andy Fiero coming out of the office hallway. He was walking down the hall with a cell phone pressed to his ear.

"Andy?"

He flipped his phone shut. "Jordan! What happened to your lip?"

"Aggressive dentistry. I didn't know you were coming in. I thought you'd be at Wimbledon."

"We were just going over some final details of the licensing agreement when this comment from the White House broke. I was going to leave today, but now I don't think so. I'd better stick around for damage control."

"Surely there wouldn't be any damage to LaserGlass."

"This whole licensing co-venture could blow up in our faces, Jordan. Don't you realize that the First Lady has just made this a national issue? People are going to be forced to take sides in debates at every dinner table in America. It's not the ideal environment to launch a new venture, to say the least."

"How did this happen?"

"She and the vice president's wife had played a game of tennis, an exhibition for disabled children. A swarm of reporters was waiting, and of course one of them had the question and she made the comment."

"It doesn't sound like something a president's wife would comment on. Especially since nobody knows the facts yet. She's opening up a political hotbed."

"It's horrible, but how do you defuse the First Lady of the United States?"

"Do you have a plan?"

"Well, we do have Kevin. He's very plugged in in Washington, but he couldn't stop this thing. It's like a boulder rolling downhill." Andy sighed and looked up at the ceiling. "I can't believe it, Jordan. We all worked so hard. There was no downside to this venture. I talked LaserGlass into making this commitment—major financing was involved—and now this." He looked at me and I saw the hesitation behind his polished assurance. "This is bad, Jordan. I talked the company into staking a lot on the Desert Springs franchise. I made it a priority. It could cost me my job."

"Really? But it's not your fault."

"Too bad you're not on our board of directors."

I linked my arm through his. "It's a terrible thing for everybody," I said. "But most of all for Dagmar. I simply don't think she did what she's accused of."

"Then why did the girl accuse her?"

"Insecurity, maybe. Or maybe she misinterpreted something. Who knows? I know her mother. I'm going to call her. The worst she can do is hang up on me."

Andy sagged against the wall, as if it were the only thing propping him up. "I was going to go for a drive, just to clear my head. Maybe you'd like to come?"

"There's a base camp of press at the gate. We'd have to run the gauntlet. But I have a better idea. It's starting to cool off. I've got a clinic Jeep. We could head back behind the clinic, past the golf course, and up toward the mountains."

"Sounds great. I'll drop these papers and meet you."

"I'll be in the parking lot."

I had a lot in common with Andy, I realized. We were both potential victims.

FOURTEEN

At the very edge of the desert, the world as we know it comes to an end. The edge of the clinic golf course marks the edge of civilization, and the dropoff from manicured putting green to desolate sand-gray scrub desert is dramatic, as if the earth had been scorched by a close encounter with the sun sometime long ago. Mountains cup the region on either side, and an asphalt line of highway bisects the terrain. Homes of a few millionaires and celebrities dot the Chocolate Hills, but otherwise it is like the landscape of the moon—dusty, rocky, and pockmarked. I like to climb here sometimes, to be alone and isolated in the midst of this timeless scene. I knew a spectacular lookout point, and I drove the Jeep in that direction.

"Why do you think the First Lady would become involved in this?" I asked.

"She has aligned herself very strongly with the social issues platform. She heads a committee to help get American youth back to basics—wholesome values, strong work ethic."

"But there's no proof of any sort in this situation. Either way."

"Well, she doesn't specifically come out against Olafsen, just against situations like the one involving her and Meg Zaresky. It's an election year, you know." He stared straight ahead, ignoring the view. "It's only a matter of time before the clinic gets linked to this, and then LaserGlass."

"The clinic's already under fire," I said. "The reporters are all over us."

"Maybe I should look for a job while we're up here," Andy said, surveying the parched and desolate desert. "Say, landscape gardener." He pulled off his tie and stuffed it into his pocket.

"Don't be so hard on yourself, Andy. You're not at fault for anything. Nobody is."

"Frankly, and off the record, Kevin Curry was very opposed to this co-venture. He put up a royal stink over it, because—well, actually, once it goes through and the focus is off sunglasses as the only core business, his future role is unclear."

"I thought he was one of the top management team." I shifted gears and drove off the road and over the rugged terrain at a 45-degree angle. The Jeep bumped and swayed but was sure-footed in its climb.

"He is. For the sunglass business. But once we go beyond sunglasses, he's not as involved. So even if this expansion is better for the business as a whole, it's not necessarily better for his career."

"I see."

"He argued to the board that we'd be walking away from our roots, throwing our heritage in the trash, so to speak."

"What changed his mind?"

"Common sense. The upside was too obvious to ignore. Eventually, Kevin came around, and so did the board. I'm absolutely convinced that licensing is the way to expand our brand franchise and grow the business, and partners like the Desert Springs Sports Science Clinic are an ideal way to do it. I worked up a model that proves the payout—of course Kevin calls it theoretical, but who could program in this kind of complication? Some of our board members are going to have a heart attack when they hear about it. There's going to be a call for blood. Probably mine."

We reached a place that was flat enough to pull over and get out, and I stopped the car and set the emergency brake. "What kind of shoes do you have on?" I asked. "The rocks can get slippery."

Andy lifted a foot. "From our new line. Not even broken in."

"If we spend thirty minutes here, I guarantee we will feel better."

"About what?"

"Anything." We got out of the car, and Andy scanned the view.

"Not a good place for an attack of vertigo," he said. The clinic and, beyond it, the buildings of the town were spread out below us like loose gems that had spilled onto the rich green velvet of the lawns, crisscrossed by the geometrics of roads and highway. It had the feel of coming in for a landing in a small plane. For someone else, the view was no doubt spectacular, but since my accident I've had trouble appreciating heights. I walked around the front of the car and tried to sit on the hood, but it was too hot to be comfortable, so we found some rocks and perched there.

"Is this typical of the corporate world?" I asked.

"I don't know. Is it typical of the sports world?"

"I don't think anything is typical anymore." The sun was still high in the sky above the mountains.

"I think I offended you in Paris. I'm sorry about that. It's just that I was intimidated."

"By me? How so?"

"You're a former champion. You're very smart."

"So is Billie Jean King."

"Well, what did you think of *me*? I really want to know."

"I thought you were a suit. A walking calculator, figuring out how much you could squeeze out of your next deal, and we happened to be it."

"And what do you think now?"

I looked at him. "Maybe you know what you were. Maybe you're not too happy about it. I think you see the people behind the numbers now—and you happen to be one of them."

He laughed, a short, brittle bark. "True. So I am. Too bad things didn't turn out quite like the annual report I had in my head. God, was I stupid! I had everything covered except the human element."

"A minor detail."

"Now that I've admitted I was an idiot, will you forgive me for being so crassly capitalistic?"

"No problem."

"Can we start over?"

He really was endearing, in a naïve sort of way. Andy wasn't like most of the other people I knew—confident, physically trained, coordinated. His bravado was all on the surface, and now he was verging on bumbling, like an overgrown teenage boy. I had to smile. "I don't know what you're talking about." But of course he knew that I did.

"So what's the view like on the other side of this little ridge?"

"I've never gone over there because the car can't go any farther. I usually just sit here. Sometimes I read a book. I used to mountain-climb, but a few years ago that fall put me away for months and months. Since then, I've avoided scrambling around the mountains."

"It's probably just like riding a bike. When you fall, you should get right back up. Let me go check it out. This isn't exactly Mount Everest. It's not mountain climbing—it's hiking. I'll make sure there's a good path. Then I'll come back and get you. Or we'll go back down. Or just sit here a while longer. Whatever you say."

"Fine. I'll be here."

Andy pushed himself up with his hands, gave me the thumbs-up, and tramped off purposefully toward the ridge. I sat quietly for about fifteen minutes, just soaking in the solitude. Occasionally, I glanced toward the view, but it was still hard for me to appreciate heights. If I let myself, I could still remember what it felt like to fall, the terror of the ground rushing toward me.

"Jordan!" Andy's voice, thinned by distance but still sharp, broke the silence, carried on the clear high air. I supposed this was his way of getting me to hike over the ridge. Well, I thought, why not? I stood up, stretched, and picked my way along the rocky path, around a wide abutment, to a flat area that pointed out like the prow of a ship. There was no sign of Andy, but the path came to a dead end. I still had a lingering fear of falling, so I avoided the ledge and instead found small toeholds in the rock behind me and used them like a ladder, to shimmy up another ten feet in hopes of seeing around the edge of the next abutment. Planting my feet, I steadied myself and inched my way down. My breath was shallow and unsure.

"Hi," said Andy.

"You worried the hell out of me." I gasped. "I thought you'd fallen or run off with a mountain goat."

"See? You weren't thinking about being scared."

He was right. For the first time since the accident, I was on a mountain and I wasn't scared at all. It was exhilarating, all of a sudden.

"You did it," he said. "Now let's go."

"You tricked me," I grumbled.

"No. You would have done this sooner or later. How many times could you sit there in the car? Besides, I knew you'd think, 'If that wimp can do it, I can do it.' "

"Not true. I thought you might be dead or something."

"Oh, come on. Nobody's dying. Didn't you enjoy it?"

"I won't be crawling around up here again anytime soon." We hiked back to the Jeep and drove down the steep mountainside to the Springs. I dropped Andy at his car and dashed into the building to pick up a few papers. Tony was still working at the computer.

"Jordan, I'm getting some interesting information," he said.

"Show me." I leaned over his shoulder, and he tinkered with the keyboard for about fifteen minutes.

"Sorry," Tony finally said. "Looks like it'll be a few more minutes. But I'm close—real close."

I realized that I still hadn't called Janie, Meg's mother. But I also hadn't fed or walked A.M. in a very long time. "Hey, Tony, it's getting late. Maybe you could do me a huge favor and run out and feed and walk A.M. Then you could come back and pick me up and we could grab a bite to eat. I'm exhausted, but I have to make this call." I looked up. "If you've got something else to do, that's fine. I'll understand."

"No problem, Jordan. Where do you want to eat?" He stood up and stretched.

"Wherever." I was already distracted, sorting through papers to try to find Janie's number. "The keys are in the car."

"Back in a flash."

I didn't hear Tony leave; I was too busy figuring out what I was going to say to Janie, in case she answered the phone. A few minutes later, just as I was dialing, a shuddering boom rocked my office, jolting the phone receiver out of my hand and onto the tabletop. The entire building shook. I leaped up and raced down the hall. Everybody seemed to be swarming toward the exits. When I reached the lobby, I could see that the entire glass picture window in the reception area was blown out. Jana, the receptionist, stood sobbing and dabbing at cuts on her face. Glittering bits of broken glass covered the lobby floor, like tiny crystal daggers. People started swarming into the lobby, and Andy found me and gripped my arm. Terrified of what I might see, I looked out through the jagged, gaping hole of what was left of the window and my breath completely stopped. Inside a cloud of thick black smoke, a molten fireball raged on the spot where I had parked my Jeep. Small pools of flames blazed on the asphalt of the parking lot.

Tony.

"She's still in shock," Gus said, talking about me as if I were a patient or a third party who couldn't hear. He had flown back to the Springs immediately upon hearing the news two weeks ago.

As in any crisis, he was adept at dealing with the aftermath, a trained psychologist who could do everything except turn back the clock and prevent the problem. The entire Springs senior staff had flown to Chicago for Tony's funeral, and the clinic had closed for the day in remembrance. Andy attended the funeral with me, then returned to LaserGlass headquarters in New Jersey. The glaziers had repaired the plate glass window. The incinerated Jeep had been declared police evidence and removed from the scene. The yellow tape that marked off the location of the explosion had been removed from the parking lot. Dagmar received a death threat and left the complex for security reasons; she and Woody went to Europe to complete her rehab and training for the Crown Jewel. Wimbledon wound to a close, with Heather losing in the semifinals to a Romanian newcomer.

Life went on, but for me there was no refuge. I had to live not only with the loss of a dear friend but with the fact that Tony had died instead of me. It could have, should have been me. Tony had been such a big part of my life—even my house was filled with reminders of him, since he had been staying with me when he was killed. I had carefully boxed up all his clothes and belongings, including his prized French copper omelet pan and professional knife set, and sent them to his parents in Chicago. At the funeral, his sisters had put their arms around me and assured me that they didn't blame me, but his mother couldn't look at me. I knew I would blame myself for Tony's death for the rest of my life, just as I would miss him for the rest of my life. The night of Tony's funeral, in a hotel in Chicago, I cried myself to sleep.

Catherine. Mila. Noel Fisher. Tony. I was not quite so self-centered to think that they were all dead, or threatened with death, because of me, but I knew I was connected to some reason why they had all died, or almost died. There was a link forged in blood that I had so far managed to escape. I also knew that nothing short of my own death would stop me from finding it.

I became incensed with a fury I had never known. The anger replaced the sadness and allowed me to function. I spent hours in my office, unable to return home. Even A.M. mourned, in her own way, waiting patiently for Tony to return and slip her a forbidden treat. Outside my door today, at the desk where Tony had worked, sat one of three round-the-clock bodyguards the clinic had hired for me. Paula looked like a secretary, in her business suit and silk shirt, but she had a black belt in karate and was capable of shooting the eye out of a needle with the pistol in her shoulder holster. I supposed I was safe, but I didn't care. I only cared about finding who killed Tony, and I resolved to do so with every ounce of energy in my body.

Now, two weeks after Tony's death, I was finally able to make the call to Janie.

"Good grief, Jordan. I don't know whether to tell you I'm glad to hear from you or to cry," she said, upon hearing my voice for the first time in years. "I've heard about everything, of course. That car bomb at the clinic. It's terrible. I'm so sorry."

"It's surreal," I said. "Things can't get much worse. But, Janie, maybe we can talk about Meg for a minute."

"Meg? What about her? Where is she?" Janie's voice was anxious.

"I don't know at the moment, but this lawsuit, the harassment issue—"

"Frankly, Jordan, I read about it and I was very upset. I tried to reach Meg, but she never calls me back, and now I don't know where she is. Meg and I—well, we don't keep in touch. She lives with her father." She laughed bitterly. "If you can believe it, when we got divorced, he won custody. Meg was very young and I traveled too much, the judge said. God, if I hadn't traveled, who would have paid the bills? Anyhow, after she started living with her father, the custody agreement got more and more loose. Some holidays, he would keep her. Some summers, I was on the road, so she was better off with him. She just drifted away from me, and I saw less and less of her as she got older. Now I never hear from her. I can't stand it."

"I'm so sorry, Janie. But didn't you refer her to me as an intern?"

"No. She never asked me about being an intern. She must have done that on her own. Well, at least she's resourceful. This—harassment suit. Tell me the truth. What happened?"

"Nobody really knows, except Meg and Dagmar. But it seems blown out of proportion. The way Meg was talking to the press right away—do you think she's so sophisticated that she would be calling the tabloids?"

"I don't know what she'd do. I really don't anymore."

"So you haven't heard from her?"

"No. Not for at least three months. She sent me a forwarding address then—in LA. I suppose she's still there. And she attached a note. She'd gotten a part-time job that paid really well."

"Before she came to the clinic?"

"Yes. With a talent agency."

Talent agency. There were hundreds of them in LA. Still . . . "Does the name Jimmy Bennett mean anything to you?" I asked.

"No. Meg didn't mention anyone's name."

"What about the company? Could it have been TalentMasters?"

Janie paused. "I don't think she ever told me the name of her company either. It was a very brief conversation. Like most of our conversations, I'm afraid."

"What about her father? Do you know how I can reach him?"

I could sense over the phone that Janie bristled.

"I don't mean to intrude on your personal life, but this could be very important to Meg. She's young, Janie, and naïve. I think she's being manipulated by some very slick operators. In the process, innocent people may be destroyed. One day she's going to wake up and realize what she did, and she'll never forgive herself. I know you wouldn't want that." I couldn't tell her what was in the back of my mind—that Meg could find herself in the same kind of jeopardy as Catherine had. If she knew too much, came too close, her own life could be in terrible danger, perhaps at this very minute.

Janie gave me her ex-husband's addresses and phone numbers. He worked at a carpet showroom in Los Angeles. "Let me know when you find her, will you?" she asked quietly.

"You can be sure of it, Janie."

"Tell her—I love her."

"I will, Janie. I'll see that she calls you."

I was sitting grimly at my desk when Gus came in. His denim shirt was rolled up at the sleeves and he was polishing his glasses on it. He had his usual placid air, an unruffled surface that masked his turbulent intelligence. Our relationship had had many incarnations, but I had never figured him out. Since Tony's death, however, it was clear that Gus was making an effort to drop by my office or my house on a more or less regular basis.

"How're you doing?" he asked.

"Lousy."

Gus leaned over and scooped A.M. under his arm as he walked in. He had no comeback because I knew he felt lousy too. We all did.

"Guess what?" I said.

"I hate games. You know that."

"I'm betting that Meg Zaresky is connected to Jimmy Bennett. I just talked to her mother. Meg worked for a talent agency before she came here. And she lied when she said her mother had her apply for an internship. Janie hasn't spoken to her in months; they've been estranged for years. I think Bennett put her up for the job to get somebody on the inside."

Gus sat on the edge of my table. "Why would he do that?"

"Any number of reasons. A: to get a story on Dagmar that Heather could use as a competitive advantage. Or B: to snoop around and find out what I know about his assistant's murder."

"Isn't it possible that Meg just used her mother's name on her own to get an edge on the internship? Kids have been known to do such things." Gus rubbed the wire frames of his glasses on

A.M.'s forehead. "How can you prove she was working for Bennett?"

"That part, my friend, is easy. We're going to surf the net."

Of course we had her Social Security number, and within two hours Jason had located a routine credit check for Meg Zaresky that had been conducted when she applied to rent an apartment in Los Angeles. On it, she listed TalentMasters as her employer.

"Did this girl know Catherine?" I asked Jason.

"I don't think so. At least it's not a name I heard."

"Well, in any case they had something in common."

"What's that?"

"A weakness for whatever bait Jimmy Bennett was throwing around. Mr. Bennett seems especially adept at luring young women into his fold and deploying them for his purposes. I think he gave Meg a script, and she followed it. That entire harassment thing had to be a setup, either a PR stunt or just plain character assassination to benefit his client."

"And what was Jimmy Bennett's purpose for Catherine?"

"What did you find out about that last fax you made for Catherine?"

"I got the phone number. It was the French Tennis Federation. Roland Garros Stadium."

"Which makes sense, since she faxed you a list of tennis players. I'm sure he was manipulating Catherine. Maybe using her somehow to undermine Dagmar, the way he was using Meg."

"I'll kill him."

The emotionless tone of his voice frightened me. "Please, Jason. I know how you feel. But give me the fax number. I can probably trace the exact office in Roland Garros, see whose line was at the other end. Maybe it was Jimmy."

"Where's the little creep now?"

"Probably in Las Vegas, doing advance work for his tournament. It starts this weekend, you know."

"Are you going?"

"I wasn't planning to. Until now." I decided to leave in the morning, with a quick detour through LA—to shop for some new carpeting.

Before I left the office to go home and pack for Las Vegas, I put in a call to my friend Arlene at the Women's Tennis Foundation in St. Petersburg. It was late there, but Arlene was in administration and she always stayed after hours. When I'd been on the tour, Arlene was the one I always called for the practical details—itinerary information, how to get messages through to people, credentials details. She had access to tournament records and the names and numbers of all Grand Slam officials and administration staff members. The extensions at Roland Garros would be relatively easy to track down, since it was also the headquarters of the French Tennis Federation.

"God, Jordan, we all feel so sorry about Tony," was the first thing Arlene said. "I talked to him every week. He was like family." She started to cry. "I'm sorry. It has to be awful for you. I'm not helping." I could hear her blowing her nose. "Now. What can I do to help? Anything!"

"Actually, Arlene, there *is* something. If I gave you a number at Roland Garros, and a date, around the time of the French Open, could you tell me whose extension it is?"

"Probably. What is it?"

I gave her the numbers.

"You need this right away?"

"Can you get it right away?"

"I'm going to put you on hold, okay?"

Within five minutes, Arlene was back on the line. "It's not a phone—it's a fax number."

"I know. But whose?"

"Nobody's. It's a line to their central data system."

"What happens on there?"

"They keep the files, the records. That system probably is similar to ours, since it's the French Federation. They'd have all

the files of all the French players, all the Federation correspondence, but if the Open was happening, they'd also have information like the draw—"

"The draw. Records of the official draw?"

"That's probably where they'd be, yes."

"Could somebody get records of the draw for the French
Open off that database?"

"*Somebody* might be able to, but not you or me or the average
person. We'd be going through, say, the press office or tournament officials. The Federation system would be like ours—you'd
have to know what they call an encryption key to get into it, and
only certain people would know that key."

"What sort of key?"

"A computer code, a series of numbers, like a PIN number."

"Could I figure it out?" My antennae shot up. *A number.*
Maybe like the number on the back of Catherine's business card.

"Let me put it this way—only if you were some kind of genius
hacker, like that kid who broke into the Pentagon system."

"What if you were trained in encryptions?" The key would
have been Catherine's proof of what she had done.

"Oh, well, then it's conceivable. But why would anybody
want to do that?"

"Do you think they would use the same computer system to
set the draw as well as to keep records?"

"Well, *we* use a centralized system. I'd be surprised if they
didn't in France."

"Could a person with access to the system via the encryption
key change the draw somehow? Would that be possible?"

"Hm. Theoretically, I suppose it would. Although I don't think
there's a record of its ever happening."

"But there *wouldn't* be any record, would there, if somebody
got into the system at the right time and place?"

"Sometimes they put technical booby traps into these systems
for security reasons."

"Would they have done that at Roland Garros?"

"Listen, let's face it. If some nut who's determined enough can get past guards during a tournament in play and get onto the court and knife a number-one player in the back in front of thousands of fans, I'd say there's certainly a chance that somebody could get into the French Federation computer system. The question is, why would they want to?"

"I agree, Arlene," I said. "That *is* the question."

I hung up, fairly certain that Catherine had managed to get an unwitting Jason to tap into the French Federation system with a code that was factored into the fax transmission but was meaningless to him, as she knew it would be. She would have realized, of course, that he knew very little about tennis. To Jason, a list of player names was just a list of names. The number would have seemed like a phone number. No alarm bells would have gone off. In fact, hadn't Jason said the number on the back of Catherine's business card had seemed familiar?

Catherine said she had done Heather a favor. It must have been important for Heather to be in a certain part of the opening draw for some reason, and that reason had been determined in advance. It was clear to me that Catherine had been targeted and recruited by Jimmy Bennett not for romance but specifically for her extraordinary computer skills, to ensure that she would be able to execute certain computer maneuvers for his own questionable purposes.

I had some facts now, and I intended to see to it that the Crown Jewel, the richest tournament in tennis history, would be Jimmy Bennett's last.

Before I left for Las Vegas the next morning, I tried to reach Jason. He was out of the office, so I left a message on his machine at home, asking him to meet me in Las Vegas, at the Olympus Hotel, and leaving details. First, however, I felt a pressing need to buy some carpet in LA.

FIFTEEN

A certain part of Pico Avenue east of the 405 is dotted with the mid-range to discount furniture stores and carpet shops of Los Angeles, and apparently this was where Terry Zaresky, Janie's ex-husband and Meg's father, worked. I wore a half-hearted disguise consisting of a scarf and sunglasses. I hadn't seen Terry in at least fifteen years, and it was doubtful if he would recognize me in any case. I parked the car Tony had leased for me while we were waiting for the motorcycle to be repaired, cracked the window, and left A.M. to guard the floor mats. My bodyguard, Dan, was left in the backseat to guard A.M.

Carpet World was typical of its genre: swatches of shags, plush, and indoor-outdoor carpets vying with stacks of remnants for floor space. Books of samples were stacked on tabletops. A woman pushing a baby stroller and an elderly couple were the only other customers, and the sole salesman was on the phone. I browsed a pile of plush for a few minutes, while the salesman talked with the young mother. The elderly couple left. After a few minutes, I heard the young mother say she was just looking. The salesman came over to me.

"May I help you?"

You sure can, I thought. He was tall, in good shape for what looked like about forty-five years old, with thick dark hair, side-parted, and features so much like Meg's I knew I had found Terry Zaresky. "I need something for my dining room," I said, trying to recall what he had looked like fifteen years ago. It was ridiculous to have thought that either of us could have recognized the other. "Something in neutral."

"We have some very nice Berbers. And this line over here is on sale, fifteen ninety-nine a yard, pad and installation included."

"What about shag? Are these spot-resistant?" I knew absolutely nothing about carpet, but I kept the conversation going for a few more minutes. Finally I picked up a sample. "How much would this one cost if I took it for a bedroom fifteen by twelve feet?"

"I thought you were looking for the dining room."

"The bedroom too. And how long till I can get it delivered?"

"I'll have to check." I followed him to his desk, where he sat down and rifled through a notebook. There were two framed pictures on his desk. One was of him and a huge harlequin Great Dane. The other was Meg.

"Is this your daughter? She's lovely."

"Thank you."

"I suppose she's out of school for the summer."

"No, she's a go-getter, that one. She's got a job at a talent agency."

"My sister works at CAA. Maybe they know each other?"

"No, she's at TalentMasters. They're new, but very hot. They specialize in sports." He smiled and looked up. "Good news. We've got the shag in stock. No delay."

"You know, if I could have your card—I'd like to think about it."

His smile never faltered. It was the smile of a man who was used to people not buying carpet. "I'll be here all day, except I'm leaving for lunch in a few minutes. We're open till seven to-night." We shook hands and I left.

I unlocked the car, took a bottle of Evian out of the glove compartment, and poured half of it into a paper cup for A.M. After she'd finished drinking I drove over to Maple Drive, to TalentMasters. I parked on the street, then tucked A.M. into my backpack and went inside. Dan waited with the car. I felt sorry for him, but I had learned on the drive from Palm Springs that Dan was a monosyllabic conversationalist. He was being paid to watch, not to talk, and it showed. Since you could see through the glass doors of the TalentMasters lobby from the street, he was fine with waiting outside again.

"I'd like to see Meg Zaresky," I said to the receptionist. "What floor is she on?"

"Three, but you can't go up unless you've got an appointment." The British receptionist had the usual orders.

"Tell her her father sent me." I showed the receptionist Terry's card, and she nodded and dialed the phone.

Three minutes later, the elevator doors opened and Meg appeared. Her mouth dropped when she saw me, and she stood frozen to the spot.

"Hi, Meg," I said. "I just saw your dad." I produced the card. "He thought we should have lunch." I knew that Jimmy was in Las Vegas. Meg was probably on her own for the time being, with orders to talk to nobody.

"Dad thought that?" She frowned.

"There's a restaurant in the building." I gripped her arm firmly. "Let's grab a bite." I walked her toward the door. Meg was clearly confused. She wasn't sure whether she should stay where she was or go with me.

"Maybe I should call my dad," she said quickly.

"Good idea." I nodded.

There was a courtesy phone on a corner table. Meg walked over and made the call. Terry Zaresky had said he was going to lunch, and I hoped it was a long one. Meg hung up without speaking, so I was in luck.

"It'll be fast," I promised. Meg looked uncertain as we walked out, but she came with me.

The restaurant was glass-fronted and just beside the entrance of the building. It was a casually elegant Beverly Hills hangout, where torn jeans mixed with Armani suits. We settled in with menus that neither of us opened, and the waiter took an order for two iced teas. Since there are always dog ordinances in food establishments, A.M. remained hidden in my backpack, on the floor beside the table, as she did wherever she went where she was forbidden. A few minutes after we were seated, I noticed Dan the bodyguard take a seat at the bar. I felt sorry for the guy. I felt like sending him a sandwich or something.

"What did my dad want?" Meg asked.

"First let's talk about the lawsuit."

"I'm not supposed to," Meg said.

"Fine. Then I'll talk about it. You're being used, Meg."

Her lips tightened and she stared at me defiantly.

"Jimmy Bennett used another young woman who worked for him. Her name was Catherine Richie and she's dead. Perhaps you heard her name around the office."

"It was an accident," Meg said, her voice barely audible.

"It was murder, Meg. Stop deluding yourself." The waiter set our iced teas at our places. "Catherine was a computer whiz. Jimmy recruited her and hired her to hack into certain systems and databases. I don't care what you've heard. That was the fact. When she was no longer useful, when she quit, she was murdered."

Meg put her hands over her ears. "I refuse to listen to this. I'm leaving." She started to stand up.

"Maybe you have a death wish," I said. "Meg, I believe you're in very serious danger. Too many people are dead or missing. Do you want to be next?"

"I don't believe you," she said.

"What about Tony? He was your friend."

Her face softened. "I heard about Tony."

"Somebody blew up a car that he happened to start. He was murdered just like Catherine. Tony liked you, Meg. He tried to help you. You should have some feelings about that. If you don't care about yourself, you should at least care about Tony."

Meg sank slowly back into her seat, as if the bones in her legs had suddenly dissolved.

"What makes you think you'll come out of this any better than Catherine?" I asked. "Those abuse charges are not going to stick. As I'm sure you're aware, sexual abuse is a very hard thing to prove in any case. You're the one whose name is going to get dragged through the mud by Dagmar's attorneys, who will do what they have to do. Are you ready for this? If anyone coached you to say that Dagmar came on to you, you should rethink this immediately. Worse, when it's over, when they've gotten their public relations buzz, what will happen to you? You're not even out of school. This will stick with you the rest of your life. Unless you're too dangerous to have around—like Catherine was. Or you get in the way—like Tony did."

Meg blinked away tears, her face white.

"I knew you when you were a baby, Meg. Whatever you're being paid at that place isn't worth it. It's blood money. Your mother and father both love you. Don't do this to them."

Meg's tears splashed on the white tablecloth. "It was supposed to be a little thing, like a—joke. Just some PR for the tournament. But then the First Lady got into it."

"How do you think the First Lady got into it?"

"I guess she read about it."

"Let me fill you in. What the First Lady says and does is very carefully orchestrated. No public position is by chance. This was brought to her attention by powerful people who have something at stake. You were just a pawn. Like I said, they are using you. I can understand how someone might try to do that. What I can't understand is why you'd let it happen." A white-coated waiter headed in our direction, dropped menus on the table, opened his mouth to introduce himself and recite specials, then noticed Meg's tears and backed off.

Meg drew herself up stiffly. "You can't? Does your father work twelve hours a day selling carpet so you can go to school? Mine does. His business is bad, really bad. Nobody's buying carpet anymore. I helped at the store, I saw how hard it was for him. He used to have a wonderful business, a contracting business. Now all he has is this carpet thing, and it's not much. I wanted to help him."

"Do you really think that lying and hurting other people and, in the end, putting yourself in danger is *helping* him?"

"That's not how it started out. I was just going to be an intern at TalentMasters. It seemed like such a great opportunity."

"Why did you apply to the clinic?"

"Mr. Bennett suggested it might be a good way to round out my experience. Actually, he sent in the application for me. He said he knew people there."

And he would have known that Janie's name would pull some weight and that, given her distance from the tour and the fact that we were all preoccupied in France, it was unlikely that anyone would try to contact her.

"Once you got to the clinic, did Jimmy ask you to do anything?"

"He asked me to find some papers, notes of yours. I never found them."

"What about Dagmar?"

"He said it was part of a publicity plan."

"You had to know better, Meg."

She nodded miserably. "There was a very big bonus. And my dad needed the money, so—"

"A bonus?"

"Fifty thousand dollars if I did what Mr. Bennett asked. And I'd get a full-time job with TalentMasters. But I never thought it would turn out this way."

Jimmy certainly had a pattern of picking young, susceptible women and using them to do his dirty work.

"Did Dagmar actually try to molest you, Meg?"

"No." Her shoulders sagged with hopelessness. "I was supposed to say she did so the press would make a big deal of it and everybody would want to come the Crown Jewel and root for Heather. That was the PR angle."

"What about what it did to Dagmar? Didn't anybody ever think of that? The impact of these kinds of charges on an innocent person?"

"I thought of it," Meg said quietly.

"And?"

"I asked Mr. Bennett first thing. He said not to worry, that Dagmar knew it was going to happen and she'd go right along with it. It was like a script. That's why I didn't think it was all that wrong; that's why I did it."

This stopped me cold. Was it possible that Dagmar *really* knew, or was this another of Jimmy Bennett's manipulative lies? Meg mentioned a script. What if the entire episode had been just that: a massive stunt to escalate the rivalry between Heather and Dagmar, to drum up attention for them at the Crown Jewel? It didn't seem possible—there was no benefit to Dagmar, and her entire career and all her hard work at the comeback was at risk.

"Did you ever speak to Dagmar about this yourself?" I asked. "Do you know for a fact that she knew about this scheme?"

"Well, that's what Mr. Bennett said."

Jimmy, of course, could be counted on to say whatever it took.

"Meg," I said. "Some terrible things have happened, but, believe me, it can get much worse, especially for you. The thing is, you have to look at yourself responsibly in light of what you know now, not based on something Jimmy Bennett told you."

She looked frightened. "I don't know what to do. Everything is such a mess."

"I'm on my way to Las Vegas. Do you think you could come along and talk to Jimmy with me, face-to-face?"

"No! No, I can't do that." Meg gripped the edge of the table so tightly that the tablecloth inched toward her. "He can't even know that I talked to you! Maybe I didn't understand. Maybe he didn't tell me anything!"

Making Meg feel trapped and cornered, perhaps hysterical, would not help things now. Besides, I wasn't about to sit here and put a young girl's back up against the wall, pressure her into answers that would not hold up later and would only panic her now. "Then let's start with something you can do," I said. "Your mother wants to see you. Why don't you give her a call."

By sunset, A.M. and I were in Las Vegas. You know you are in Las Vegas from the moment you land there, because McCarran International Airport is like a giant fusion of mall and arcade. The first sights when you step off the plane are slot machines with names like Dream 7's and Cherry Delight, inviting you to feed them money, and the first sound is the clink of coins hitting the tray as someone wins—the city's siren song.

The clinic had booked a suite for me at the Grand Olympus Hotel, which was the newest extravaganza on the Strip and the host hotel to the Crown Jewel. As the sun was setting, the Strip generated its own brand of daylight: neon lights in every color, shape, and configuration—blinking, pulsing, twinkling, beckoning. Like a hooker in a sequin dress, the town can look worn and overdone by day, but at night it shimmied and glittered.

Traffic on the Strip was bumper to bumper as my cab crawled toward the Grand Olympus. Located in the heart of the newer part of the action, virtually next door to Caesar's Palace and the Mirage, the hotel was debuting its new fourteen-thousand-seat, all-weather, indoor-outdoor dome complex with the Crown Jewel tournament. Because of the extreme heat of summer temperatures, in the hundred-and-teens, Las Vegas has always been a problem for sports events there, but the Olympus had solved it by installing this incredible dome setup. The domes were automated to roll back during good weather but could be closed up whenever needed. For this tournament they would be setting up three courts, one under each of the three domes.

The field at the Crown Jewel was a select four players: Harriet Craig, the number-one woman player; Celine Gilbert, the number three; plus Heather and Dagmar. The money was exceptional—appearance fees of half a million dollars to each player, guaranteed win or lose, plus another half million to the winner. Also, this was an opportunity for the top players to prepare for the upcoming U.S. Open. The all-court championship was scheduled to last two days—a semifinal and a final. Part of the excitement arose from the players' being unaware of what surface they'd draw, had to practice on all three—clay, grass, and hard courts.

"Welcome to the Grand Olympus," said the doorman as he swept the cab door open. He was wearing a robe, a crown, and a lightning bolt: only in Las Vegas. I handed him A.M. and climbed out, followed by Dan on the other side. The hotel itself was a majestic cerulean-blue mirrored-glass structure, angled upward in the style of a mountain. A gigantic neon lightning bolt slashed its way from the top of the building down the side to just above street level. It coordinated nicely with the hundred-foot-high "volcano" fountain that was erupting spectacularly in twin rings of water and fire across the street at the Mirage, a tourist attraction in itself.

While we waited at the check-in desk, I looked around. Brochures about the Crown Jewel were stacked on the pink marble counter. White-shirted dealers and tuxedoed croupiers led the action at the tables, while waitresses in Greek mini-togas and gold stiletto sandals circulated through the crowd. A bank of video keno machines was in full use. The room was chilly and serious, full of the feeling of money changing hands.

"Please tell Mr. Jimmy Bennett that I'd like to see him as soon as possible," I told the clerk.

"He's holding a champagne press conference in an hour," he

said. "They are setting up in the Neptune Room, and I'm not sure where he is right now, but I'll leave a message with his pager."

Dan accompanied me to my suite, where he sat in the living room, leafing through a magazine. In about an hour, he would be replaced by the night shift bodyguard, someone they had hired in Las Vegas. I ordered A.M. a rare hamburger from room service and flicked on the TV. Jimmy Bennett's face appeared on the screen.

"You're going to see some incredible action, I think, Jane," he was telling a CNN interviewer. "We have Harriet Craig, number one in the world. We have Celine Gilbert, number three, the woman with the fastest serve in the world. We have Heather Knight, making her phenomenal comeback—you know she came close at Wimbledon this year, and when have we ever heard a comeback story like this one? And then there's Dagmar Olafsen, a master of the clay court. A very controversial woman right now, but nothing about her game is controversial. She's got what it takes. As an interesting sidebar, Dagmar and Heather have been locked in a head-to-head rivalry on and off court this year. It should be a fascinating match, with the biggest prize money in history at stake. No tennis fan should miss this tournament."

I switched off the set. There was a knock at the door. Dan answered it warily and let in room service with the hamburger. I scraped off the fries, broke the burger into little bites, and left the plate on the floor for A.M., who looked at me as if to say, "What? No fries?"

Quickly, I changed out of my jeans and into a tailored pants suit and heels. These press conferences were usually dressy events, and I wanted to be able to blend in with the crowd if I had to. There was still half an hour before this one began, and I wanted to catch Jimmy off guard.

Dan and I got to the Neptune Room just as a phalanx of waiters was pushing in a flotilla of carts stacked with bottles of chilled champagne. The room's undersea motif extended to the walls, which were lined floor to ceiling with huge aquariums filled with a rainbow assortment of tropical fish. A huge screen was set up at the front of the room, as well as four thronelike seats and a podium with a microphone. Two TV camera crews were set up by the gold-lamé-draped podium. Stacks of press kits were neatly aligned on long tables swagged in purple velvet, and gigantic purple velvet banners with the Crown Jewel logo of a jeweled crown and scepter hung from the ceiling. At the back of the room, ten trumpeters in white togas stood at the ready on risers. A woman in a strapless with a clipboard and wireless miked headphones circled the room, directing the action.

"The players will enter from the grand parade and will be seated here." She indicated the thrones. "The mayor of Las Vegas will present them with keys to the city. We will show film clips of each of them winning various championships, in a montage. Then Jimmy will speak for approximately ten minutes, after which there will be an open Q and A from the floor." She motioned to the headwaiter. "Champagne will be served and we hope to conclude by nine."

I sat quietly off to one side. Dan took a seat in the row behind me.

"Jimmy, where do you want the champagne? I think it's distracting up front. It could block their view of the podium."

Jimmy hurried in through an open side doorway, adjusting a lapel microphone and trailed by a note-taking assistant and a security guard. "Is the money set?" he asked.

"Right here, Jimmy," said an assistant, indicating a large gilded wheelbarrow that appeared to be stacked with bundles of cash. The wheelbarrow was piloted by a showgirl in a gold sequin evening gown, flanked by two Brinks guards. The girl tripped on the carpet.

"Have her practice pushing," ordered Jimmy. "Are we ready at the main entrance? Is the mayor here?"

"His Honor is pulling up now."

"Are the people from Equinox taken care of?"

"Check."

"Let's go!" Jimmy snapped his fingers and headed down the aisle toward the ballroom doors.

I stepped into the aisle. "Hello, Jimmy. Do you have a minute?" I pretended not to know this was the most inconvenient time possible.

Jimmy glared at me. "Where's your invitation, Jordan?"

"Dagmar has it," I said. "She's my client. I'm part of her training team. If she doesn't see me here, her motivation will be affected." Jimmy laughed, and I said, "It would be best if we talked now."

"You're finished in this industry, Jordan. You have zero credibility. After this tournament, I'll see to it that your only involvement with sports is watching the late news. Bill is going to get you voted off the staff of the Springs. You're going to take early retirement." He swept past me. "Security, please eighty-six this woman off the premises."

A guard materialized. "This is private property, miss. You'll have to leave."

Dan stepped between us, and I pushed him aside.

"I have a sworn statement from Meg Zaresky," I called out.

Jimmy froze, then turned slowly back toward me. "Sworn to what?"

"I think you know."

He stared at me through narrowed eyes, a gambler assessing the odds of his opponent's hand. "I don't believe you." He turned and kept walking.

"You still want to throw me out?" I called after him. "I'll have my own press conference at the edge of the property right now." Jimmy happened to be right. I didn't have any signed statement from Meg, at least not yet. But I was prepared to bluff for time—and he had far more to lose. Members of the press were starting to filter into the room.

I followed Jimmy to the front lobby, which was a swarm of activity. A wide red carpet had been laid down, flanked by velvet ropes. "Stop right there," said a guard as Jimmy ducked under the ropes and sprinted outside.

For the next few minutes, I was jostled by the crowd as I edged toward the entrance, causing Dan, who was overdue to be replaced by the night man, to break out in a sweat. Under a crimson canopy, Jimmy, the mayor, Kevin Curry, a woman in a white Chanel suit, Kelly Kendall, and a dignified Japanese gentleman posed for the press. I noticed a large contingent of Japanese in the VIP area, including the Sumo wrestler type acupuncturist from the French Open. Clearly, this was the Equinox sponsor group. Suddenly a trumpet volley announced the arrival of the players in four horse-drawn golden chariots, each driven by men in ancient Greek battle garb, complete with breastplates and plumed helmets. Harriet came first, followed by Celine, Heather, and then Dagmar. Each horse came to a halt under the hotel marquee and a togaed and sandaled muscleman stepped forward with a scroll.

"In the name of the gods of Mount Olympus and the Grand Olympus Hotel, I welcome these championship athletes to the Crown Jewel Tournament. Let the games begin!"

The crowd applauded, cameras flashed, and each player was escorted out of her chariot by an Adonis-like muscleman. I noticed that many people in the crowd were wearing buttons proclaiming their support of their favorite player: I PICKED HARRIET! or MY MONEY'S ON HEATHER! Harriet, I noticed, seemed almost bothered by all the fuss and had on a professional face, a smiling mask. When I looked closely, her eyes were red-rimmed as if she'd been crying. Celine was expressionless. This was clearly a walk-through for her. Dagmar, on the other hand, looked embarrassed. Only Heather seemed to be enjoying herself, smiling and waving to the crowd and the cameras. Jimmy, the mayor, and the sponsors greeted each woman, and each was handed a massive bouquet of red roses. After this formal greeting, a procession formed down the red carpet and into the ballroom. I struggled to the front of the crowd to get Dagmar's attention. "Dagmar!" I called out.

She looked at me in surprise and gave a little wave with her roses.

"Where's Woody? I've got to talk to you both!"

She nodded, but there was no way we could communicate any further. As the group swept into the ballroom, a security guard stepped in front of me and stood there firmly until the doors were closed.

I looked around for Dan, but we had gotten separated in the confusion of the grand entrance. I then found myself between two extremely large guards, one gripping each of my arms, and being propelled through the crowd. I struggled but could not break free, and I quickly found myself deposited at a service entrance.

"Hey!" I yelled. "Let go of me!" Nobody heard my voice, as a trumpet fanfare echoed through the lobby.

Backing through the door, the two men pulled me along as I struggled, and I could see that at least one of them was wearing a shoulder holster. I managed to wrench an arm free and elbow one of them in the diaphragm and bring my heel down on the instep of the other. There was absolutely no way in hell that I was going down that service hall. These so-called guards were clearly not legitimate hotel security. Casino security is never armed. There are too many people on the casino floor to risk the downside. Except in extreme cases, the role of house security is usually limited to getting problem people off the premises, where the police can step in to carry out any really serious action. You could probably blatantly rob a casino of millions of dollars and walk out unrestrained with the money—although you would be arrested the minute you stepped out the door.

I realized that no one would hear me if I screamed for help here in the bowels of the service corridor, with only the air-conditioning vents as my witness. It was possible I was simply being ejected from the premises, but I was certainly not going to take the chance and allow myself to be ushered into oblivion. I felt a hand grasp my shoulder from behind, a third man. The odds in my favor were definitely decreasing, and I knew I had to act before they got any worse. I feinted to the left, then tripped one of the men as he lunged toward me. Whirling around, head down, chin tucked, I bulldozed my shoulder into the man behind me, shoving him off balance as I charged back toward the exit.

"Jordan!" yelled a voice from the floor, and I froze where I stood.

It was Noel Fisher.

SIXTEEN

"**I** ought to kill you for not being dead. For a while there, I thought you were," I said to the Fish as we sat at the bar. For a guy who had almost died, he looked remarkably robust.

"Good," he said. "That was the point."

"But why?" I refrained from telling him how distraught I'd been about his disappearance. He probably knew. In retrospect, my being distraught was probably key to making his disappearance seem legitimate. "I do deserve some sort of explanation," I said.

"It was necessary to work behind the scenes. I was just sitting there like a target. Besides, it was almost true. I practically lost it dragging myself out of that room."

"How'd you do it? You were completely immobile when I saw you. Barely breathing. To be honest, I wasn't sure you were going to make it."

He nodded and blotted some sweat off his forehead with a paper cocktail napkin. "Neither was I. But I *knew* I wasn't going to make it if I stayed where I was, so I relocated. Another room, another name. My mother helped me. She's stronger than she looks."

"But nobody saw either of you leave."

He waved his hand, dismissing the question. "Houdini never told how he did his tricks. Neither do I." His eyes flicked around the perimeter of the bar.

"What about Inspector Lemire? Was he in on this?"

"He didn't want to take the responsibility, so they sent him on a little vacation."

"It wasn't very considerate of you to worry me like that," I grumbled.

"I sent word."

"That postcard could have come from anybody. I wasn't sure you were okay until I saw your mother on TV during Wimbledon."

"I figured you'd pick up on that. It was a signal." He swished his index finger in his drink, pulled out a maraschino cherry by the stem, and slurped it down.

"So, how are you?"

"I lost a little flexibility in my wrist, but then I'm not going out for the javelin throw this year."

I laughed. The only thing I could ever imagine the Fish throwing was a potato chip—from a bag into his mouth. But I noticed that he was limping slightly, walking with one knee stiffened. Not that it slowed him down. The Fish had always moved at the approximate speed of glue.

"Listen, I'm sorry I pushed you down," I said. "But you were the last person on earth I expected to see in that service hall."

"Well, I'm big on surprises, as you know. I couldn't believe those bozo bodyguards of yours, and I use the term loosely."

"I think there was a shift change."

"That would have done us a lot of good if you'd ended up stuffed like a sausage into an airshaft."

My skin prickled. Somehow, danger never affects me till it's over. "What about your mother?"

He gestured to a blackjack game three tables away. There, behind a gigantic pile of chips and markers, wearing blue-tinted glasses and a little print dress, stood Mrs. Fisher. "The woman has a photographic memory," said the Fish. "The house is gonna lose big."

"I should know better than to worry about her. Did you ever find out who went after you in the hotel?"

"In general."

"Was it Jimmy Bennett?"

He laughed. "Please. Don't insult me. Or him. That's a guy who wouldn't want to wreck his manicure. No, it was the hired help."

"Hired by Bennett?"

"It was a large guy, that's all I know. I saw his back for about half a second, from the floor."

"I think Bennett knows exactly what happened to Catherine, and he's probably behind Tony's death too," I said.

"Why do you say that? Anything concrete?"

"Well, he had Catherine hack into the system at Roland Garros to change the opening draw."

His eyes snapped back to me. "That's it! That's the connection I couldn't figure out. Can you prove it?"

"She had the program faxed from the States by her former boyfriend and ex-supervisor, Jason Campbell, who works for KRW in San Francisco. They monitor all phone transactions, so he has records."

"Jason Campbell? Did he help her do this?"

"No. He had no idea *what* he was faxing. He was helping her out. They were having a relationship."

"He was the boyfriend? Where is he now?"

"He's meeting me here. Poor guy. He really cared about her. You can't believe how concerned he's been about the case since she died."

"Good. I'll be anxious to make his acquaintance. So why would Catherine change the opening draw at the French Open?"

"To make sure that certain players ended up playing each other. I think Jimmy wanted to build up the rivalry between

Heather and Dagmar. The more chances they had to clash, the better the hype, the more they would be worth when they got here, and the more dollars he could attract to his tournament." I glanced at the ballroom. The doors remained closed, although I could hear swells of applause from inside. "You see, Heather and Dagmar would have been very eager to cooperate with Jimmy. They were both former stars who were out of the limelight and wanted to get back in. Catherine told Jason she was doing Heather a favor, and I think that's what she meant. She was resurrecting her career for her before she'd even played a stroke."

"But neither of them won."

"No, but they got put head-to-head; that was what was important. The chances would normally only be fifty-fifty that they'd be in the same half. If Heather and Dagmar had been on the same side of the draw, they wouldn't have played each other. For the quarters, the odds that they'd play each other would even be worse. If Jimmy wanted them to play each other when he needed them to, he had to improve the odds. Once he got them on the same court, how they played was much less important than the publicity spin he knew he could put on the match."

"So that's why they concocted those scenes and screaming matches on and off the court," the Fish said. "Publicity stunts and sound bites."

"You got it. After the French, Jimmy just had to be sure that they both played well enough—and attracted enough interest— to stay in the limelight. That's why Heather went into training and Dagmar into rehab. And that's why Meg accused Dagmar of molesting her."

"Well, it certainly got national attention. Jimmy should have stayed out of sports and gone into PR. He missed his calling. So you think Heather and Dagmar were involved all along?"

"I'm not sure to what extent, but, yes, I do."

"What about the coaches?"

"I don't know yet."

"And Catherine's murder?"

"That's another story." I still wasn't sure who murdered Catherine—or Tony. "But tell me what you found out." I had no doubt that, even flat on his back in a hospital bed, the Fish was capable of finding out almost anything.

"Well, there's big money here. Follow the blood, you usually find the money."

"The Crown Jewel is the richest tournament ever," I said.

"That's pocket change compared to the money behind Talent-Masters. You've got money in there yourself."

I was stunned. "Me? That's ridiculous."

The Fish pulled a small spiral notebook from his lapel pocket and flipped it open. "Well, Desert Springs Sports Science Clinic is partners with LaserGlass in promoting a new line of products, is it not?"

"Yes."

"And according to my financial sources, the clinic put up quite a chunk of change. And a certain Kevin Curry, who is an officer in LaserGlass, has put major LaserGlass backing into the funding of TalentMasters. So there's some commingling of funds going on."

"Is that illegal?"

"Not at all. But it puts you in bed with them."

"If this tournament doesn't do well, what will happen to the clinic's investment in the LaserGlass project?"

"Depending on how the money is set up, it could come up short. Do you think this tournament has a chance of failure?"

"It would be tough at this point," I said. "They've sold their tickets, sold their TV sponsorship time, got their pay-per-view special set up. But this puts me in a terrible position."

"Why?" The Fish gnawed on a toothpick.

"I want to confront Jimmy with what I know right now. And if I do, and if it hurts the tournament, you're telling me it will hurt my company."

"Possibly. That's a decision you're going to have to make, Jordan."

I wondered if Andy knew about this. Or was behind this. I doubted it; Kevin seemed too competitive with him. I imagined this would be Kevin's attempt at a coup. If TalentMasters was the name behind a major new tournament that Kevin had helped launch, his job would regain its former importance and prestige, which was otherwise threatened by Andy's strategic plans for diversification of the business. Ultimately, for Kevin to succeed, TalentMasters would have to succeed. "You know what? The finals will be on clay," I predicted.

"What's the difference?"

"Clay is the surface where the unpredictable can happen. Upsets are more likely to occur. It's not uncommon for established champions to be overthrown on clay. Dagmar is a clay court specialist."

"You think she's being set up to win?"

"Or lose. She'll be the player who can control the ball best on clay. It could go either way, actually."

"What about the other surfaces? Don't they have to play on them all?"

"True. And they do have some pretty good players involved. Even Jimmy can't force Harriet or Celine to lose this tournament."

"How can we get a lock on any of this?" The Fish signaled a thumbs-up to his mother, who was raking chips into her purse.

"Meg Zaresky, the girl who accused Dagmar of molesting her, knows the story. She told me that Dagmar and Heather were playing out a prewritten script. And Jason put through the fax for Catherine from his office in San Francisco. But frankly I don't care about it anymore. Tony is dead. I have to live with that."

"Yeah," said the Fish softly. "I wish I could have done something."

"I intend to find out who killed him, whatever it takes. I've made it my job in life."

"And my job is finding out who killed Catherine Richie."

"Maybe it's the same person. Or maybe the same person was

behind it," I said. "A person who didn't want anybody finding out that these matches were fixed."

"Who would have the most to lose? Bennett?"

Jimmy Bennett had a lot to lose. Before he formed TalentMasters he was a very unstellar agent who had no cash on hand. To raise the necessary capital, he would have had to borrow and leverage to the limit—which is one reason why he needed world-class stunts to attract press and hold on to big-name sponsors. Besides LaserGlass, I wonder where the cash came from.

"They're coming out," said the Fish, dragging his tie through his drink as he leaned forward.

The ballroom doors opened, and the triumphal entry procession was repeated in reverse. Promoters are always careful not to trap stars in a sea of fans and press. Harriet, Heather, Dagmar, and Celine emerged and were led to the banquet room for the gala kickoff dinner. I spotted Woody in the crowd surrounding the stars. I knew I could never get to Dagmar; security was swarming around the players. I saw the two who had unceremoniously escorted me out earlier. "Who are those guys?" I asked the Fish. "Not casino security."

"No, I think they're bouncers, on loan from some strip joint." He blotted his tie with a paper cocktail napkin. "I talked to some of the guys. Twenty-four-hour men are posted by the doors of all the players' rooms. Plus each player is assigned two New York City cops, two LA swat team cops, three bouncers, several of whom are recently out of prison, one Pinkerton detective, and two fifth-degree black belt martial artists. They even had people checking the air-conditioning vents. Then there's the detail that's guarding the jewels, which are on loan from Harry Winston."

"Let's go talk to my buddy Woody." I jumped up and sprinted toward Woody through the masses of people surging toward the banquet.

"Hi, Woody," I said, catching up with him as he headed toward the dining room.

"Jordan! God, look at this spectacle. It's worse than the Olympics."

"I have good news and bad news," I said.

"I heard the good news: Harriet broke up with her fiancé just before she got here last week. She's a mess. Concentration's shot. We're gonna roll right past her."

"This is more serious, Woody. My news is, I know Dagmar didn't molest Meg Zaresky. Meg's admitted it to me."

"Well, thank God!" Woody sighed. "Not that I didn't know it already."

"Wait. I have to tell you something, and you must be honest with me."

"Shoot."

I took a deep breath and spoke carefully. "I think this whole thing is a setup and there's a chance Dag's a part of it. If she is, and you want any shred of a career left, get her out now. It's all going to blow up."

Woody frowned. "Where'd you hear this?"

"Meg Zaresky."

"Oh, the voice of truth, as we have seen by her record." Woody draped his arm around my shoulders as we walked. The Fish followed behind. "Let me tell you something, Jordan. I've been in this sport for longer than you've been alive. And I've never seen anybody work harder and in more physical pain than Dagmar Olafsen. If she was going to throw a match, all she had to do was stand there with a bad shoulder and lose. She went through too much pain for me to believe she is not out there to win. So get on with your life and get out of here. We have a match to win tomorrow. I don't know about anybody else, but I'm gonna stop by the booking office and place a bet on Dagmar with the manager. I don't spend my own money unless I'm sure about it, I can tell you that." He turned and waved to a photographer. "Joe! Good to see you!"

We passed through a gigantic model of the Acropolis, complete with faux-crumbling columns, and ahead in the crowd I saw Andy Fiero and Kevin Curry, in tuxedos, walking with Kelly. I pushed closer and tapped Andy on the shoulder.

"Jordan! Nobody told me you'd be here." He seemed delighted to see me.

"It was sort of a last-minute decision. Andy, can I talk to you for a minute?" We edged out of the current of the crowd and into yet another casino area. One seemed to flow seamlessly into another.

"I hope you'll sit at our table at dinner." Andy smiled. "I'm so glad to see you out and around after . . . what happened. I've been concerned." His voice was gentle.

"This isn't really a social visit. I have a serious question. You don't have to answer it, but I hope you will." I braced myself. I liked Andy, and I knew if he evaded my questions, or misled me, or, worse, lied to me, he was part of Jimmy's team and would have been all along. He would have been sent to divert me, keep an eye on me, use me.

"What is it?"

"Who's the financing behind TalentMasters? Is it LaserGlass?"

"That's a pretty basic question. Well, we're a sponsor," said Andy. "But the lion's share of the money is coming from Equinox."

"The Asian group?"

"They've got a big promotional exhibition after this for the winner that launches in Japan. It's been presold to pay-per-view TV."

"Who set that up?"

"Jimmy, of course. The Japanese are ecstatic. You should see them. They're ready to make Jimmy the next ambassador. And there's a movie deal too, a documentary. Equinox is funding that as well, I understand, in addition to a whole related product line. Our stake is relatively small by comparison. In fact, I made sure of it. I thought it was a rather risky venture, considering Talent-Masters is a new agency with no track record. And everything there relies on Jimmy. I've never put too much stock in one-man shows. What if the man quits the picture?"

"Thanks, Andy. They're lucky they have you."

"I appreciate the vote of confidence. I have to tell you, Kevin took the opposite position. He was ready to leverage to the hilt just to maximize our position." He smiled slightly. "You should have seen him at the meetings. He blasted me up, down, and sideways for my so-called lack of vision."

"Well, that's just him being defensive. Protecting his own rear end."

"Will I see you later?"

"You may not want to. I don't think I'm going to be winning any popularity contests."

"You do what you have to. I know that." He nodded encouragement. "Don't worry about it. Can I do anything to help?"

"Thanks, you already have. You'd better get going." I smiled reassuringly, feeling relieved. Andy reluctantly walked back into the lobby and caught up with the crowd as it washed into the banquet room. The Fish remained, leaning against a column, almost part of the scenery.

"The tournament starts tomorrow," he said. "There's still time."

"Nobody's going to listen to anything I have to say," I said. "What do you know about Equinox?" We left the Acropolis and found ourselves on a glass-enclosed skywalk with a moving sidewalk.

"A secretive privately held company. Very powerful in financial circles," said the Fish. "Finding out about Japanese companies is almost impossible."

Looking out the glass walls, I could see the all-weather domes rising up to dominate the landscape, shimmering in the night. They were incredibly impressive.

"Let's check out the courts," I said.

An escalator banked by two indoor waterfalls brought us to the pool exit, which in turn led to the patio area and the dome beyond. The arenas were swarming with activity. The enormity of the area was stunning—at least fourteen thousand people could be seated in each one. We went first to the hard court, which was being resurfaced.

"Why are you doing this now?" the Fish asked one of the workers who was painting a baseline.

"Harriet Craig looked the courts over, hit a couple of balls, and said the surface was too slow." The workman rolled his eyes, as if he were speaking of the princess and the pea. "The number one in the world says the court is off, you fix it."

"The speed of the court depends on how much sand they put in the paint," I explained to the Fish. "Sand acts as a deterrent, slows the ball down by adding friction. If you want the court faster, you put in less sand. A faster court will be good for Heather. Clay-courters like Dagmar usually prefer a slower court."

"Well, lady," said the workman, "everybody's ticked off now, seeing as how they can't practice on the main court. Just goes to show you can't please everybody."

"Where's the grass court?" the Fish asked.

"Through the big archway, but you can't walk on it. They got it taped off. You'd think the stuff was gold-plated. Get this: They brought in the head groundskeeper from Wimbledon to supervise it, blade by blade. I made a few crabgrass jokes, but, hey, the guy's a stiff—zero sense of humor. You know it costs thirty-eight thousand to put in a clay court? Forty-five for grass."

"It should be quite a spectacle," said the Fish.

"More like a circus," I said. "A very expensive circus. There's ticket sales, at seventy-five dollars per seat, there's the satellite TV sale, the overseas deal, the merchandising. And then there's the betting. What are the odds?"

"On what?" said the Fish. "They've got odds on everything from the winner to the point spread to the sets to the speed of the serves." He yawned. "Let's get some sleep."

"Where? They're throwing me out of the hotel."

"I got a big suite at the Mirage. You can share it. I'd feel better about knowing where you are, anyhow."

We headed back through the complex to the lobby. The elevators were just past the registration desk. It was late, so there were only a few people checking in. I recognized two of them: Janie and Meg Zaresky. Janie looked much as she always had, only a little heavier, with glasses. Even in middle age, she managed a vestige of perkiness.

"Janie!" I called out.

She turned and motioned me over, tucking her arm through Meg's.

"My daughter called me," she said, putting a hand on my arm. "She was very confused, but she isn't anymore. She knows she has her family behind her—both me and her father. We've all talked about it, and she knows we love her. Go ahead, Meggie."

Meg gripped her mother's arm. "I lied," she said. "It was a terrible thing for me to do, but I'll set it straight. I already quit the talent agency. I'm going to tell Mr. Bennett as soon as I can reach him. I've left messages, but he hasn't called back."

"Our lawyer is meeting us here," said Janie. "Meg is a minor. She was covered. If she handles this right, her life won't be ruined. She can start fresh. And I'm going to help her. I'm going to be a real mother at last."

"Meg, that's wonderful," I said. "I know it took a lot of courage. And I'm so happy that you two are together again." I pulled Janie aside. "You know, Janie, you have to be very careful how you handle this. There is real danger involved. If Jimmy thought Meg could threaten the success of this tournament in any way, it would be very bad for her. Who knows what he could do? I have an idea. Will you go along with me?"

"If it involves getting even with that lowlife Jimmy Bennett, I'll do anything," said Janie determinedly. "Nobody takes advantage of my kid."

That was the difference between Meg and Catherine, I thought. They were both manipulated. But nobody had fought for Catherine. She'd taken on Jimmy on her own—and lost. But I was going to make sure that this time she would finally win.

A.M. and I moved in with the Fish, and the next morning we began to line up the facts as we knew them, sharing notes and information. Within two hours, the floor of the suite's living room was covered with papers, notes, and files.

"We have to be sure that all the information is on the table before we make a move," I said.

"Thank you for reminding me," cracked the Fish. "Now exactly what is it that we don't know?"

"We don't know why Catherine was killed, although I suspect she was refusing to go along with Jimmy's program of fixing the draw."

"But she'd already quit, and the draw at Roland Garros was already fixed," said the Fish.

"Maybe she was going to turn Jimmy in," I said. "Maybe her conscience got to her. You know, that bothers me. It seems like a lot of risk for Catherine to take without much reward."

"She had the job. It must have seemed like a big salary."

"Maybe there was a bonus. But she lived pretty modestly, and no big money turned up after she died, did it?"

"Not in her accounts, or her parents'," said the Fish, scribbling a note.

"Well, why did she do it? Was there a payout coming? The other question is, Who was trying to kill us and why?" I said. "What is it that you knew or saw and that I knew?"

"I don't think it's what we knew, it was more that we were poking around, that we were involved. Nobody else seemed to be paying attention. Look, you cared enough to climb up on that greenhouse, to re-create the action. I was being paid to care by the Richie family. Everybody else was willing to ship the body home and forget it." He slathered a bagel with butter. "Don't forget, you're a high-profile person in tennis. What you do attracts attention. That's not something any killer is going to welcome with open arms."

"Jason was supposed to meet me here with some more information," I said. "He has the phone records. I'd better call him and leave a message where he can find me."

I dialed Jason's office at KRW, expecting his phone mail to pick up.

"Hello?"

I didn't recognize the voice. "Is Jason Campbell there?" I hoped he wasn't.

"No."

"Thank you. Do you know when he left?" He probably didn't know how to reach me.

"He's left the company," said the voice.

"What?"

"I'm just cleaning out his office before I move into it next week."

"Where can I get in touch with him?" I tried not to sound as anxious as I felt.

"I don't know," said the voice. "I'm just starting in the department. You might try personnel on Monday."

"Thank you." I hung up. "Jason quit his job," I said. I tried his home number. It was disconnected. "He seems to have dropped out," I told the Fish. "This bothers me. He had the phone records. Now I won't be able to prove what Catherine did."

"The company will have backup records," said the Fish.

"I hope he's still coming here with the information. I'll leave a note with his name at the front desk."

"How long do you want to wait?" asked the Fish.

"Till tomorrow. Meg and Janie are here, but Jason can really put the nail in the coffin. He's our direct link to Catherine. Jimmy can brush me off or try to strong-arm me, but he's not going to be able to roll by this wall of people. I want to surround him, leave him with no way out."

"I hope you're right," said the Fish.

SEVENTEEN

The semifinals went as expected, meaning that Dagmar and Heather won. I wish I'd been the betting type; I would have cleaned up. Nobody could have known that the number three player in the world, Celine Gilbert, would play so poorly, or that the number one player, Harriet Craig, would have a blowup with her boyfriend that put her off her game. This meant Heather and Dagmar would face each other on clay tonight. Funny how things work out sometimes.

I couldn't get near the court, but the Fish and I went out to the airport and intercepted Harriet as she headed for her flight the next morning. Celine had left the night before, immediately after the match, by private jet. I took a seat beside Harriet in the Platinum Miles Lounge and pretended to be leaving too. She was still steaming.

"Unbelievable!" she exclaimed, slamming the arm of the chair with her palm. Her short brown hair was slicked back off her face with gel and looked like it was still wet from the shower. "You wouldn't believe it, Jordan. Everything was off. My skirt was so tight I could barely breathe."

"You gained weight?"

"No, that's the ridiculous thing. I weighed myself before and after the match. I'm the same as always. I must be getting my period. Or maybe it was so dry I took too much salt and was retaining water. And my timing was just shot. It was a disaster. I should have won. I wouldn't have even played this rinky-dink tournament except that I was sure I would win. My game was off so far I wasn't even on the planet. Beaten by Heather, the Blast from the Past. God, I can't stand it!" She shifted her equipment bag on her shoulder.

"Are those your match clothes?"

"No, they kept those, and my match rackets. Jimmy's doing some sort of tennis theme restaurant—like the Hard Rock. Of course, when I promised him the clothes and the rackets, I assumed I'd win." She laughed mirthlessly. "Now I wish he'd just burn them or donate them to the junkyard."

Her flight was called and she stormed off.

"You think she threw her match?" asked the Fish as he watched her head for the boarding gate.

"Her game was so bad, I thought it was possible," I said. "But why would she? Harriet is a reigning number one. She'd have nothing to gain and everything to lose. On a decent day, she can wipe the court with either Dagmar or Heather. She has all the money she needs, and wherever she appears the crowd shows up. You know, that's the funny thing about tennis fans. They complain that tennis is too predictable, and then if anybody except the top people are playing, they *really* complain."

"Well, they've got Dagmar and Heather now," said the Fish as we headed back through the gauntlet of shops and food stands.

"It's like they paid for a Las Vegas show," I said. "And that's just about what they'll get tonight."

"Who will win?" asked the Fish.

"Who do you think? Who's the one with the most commercial value—or, should I say at this point, the *only* one with commercial value? Heather will win. That's got to be their script for the tournament. If Dagmar won, she wouldn't be worth much on the commercial marketplace, would she? Jimmy's seen to that. Her only value is in a match against Heather. But Heather can be trotted out and pitted against Harriet in big bucks rematches. Imagine the marquee value."

The Fish's car was waiting in front of the terminal, with a parking ticket on the windshield.

"I'll add this to my collection," he said.

"You know," I said, "There's one person I really should talk to."

"Who's that?"

"Kelly Kendall. She's up to her neck in this, but I don't think it's her fault. She has absolutely no reason to be involved. What could Jimmy Bennett offer a woman who already has everything?"

"More everything?"

"No. She goes for prestige. Being the best. Now she's launching a career in coaching, and she wants to be the person behind this huge comeback of Heather's. She's got a world-class image, and it's all going to backfire in her face."

"Where is she?"

"She's not at the hotel—that would be too accessible for her. She's got a house in one of those expensive gated communities on the edge of town. One of the local bodyguards gave me directions. Or she could be at practice, but it's awfully hot right now for practice."

"Maybe they're at the dome. It's air-conditioned."

"No, Heather wouldn't practice out in the open like that."

"Let's go." The Fish wadded the ticket into his pocket, and we lurched away from the curb.

"Are they expecting you?" questioned the guard at the gatehouse of Los Gatos. The community of expansive modern homes, where Andre Agassi also lived, is fifteen minutes from the Strip at the very edge of town, facing the mountains. Unlike Palm Springs, there is very little vegetation in Las Vegas. What trees there are look like they are clinging desperately to life, and the few plants and flowers have a weathered quality that make them look like dusty plastic. High winds in certain seasons make walls around most of the houses necessary, and there are no lush yards or expanses of lawn or greenery.

"Please call the house and let me talk to Kelly Kendall," I said. "I'm an old friend, Jordan Myles."

The guard lit up. "Jordan Myles! I saw you play Wimbledon!" He immediately dialed the phone and handed it to me.

"Kelly, it's Jordan. I'm out at the gate and I'd like to talk to you."

"I heard you've been making a nuisance of yourself," she said, laughing.

"Come on, Kelly. This is important."

Ten minutes later, I was sitting in a vaulted marble-floored living room. Kelly, in sand-colored cashmere slacks and a matching sweater, stared at me askance.

"Kelly, you have to disassociate yourself from this right now. It's going to be a major scandal, with criminal indictments," I said.

"Oh, come on, Jordan," she said. "You're getting carried away."

"Am I? You remember Janie Pierce, Meg's mother? She was on the doubles tour a few years back. Well, she's here at the Olympus with Meg. You don't have to believe me. You can call Janie." I picked up the phone. "I'll even dial for you."

Kelly rubbed her forehead nervously. "Janie's here?"

"She's going to make a statement saying that her daughter was manipulated into lying by Jimmy Bennett. There's some very bad stuff going on, Kelly. I don't want to believe you're part of it."

"What are you insinuating? Of course I'm not!"

"Well, then, you'd better do something about it."

"You're not doing this to embarrass me, Jordan?" she asked.

"Kelly, think about that girl who died for a minute. Think about Meg Zaresky. Talk to Janie. And then make your own decision." I got up and left.

"What's she going to do?" said the Fish as we drove back to the hotel.

"Leave town," I said. "Something will suddenly come up. The press will conveniently forget her involvement and blame CiCi. Kelly's a genius at avoiding bad press. Even when she loses, it comes off like she's won. The woman is made of Teflon. Nothing bad will ever stick to her. You know, when we were on the circuit she was no Miss Priss. She'd drink, stay out all night with guys, swear like a sailor sometimes. And what would they report? That she went to tea at Buckingham Palace, wore white gloves, and ate cucumber sandwiches."

The Fish and I went back to the Mirage and planned what we were going to do. "We could have your friend Janie hold a press conference right now," he suggested.

"I don't want to do that," I said. I'd thought of it. With far bigger issues at stake, I didn't want to alert Jimmy and give him a chance to slither away. I did have one thought, though. It was far-fetched, but being rational hadn't gotten us very far. "Let's see if we can get hold of Harriet's match clothes and her rackets."

"What's that going to prove?" asked the Fish.

"You never know."

"What if she took them with her?"

"She didn't. She said Jimmy kept her clothes and rackets for some tennis-theme restaurant he was launching. They might still be in the locker room. Let's see if we can scrounge them up." I frowned dubiously, knowing full well the challenging effect of my next words. "Though, let's face it, it's probably impossible to get our hands on that stuff." I groaned, suggesting the impossibility of the task.

The Fish grinned. "Yeah, it's impossible, all right."

It only took one phone call to track down Harriet's match clothes and rackets. The PR director of the tournament was only too happy to tell an inquiring newspaper editor what had happened to the historic outfit and equipment, and how Mr. Bennett was going to use them as the keystone of his new collection for the tennis-theme restaurant. They'd be announcing the full story at an upcoming press conference: Did I want to come? Did I want to speak with the curator they'd hired? In fact, he had Harriet's things already; he'd sent the dress out to be cleaned before putting it on display at the press conference. Did I want a press release faxed to my office? A press kit FedExed overnight? And the rackets? They were right there in the PR office. So were the shoes. A man was picking up the rackets to install them in Plexiglas display cases, and the shoes were going to be bronzed and engraved. My reporters were welcome to inspect these historic artifacts. Of course, the PR director had no idea that the so-called editor he spoke with was Jordan Myles.

The Fish placed the next call, to the in-house valet service at the Olympus. "I have a tuxedo to send out to be dry cleaned," he said. "I'd prefer to handle it myself. The tuxedo has sentimental value. Who do you use for laundry and dry cleaning service?" He scribbled down a name and address and waved the paper at me.

We got to the Lucky Lady dry cleaner's within fifteen minutes. "A thematic dry cleaner's," I said. "How quaint." I jumped out of the car and caught the attention of a clerk.

"I'm from the Olympus," I said. They sent me over to pick up the tennis outfit you picked up today from the PR office."

The clerk was busy but accommodating. "We picked up hundreds of items from the Olympus," he said. "You got a receipt?"

"No, but it was sent out by mistake. I need it. Can I look?"

He shrugged and opened a gate in the counter. "It's all back there. We got the plant on premises."

I spent the next thirty minutes sorting through bags of dirty laundry and dry cleaning, during which I located five tennis dresses, none of them Harriet's. She always wore Apex clothing for her matches; it was in her endorsement contract. Finally, I

found what I was looking for: an Apex tennis skirt and shirt, size
ten, with Harriet's autograph stitched onto the sleeve. I wadded
the dress into a ball, tucked it under my arm, handed the clerk
a twenty-dollar tip, and told him to have lunch on me.

Next the Fish went up to the Olympus PR office while I waited
outside in the car. Ten minutes later he returned, carrying the
rackets and the shoes. "This was too easy," he said. "Everybody
was at lunch. I told the secretary that I was the messenger for the
display and bronzing company." He tossed his booty into the
backseat, and I wheeled the car around past the gigantic and
dazzling volcano fountain, a Las Vegas landmark that was dor-
mant until dusk, at the entrance to the Mirage.

"Now what?" asked the Fish, after we deposited the clothes
and rackets in our suite, where my patient bodyguard sat waiting, guarding A.M.

"I'm going to perform a minor medical procedure," I said. "It's
called *dissection.*" I zipped open my manicure kit, took out
cuticle scissors, a razor, and tweezers, and began by examining
the skirt, seam by seam. "When I was starting my tennis career,
we didn't have much money. My mom and I used to sew my
tennis clothes, and I got to be pretty good at it, even before I was
thirteen. I could follow a pattern, put in a zipper, pleats, button-
holes." I held a seam to the light. "See here? I can tell you right
now that this dress has been taken in. See the little pinholes from
the former seam? And the tiny bits of thread? And the stitch size
is different."

The Fish peered over my shoulder. "Proving what?"

"That the dress was taken in, that's all," I said. "Look here, I
think they moved the zipper, too. Harriet must have lost a lot of
weight right before the match."

"Maybe they altered it before?"

I shook my head. "I can call her and clarify this, but Harriet
never wears the same outfit twice. She's known for it, and Apex
expects it. All her tennis clothes are custom-made to her mea-
surements, so they fit perfectly. I doubt she'd retread an outfit
like this, or that it would be so far off it required extensive

alteration." Players are paranoid about their weight and the fit of their match clothes. A too-tight skirt, trivial as it may seem to the average person, could certainly throw off a top player's game.

I set the skirt aside and turned to the shoes, pulling out the innersoles and examining the soles. Immediately, I could see that—ever so slightly—the orthotics had been altered. The area under the toes had been shaved. I poked with my tweezers. Small pieces of paper had been glued under the heels. The total effect would be to pitch the player forward very slightly. Not enough for her to notice, but enough to disrupt her game. I looked up at the Fish.

"That's it," I said. "And if we get this racket pulled apart, I'll bet we find they've weighted the handle—maybe a couple of strips of lead tape wrapped up in there."

We'd have to compare it with other rackets of hers to be certain, but I was pretty positive of what we'd find. And even if the rackets hadn't been weighted, the skirt and shoes would have been enough to put Harriet off balance.

"I guess Jimmy figured to hide the evidence in the most public place he could find," I said, "a display case in his new restaurant. Can't you just picture it? As they ordered their hamburgers, everybody would be staring at equipment that supposedly immortalized Harriet Craig but which actually caused her to lose the most lucrative match in tennis history, and nobody would ever know it." How typical of Jimmy's egocentric approach—lording it over everybody that he'd pulled off the con of the tennis world. Catherine, Tony, Harriet, Dagmar, me: he'd conned us all. Now, failing to con us, would he dispose of the rest of us?

There was no way I could get access to Jimmy Bennett, and I knew it. But I had access to someone who did. I called Kelly Kendall. She was still at the Olympus. "I have specific evidence that someone tampered with Harriet's clothing and rackets," I said. I proceeded to explain. "You can come see for yourself."

"Are you crazy?" ranted the Fish when I hung up. "That woman hates your guts. We need to get to the authorities."

"The authorities do not understand tennis," I said. "It would take weeks to prove anything, and by then who knows what will happen? Kelly is instant credibility."

"What about that boss of yours, the Olympian marathoner?"

"He's too close to me," I said. "People will think he's biased. It's good that everyone knows Kelly and I are famous worldwide for hating each other's guts. If she believes me, everyone will."

Kelly arrived with her bodyguard, who waited outside the suite as I took her through what I'd found. She took one look at the clothes and understood immediately—to a point. "Could it be you're jumping to conclusions?" she asked. "Maybe Dagmar did this. She's the one with a lot to lose. You can't prove it's Jimmy." She was already in full TV makeup. The match was starting earlier tonight to be broadcast live to the East Coast.

"Have you talked to Janie?"

"Yes," she said, and I could see she was troubled. Kelly never liked to align herself on anything but the winning side. It was now clear that Jimmy Bennett was not a winner.

"Will you go with me to talk to him now?" I asked.

She tightened her lips into a firm, straight line and nodded.

Out in the street, there was total bedlam. A huge trailer was unloading three elephants, and all traffic was at a standstill. The elephants were bedecked in jeweled headdresses that bowed and dipped as the animals rumbled across the street to the Olympus marquee, escorted by five handlers and a police guard. All eyes were focused on the elephants, so nobody noticed as Kelly, the Fish, and I made our way through the crowd.

"Where are they taking them?" I asked Kelly.

"Wherever elephants go," she said, clearly relieved that she would not have to ride one of the monster pachyderms.

Dagmar, Heather, Jimmy, Andy, Kevin Curry, and a contingent that must have been from Equinox met the elephants under the marquee for photo opportunities. The lead elephant knelt down, and to my amazement Jimmy—not Heather or Dagmar—

climbed aboard. There was a blaze of light as photographers and videocameramen jostled for position. A handler led the elephant Jimmy was riding forward, and I realized that he was about to lead a parade down the Strip. This was why traffic was blocked. The next two elephants followed, ridden by Dagmar and Heather. All were followed by a gigantic float where showgirls in togas re-created tableaux from friezes on ancient Greek carvings.

"You'll have to catch him before the match," said Kelly.

Since I couldn't see myself chasing three lumbering elephants down Las Vegas Boulevard screaming accusations, I reluctantly agreed. The delay could work in my favor, giving me time to talk to Gus and Bill and to locate Jason Campbell.

My wish was granted soon enough. Gus and Bill, standing off to the side of the marquee with Andy and Kevin, waved us over.

"So where have you been?" asked Gus.

"Didn't you hear? They eighty-sixed me off the property. You remember Noel Fisher?" I motioned Gus aside. In spite of his many shortcomings, like his irrational penchant for women who do macramé, he is still the only person in the world whom I completely trust. "Gus, I have proof that the semifinals were a fix," I said. "The draw at the French Open was fixed too. Meg Zaresky is ready to recant her claim against Dagmar. She says it was a setup. And Harriet Craig's match clothes were tampered with. The orthotics of the shoes were shaved, the dress was nipped in to the point where it interfered with her game—"

Gus raised his hands, as if he didn't want to hear.

"Wait, that's just the tip of the iceberg. Catherine Richie was put in her job by Jimmy so she could hack into the tournament computers and move players around like pieces on a chessboard. Once she bailed, and threatened to talk, she was too dangerous to be left alive."

Gus stared at me. "My God, Jordan. Can you prove all this?"

"Well, some of it. I have Harriet's clothes."

"Go to the police right now!" he said urgently.

"I need Jason Campbell, Catherine's boyfriend and also her ex-boss. He's got the hard proof about rigging the draw at the French Open: phone records, computer transaction records. He's supposed to meet me here."

The crowd had thinned out as people either followed the parade or moved back through the hotel toward the arena area. "What do you think, Kelly?" asked Gus.

"I'm not sure I know what to think," Kelly said. Her bodyguard was unreadable behind reflective sunglasses.

Bill stood with his back to me, talking loudly to Kevin and Andy in hopes of diverting them from our conversation. The Equinox executives had already disappeared inside.

Kelly's brow furrowed, and her eyes glared with the icy intensity that had won her the mantle of best tennis player in the world. I recognized that look. I'd seen it across the net: Kelly was ready to fight. "I will not be involved with anything that is less than one hundred percent aboveboard, and if I was brought here under false pretenses, I will personally see to it that the people involved are nailed to the mat."

Gus turned to me. "You realize, Jordan, that if it comes out that Jimmy and TalentMasters were doing something illegal, or are linked with these murders, the Springs is going to be in major trouble? We're a business partner. Like it or not, we've invested in TalentMasters. There's a direct money trail. Our business could be linked to this. You could be linked to this. I just hope you understand what the significance is. You bring down Jimmy, you could well bring us all down, yourself included. You have to make a choice."

"I know," I said, although my knees were slightly weak with the impact of what Gus was saying. "I wish I had a choice."

"Well, think about it," said Gus. "I'm just laying out the options—and believe me, I'm not forgetting about Tony. We're all as concerned as you are. But you can't go on a vendetta."

"This is not a vendetta." Sometimes Gus makes me furious. This was one of those times.

"It won't help anybody if you end up getting yourself killed too," he continued. "I'm just saying maybe you'd better leave matters to the police. It's your own safety I'm concerned about, even if you're not. This reckless pursuit of yours—I just don't understand it." We faced each other for a minute, and then he turned and walked slowly through the hotel doors.

Gus was right. I was certainly being reckless. But I also felt I had a responsibility.

Andy stepped closer. "I heard everything you both said," he told me. "I was listening. You're right to do what you're doing, Jordan."

"But your company is involved too," I said. "I'm sorry for that, but there's been too much damage to worry about the business implications."

He nodded. "I agree. I know how you felt about Tony, and I saw what they did to him. You have to live with that."

"I want to keep this quiet, but the problem is, I can't pin down Jimmy. He's either surrounded by people or he's inaccessible. He keeps getting away from me or having me thrown out or chased down. What am I going to do, tackle a herd of elephants?"

"Well, you know he's going to be at the match, front and center. And the party after, no matter who wins."

"I can't imagine his goon squad will let me within fifty feet of him," I said. I looked toward Kelly, who was huddling with her bodyguard, and at that moment I knew how I would get to Jimmy. Kelly and I had been rivals for about as long as I'd been involved in sports. It was ironic, but at this critical point, when it was no longer a game, when careers, reputations, and lives were at stake, the person who had caused me the greatest grief, who had done the most to thwart me at every juncture, was the only person who could help me now.

EIGHTEEN

Fourteen thousand people, including the Fish, watched the Crown Jewel finals in the amphitheater. Hundreds of thousands more watched on pay TV. Kelly Kendall watched from her seat beside CiCi in the players' box. But I didn't see it. I waited inside playing roulette in the gaming room, with no clocks and no windows, only murals of ancient Greece.

Inside a Las Vegas casino, you are unaware of the outside world or the passage of time. That's purposeful—they design them that way in hopes that you will while away more hours than you'd planned at the table, feeding more money to the house.

I was standing under the watchful gaze of my bodyguard, losing five dollars every time I put a chip on a number. The polished wheel would spin, the little ball would dance around it and come to rest on a number that didn't seem to be in my vocabulary, and we would do it again. But at least my mind was momentarily off the confrontation I knew was coming when the match was over and Jimmy Bennett was toasting Heather's victory in the crystal-chandeliered Penthouse Room. Kelly had agreed to meet me at the elevator on the penthouse floor, and she would front my entrance into the room. That was the thing about Kelly: The world was an open door to her and her party. And as co-coach of the new Crown Jewel champion, she could risk a scene if the guards denied her guest entry.

My pile of chips had disappeared. I looked up to see Mrs. Fisher across the table, raking in a stack of markers. She gave me a cheery little wave as she tucked them into her handbag, straightened her hat—this one was trimmed with violets and a tiny cloud of net—and moved on toward the next table.

I intercepted her. "Mrs. Fisher!"

She bestowed the sweetest smile I'd ever seen. "Hello, dear."

"You're doing so well. Maybe you should give me a few tips."

"Oh, my dear, it's all just Lady Luck, you know." She hummed happily.

I took her arm and escorted her to the blackjack table. "Mrs. Fisher, I have to ask you something."

She opened her bag and checked her markers. "Certainly."

"How did you get your son out of that hospital room, and where did you go?"

She removed a lipstick from under the markers and pursed her lips. "Now let me see—you know, dear, my memory isn't so fabulous anymore. Where was that, Atlantic City?" She dabbed on a coat of pink lipstick and snapped the lid back on the tube. "There! I feel much better. Nice to have seen you, dear." With that, she turned to the table with the finesse of a professional card counter. "Hit me," she said, thumping the felt. Clearly, our conversation was at an end.

I was startled to see Jimmy burst into the room, accompanied by hotel officials, Kevin Curry, and two of the men from Equinox, all of whom were practically running to keep up with him. I checked my watch. This had to have been one of the shortest clay court matches in history. It must have been a virtual shutout—or perhaps an injury had ended the match. The Fish materialized at his mother's side, leaned toward her, and whispered something. She nodded, collected her markers and chips, kissed his cheek, and made her way toward the room elevators.

I motioned to my bodyguard. "Go with her."

He hesitated.

"Just go!" I hissed, giving him a push. "What happened?" I asked, turning to the Fish.

"Your buddy Dagmar wiped the court with Heather. I don't think Heather got in one point."

"You're kidding!"

"I don't know tennis well enough to kid about it. Olafsen won. Straight sets."

"I'm stunned." I really couldn't believe it.

"You better get up there fast. Everybody's headed for the party."

I took the elevator to the penthouse and waited in the hall. From the suite, I could hear the muffled sounds of Jimmy yelling, but I couldn't make out what he was saying.

The elevator doors opened and Kelly leaped out and rushed up to me. "Dagmar clobbered Heather! God, you wouldn't believe it. Heather just crumbled out there. I saw her in the dressing room. She blamed the setup—said it was like a show, not like a match, and she was crying that she wasn't a trained seal who could win on command. Then she got hysterical. They had to give her a sedative. It's unbelievable!"

"Where's Dagmar?"

"On her way up. If you want to talk to Jimmy, this is the only window, but since Dagmar won are you sure your theory is right?"

"I have no theories anymore on the match. But my other theories about Catherine and Tony stand. Let's go."

Kelly linked her arm firmly through mine. "I'm scared," she whispered.

"I thought you were never scared."

"That's what you were supposed to think. But sometimes I was."

We reached the penthouse suite door.

"Invitation?" said a tuxedoed man at the door. "Hello, Miss Kendall."

"This is my personal guest," she said airily. "I'm expecting another party of three." She pushed me through the door, and in we went.

Jimmy looked to be having a heart attack. His face was ashen and sweaty, his mouth set in a grim, lipless line. The executives from Equinox were staring stonily at him, and Kevin Curry was pacing nervously. I figured I might as well give him something to really worry about.

"Hi, Jimmy." I tapped him on the shoulder.

"Oh, for God's sake. Who let you in here?"

"Kelly."

"Well, you are about to leave. I have business to take care of." He snapped his fingers nervously toward the guards.

I looked toward the door. The Fish was walking in, accompanied by Janie Pierce and Terry and Meg Zaresky. Janie, her arm around Meg, led her daughter to my side.

"Meg has dictated a notarized statement that details how you put her up to the accusations against Dagmar and planted her in my office to spy on me," I said. "Her parents, whom you can see are here with her, were witnesses to her statement."

Jimmy's skin blanched an even paler color. "She's just an impressionable child," he said. "She'll say anything."

"That's right. You counted on that. With Meg—and with Catherine Richie. There are a lot of similarities between the two of them. Then again, maybe not. Meg can't hack into computer programs in France."

He blinked as if I'd thrown sand into his face, then waved furiously to the guards, who moved to my side.

"It's over, Jimmy," I said. "Enjoy your day in the sun at this party, because when you walk out, you will be arrested. I will personally see to it." The men from Equinox stepped closer, and Jimmy's eyes flicked nervously back and forth between me and them.

A burst of applause at the door to the suite announced the

arrival of Dagmar and Woody. Dagmar was carrying an armful of long-stemmed roses, a jeweled scepter, and a serious frown. Woody just stood there and beamed; then he saw me. "Jordan!" He rushed across the room, thrusting himself between me and Jimmy. "We did it, kid, we did it!" He threw his arms around me and clinched me in a bear hug, jumping up and down. "She was great! She couldn't miss! Heather choked. Did you see it?"

Over his shoulder I saw Dagmar walk up to Jimmy and, with a defiant expression, throw her flowers pointedly onto the floor in front of him. In case he missed her point, she ground the crimson petals into the carpet with her heel. Then she walked over to Woody and me. "I had to do it," she said. "You were right, Jordan. I'm not a loser."

I wrestled free of Woody's embrace, but the few seconds he'd had me in his enthusiastic grasp had been just enough for Jimmy to slip away and head out the door. The Fish followed, but I noticed that as he tried to run he was limping. His injuries were clearly not as far behind him as he'd had me believe. I took off at a run.

Jimmy dashed down the hall and disappeared into an elevator. I jumped in just as the door closed, and the two of us were alone for the long ride down.

"Why did you do it, Jimmy?" I asked.

"Jordan, I didn't do anything. Well, maybe a little bit of PR, that I admit to—the thing with Dagmar. But she was in on it, she was part of it. It was all part of the show."

"Was it part of the show for people to die?"

"I never planned that," he said. "I don't know how it happened. For what it's worth, Jordan, you're fixated on me, but I'm not the one you should be worried about. All I wanted to do was have a spectacular event and keep my business together. Is that a crime?"

"Fixing the French Open by tampering with the draw and doctoring Mila Karacek's drink is probably a crime. Fixing the matches here is probably a crime. Or maybe the Nevada State

Athletic Commission and the U.S. Tennis Association will see it differently."

"Don't tell me people haven't dropped tennis matches before, Jordan. I've seen guys lose a match just to make a plane." He looked nervously at the floor indicator as we moved down. It felt strange being on this elevator alone with him, like being trapped in a sarcophagus. We both knew that the instant the elevator hit the ground floor, the chase would commence. But for these few seconds, we were suspended in the eye of the storm, and I seized the opportunity to press my case.

"You recruited Catherine," I said, speaking quickly, my eye on the floors as we went down. "You went after her purposefully, to get into the computers at the French and wherever else you had in mind."

"You should write novels."

"Oh, don't worry, I can prove it. Her former boss—and boy-friend—has the records."

Jimmy exhaled slowly. "Yeah? Just try and find him." I got the distinct impression that Jimmy knew far more than I did about Jason Campbell. With a sinking feeling, I realized that Jason's absence—from his job and his apartment—were not due to a missed connection or a prior commitment.

He was probably dead.

The elevator doors opened at the lobby level. Jimmy turned to me briefly. "If you enjoy breathing, drop this now. I'm doing you a favor, Jordan. *Drop it!*" He took off, but I stayed right with him.

"Oh, for God's sake," he said. He started to run, dodging through the crowd in formal attire, which was now swelling toward the elevators in search of the victory celebration upstairs.

Suddenly a man in a wheelchair blocked my path, and I stumbled almost into his lap. "Excuse me, sir," I mumbled. Jimmy, now yards ahead of me, disappeared out the front doors into the night.

I had lost him. I stood scanning the darkness, illuminated by all the neon Las Vegas could muster. Across the street, the volcano fountain was erupting "lava" of red and orange water a hundred feet into the air, ringing bursts of real flame at the center of the fountain. A double line of about fifty limousines, white and black, blocked the driveway. There was no way Jimmy, or anyone else, was going to get a car out of here. But across the street—I took off for the Mirage, where Jimmy could get a car and escape. Dodging through traffic as I crossed the street, I spotted him. A white stretch limo screeched to a halt inches from my knees, and the driver leaned out to scream at me, but I raced ahead, vaulting over the bumper of a stopped car, up the driveway of the Mirage, to Jimmy's side.

Jimmy faced me with eyes glazed by fear, and I realized he was looking *past* me at someone else. He whirled and ran. I followed as he went toward the underground garage where the valet parkers were taking the cars. Looking over my shoulder, I tried to discover who or what had frightened him, but I couldn't distinguish any one person clearly, certainly no one I recognized.

I followed Jimmy into the garage, dodging between rows of parked cars. Cars came and went, oblivious to us, as Jimmy wove in and out at a trot and came finally to a doorway, which he opened and disappeared behind.

Within seconds, I had caught up. There was a sign on the door that said MAINTENANCE ONLY. Inside, I entered a small room with dim lights, the walls lined with controls, the ceiling a web of pipes like a submarine. A small metal ladder led to a hatch overhead. I had one foot on the ladder when I heard the metallic sound of door to the maintenance room opening behind me. Before I could turn my head, I was virtually tackled and shoved off the ladder. I fell sideways only a few feet, but I hit the floor awkwardly, my head striking the concrete. The wind had been knocked out of me. I lay there, hardly able to breathe, my eyes shut tight, pretending to be unconscious as someone scrambled up the ladder in my place.

Painfully, I pulled myself up. My forehead was scraped and

bleeding. I scrambled up the ladder, pushed the hatch open, and emerged outside, on a catwalk. All around in the darkening sky, which still clung to streaks of sunset colors, were the hot neons and sparkling lights of the Vegas night, and I seemed very small, dwarfed by the golden glitter that winked and blinked from every possible surface. Looking ahead, I could see that the catwalk led straight through a stand of giant palms and boulders to the domelike volcano fountain. The crater in the center was momentarily quiet. In silhouette, I could see Jimmy, off the catwalk, picking his way toward the crater's edge and, I supposed, the street beyond.

"Jimmy, stop!" I yelled.

He looked up momentarily. But how could I warn him from a hundred feet away that there was a greater danger between us? A real killer, perhaps. *The* real killer. I realized now that Jimmy knew it, had probably known it all along. The person who hadn't known it was me. Perhaps the killer was after both of us, although he had brushed me aside for Jimmy. I looked for a way off the catwalk, but there was none. I could go back down the hatch or forward to the volcano.

A large crowd had assembled in the street in front of the fence to watch the next eruption. No one seemed to notice the figure of a man making his way to the rim of the volcano. Suddenly, the crater erupted again, spouting a blaze of orange and red flames and water a hundred feet up, spewing a strangely sweet smell, like piña colada, and clouds of molten mist. I saw Jimmy, backlit in silhouette, stop in front of the white-hot blaze and merge with the figure of a second, much larger, man. The figures wavered, and then one shoved the other directly into the flaming mouth of the fountain's crater. There was a quick, hoarse scream, muffled by the roar of the rushing water.

I froze for a second, horrified, realizing there was nothing I could do to help, then quickly cleared my head to remind myself that the surviving man, whether he was Jimmy or someone else, could easily have targeted me as the second victim: after all, I was a witness. I felt the catwalk vibrate as a dark figure approached—it was impossible to tell who. I turned to run, assessing my chances of vaulting over the catwalk railing and scrambling down the steep sheer drop of an artificial rock cliff to the street, and then I froze. Ahead of me was another silhouette, pointing a gun directly at me. There was no way to escape. I was trapped between them.

The silhouette stepped into the lights of the fountain. It was a very tall man. For a split second, my heart stopped—and then I recognized him; it was Kelly's bodyguard. From behind him darted Kelly, vaulting past him with a gun in her hand. "Jordan!" she screamed, "you're blocking my shot! Catch!" She tossed me her gun, just as I heard footsteps on the catwalk coming toward me, sensed the heavy vibration of a person approaching.

I felt the cold, hard metal in my hand, turned, and pulled the trigger. Nothing happened. I could see the backlit form of the man approaching clearly now, glowing like an ember coughed up from the bowels of hell. He was only feet away.

"The safety!" shouted Kelly.

I flashed on the gun she had showed me at the Springs, flicking the lever on the left side of the weapon even as she spoke, then leveled the gun and fired again. The figure of the man looming now just in front of me toppled over and slid silently down the sloping side of the volcano and into the steaming froth fifty feet down at the bottom of the pool. This time, alerted by the gunshot that had burst out even over the roar of the fountain, at least some people in the crowd saw him fall. In the distance, a woman's scream pierced the neon night, and I stood there beside Kelly in the glowing mist of the volcano, staring and trembling.

"**H**e's going to make it." The Fish put down the phone and I dropped my head into my hands. It was over. I had shot a man, a murderer—for Jimmy Bennett had been dead when they pulled him from the fire, roasted alive in the midst of a gushing fountain of water. Did the fact that I wished my shot had been fatal make me as morally bankrupt as my victim? I didn't care. I wished I'd killed him. At this point, I was incapable of feeling anything but the most primal desire for revenge.

The volcano fountain, as it turned out, was controlled by valves and pipes that ran beneath the parking lot for maintenance, and in fact the little room where I had been yanked off the ladder was the control room. The hotel management had turned off the water and gas the instant they were alerted to the problem, and a mobile command post in a trailer, which was always standing by, fully set up and equipped for such emergencies, had been whisked into the parking lot. Police, federal agents, and medical authorities had taken over, manning phones, directing ambulances, and keeping the crowds and media people at bay.

Grateful to be a spectator, I sat in the trailer with the Fish, wet and shivering in a blanket, in the midst of a chaos of ringing phones and barked orders. Somehow I hadn't even known that I'd been drenched by mist from the fountain. Gus and Bill were in the front of the trailer, conferring with the police and the hotel manager.

"Who was he?" I managed to ask. Clearly, he was no mere acupuncturist.

"A martial arts specialist from Tokyo. He's conscious, and I predict he's gonna do some big-time talking when he hears his buddies split the country and left him holding the bag. The bullet got him in the kneecap. He'll need surgery, but it's not that serious. Under questioning, he admitted he was working for Equinox. Says he was a management consultant. My guess is he's some renegade from the Japanese mob. Sort of a quasi-professional. A freelancer."

"What about the Equinox executives?"

"The bosses took off for Japan the minute things got hot. They had a private jet waiting at the airport. They were here on diplomatic passports. You need consulate intervention to detain them. They're out of here."

"But what about the Americans with Equinox?"

"Claim they're completely in the dark—and they probably are. Jimmy, that's another story. He was up to his neck on both ends."

I pulled the blanket closer around me. "So Jimmy was tied up with his Japanese sponsor. He had promised to deliver a highly promotable champion for the Asian tour coming off the Crown Jewel, and he had set Heather up for it."

"He almost succeeded," said the Fish, handing me a cup of hot tea.

"Well, Jimmy always was a little light in understanding sports personalities," I said, blowing on the tea. "He preferred the glamour of the business, the show biz parts. The fact is, he hadn't counted on the fact that Dagmar Olafsen is a true champion in her heart. And you can't take the champion out of the player."

The Fish shook his head. "I don't get it. She could have just taken the fall, and they all would have walked away rich. But she told the police that something came over her and she just couldn't lose to Heather, especially since Heather couldn't seem to rise to the occasion and take the victory."

I nodded. I understood completely. You have to work to win on clay—and work hadn't been in Heather's vocabulary for quite a while. The time you know you're supposed to win, as is sometimes the case in exhibitions, is often the time you choke. Meanwhile, the pressure is off the person who is supposed to lose, and suddenly they can't miss. Heather had just kept giving points to Dagmar, and finally Dagmar snapped.

"What about the other sponsors?" I asked, fearful of the clinic's position.

"Smokescreens, from the looks of things. Jimmy brought in just enough participation to hide the fact that the big money was from Equinox. And the real payoff would have been in the stock value, after the company got bought out by a bigger fish."

"So Jimmy didn't kill Catherine after all," I said slowly. "My guess is that she quit, and then she came back to tell Jimmy something, maybe argue with him. He probably tried to grease his way out of it, or maybe he wanted to placate her, that would have been his style, but his partners realized she knew too much. She was dangerous, a loose cannon. They had to move fast to keep her quiet. That thug that I shot. He was in Paris during the French."

The Fish nodded. "Quite a coincidence."

"He killed Catherine." I said it flatly. "She tried to make trouble, and he killed her. Her neck was broken before the fall, wasn't it?"

"Yes," recollected the Fish. "But . . ."

"There was a large handprint-shaped bruise on her neck. Wouldn't a martial arts specialist be more likely to break somebody's neck than to shoot?"

"Sounds plausible. Forensics can compare his hands with the handprint on her neck."

I shuddered. "Was he the guy in your hotel room?"

"It wasn't room service, but I can't prove it was him. Anyway, it doesn't matter. We have enough on him."

"I wonder if he got to Jason," I said. "I wonder if he's dead."

"Dead," said the Fish slowly, "or let me toss out another possibility: very rich. My buddies at the IRS had a thing or two on Mr. Campbell. He had some very large unreported sums deposited in Monaco. They were monitoring the situation, waiting for him to make a withdrawal."

"So that's what you were up to in Monte Carlo," I said.

The Fish merely smiled.

"And did he make a withdrawal?" I asked.

"Yes. Yesterday. In Monaco. The Monegasque cooperate with the French. Our friend Inspector Lemire just happened to be in the neighborhood."

I had to let this sink in. "God. He was in on it. *They* were in on it together." Jason was a brilliant computer programmer. It all came together. He had to have known what Catherine was doing, and they had to have agreed to do it as a team.

"There was a lot of money at stake—huge money, as a matter of fact. It was a leveraged deal. If the Crown Jewel didn't make money, the Japanese tour wouldn't come off. It the Japanese tour didn't come off, the buyout Equinox was counting on from Hiro International, who was waiting in the wings, might not come through. No buyout, no big stock windfall. But Catherine got cold feet and without her, the dominoes would have fallen."

"Her mother said she was a bit of a rebel. But let me build on that. Let's say she tried to blackmail Jimmy, she and Jason. They had the evidence—and the whip hand."

"That's why they got rid of her. Catherine Richie wasn't as naïve as they thought. She was for sure smarter than Bennett. Besides, she was expendable; that's why they picked her."

"And that's why Jason wanted me to expose Jimmy. It would have taken him off the hook—and out of the country." It sickened me to realize that I had told Jason almost every move I'd been making, almost every suspicion I'd had. I'd played right into his hands. He'd been in the perfect position to follow me, threaten me, and make me suspect Jimmy all the more. Hadn't I told Jason that I was planning to go to Jimmy's house? I'd given him a play-by-play description of almost every move I'd made. He could have certainly arranged to have me followed, have my office searched, have me run down on my motorcycle, and led me to suspect Jimmy. In fact, he was the *only* person who knew when I went to Jimmy's house. I felt sick. Jimmy wouldn't have wanted to kill me. In fact, he had been trying to warn me off all along. "Where is Jason now?" I asked.

"Inspector Lemire has him in custody in Nice. They'll be extraditing him back to the U.S., nice, wholesome American boy that he is."

Then there was Tony, killed in my car. For being in the wrong place at the wrong time? Tony had also been brilliant at computers, and he'd been sure he was on to something that had

warranted the search of my office and his. Tony knew computers—probably well enough to at least get close to figuring out
what the numbers on Catherine's business card meant. Unlike
me, he had not taken Jason's answers at face value. He'd never
met Jason, never been taken in by his show of grief. I'd told
Jason that Tony carried the discs in his pocket. The bomb in my
car had been a sophisticated computerized explosive, not a
homemade device thrown together by some thug. Suddenly, I
could only think of Jason. Perhaps it had been set to be deto-
nated by remote control, rather than by turning on the ignition.
Jason, who knew my patterns in Palm Springs, would have been
in the perfect position to set this up and make it look like I had
been the target. "I want the police to reexamine that bomb
evidence," I said, "and all of Jason's charge receipts. Did he buy
a plane ticket to Palm Springs or LA at the time Tony was killed?
Or did he buy gas on the way?"

One of the detectives handed the Fish a fax. "Well, what do
you know," he said, handing it on to me. "This is from Nice. It
seems Mr. Jason Campbell was quite the traveler. Lemire
checked his passport. Looks like he was in France during the
French Open—including the day that Catherine Richie was
killed. So, we've finally found our missing link. As soon as you
tell Lemire everything you know about Catherine and Jason, he'll
have plenty to go on."

"Maybe he intercepted Catherine on her way to meet Jimmy at
the reception. She already had told him she quit working for
Jimmy, and maybe now she told him she was going to the authorities. Maybe even tell the press right then and there. That
would have explained her message to Bob Riordan, with Kelly's
camera crew. Actually, that would have been very smart of her.
It would have put her immediately in the spotlight and practically guaranteed her safety."

"Then who chased her up onto the roof?" wondered the Fish,
frowning intently.

"I'd like to think it wasn't Jason, but, frankly, after all that's happened, I don't think it was that Sumo type. He's an animal, he's got brute strength, but I was up there and, in my opinion, he's too big to scramble up that flimsy catwalk in the dark. If it wasn't Jason, it was somebody he hired. But I think this was too public, too spontaneous, for a professional to have done it."

"Then who chased you when you were up there?"

"That was more of a grab than a chase. Actually, I think that could have been Mr. Big." I remembered the brutish tug on my leg. "He wasn't that far up. He grabbed me from below, remember? Besides, I don't think he was trying to kill me. He could have done that any time. I think he was there to scare me off."

The Fish smirked. "A thankless task if there ever was one."

"Same as the security guard at the Springs. I'm sure Jimmy hired him." I sighed as I felt all the remaining energy drain from my body. "I bet the bruise pattern on Catherine's neck will match Jason's handprint."

"You think a computer nerd like him would have actually killed Catherine with his bare hands?"

"I'd never have thought of Jason Campbell as being overtly violent, but who knows about people who do these kinds of things? There is no 'type'—isn't that what you told me? I guess it started out with him being desperate. Let's say Catherine was going to confront Jimmy at the reception, and she ran into Jason on the grounds. Or he followed her there, or intercepted her. Maybe she told him she was going to talk to the press. Whatever. They fought. She ran. He followed her. He couldn't allow her to get inside the greenhouse."

"And Jimmy?"

"A pathetic chump. It's sort of ironic—the ultimate user gets used. He was strictly your level one, a small timer. They had him totally—except that Catherine was too moral in the end to see the scam through. In the end, she refused to be used any longer. But Jimmy was right about one thing: I was definitely on the wrong track. I can't say he didn't try to warn me, in his own way."

"The computerized components of the car bomb should be

traceable," said the Fish. "With Catherine, it's going to be tougher, a circumstantial case."

One of the detectives leaned down and whispered into the Fish's ear. He nodded. "Well, imagine that. Jason confessed. They just got word."

"Why would he confess?" I wondered aloud. "With Jimmy dead, Jason could blame everything on him. At least until some forensic evidence or some other evidence nailed him."

The Fish arched his eyebrows.

"Ah. Of course. He doesn't know Jimmy's dead."

The Fish leaned back in his chair and rubbed his chin thoughtfully. "Well, you know, he's a wild man sometimes, that Lemire. Who's to say he didn't let that fact completely slip his mind? Let's say he was on a roll—he might have even implied that *Jimmy* confessed." The Fish shrugged helplessly. "Or maybe there was a language barrier. He said 'confessed,' when he really meant 'dead.' It happens."

In another corner of the trailer, CiCi and Woody were being questioned. I had to walk over and listen.

CiCi just sat there, shaking her head numbly.

"I had no knowledge of this," Woody said fiercely. "None at all." I believed him. He had worked too hard, believed in Dagmar too much. Of everyone, I felt sorriest for Woody. Dagmar had clarified a renewed sense of purpose in his long and fading career and taken him close to the final victory that would have brought him the validation it would have been far easier not to seek.

"Ms. Knight has confessed," said the detective. "She confirms what you say, Mr. Solister."

I was relieved, but I knew this was scant consolation for Woody.

The detective continued, reading from a small spiral notebook. "But she claims her coach, CiCi McBain, was a party to everything since last spring, as was Ms. Olafsen. I also have a signed statement from Ms. Olafsen."

CiCi leaped to her feet in a fury. "Oh, she confessed, did she?

On my behalf? Well, let me tell you, I was not the one on court, playing the game. I was *recruited* to be a coach. Sure, money changed hands. I don't deny that I got money from Jimmy Bennett. It was a *signing bonus*. That's not the same as throwing a match! That's a business matter! Where's my lawyer? And what about holier-than-thou Miss Kelly Kendall? Don't tell me she's as clean as the driven snow!" The detective led her away.

Kelly stepped into the trailer, and CiCi glared as they passed each other. Kelly spoke briefly to Gus and Bill, then came immediately to my side.

"You know I had no idea," she said quietly. "I would have done anything to stop it."

"Yes," I said. "I know that. You put your life on the line, Kelly. I misjudged you. I'm sorry."

"We misjudged each other. But we did it." Kelly and I hugged each other wordlessly. There was nothing more to say, no more games to play.

The duel was over. We were both, we knew, champions.

MARTINA NAVRATILOVA has won more tournaments and set more records than any other player in the history of professional tennis, and experts have suggested that her career achievement of 168 singles titles and 9 Wimbledon singles crowns may never be surpassed. Her autobiography, *Martina,* was number one on the *New York Times* bestseller list for ten weeks when it was published in 1985. An avid reader—especially of mysteries—Martina admits, "Clive Cussler's Dirk Pitt is my hero."

LIZ NICKLES is the author of the novels *Hype* and *Baby, Baby,* and a work of nonfiction, *The Coming Matriarchy*. She is also a marketing executive who has won numerous awards in the advertising industry; she was named one of the most outstanding professional women in the United States by the National Council of Women, and was one of *Glamour* magazine's Top Ten Working Women. An expert on women's issues, she lives in Los Angeles with her husband and son.